Arnold Metz ran his fingers carefully over the smooth, twelve-inch long casing of the weapon he had been given. The man known as Lynx wasted no time in explaining what he was to do with it.

"You have until Friday to practice with the projectile, Metz. Absolute secrecy, of course, is in order. I trust you have access to isolated test facilities?"

Metz nodded. His eyes were glued to his weapon.

Lynx's cold, even voice continued. "You will be hidden in the rear of a truck just off Constitution Avenue, the route the President's limousine will take after he leaves the Capitol. We will provide you with a small TV, that you may see the President's speech.

"If the President resigns, there will be no further need for your services in Washington. If he does not, you will fire into the Presidential limousine."

Metz ran his palm over the death's-head tattoo on his left forearm. "The assignment," he replied, "is like shooting fish in a barrel."

AMERICAN REICH

DOUGLAS MUIR

CHARTER BOOKS, NEW YORK

This effort is dedicated to the memory of former co-worker and admired mentor Rod Serling—a rare talent who taught many of us a thing or two about dramatic timing and tension.

For a thriller novel to pulse with movement, its characters must be outrageous and frightening, but at the same time believable. The nefarious cast of AMERICAN REICH exists, we'll hope, only in the author's super-charged imagination. All characters and events portrayed in this work are, of course, fictional; any resemblance to real people or incidents is coincidental.

AMERICAN REICH

A Charter Book/published by arrangement with
the author

PRINTING HISTORY
Charter edition/November 1985

ISBN: 0-441-01972-2

Charter Books are published by The Berkley Publishing Group,
200 Madison Avenue, New York, New York 10016.
PRINTED IN THE UNITED STATES OF AMERICA

ACKNOWLEDGMENTS

I'm indebted to agent Robert Gottlieb at William Morris for the germ of an idea and his untiring assistance, and to Laura Shapiro for keeping the traffic moving in both directions. My gratitude also to Berkley's Editor-in-Chief, Nancy Coffey, who believed in the project.

Without the encouragement and aid of some special people, AMERICAN REICH might not have come to fruition. Naturally, some of these friends may disagree with my creative license. My thanks to my mother, Elsie; to Suzanne Forster, Patricia Kubis, Glenn and Dorothy Lewis, Harold Metz, Robert and Corrine Pilling, Jean Marie Sparling, Andrew Swavely, Stan Szarkowicz, Wayne Wright, and especially to Marshall and Nell Stamper.

A society of sheep must in time beget a government of wolves.

Bertrand de Jouvenal

No one man can terrorize a whole nation unless we are all his accomplices.

Edward R. Murrow

PROLOGUE

THE NIGHT SKY over New York was cloudy, as threatening as the burnished steel of a terrorist's carbine. It was just after two-thirty, and the brick warehouse in the south Bronx appeared deserted, one more graffiti-smeared edifice consigned to urban renewal. The structure's high windows were covered with paint and thick iron bars, while the twelve-foot-wide door, double-metal plated, bore several formidable locks. A thing apart from its surroundings, the rat-infested building looked like an abandoned fortress.

Sweat coursed off the face of the FBI agent as he climbed a stack of refuse containers outside one of the structure's lofty windows. He scraped away a hole in the paint with his pocket knife and peered inside. For ten minutes he kept his lonely vigil. Inside the warehouse he could see a lantern burning on the tailgate of a large truck and several men struggling to unload long wooden crates. The agent continued his silent count: forty-eight, forty-nine, fifty. *Christ,* he thought. Fifty cases of government-issue M-16s!

Suddenly, two of the men beside the truck looked up, swinging their flashlights in his direction. The agent lowered his head and cursed softly as the garbage can beneath his feet rattled again. Leaping to the ground, he held his walkie-talkie to his mouth and whispered, "Five one. No time for acknowledge! Davis, Ryerson, you read me? Slip over to sixteen Blacker Street, double-time. The action's here. Moved in prematurely and I'm in shit city."

The heavy warehouse door clattered open, and several men rushed outside. From within the building came the start-up roar of the diesel rig's engine. Harsh headlights pierced the doorway, silhouetting a half-dozen men. All were armed with submachine guns.

Pressing alongside the building, the agent tried to escape, but too quickly they were on top of him, flashlight beams probing. From somewhere off in the distance a siren knifed through the night. The strident wail came nearer, but the men ignored it and leveled their automatic weapons. The Bureau man managed to get off one wild shot from his .38 Police Special before the hailstorm of automatic fire tore into him, driving shreds of his suit and shirt through his body, bloodily enhancing the graffiti on the warehouse wall.

The screaming siren was closing fast. The men dashed for the truck, jumped inside, and quickly drove off. Behind them they left the open warehouse door, fifty cases of automatic rifles, a brick wall blotched with blood and clothing fragments, and a body barely recognizable on the street. In their zeal, two of the gunmen had aimed for the agent's head; the others had shot lower, the deadly fusillade from their weapons nearly cutting their victim in half.

The grim-faced men in the rig did not congratulate one another for their luck in getting away, for though they had escaped certain arrest and interrogation, they'd lost an important arms stash. None of the participants in the incident considered himself an assassin or cop-killer. Each wore a three-by-four-inch American flag sewn on the right shoulder of his brown leather bomber jacket. Each man thought of himself only as a patriot.

En route to an automobile body shop in south Queens, the truck made several stops to let out men at their homes. When the driver arrived alone at his destination on Rockaway Boulevard, he pulled the rig inside the garage, rolled down the overhead door, and hurried to the office phone. From memory he dialed a residential number in Washington, D. C., and seconds later, thick with sleep, a familiar voice came on the line.

"Yes? What is it?"

"Sorry to rouse you at this hour, but we've got trouble in New York. They're on to the Bronx armory. A half-hour ago."

The voice at the other end tightened. "Any casualties?"

"Only an FBI agent. Our trail's clean enough."

An uncomfortable breath, followed by *"Only?* You should have let him escape. Retribution runs fierce in the Bureau."

"What about the guns? We can't function here without them."

"We have a full week to bring in replacements. You'll have all you need. Activate that alternate storage facility in Jersey. Alert the others tomorrow."

"For not knowing your name, I'm taking a heap of orders and responsibility. All we know about you is your fucking telephone number."

"Just do your job, I'll do mine. If it'll make you more comfortable, my code name is Lynx."

The click of the receiver indicated the conversation was over.

1

STEREO MUSIC FLOATED in from the hallway, a Pat Benatar cassette repeating itself for the third time. Outside, the early January evening was cold with a brisk offshore wind pressing relentlessly against the window of their shared fourth-floor Greenwich Village apartment. The ancient radiator in the corner was functioning, though noisily.

Faster and faster their feverish bodies came together. Kicking the rumpled sheets away with his toes, Kirk pumped violently. Shira gasped with pleasure, responding to his advances like a maddened Gypsy violin. As always, he'd found just the right strings, touched them at the right time. Finally, they rolled onto their backs, sated, breathless, and still shivering from their orgasms.

Kirk Stewart's body glistened with sweat. Wiping his forehead and collar-length sandy hair with a T-shirt he'd draped over the bedpost, he fixed his turquoise eyes on the reflection in the five-by-seven-foot mirror he and Shira had attached to the ceiling the day before. Stewart was six feet one and copper tan from sunlamps at the gym; his roommate and on-again, off-again lover Shira Bernstein was five feet seven and white as a polar bear. Shira had freckles not only on her pretty aquiline

4

nose but on her breasts as well. He winked at her in the reflection of the mirror. An odd couple, he mused, but the relationship had more things going for it than against it. There was a five-year gap in their ages, he being thirty-four and Shira twenty-nine. She had constantly teased Stewart that despite the slight jowls and double chin that had started to form, his baby face belied his age; his clean-cut, scrubbed features, in fact, reminded Shira of the predictably shiny faces found on the backs of breakfast cereal packages—the face of one man in particular, with ski goggles around his neck. Stewart had been a ski bum once, but that was a long time back. Shira Bernstein reminded him of a cute but officious librarian.

Abruptly, she rolled away from him, tossing her brown curly hair. Nervously, she eyed the digital clock beside the bed. So much for after-dinner quickie sex, Stewart mused.

"Have to get moving," Shira said softly.

He grabbed her ankle. "Whoa! I provide plenty of foreplay, and afterward—"

"Kirk!" she cut him off. "Let go. I've only got two hours to flight time."

Stewart watched her slip out of bed, snatch a terry-cloth robe off the floor, and trail it behind her to the dressing table. He knew what would be next: the involuntary grab for her purse, the sudden remembering, the embarrassed look as she tossed it aside. It had been just over a month since she'd given up smoking at his urging. Possibly he shouldn't have been so outspoken. There was a brazen sexiness in the way she held a cigarette in her lips, an ironic tilt of the head as she lit it. He put the picture out of his mind. "Still having nicotine fits?"

Shira glanced back to the bed, saw his wry smile. "Habits. Hard to break."

Stewart silently ravished her body, waited for her predictable twitter. "You're beautiful," he said lyrically. "Never thought for the world I'd wind up with Daddy Warbucks's little girl."

"A trifle old for Annie, love." She looked away, trying to find the case for her contact lenses on the dresser.

"It's my weakness for freckles and long curly hair, not to mention those picture-perfect legs of yours."

Shira turned, hands on her hips. "Figures I'd miss out in the tit department."

"Breasts, Ms. Bernstein. Or try 'bosom' for a little class. We writers have to consider our image."

"Merde. In my case, they're a *bust."*

Stewart tossed back the sunflower-patterned sheets, crawled out of bed, and stood facing her, idly scratching his crotch.

Shira frowned and shook her head. "And I should learn from your locker-room manners?"

"Neanderthal manners," he corrected, blowing her a kiss. "Which I suspect you secretly, subliminally crave. I read somewhere women like to fantasize about being dragged back to the cave and ravished."

"Kiss off. You've been reading those personal ads in the *Village Voice* again."

Stewart shrugged. "Flip you for the first shower?"

She looked at him. "Why hurry? Your graveyard shift at the city desk is over three hours away."

"I'm going with you to the airport," he replied, coming up behind her, slipping off her robe, and gently rubbing his hairy chest back and forth across her back.

Distracted, Shira shivered with delight. "Mmmm. I definitely like it. But you spending the cab fare, I can do without. Relax and watch the tube, for God's sake. Only crazies like me venture out to Kennedy for a flight at this hour."

Stewart laughed and nibbled playfully on her ear. "Tasty morsel," he whispered. Stepping back and lifting her chin, he smiled into her eyes. "Crazies? More like cheapies. Take that bargain red-eye to Houston and you'll be half asleep for your interview with Jimmy Hallowell tomorrow. I still say cancel out, stay home. Wait until the famous TV reverend comes to New York." Stewart watched her brush several ringlets of hair from her eyes and look up at him.

"Is the tall man about to talk down to me with another play-it-conservative lecture?" Playfully drumming his chest, she added, "Stay home and wait, forget it. Easy for you to say. You collect a steady paycheck every two weeks while I bust my back in speculative free-lance work. Want to switch places?"

He kissed her and slowly pulled away. "Out of the question. I just received a raise. You were riding high on the syndication rights for that exposé on those would-be terrorists at the Los Angeles Olympics. You've blown all that money already?"

She folded her arms. "That was three years ago. And *we* blew that money."

He nodded sharply, then suddenly grinned. "You're not the nine-to-five type. Shira Bernstein and her hell-bent bonfires would short out a newspaper's word processors." Stewart had always prided himself on his ability to keep his passions in check. He was cautious. It showed in his careful, meticulous journalism.

Shira, as usual, appeared to be reading his mind. Glowering, she said firmly, "You hold your emotions too tight, love. Like diamonds smuggled in a sphincter."

Stewart rubbed his chin. He tried to think of a clever retort, then decided to change the subject instead. Smiling, he traced circles around the tips of her breasts with his fingers. "We shower together or separately?"

Shira hunched her shoulders and gazed back at him. She looked impishly sexy, and Stewart liked what he saw. Her hands slid down his chest, explored between his legs.

"Together," she said softly.

2

THE MORNING WAS grimy, a clinging canopy of gloom that
insinuated its gray mist into every corner of the city. Even the
pigeons lining the window ledges of the New York Times
Building were sullen, unmoving. A light rain pelted the sidewalk in front of the entrance as Kirk Stewart shuffled out of
the building, sniffed the light breeze wafting over from the
Hudson, and looked along the deserted street for a cab. Scowling, Stewart pulled up the collar of his tweed jacket and started
to walk through the drizzle.

He'd forgotten his raincoat, but that didn't matter. Stewart
thought little of clothes, long aware that he could attract ladies
no matter what he wore—tuxedos, Speedos, even a monk's
robes on Halloween. Envious pals had told him it was his
posture that attracted women, the way he walked. Stewart had,
in fact, a stride that would have pleased a drill sergeant. Whether
walking, running, doing sit-ups, or dancing aerobics with Shira,
he handled his body like a trusted machine, almost with a touch
of arrogance. But this morning did not apply.

It had been a long, tedious night digging through the crime
files, and Stewart knew he looked like a hangdog and felt just
as tired. He could use some shut-eye, but wasn't in a hurry.

Shira wouldn't be there to prepare breakfast. With his lover off to Texas, the apartment would be conspicuously empty, except for her temperamental cat Rasputin, who hated him.

West Forty-third Street seemed suffocated with loneliness. A tawdry necklace of garbage cans and plastic bags of litter still lined the curb; the sanitation trucks were running late. Working the graveyard shift at the city desk left Stewart with three early morning options; a quick cab ride home, a two-mile hike, or a bus or subway ride, hopping off a few blocks from home to have breakfast at Greenblatt's Cafeteria. Had he not been wearing his favorite tweed suit, he might have jogged home, despite the drizzle. He headed for the subway.

At the corner Stewart saw three men huddled in conversation. They looked up, eyed him briefly, then disappeared into the nearby subway entrance. As Stewart crossed the street, a pitiful-looking, toothless shopping bag lady, her lips moving in a whispered conversation to herself, held out a filthy Dixie cup. She looked up, suddenly recognizing him. "Good morning, Mr. Stewart."

He paused, dropped in a couple of quarters.

"Thank you, sir. Watch the ruffians this morning."

Old Nora was at it again, Stewart thought. Nora, with her predictable bloodshot eyes and rheumy empress nose. Yesterday it was the dirty pigeons; the day before acid rain. Always some imagined, sinister premonition. Even when she was sober, Nora fell into that category of garrulous old women who say tiresome, exaggerated things with a ring of divine authority. Stewart emptied the rest of his change into her cup, keeping only a subway token.

He skipped down the steps into the IRT. As Stewart slid around the corner of the first graffiti-scrawled landing, they were there, waiting for him, the same three faces he had seen moments before on the street.

Stewart swore softly, shook his head. "You're wasting your time," he said, knowing it was a token point. "Nothing but chicken feed on me." His nerves tightened, along with his fist.

The trio inched forward, encircling him. Two were dressed in sports jackets, heavy sweaters, wore polished shoes and expensive watches; the third man wore a work shirt, Levi jacket, and a baseball cap. Abruptly, they slammed Stewart up against the cold tile wall.

The one in the work shirt and Mets cap snarled, "What the hell you take us for? Muggers? Hell, I make more money erecting steel than you do finger-fucking a typewriter." The man appeared to be in his early thirties, was short but heavily built; he had an alopecic forehead, puffy eyes, and an ugly square chin.

"How do you know I'm a writer?" asked Stewart, feeling more curious than cautious.

"Shut up! We're aware of plenty, Stewart."

They knew his name. What gives here? The other two assailants were taller. One was blond and bearded, wore glasses, a golf shirt, a corduroy jacket, and dress Levis. The other, clad in a herringbone and leather shooting tunic, striped tie, and knit slacks, had close-cropped black hair, sharply drawn features, and a Charlie Chan mustache.

"Look, you bastard," began the bearded blond, "listen and listen good. We've warned your lady friend twice already, and she seems to have deaf ears. Hints don't seem to impress this Shira Bernstein. So now it's your turn to heed some advice. And you can help apply some pressure. Certain organizations in Jersey, New York, and Connecticut don't like being smeared by political reporters. Or pinko agitators."

Stewart tried to keep his cool, to be rational. He really wanted to shove his fist down the man's throat, get the hell out of there. He thought for a moment, then said, "Politics isn't my beat. I stick to crime. Only government doors open to me are the reefers down at the morgue."

The man in the hunting jacket smiled, thick lids squeezing his small fiery eyes. "Okay, but your Jewish girlfriend takes on all subjects, no holds barred. And if she wants to stay healthy, she'll lay off the political *right*. No more trouble."

"Trouble?" Stewart asked, genuinely confused.

"Like bad-mouthing the American Nazi meeting in Newark last month. And nosing around the Navy Patriotic League's dinner party at the Sherry Netherland three days ago. Not to mention certain threatening letters to the Pentagon—specifically to the Chairman of the Joint Chiefs, Sandy Palmer."

Stewart glanced at his watch. "If you muscle boys are finished, I've had a tough shift and need some sleep. It's still a free country and Shira's a liberated lady with a tough mind of her own. As for that letter to the Department of Defense, I saw it, and the word was 'inquiring,' not 'threatening.' And you'll have to admit that the chairman of the Joint Chiefs acknowledges that he's a feisty extremist."

"That's your opinion," the blond man grunted.

Behind Stewart's facade of calm, his mind raced. More times than he could remember in the last five years he had eluded danger by sharp thinking in a crisis. He smiled thinly. "Look, unwind, pal. Why worry—"

"Up your ass," snorted the man with the Mets cap. "You're going to start worrying, Stewart. And this Shira is going to start thinking twice about the writing profession, especially the muckraking end of it."

All three men edged closer. Stewart suddenly felt sick with apprehension. He could feel the tension in the air. All the sharp thinking in the world wasn't going to help him now. He tensed, his heart pounding.

The blond man smiled thickly and rubbed his beard; behind his glasses, his eyes glittered with a childish anticipation and malice. He nodded to his companions. "Now," he said firmly. The short one with the baseball cap grabbed Stewart's left hand, gripped his index finger and, without hesitating, jerked once. A cartilage tore; a knuckle snapped.

Stewart heard his own scream echo back at him along the deserted corridor. The pain was excruciating. He felt another sharp ache, then another, as clenched fists slammed into his stomach. Stewart fell, gasping for air. Vaguely, beyond his agony, he heard excited voices, footsteps approaching in the tunnel. The men hanging over him cursed. They jumped back and, like frightened-off vultures, darted up the subway steps to the street.

Despite the near zero visibility, the twenty-foot sloop plunged ahead, its auxiliary engine at full throttle. Lower Chesapeake Bay was just past high water, on ebb tide. Satisfied that he was now fifteen miles southeast of Baltimore, the man at the tiller checked the small compass in front of him to make sure he had not strayed from the steady course of ninety degrees, then looked at his watch. It was midmorning, and the fog was still as thick as vichyssoise à la Russe.

The Soviet agent posing as a bay fisherman was short, medium-set, in his thirties; he had a strong chin, a neatly trimmed mustache that matched his dark brown hair. His eyes were a piercing, transparent blue. The name on the Israeli passport he carried in his jacket pocket read Motti Barak. He was quite used to the name by now, for he had used it for several years.

Barak pushed his visored cap back over his receding curly hair and looked up to check the rigging. All was in readiness.

Overhead, a long strip of metal foil fluttered from the top of the mast—a hastily improvised radar deflector. Once more Barak's alert eyes scanned the small portable radar set he had propped up on the cabin hatch before him. During the time he had tended the engine and changed course, a small pip had appeared on the screen. He adjusted the instrument in an attempt to brighten the pip, but it remained fuzzy. Cutting the twelve-horsepower inboard engine, he let the sloop drift with the tide.

Barak estimated the unknown object on the radar screen to be a mile away and approaching slightly from port. The fog seemed to be lifting slightly, but still he could see less than four or five boat lengths away. At two-minute intervals, he dutifully sounded the horn.

Ten minutes later a Boston Whaler with its own radar antenna slowly spinning in front of the windscreen idled up beside the sloop. Lines were made fast by two men who looked no different from any other weekend fishermen out of Annapolis, Bay Ridge, or Sandy Beach. Motti Barak knew better. The fishing poles and live herring tank at the stern might have been used on other occasions, but on this particular Saturday morning they were props and nothing more.

Barak knew all too well Soviet Ambassador Mikhail Grotski's plight. The Russian diplomat had few, if any, opportunities to escape the watchful eye of the American intelligence apparatus in Washington. After months of unproductive, if not embarrassing, efforts at following him out on the bay, the CIA had written off the ambassador's interest in fishing as genuine, their shadowing errands a waste of time and taxpayers' money. At last, thought Barak, Mikhail Grotski would make large change of their negligence.

The diplomat climbed aboard the sailboat, took off his gray sheepskin cap, and with it gently cuffed Barak on the elbow. Grotski, bald as a billiard ball with protruding eyes, grabbed his hand and shook it firmly. Too firmly, thought Barak, edging back slightly.

"Comrade!" Grotski waved at the fog and smiled grandly. "Convenient weather, you agree?" His sullen assistant remained on the Boston Whaler, continuing his vigilance over the radar screen.

The ambassador stuffed his cap into his red plaid jacket, stepped into the forward part of the cockpit, and sat down on a kapok cushion. "I regret the inconvenience this rendezvous may have caused you, dear Major, but you will no longer be able to communicate with the embassy."

Barak stiffened and bowed slightly. "Ambassador Grotski, inconveniences to further the will of the state are my duty and pleasure." He had committed the line to memory; it was an effortless lie, thought Barak. Working for the KGB had never been a pleasure, only an obligation, a simple commitment to the continued safety and welfare of his parents. "Comrade Ambassador, I have American coffee in the thermos. You and your aide would like some, perhaps?"

Grotski waved the thermos away. *"Nyet.* It disagrees with my stomach, and there isn't time. We must make haste. Back in Moscow, Colonel Koroteyev has kind words for you, Laurenti Baroski. Forgive me, I should say Major Motti Barak, yes? The Hebrew name suits you well, I must say. The colonel tells me you did well for us in Jerusalem. Exceptionally well."

"How could I have done otherwise, Comrade Ambassador? I am a Jew."

"You are a Russian, Laurenti Baroski" Grotski smiled. "It is easy for you to proclaim your nationality and religion to me here in the middle of Chesapeake Bay. But if you ever wish to obtain your KGB card—"

"Comrade Ambassador," interrupted Barak, "we have known each other for almost a year. I will never be formally admitted to the KGB. I will always be a *shpik.* Our Communist slogan is 'Brotherhood, Equality, Happiness to all Peoples.' A hollow ring, Comrade, when the doors to the KGB remain closed to certain nationalities—specifically the Crimean Tartars and the Jews."

"Times have changed before. They will change again. The head of the KGB under Stalin was a Jew. You must have faith, Major Barak. There are only two kinds of Communists. Con-

vinced and unconvinced. Which are you? And are you the one
for this American mission at hand?"

Barak poured himself a cup of coffee and slumped back
against the cockpit rail. He blew on the hot liquid and took
several cautious sips. Exhaling wearily, he finally said,
"Comrade, the KGB is made up of Communism's landed gen-
try. I am a socialist, but I am *convinced* of only one thing. I
will fulfill my part of the bargain to Colonel Koroteyev. I will
not fail in my duties, but my parents must be permitted to
emigrate to Israel. Their exit must be expedited. Soon."

Grotski nodded, all too slowly for Barak. The ambassador
lowered his eyes. "Department Ten has been quite zealous in
its suppression of counterrevolutionary nationalist elements, I
admit. But your parents back home in Ivanovo have been treated
well. You hear from them regularly, yes?"

Barak nodded.

"Tell me, Major Barak. Where were you trained?"

"KGB School Number Three Eleven in Novosibirsk."

"Were you not told, repeatedly, why the KGB considers all
applicants for exit visas to Israel to be enemies of the state?"

"Yes, Comrade Ambassador. International clout, among other
reasons."

"And still . . ." Grotski's voice trailed off. He looked off
into the fog. When his protruding eyes finally came back to
Barak, they were cold and unsympathetic.

Motti Barak felt uncomfortable. He couldn't resist blurting
out, "To be a Jew in the Soviet Union today means nearly the
same as it meant in czarist Russia during the Stolypin period."

Grotski looked at his watch and sighed. His shaved head
glistened. "I will have half a cup of that coffee. Black, please."

Barak found another cup in the galley and poured from his
thermos. Grotski took it from him and nodded. "I am not your
KGB superior, Comrade Major. I am an *ambassador,* and at
the moment, an expedient go-between. But I have some advice
for you, yes? You must develop a sense of smell to succeed in
the spy business. Never speak uncomfortable truths to your
superiors. Lean to lick and bark at the right times."

"I'm sorry. Perhaps I spoke too strongly."

Grotski waved a hand, silencing him. "Enough, enough.
We're running out of time. When do you leave for New Orleans?"

"No, it is Houston. At noon today. The meeting is being

held near Lake Charles, Louisiana, but it is closer to the Houston airport."

"You are fortunate. Texas is off limits to those with Soviet passports. Your Israeli papers are in order, in the event anything goes wrong?"

Barak sipped his coffee and smiled. "Impeccable."

Grotski reached into his pocket, withdrew two photographs, handed them to Barak. "Do not lose these. Old pictures, taken in 1970, but purportedly they are of Dr. Mengele and Martin Bormann. One of them may attend that meeting of American Nazis. I want a full transcript of any after-dinner speeches."

"I'll do my best, Comrade Ambassador, but I am one man, and I must be subtle, cautious."

Climbing to his feet, Grotski finished off the rest of his coffee and pulled his sheepskin cap over his bald head. He reached into his pocket and retrieved an envelope, handed it to Barak. "Your wages and expenses, Major. Go easy on the vodka." Pausing, he thought for a moment, then added, "Tell me, Barak, do you know what the three letters KGB mean?"

"Yes, Comrade. State Security Committee."

Grotski beamed, but shook his head. "Nyet! KGB means Kontora Grubykh Banditov—Office of Crude Bandits." Clasping his hands together, he added, "Strike with impertinence and pressure, yes? Proceed with insolence and total self-confidence and you will successfully fulfill the task we have given you. But at the same time be aware and cunning. The FBI may well be conducting its own investigation."

The man in the Boston Whaler, silent until now, suddenly looked up. "Pips on the radar, Comrade Ambassador. A long way off."

"Fishing boats, I'm sure," said Grotski, "but still, we go." He jumped back into the outboard, jabbing a pudgy finger in Barak's direction. "You are special, my friend. Not a typical apparatchik, used to living according to instructions from above and avoiding personal initiative. On the contrary, we demand you use that yeasty mind of yours. Improvise, Comrade!"

"I will be successful. And my parents?"

"They will be provided for. Dostevedanya, Major Barak."

The Mercury engine on the stern of the Whaler roared to life. Barak tossed back the mooring lines. "Comrade Ambassador!" he shouted over the fog-shrouded water.

"Yes?"

"I know too well how my people—and others like them—can be swallowed up in today's Gulag Archipelago! Please remember that when I no longer receive correspondence from my parents, I cease to be your *shpik*, Comrade!"

Kirk Stewart's splinted finger started to throb again. After leaving the East Manhattan Emergency Clinic he had returned home, tried to sleep, but had dozed only fitfully. Reaching for the aspirin bottle on top of the television, he gulped down two pills, chased them with what was left of his Budweiser Light. The volume was turned down on the replay of the Orange Bowl game, and he watched the set without interest. Shira's cat stared at him balefully from across the coffee table.

"Rasputin! You arrogant little bastard, come over here," he ordered.

Ignoring him, the cat turned and padded out of the room.

Stewart switched off the TV, fell back on the sofa, and tossed a pillow under his head. Kicking off his shoes, swallowed up by the loneliness of the empty apartment, he stared at the ceiling. Damn Shira, he thought. The confrontation in the subway signaled the beginning of her undoing. His mind began to wander. Trying to fix the blame, he thought about their political differences. Plenty of air between them, but never before had it seemed important.

You're as American as apple pie with the core tossed in for good measure, Shira and her liberal friends had taunted more times than Stewart wanted to remember. Too fucking middle-of-the-road. He couldn't argue the point. A product of the melting pot, his mother was a closet Democrat, his father an outspoken, contributing Republican. Stewart was curious about politics, often intellectualized on the subject, but he had never considered himself much more than a moderate. Recently, he had come to vote for the man, not the party. He, like countless others in the last election, had voted for the incumbent President as a compromise candidate. And he was among the multitudes who were now disappointed. Despite his father's urging that he devote his industriousness and writing talent to the campaign, Kirk had declined to pretend an interest in politics that he didn't feel.

Stewart's socially prominent, business-minded parents were

of mixed Scottish-Swedish extraction, as red, white, and blue
as the flag they flew on holidays—always the largest standard
on the block. His father was self-made, a retired highway
contractor; his doting mother, a secret drinker, was a former
nurse turned board member of a Seattle children's hospital.
Stewart had a sister who taught school in Coos Bay, Oregon,
and a young brother who was a marginally successful Hollywood stunt man. Kirk's shoulders weren't as broad as his brother's, and he wasn't as athletic, but it was commonly agreed he
was the most talented and intelligent member of the family.

Raised in the Northwest, Stewart attended Journalism School
at the University of Washington. In college his tall, trim frame
had earned him a place in the varsity rowing shell. High ac-
ademic marks and a turn as editor of the *Daily* had brought
him a graduate scholarship to Stanford. After a year and a half
at Palo Alto, instead of going to work he took an extended
vacation. His more ambitious friends accused him of dropping
out.

Life outside the parental economic fold was rougher than
Stewart envisioned. He found this out trying to make ends meet
as a ski bum at Sun Valley and Aspen, where ski instructing
jobs were feast-or-famine situations. Too often it was a game
of accepting fat tips while spurning the advances of lonely,
ugly wives and wealthy gays who took it for granted a glam-
orous ski bum was available.

Coming down to earth, making a living below seven thousand feet, had at first been as difficult for Stewart as overcoming
an allergy. Now, reflecting back on those years, he knew it
wasn't an allergy he had overcome, but the horseshit phase of
growing up.

His first real job was writing for a Bay Area travel magazine—the giveaway kind found in the back of airliner seats.
Like most good reporters, over the years Stewart tucked a good
deal of travel under his belt—much of the Orient and three
times to Europe. On his first business trip to New York he'd
fallen in love with Gotham and not long thereafter made the
big shift to the East Coast. Stewart's forte now was crime
reporting, and he knew he did it well. His superiors respected
his nose for police intelligence, his ability to probe swiftly and
quietly behind the scenes. To Stewart, words came simply
enough, but he would often sweat for hours over clever and

not-so-clever combinations. How the phrases were glued together was what made readers think and act. He had the knack, the sense of timing; he knew how to hook and hold a reader. It had been a determined climb, and working for a prestigious daily like the *Times* tickled Stewart's vanity.

When the proper day came, when he had a few extra bucks in the kitty, he'd draw from his rapidly accumulating experience and write a book. A mystery or a horror novel, possibly a thriller with a convoluted plot. With his picture on the dust jacket, perhaps with a family. The wild oats would all be sown by then, and ideally he'd be married, settled down with children. He'd write not just one novel, but several.

Stewart put his thoughts on the future aside and again fixed his mind on Shira. He thought about her for a long time, then dozed off. When he woke an hour later, his stomach, still bruised and sore from his pummeling, was now growling as well. Time to get into that salmon casserole and the bottle of Blue Nun Shira had left for him as a peace offering for her being away. Peace offering, he mused. I could use a little of that. Tonight his body felt as if it had been through a war.

The telephone on the end table shrilled in his ear. He picked it up and answered.

"Kirk? This is Carlie."

Stewart felt his heart skip a beat. Carlotta Chavez always did that to him. It took him several seconds to compose himself. Finally, he said, "A voice from the past. What's happening, lost love? Been eight months since I've seen you in the flesh."

The young woman at the other end of the line laughed. Carlie Chavez had a warm, infectious laugh uniquely her own, and Stewart liked it.

"Don't you get enough of me, God forbid, five nights a week on the tube?" she asked flippantly.

"I watch my news on Channel Five. Leslie Phelps is more animated. When her head moves, so do her tits."

"Still the sophomoric sexist? When do you take the big step and turn into a dirty old man?"

"I couldn't stand the competition. Too many of them in New York."

"Kirk, I miss you. You're as fun to talk to as ever, but this call's half social, half business. Shira asked me earlier in the week to get back to her with some information. My research crew's been swamped, and I'm just now returning the call. Put her on, please."

Stewart leaned back on the sofa, put his feet up on the coffee table. "Sorry, Carlie. She's gone. Went down south on a magazine story interview. That television witch doctor, Reverend Hallowell."

There was a moment's silence at the other end. Finally Carlie said, "Interesting. What's Shira digging for, Kirk? She asked me if she could borrow some old program tapes—interviews with Episcopal Bishop Elliott and a panel show featuring two prominent rabbis. She seemed to be fencing with some ultra right wing extremists—Nazis and paramilitary groups. Wanted to know how they were infiltrating the establishment, what ways they were attacking the news media."

Stewart grimaced, looked at his bandaged finger. "They're attacking me. For all I know this could be that German underground—the Odessa."

"What are you talking about?"

"SS. Gestapo. It's a long story. You available for lunch this week?"

"For you I'm always available, provided Ms. Bernstein isn't still jealous of me." Carlie paused. "If she's out of town tonight, maybe you want to stop over for a pizza and beer?"

Stewart considered the invitation. Tempting, he thought. "Love to another night, Carlie. Shira left dinner in the refrigerator and plans to call me later. I'll tell her you tried to get in touch. If it's important, she'll probably get back to you this weekend."

"Kirk, mind if I tell you something?"

"Shoot." There was an uncomfortable silence. "Well? I'm holding," he said smartly. "The camera's on you, Anchorwoman."

Again, a short silence, followed by "Nothing. Changed my mind. Don't forget to call me for lunch."

"You're on. Good-bye, Carlie."

Stewart placed the phone back on the end table and was about to trudge to the kitchen when it rang again. He answered it quickly. "Forget something?"

It wasn't Carlie. "Mr. Stewart?" The gruff individual at the other end didn't identify himself, but the voice was uncomfortably familiar. "I trust you've had a little time to reflect on our discussion this morning in the subway?"

"I have. Get to the point.

"Call off the bloodhound bitch, Stewart. Keep Shira Bernstein muzzled and in the kennel."

3

THE HALFWAY HOUSE was known throughout five Texas and Louisiana counties, if not the entire Sunbelt, for its lake-to-plate catfish dinners. Despite its rural location midway between Lake Charles and Houston, the dining room, run by the German-American proprietor and his wife, always had a waiting line. Even the huge banquet chamber, a frog's jump to the rear of the parking lot, was booked for months in advance. But the catering for tonight's fund-raising dinner and joint policy meeting of the Freedom Militia and the Nazi Alliance of America, had been carefully planned a full year earlier.

Banquet room waiter Tyrone Jackson felt about as much warmth for his employers as he did for a water moccasin, for he knew the restaurant owner and his fat wife were racists of the first order. Having been on the payroll for the last month, the black man's survival, fortunately, had not been dependent on the roadhouse's skimpy pay and part-time employment. Jackson's real income came from undercover funds dispersed out of the FBI regional office in New Orleans. That same source had also furnished the Nikon camera, 300mm telephoto lens, and supply of infrared film he now hastened to set up in the tangled canopy of ferns beyond the parking lot.

Jackson had heard only scraps of the proprietor's heavily accented conversation the day before—terse, disquieting words to an assistant, demanding that the premises be "niggerproofed" for this one night. Jackson knew these orders meant a clandestine meeting with some notorious Nazi from Paraguay as guest speaker. And it would be an unauthorized, illegal visit.

Once more Jackson checked his watch. Just after 7:00 P.M. Squinting through the camera viewfinder, he focused the telephoto lens on the banquet hall entrance at the end of the driveway. He cursed, discovering that the nearby trees threw long dark arms across the area. He needed a better position.

Tyrone Jackson's heart skipped a beat as he heard a twig snap behind him. Suddenly, massive arms closed around his neck, pulling him swiftly backward, choking him. He felt a terrible pressure, as if his throat, lungs, and heart were being compacted. His arms flailed wildly, but uselessly. The choke hold was gradually tightened, and the last thing Jackson saw before everything went black was the camera tripod smashing against his head.

"He's out cold. Now what?" snapped one of the muscular men hovering over Jackson's still form.

"Take him out in the swamp. Feed the spying nigger to the 'gators."

The twenty-foot-long black Mercedes 600 pulled slowly into the driveway. Two alert-eyed men with telltale bulges beneath their suit jackets stepped forward and opened the limousine door. The old man in the rear seat hesitated, then pushed himself forward. Despite his silver hair and gold-tipped maplewood cane, the arriving dignitary could have filled the Hollywood role of an arrogant German SS officer perfectly. Appearing to be in his early seventies, of slender build, the guest of honor stood ramrod stiff after he climbed out of the vehicle, giving the immediate impression that he was still a man of stern stuff. Peering out from a sun-bronzed face were hard, uncompromising eyes that betrayed considerable energy and icelike fanaticism.

A second limo pulled into the driveway, and several additional security men, any of whom might easily have played defense for the Houston Oilers, moved swiftly inside the restaurant ahead of the man with the cane. A grossly overweight middle-aged businessman in a gray knit suit officiously stepped forward from the entranceway, his eyes glittering with anticipation.

Karl Frober's crew-cut red hair was shot with gray. He had a fleshy, pock-marked face with thick lips and wore a bow tie the same color as his mouse-gray eyes. Behind him stood two younger men, apparently assistants, also expensively attired. One of these wore a red, white, and black swastika arm band as did several surly individuals who lined the walkway leading to the banquet chamber.

Frober tried unsuccessfully to button his jacket over his considerable paunch as he rushed forward and shook the hand of the guest of honor.

The old man looked at the reception committee stonily and held up a Canadian passport. "For purposes of my visit here and introduction to your membership, I am officially Dr. W. Schmidt. From Edmonton. Simple enough, gentlemen?"

The men standing before him nodded like automatons, glanced at one another with bewildered looks.

Scalp glistening beneath his crew-cut hair, Frober edged his bulk forward, extended his hand. "I'm Karl Frober, in the hotel business—worldwide operations. As well as national chairman of the Freedom Militia. Came out from Glendale, California, to chair the meeting."

"Ah, yes," said Schmidt thoughtfully. "My friend Norman Gifford, the chairman of Condor Defense Industries, speaks highly of you. You're the one with friends in Haiti." He paused, making a clicking sound with his tongue, then bobbed his head and added, "The organization you head is the one with the weapons, correct?"

Frober beamed, rocking back and forth on his heels. "From Alaska to Florida, we can muster nine thousand men. And we have four hidden armories with enough weaponry to restage the Battle of the Bulge."

"And the others here?" asked the old man, glancing around him.

Frober replied quickly, "Officers of the Patriot Cause and the Nazi Alliance of America. Gentlemen, introduce yourselves to our guest of honor."

The men quickly complied. After shaking their hands, the old man looked sternly at Frober. "It has been twenty years since I last set foot in America. The last time, I was very nearly apprehended by some clever Jews." He sighed wearily, gazing out across the parking lot. "And now I see this land only at night and through the tinted windows of a limousine. Swamp country fatigues me. I've seen too much of it in Brazil and Paraguay."

"The remote location was a matter of security, my friend," said Frober quickly. "But I believe you will find the fresh catfish feast a rewarding experience."

One of the burly men behind Frober stepped forward and added, "The secrecy of your visit will not be compromised. Your personal safety was of utmost consideration in our planning."

Schmidt smiled thinly. "At seventy-one, Kameraden, my personal welfare is not the cause of a consuming fear. I only worry that I may not live long enough to see America confronted with its own *Schicksalsstunde*."

"I'm sorry," apologized Frober, "my German is quite elementary."

"The hour of destiny, *Kamerad*," explained Schmidt. "Tonight I will provide you with a refresher course in National Socialist ideology."

Hands folded over his stomach, Karl Frober grinned. "America's hour of destiny is imminent, *Herr Doktor;* of that I can assure you."

The two men clasped arms and entered the building. Several security guards remained outside, watchful and vigilant.

Inside her rented Pinto, Shira Bernstein turned on the dashboard light, glanced in the rearview mirror, and checked her lipstick and hair. Pushing back the thick mop of brown ringlets that framed her face, she cursed herself for not having worn her contacts. The crowd inside, from all appearances, was mostly men. In all probability loudmouth, macho reactionaries, but nonetheless men, a few of whom might be good-looking and flirtatious. A probing journalist had to play all her cards. She put her glasses back on. The professional look of the oversized square frames was ideally suited, almost *de rigueur,* for business luncheons ordered from blackboard menus in Manhattan. But out here? Dorothy Parker's poem skitted through her mind: "Men seldom make passes at girls who wear glasses." No, her image was right; she wanted to come off as a studious South African magazine editor. To hell with sexist allure, she mused.

Infiltrating the Tallahassee-based Association for White

Rights had been simple enough. Once she had paid the dues she was on their mailing list, and from the material the organization had sent her, she had devised a cover packet to get her into this important meeting. According to the engraved invitation she now carried in her purse, she was Sally Brudde, editor of *Viking,* a neo-Nazi, South African youth publication. All this was a far cry from the young woman who preferred bagels to bratwurst, the free-lance magazine writer who shared an apartment in Greenwich Village with a handsome reporter for the *New York Times.* Her outspoken activism and muckraking had sometimes alienated her lover Kirk and even her friends in the Anti-Defamation League of B'nai B'rith had found Shira Bernstein a trifle aggressive. She disliked that word, thought of herself as assertive.

Shira checked her watch, then once more examined the miniature tape recorder in her purse. The cartridge was full, the battery replaced only the day before in New York. Kirk had helped her conceal the miniature microphone beneath the bag's wooden clasp. Climbing out of the Pinto, she hastened across the parking lot, avoided the main entrance, and headed around to the side door of the large banquet hall. At the doorway she heard loud applause, followed by raised voices singing "The Star-Spangled Banner."

"Your identification, please." The tall, burly doorman played the beam of a small pencil flashlight over her face, across her breasts. An assistant came up beside him.

Heart trembling, Shira thrust forward her forged press credentials. "I'm Sally Brudde. *Viking* magazine. Will this ID suffice?"

The pair checked her name against a master guest list, nodded, and handed back the papers. "Y'all are late, ma'am. The ushers inside will show you to your table, Miss Brudde."

Shira smiled hesitantly and hurried inside.

The deep-fried catfish were served family style, the assembled crowd wolfing down platter after platter and chasing it with imported beer or Riesling wine. At the microphone, the proprietor explained that his usual army of black and Hispanic service workers had been replaced with volunteers—wives and family members of the various delegates—to ensure absolute privacy, both for their honored guest's secret appearance and for any post-dinner deliberations.

Shira wondered about the guest of honor. Was he who she

suspected? There was only one familiar face at the head table, multimillionaire hotel chain owner Karl Frober, his plump face and crew cut easily recognized from news photographs. Frober was known on Wall Street as the boy wonder entrepreneur, the owner of Worldwide Hotels, as well as an outspoken anti-Semite. Shira knew he was anti-alien, anti-minority, anti-everything. He was also chairman of the controversial Freedom Militia. Frober had never been known to give interviews to journalists, and his own poisonous political newsletters were enough to burn the ears of the soberest reader and sicken the soul of a Jew like Shira whose grandmother had been gassed at Treblinka.

Shira picked at her food, unable to relax. Her table companions, five men who introduced themselves as representatives from the United Klan Brotherhood of Cobb County, Georgia, not only had crude table manners but constantly ogled her. Shira felt awkward. All through the peach cobbler, she dispensed with small talk—the night somehow didn't deserve it. She was relieved when the entertainment began. Her eyes went to the dais, where before a ten- by sixteen-foot American flag, banquet chairman Frober sluggishly got to his feet. He introduced a guest soloist, a plump Teutonic contralto in a floor-length burgundy dress who belted out "God Bless America" in a style remarkably similar to that of Kate Smith.

At the song's conclusion, the vocalist bowed unctuously to heavy applause and turned to the guest of honor. "To our illustrious visitor," she soothed, "I dedicate my next number, in the hope that he might live to see the imposed guilt of his cause and his Fatherland forever purged from the history books." The woman nodded toward the old man at the center of the dais, then sang "Deutschland Über Alles." The yet to be identified guest of honor, as well as some two dozen other men and women in the room, stood stiffly at attention as her Wagnerian voice rang out. At the kitchen door, the restaurant owner and his wife wept.

The men seated around Shira twisted uncomfortably in their seats. One cursed under his breath. "I didn't come down here for this Kraut crap," he grumbled, swilling his wine.

Shira ignored him and scanned the printed program. Two more entertainers to go, then the guest speaker. She glanced at her watch and measured the distance to the adjoining lounge.

She had promised to call Kirk in New York before eight. And
there was still Carlie Chavez to contact. Now was the time to
slip briefly away from the table; she would return in time for
the guest of honor's speech and the important business meeting.
Grabbing her purse, Shira excused herself and tiptoed out of
the banquet hall. At the exit, two security cops with swastika
arm bands idly watched her pass, then returned their attention
to the vocalist. But a third duty man, heavy-set, in a rumpled
suit without a Nazi arm band, sat smoking a cigar at the reception desk and continued to observe her with obvious interest.

Smiling briefly, Shira walked past the surly face and headed
for the telephone at the end of the hall by the ladies' room.
Too conspicuous, she decided, reconsidering. Retracing her
steps to the banquet hall lobby, she walked outside and hastened
to the phone booth in the parking lot near the highway. Glancing
nervously around to make sure she was alone, she closed the
door and dialed the operator. Seconds later, after reversing the
charges to New York, she heard the reassuring voice of Kirk
Stewart on the line. "Hi, roomie," she said quickly. "Only have
a minute. I think I'm on to something big. Very big."

There was a gentle laugh in New York. "What else is new?
So tell me about Houston. How goes the interview with the
great Reverend Mr. Jimmy Hallowell? He still uptight about
tape recorders?"

Shira hesitated. "Uh, I haven't seen him yet. I might get in
for an interview tomorrow."

"I thought you were flying home in the morning. Something's come up we need to talk about."

Shira detected a vague uneasiness in Kirk's usually sunny
voice.

"I'll catch the late flight, try to get out of here tomorrow
after dinner at the latest. Miss me, Grumpy?"

"Silly question. You want a dumb answer or just some heavy
breathing? What's going on down there? Have Hallowell and
his Moral Confederation cleaned up your act?"

Shira held the mouthpiece closer and lowered her voice.
"Kirk, be serious for a minute. Remember that World War Two
SS doctor who died in Brazil? Josef Mengele? It appears I've
come on to one of his pals."

"Shira! What's this got to do with the preacher? Damn it,
you promised!"

"I know, I know. Don't worry. I'll be all right. I'm safe."

"Bullshit. That's what I want to talk about. Our mutual friend, the newscast lady, wants to talk to you. Same subject. What's more, a trio of your admirers left their calling card this morning."

"Who? What are you talking about?"

"You said you were heading down there to interview that money-grubbing bigot Hallowell. So where are you and what's really going on?"

Shira hesitated, biting her knuckle. The big man with the cigar had followed her outside. He was now standing next to the phone booth, studying her face as though he had seen it somewhere before.

"Shira? Answer me! Are you there?"

"Kirk, look—I'll call you when I get back to the hotel. I promise. Wait up, okay?"

The voice at the other end of the line tightened. "Where are you calling from right now? I want the number."

"I'm sorry. I can't talk now. Don't worry, all right? I'll call you back in a couple of hours. Bye, love." She slowly replaced the phone on its hook.

When Shira opened the door to the booth she was confronted by a cloud of pungent cigar smoke from the man in the rumpled suit. His porcine eyes surveyed her with obvious distrust, and now to one side of him stood two men with swastika arm bands. The tallest, a broad-shouldered individual with penetrating green eyes, snapped his fingers and extended his hand. "Your identification, Miss Brudde. Our sergeant-at-arms here would like to see it."

"Of course," she said as calmly as she could, reaching for her purse. She paused, suddenly remembering the tape recorder. "I'm sorry. My wallet. I left it at my table inside. If you'll permit me to go after it—" She started to edge away.

Eyes fixed on her, the man with the cigar blocked her way. Before Shira knew what was happening he held her bag in his hands, his plump fingers probing inside it like hungry ferrets. An instant later his lips twisted in satisfaction as he withdrew not only her press pass but the miniature tape recorder and the hidden microphone as well.

"You very nearly succeeded, Miss Brudde, or whoever you are. I seriously doubt that you are South African." He smiled, exposing gold-capped teeth. "You see, I had the pleasure of meeting the real Sally Brudde in London only last year at an editorial conference. I'm a writer myself, from *Liberty Bell* magazine. Also, incidentally, I am security coordinator for the meeting tonight." He turned to his companions who stood to one side, waiting like hungry carrion birds. "Use your usual persuasion. Find out the name and number of the party she was calling. I want to know *everything*, understand? Meanwhile, I'll inform Karl Frober of our little discovery."

Shira felt trapped. Frantically, she swung a fist and brought up her knee, but missed her targets. The three men easily subdued her. The security coordinator strode off toward the banquet hall.

Inside the dining room, the guest speaker's voice rose in pitch, firing the enthusiasm of the assembled delegates. Several times he had to pause while the crowd clapped. The man who called himself Dr. Schmidt pounded his fist on the lectern. "I can understand your loneliness, the terrible isolation you sometimes feel in your conservative, patriotic endeavors. But now you must unite, not only the two groups sponsoring this banquet tonight but all others of like political and intellectual belief. The Marxist plague, I remind you, is insidious! The voices of power in the communications industry—American newspapers, television, motion pictures—these are Jewish voices that would betray their country rather than fight an earnest war against creeping socialism, moral decay, and the ineptitude of the welfare state."

Schmidt paused, his intense eyes surveying the sea of expectant faces before him. "Why, you ask? Because both the bourgeois Jew and the intellectual Jew are afraid of us! Why else, year after year, would they rekindle the ugly propaganda bonfire, memorializing the purported Holocaust? They invent and fabricate beyond any reasonable man's sense of proportion." The old man hesitated again, glancing down at the hotel executive seated to his left. Karl Frober nodded in swift agreement.

Schmidt sipped from a glass of water, then continued. "Hitler made Germany *judenrein*—free of Jews. He was forced to arrest them because they constituted a danger to the security of the state. Jews in the camps were well fed, and when co-operative and productive, they were well treated. After the war, all of them received huge sums of money. But me? What of this old German? I hide behind one more false name, yes? Like many others, I cannot return to the Fatherland. Legally, I cannot set foot in America. Who pays me for what I have suffered because of the war's outcome?"

The audience vigorously applauded. Karl Frober sat attentively, mesmerized by Schmidt's speech. He repeatedly nodded his head as the German lowered his voice, continuing his condemnation of the unhealthy state of affairs in the United States. Schmidt spoke of impending doom. He backtracked, quoting Joe McCarthy, then author Ayn Rand. He probed into distant history, echoing the words of Schiller, Bismarck, and Nietzsche, adapting them to his own argument. Schmidt insisted that there would always be war between the producers of the world and the parasites. "The races can never be equal!" he shouted.

At this point, the old man was momentarily distracted as the sergeant-at-arms stepped softly across the dais and beckoned to Banquet Chairman Frober to follow him outside. The two men conferred briefly in hushed tones, then quietly slipped out of the dining room.

Pausing at the edge of the parking lot, Frober rubbed a hand over his fleshy jowls and whispered. "You're positive she's a spy?"

"Beyond any doubt. Nasty bitch kicked and spit in the guard's face. She's either a goddamn member of the liberal press or from some branch of Israeli intelligence. We're still working on her. She was in the process of calling a reporter in New York. The *Times* staff."

Frober exhaled sharply. "The *name* of the reporter? You have it?"

"Stewart. A Kirk Stewart. She lives with him in the Village."

"I'll have to consult with Lynx. Steps will have to be taken immediately. As for the woman, I can't get mixed up in this. Security is your province. I'll accept your judgment and expertise."

The second man unwrapped a fresh cigar, shifted uneasily on his feet. "I can have the boys make another trip out into the swamp. The same fate as our black friend?"

"However it is accomplished is your business," Frober snapped, heading back toward the banquet hall. Nervously, he turned and added, "Just get rid of her. And quickly. Bad enough the FBI agent, now this woman and her reporter friend." Frober looked off into the distance at the two grim-faced robots who waited with their female captive. "Whoever takes care of it must leave the area immediately. Give them enough funds to disappear for the rest of this critical week."

4

TOSSING RESTLESSLY, STEWART reached out for Shira, but the other side of the bed was empty. Groggily, he blinked at the vacant pillow. It came back to him that he was alone in the apartment. Stewart looked at his watch, reluctantly pulled himself out of bed, and shuffled down the hall to the bathroom. Staring into the mirror, he scowled at his reflection. He looked like a piece of dog crap and felt worse. His splinted finger still throbbed, and he was made doubly miserable by a prize hangover from the night before. No barbells this morning, he decided.

Not that he had been down at the local watering hole. Far from it, he had remained at home, close to the phone, waiting up until three in the morning for Shira's call, nursing his disquietude with scotch and Perrier and watching a rerun of Jean Renoir's *Grand Illusion* on cable. He had expected Shira to phone back from wherever her mysterious call had originated, but he had heard nothing. At first he was profoundly annoyed. By midnight he felt anguish and genuine fear.

Had she been in New York and not returned a phone call he might have halfway understood. Shira demanded her freedom, and he gave it to her. She had an independent, impish streak he would never fathom, but in spite of it he loved her. She was a brilliant conversationalist when the mood hit her, an excellent cook, good in bed, and most important, she seemed to understand his needs perfectly. But too often she had reminded him that she was an emancipated woman, success-oriented, that her career came first, and that she wasn't about to be restrained or owned by any man, Kirk Stewart included.

Stewart's parents considered the affair lopsided, his love unrequited. A roommate is a roommate, his prying mother reminded him in her once-a-month calls from Seattle. On one memorable occasion when she had visited New York she had been less than polite, advising Shira in a matriarchal tone, "A lover is a lover, make up your mind." So much for meddling. Old World parents and the uxorial ideal, Stewart reasoned. If there were long-range plans between Shira and himself, never had they found voice. Granted, they had plenty of laughs and serious conversations together. But if this was only a will-o'-the-wisp affair, why had he drunk so much and then tossed fitfully all night long? Obviously he cared. A mixed-up arrangement for the eighties, but it worked. Shira was an enigma, but a satisfying one.

Throwing on a robe, he trudged down the hallway. The kitchen, overlooking a courtyard that was little more than a fresh air shaft, was a mess, stacked with two days' worth of unwashed dishes and empty beer bottles. Feeling a sudden urgency, he grabbed the wall telephone and dialed the operator.

Rasputin leaped to the tile counter, eyed him curiously.

The operator finally picked up.

"I'd like some information. Last night around seven-thirty I accepted a collect phone call from some small town in Louisiana. Near the Texas border, I suspect. Can't remember the name. Will you check my charge record? I need to know the number where the call originated."

"I'm sorry, sir, I don't have access to billing information, but I'm sure the business office can assist you."

Stewart grimaced at the metallic, computerlike response. "But this is Sunday. They're closed, and I need the number now."

"Sorry. You'll have to call after eight tomorrow morning."

"Thanks for nothing." Stewart slammed the phone back on the hook, held up his digital watch, and checked the time. Rasputin was crying, waiting to be fed. Stewart looked at the cat narrowly. No time to fool with can openers now. Rummaging through the refrigerator he found some leftover chicken, tossed it on the kitchen floor. Sleepily, he put coffee in the mill and listened to it grind. His reporter's mind finally clicked into high gear.

Shira wasn't much of a creature of habit, he reasoned, but she did play the credit card game for all it was worth. And that might narrow the possibilities of where she had holed up in Houston. She had only four cards: Saks, Macy's, MasterCard, and Avis. Having seen her off on a Delta flight to Texas, he knew the car rental office might be his first lead. He would call Avis in Houston and check for a local address she may have given the attendants there.

Fifteen minutes later Stewart had filled the small pad beside the kitchen phone with scribbled notations. Howard Johnson's Motel, a new light blue Pinto, license 277-GRZ. But the motel clerk claimed there was no answer in Shira Bernstein's room. Odd, Stewart thought. As long as he had known Shira, not even a jackhammer could dislodge her from the sack before ten on Sunday, her sleep-in morning. The more he thought about her terse voice on long distance the night before, the more his apprehension mounted, and the more he cursed to himself. If he didn't reach her at the motel before nightfall, he would book a morning flight south to investigate.

Immediately following the early Sunday Bible-study class at the Congregational church near his official mansion on Massachusetts Avenue, the Vice-President of the United States had driven to the Executive Office Building. Paul Chandler wanted to be alone to polish up his notes for an afternoon guest appearance on "Face the Nation." Ordinarily, he would have preferred spending the late morning on the golf greens, but today, and in the seven days ahead, he knew there would be little time for personal pleasure.

The fifty-one-year-old Vice-President was a man of medium height, slightly built, with a thin, ascetic face and deeply recessed eyes. The high-backed green leather chair and his broad, inlaid mahogany desk made him look small by comparison. Paul Chandler pushed a button next to his telephone, and almost immediately an aide appeared and placed before him a carafe of coffee. Chandler poured himself a cup, sipped it slowly, and gazed out the window toward the White House. He smiled smugly to himself, for he knew that after the maelstrom of events in the coming week, the decadent liberal in the Oval Office would be eliminated and he would move across the street. Chandler exhaled sharply. It seemed a long time ago that CIA Director Walter Singer and the Committee had enlisted his active support. The months had passed quickly, and the personnel, the funding, the careful planning had all built up to these final moments before the big push. For only five more days would he stand in the shadow of the President. No more would he have to endure this man who was an insult to his party. Never again would he have to put up with that condescending face he despised.

Things weren't quite the same as they had been during the Ronald Reagan years when Paul Chandler had been a senior senator and the nation's most outspoken conservative. Even that administration had once labeled Paul Chandler as the ultimate reactionary. His invitation to share the presidential ticket was itself a supreme act of condescension, an irritating kindness from the current tenant of the Oval Office, who had no real choice in the matter. The ultraconservatives had missed the top of the slate by the narrowest of margins. Paul Chandler may have owed his skyrocketing political fortunes to financial backers like U.S. Motors, Texas-Atlantic Petroleum, Condor Defense Industries, and Frober's Worldwide Hotels, but he was indebted to the hard-right man on the street for his final triumph, the invitation to share the ticket and the subsequent endorsement by the convention. He owed everything to the hard-core right, whose demands had been met to balance the slate. Chandler felt no gratitude whatever toward the man across the way in the White House, an individual whose mistakes had long past caught up with him. He suspected that countless Americans, like himself, disliked the Chief Executive. The polls said otherwise, but Chandler was convinced the polls were manipulated by the liberals.

The Vice-President glanced up at the grandfather clock in the corner—a timepiece that came with the office and was reputedly once owned by John Quincy Adams. It chimed eleven. Time for his friend Jimmy Hallowell's revival on nationwide television. "The electronic church," Chandler reflected. The Puritan ethic was another virtue the nation's purportedly pro-humanist, pro-atheist Commander-in-Chief completely misunderstood.

For twenty minutes Chandler watched and listened to Hallowell's sermon, taped an hour earlier in Houston. One minute the TV reverend waved his Bible, pontificating, the next hě was low key, the master of the understatement. Leaning over his TV pulpit, Hallowell was tall—very tall and stringy-framed with a mane of silver hair parted in the middle. He had a sanguine face with close-set eyes and a slightly turned-up, implike nose. He's good, mused Chandler, as he listened. Clever. A very powerful persuader indeed. The Vice-President turned up the volume on the television and said to himself, "Keep at it Jimmy, juice them up for us."

"Yes, there's going to be a battle in this country, and you people out there are going to be a part of it! But take heart! I believe in America. I believe in the American people. I'm an optimist. I think we're going to have a dramatic turnaround and not a doomsday, as some of the weak-hearted among you are prone to predict. There are even those who tell us we have reached a fork in the road—one cause or another." Jimmy Hallowell paused, slowly shaking his head. "Black against white. Either an empty, immoral socialist empire or a country turning from exhaustion to fascism. A gloomy picture, perhaps, for those who haven't read their Bible, for those who are without hope."

The TV camera moved in closer to Hallowell's pulpit as he mopped his sweating brow with a monogrammed handkerchief. "But I believe in moral rebirth, my fellow Americans, and I'm not afraid for you. Neither I nor my children nor their children will surrender to the Godless world of Communism. There is no room for white flags or red flags in the house of the Lord."

The Vice-President rocked gently in his leather chair, eyes glued to the TV. He watched Hallowell hesitate and lean forward across the lectern. The TV sermon continued: "The other day a group of young people—I suspect they were Jewish college students—picketed me as I left O'Hare Airport in Chicago. One of the more assertive young men asked me why I was such a neo-fascist. I must confess to you that I'm not sure what a neo-fascist is. But I do know that, unlike the Communists, few dictators ever promoted atheism, turned cathedrals into museums, or discouraged the worship of Jesus Christ the Savior. If I'm a fascist, then God must be a fascist, too."

The Vice-President smiled, poured himself another cup of coffee, this time passing up the sugar. Chandler considered

Hallowell's address excellent and made a mental note to paraphrase parts of it and use them during his "Face the Nation" interview. He would be shooting a few sacred cows later this day, speaking his mind as he had never done before. Yes, it was a matter of spiritual versus socialist discipline. Time was running out, and he would be testing the national mood, at the same time softening the country up for the apocalyptic shock that lay ahead.

Stewart canceled his usual Sunday jog in Central Park. Keeping fit would have to wait, for Shira might still return his call at any time. He shuffled to the TV, flicked through the channels hoping to pick up a Masters tournament. Nothing but old cartoons, church sermons, and talk shows. He checked his watch, pushed the button again. The familiar face of Jimmy Hallowell filled the screen—the millionaire preacher Shira had purportedly traveled south to interview. The popular TV revivalist was making a guest appearance in Houston, just as Shira had claimed. Spiritual gin, thought Stewart, as he turned up the volume and watched Hallowell shake his fist and speak quickly in a voice sharp with self-righteousness.

"There's nothing wrong with entrepreneurial America that clean living and prayers won't cure," he urged. "It's time to get the government off our backs!"

True enough, thought Stewart, but that's going to take a heap more than medicine-show grandstanding. He thought about what Shira had told him of Hallowell's wealth, his outspoken bigotry, his reactionary connections. Stewart stood in front of the TV feeling a strange numbness as the spellbinder's words repeatedly crashed in his ears.

He turned down the volume. Shira was right, calling it "apple-pie authoritarianism." She had insisted a week earlier that if Hallowell wasn't slowed down, something nasty could come next, and that was why she had to do an in-depth, no-holds-barred story on the man. But was James Hallowell in any way responsible for Shira's disappearance? Or had she really disappeared?

Carlie Chavez, months earlier, had discussed the TV reverend with Stewart, and she had then come to the conclusion that Hallowell was harmless in his place. Carlie had even used the phrase in a TV news editorial, calling the electronic church fulfilling, "harmless in its place." Damn Carlie's naiveté! And damn James Hallowell, for capturing Shira's interest. Stewart turned off the television set, thinking again, "harmless in its place." Everything is relative. A Rolls-Royce is a splendid automobile *in its place,* but not when driven across a schoolyard with a homicidal nut at the wheel. Stewart wondered what kind of luxury automobile Hallowell owned.

Stewart felt himself getting angry. That's what Shira always wanted. But not Carlie. She was another story. Strange how two women saw him so differently. Shira criticized him for being too pragmatic, basically a realist. Carlie Chavez laughed at this suggestion, insisting that he was an incurable romantic. Stewart sighed; obviously his insides were a confused dichotomy.

Stewart tried to shut out any more thoughts of Carlie Chavez, but he couldn't. He closed his eyes and clenched his fists. Slumping down in the sofa, he reached for the phone. He had to talk with someone. The number his trembling fingers dialed was Carlie's.

The blue and white Lockheed JetStar owned by Condor Defense Industries finished its climb out of Houston, banked, throttled back to cruise speed, and headed west. Relinquishing his duties to the copilot, the flight engineer ducked into the back of the plush executive jet, where for the next half-hour he would serve as flight attendant for Condor Defense Industries' special guests. His work would be light this trip, for only three of the seven seats were occupied. Still, the cabin was crowded. Stacked and secured on one side were several boxes containing Uzi 9mm automatic carbines as well as a crate of electronics equipment—high-technology eavesdropping gear manufactured by Condor's Military Communications Division.

The flight-engineer-turned-steward looked at the passenger with the mouse-gray eyes and thin, almost cruel mouth who sat in the first seat across from the cargo. The man ignored him, staring fixedly out the aircraft's window. It was the first time the engineer had seen the director of the U. S. Central Intelligence Agency in person. Walter Singer looked young— very young and in excellent shape for his late forties. Singer's sandy hair was curly and thatched with gray, and he sported a neatly trimmed mustache. He was dressed in a finely tailored suit and Gucci shoes. Word had it that Singer was one of those government whiz kids who had made it to the top by a combination of statistical cleverness and political savvy. The man's eyes were unsettling, cold as a crypt. The flight attendant decided to tread lightly. Singer was also known to have a short fuse.

The Condor Defense Industries crewman surveyed the other guests. They had both been aboard the executive jet before. Facing Walter Singer, separated from him by a small table, sat hotel magnate Karl Frober. Behind them, by himself and sprawled on the small divan, the third passenger, the TV preacher, Jimmy Hallowell, had his face buried in the *Los Angeles Times*.

The first time Singer heard the voice it didn't register. His mind was miles away. He only turned away from the JetStar window when the flight engineer tapped him on the shoulder, again inquiring what he wanted to drink.

"Bourbon. On the rocks," the CIA director replied dully, shifting his frame and loosening his seat belt. Singer looked across the fold-up table at the putty-faced, obese man opposite him.

Karl Frober slipped cigarettes into a brushed gold filter holder and glanced up at the waiting attendant. "Make mine a vodka martini."

Singer couldn't decide what he most disliked about Frober— his corpulence, the ostentatious three-carat diamond on his pinkie, or the contented smile on the hotel executive's face. Perhaps it was the sluggish pop eyes staring back at him that looked as if they belonged to a gargantuan flounder. Frober, as usual, looked quizzical.

Walter Singer gloated. He relished the facade of equanimity he presented to others. Woe to them if they knew of his true strength, compulsion, and weakness. No, he thought. "Weakness" was the wrong word. He had no weakness unless it was his compulsion for clothes priced beyond the range of his budget, like the fine shirts he ordered by the half-dozen from Rome, or his taste for expensive Crimean caviar and contraband Havana cigars. Anything was obtainable through the CIA. Even exotic ladies, though he had no unsatisfied needs in that department. Singer, a bachelor, knew he was handsome enough to appeal to younger women. He spent few solitary nights. To bed partners, business associates, and government bureaucrats alike— to all those who pleased him Singer was capable of affection, gratitude, and unswerving loyalty. But to his enemies, he was as deadly as a cobra.

Singer corrected the exposure of his French cuffs and looked at Frober, finally permitting his handsomely capped teeth to show in a smile. "The meeting at the restaurant," Singer said calmly, "you still claim it was one hundred percent successful?"

Frober frowned. "You heard correctly the first time Walter. One hundred percent."

The CIA director felt annoyed with himself, but pleased with Frober's efforts. Singer had predicted only partial cooperation from the obdurate Nazis, sixty percent of the delegates at the most.

"They may not bring money into the kitty, but the Nazis can offer manpower," Frober suddenly added.

Singer glared back at him. "The quality of that muscle is debatable. Still, any time our ranks swell—" The CIA head paused to accept the drink offered by the flight engineer, noting that the faceted cocktail glass bore a representation of the nearly extinct California condor, fired in gold. Beneath it, in elegant, cursive script, the initials NG. Singer thought of Norman Gifford, the chairman of the board of giant Condor Defense Industries, who would be waiting for them when the executive jet reached Los Angeles. The slender, patrician Gifford was the nation's foremost archconservative, an inseparable friend of Vice-President Chandler, and the Committee's strongest link to Wall Street. By a narrow vote, Singer had lost out to Gifford for the Committee's secret chairmanship. Singer felt no regrets. The real power was in his hands, to use when and where he chose. But Norman Gifford had pulled the financing together. Huge, unbelievable sums had accumulated in the war coffers. He knew that Karl Frober, too, was indebted to the defense plant executive for far more than the use of his private jet. Gifford was the major financial sponsor for the Freedom Militia Press, an educational lobby Frober and other anti-Semites had set up to disprove the historical accounts of the Holocaust.

Looking up from his drink, Frober grinned superficially. He said, "I still say you should have come out to that catfish feed to meet the men, Walter."

Singer grimaced. "Dine with that rabble? Absurd. Even if secrecy were not a factor."

"Our man from Paraguay was responsible for the large turnout. Better than we expected."

"Every minute counts, Frober. The clock's running out. Some of us don't have the luxury of time to listen to the diatribes of infamous has-beens."

Frober looked confused. "Meaning?"

The man sprawled behind the newspaper shook himself upright. Jimmy Hallowell tapped Frober on the shoulder and quickly interjected, "Meaning the money you spent to bring that senile fascist out of South America was a waste of Committee funds. Funds provided, in part, I'll remind you, by my Moral Confederation.

Singer looked at Hallowell speculatively. "I thought you were asleep, Reverend."

"Tired, but not that tired," replied Hallowell. "Well, Walter, do you agree it was misused?"

The CIA head shrugged, took a swift sip of his bourbon. "If he inspired the delegates—"

"No other living fascist has his gift for clever rhetoric," added Frober. "Without the old man's appearance, the American Nazis would never have supported us. Not a chance in hell."

Singer ignored both Frober and Hallowell, flicking a piece of lint from the sleeve of his banker's striped suit as he gazed idly out the window.

Hallowell tapped Frober on the shoulder again. "Your unoccupied resort in Haiti, Karl. I'm curious to know how you finalized the deal. As president of the world's largest hotel chain, you surely didn't erect a twelve-hundred-unit seaside resort to *lose* money. And yet you allow our Committee to use this new facility rent free? With no obligations whatsoever?"

Frober shifted his bulk around in his seat. "Minimal obligations, Reverend. A loan, shall we say? The Committee wishes exclusive use of the facility for eighteen months only, agreed? At the end of that time, the resort returns to my control, to utilize as I see fit."

Hallowell dropped his newspaper and leaned forward slightly in his seat. "And then what?"

Walter Singer smiled sagely to himself. He knew Frober was carefully weighing his words; it was premature to tell the other Committeemen about the potential profit that could be realized from their negotiations with the Haitian government.

Frober's response, predictably, was vague. "If we are successful with our endeavors, I expect the Haitian government to purchase the property from me."

Hallowell winced. "And what, precisely, is our obligation to President Mouffetard in the meantime? Or is that a query I should address to our suddenly uncommunicative CIA friend?"

Whatever reservations Singer had about the Moral Confederation and driven men like Jimmy Hallowell, he was forced to admit they were talented, damned talented, at finding exact phrases to describe a situation. They were also good at asking the right question at the wrong time.

"This isn't the time to discuss the weapons trade-off," Singer snarled, defying Hallowell. "We'll go into the details in Los Angeles. Try to remember, Reverend Hallowell, that you're just *one* member of a four-man Committee."

"Calm down, Walter," soothed Frober, wagging his thickly padded fingers. "I suspect the Reverend merely wants to ensure that the arrangements and accommodations for the President, Supreme Court justices, senators, and congressmen will be suitably comfortable."

Walter Singer's blue eyes flashed from Frober to Hallowell. "Since when is a goddamn concentration camp supposed to be comfortable?"

It was midmorning and the main street of Vinton, Louisiana, was quiet. The Russian Jew who called himself Motti Barak drove his rental car slowly in the curb lane until he spotted a gas station with a pay phone booth out front. Pulling up to the pump, he instructed the attendant to fill the tank. Once again he nervously checked his watch, then strolled over to the phone booth. Barak withdrew a handful of quarters from his pocket, made sure he had enough change. Three minutes later, precisely at ten-thirty, he punched out the number of another pay phone near a Washington, D.C., supermarket. The operator came on the line, and Barak deposited two dollars and fifty cents. Seconds passed, and a gruff, heavily accented voice answered.

"Yes?"

Recognizing Ambassador Grotski's voice, Barak breathed easier. Identifying himself, he swiftly said, "Implications of the restaurant meeting are now clear to us. For the first time, the hierarchy leaders of three extremist groups have come to an agreement. They will join forces. As for the German, he got away and is headed back to Paraguay. His appearance was little more than —shall we say, as the Americans put it—a pep talk."

"Pep talk? I do not understand the colloquialism" was Grotski's coarse reply.

"Inspirational speech, sir." Barak had carefully used "sir" instead of "comrade." "Everything else is going smoothly enough here. Has your other observer left the capital for that Haiti resort yet?"

"Yes. He should be in Puerto Rico by nightfall. In the morning a pilot will take him from San Juan to the Dominican Republic in a private plane."

Barak thought for a moment. "The guide has been notified?"

"He will be waiting and will take our man across the mountains into Haiti as expeditiously as possible. You've done good work for us down there, Barak. You will return to Washington immediately?"

"No. I must remain here several hours longer, perhaps even a day or two. A local FBI agent is still missing, and I suspect he is still alive. There are other developments; a woman was forcibly expelled from the meeting and taken away."

"Be careful. You will report at the same time tomorrow then?"

"Whatever you command," replied Barak dully.

"Good-bye."

Coming to at last, FBI agent Tyrone Jackson raised a limp arm and felt his head. Flies buzzed above him and covered the ceiling. A radio blared somewhere nearby. Jackson turned slightly and saw a cherubic-faced black man in a sweat-stained felt hat staring at him. The old man's eyes were red-lined and tired.

"You been out for a long time, man. How's your head feelin'?"

Jackson hesitated, unable to collect his thoughts. His head ached. The room at last took solid shape and meaning: a bayou cabin, apparently a fisherman's hut back in the swamp. Behind a wood-burning stove made from an oil drum hung a grease-covered Norman Rockwell 1958 calendar. A spotted coon hound darted into the room, sniffed his hand, and tried to jump up on the sagging bed. The old man, still hovering over Jackson, nudged the animal away.

"Saw them dump you in the swamp when I was checkin' my traps. Jus' wasn't your time to die, I s'pose. Had to poke off a pair of water mocs to get you out of the water."

Jackson shivered. He hated snakes, especially swamp snakes. "What can I say? Thanks, Good Samaritan."

The unshaven old man grinned, revealing several broken teeth. "Mocs might not have fed on you, but five more minutes and the 'gators have a dandy feast for themselves. Them boys returned a little later, draggin' somebody else out there. Sounded like a woman screamin'. I heard a shot that time, so I was scared shit to go out there again."

Jackson raised himself slightly. "I need a telephone, and quickly. I'm an FBI agent."

"Easy, man, easy. First things first. Wowee! Goddamn if you don't sound educated. You miles from civilization, boy. I already done sent my son hikin' over to d'neighbors. They got a truck, if the bailin' wire still holdin' it together. Meantime, you just lay there and relax.

Jackson swatted a fly away from his face. Relax, he mused. Jesus Almighty!

5

STEWART ARRIVED AT the Times Building twenty minutes early.
For two weeks he would have the pleasure of working the day
shift, but his job was the farthest thing from his mind this
morning. All he wanted to do was clear his proposed absence
with City Editor Mike Murphy and hustle out to Kennedy for
a ten-thirty flight to Houston. Asking for two days off, he
reasoned, wouldn't be out of line. He'd never sought special
favors before, and had accumulated plenty of sick leave. Stepping into the elevator, he heard a gentle shout behind him.

"Kirk! Hold the door, please."

Sweeping toward him across the lobby, red and white checked
silk scarf trailing from her neck, her face beaming, was Carlie
Chavez.

"Good morning, beautiful," Stewart said somewhat cheer-
lessly. "Come to apply for a job as a junior reporter?"

Ignoring his tease, she winked and strode into the elevator.
Stewart sniffed her light cologne. Even without it, Carlie had
an aura that was all her own. Her eyes were deep brown, sooty,
hauntingly beautiful. One of the original feminists, she walked
and talked with authority and self-assurance. The night three
years back when they had slept together came rushing back to

Stewart once again in infinite detail, stabbing at his mind like a sharp needle. As a reporter, Carlie's professional manner was a delicate balance of attitudes, but in bed her passions ran to the extremes of dominance and complete passivity; she had, in Stewart's appraisal, been a sexy yo-yo.

"Are you just going to stand there drinking me in or do you plan to say something intelligent?" she asked, smiling casually and tossing her long, silky black hair over her shoulder. "On the phone yesterday you sounded lonely. I considered asking you to go with me to the Guggenheim, but figured you were determined to sit there and wait for Shira's call."

Stewart felt a familiar surge in his pulse. His last date with Carlie seemed like eons ago; they had gone to a museum. He remembered that Carlie loved art, or made a good pretense of enjoying it. She was also one of those eager movie buffs who haunted the Museum of Modern Art film showings.

"Did you come to see me," he asked, "or do you have official business upstairs?"

"Strictly work. So what about Shira? I trust she finally called?"

Stewart grimaced. "No. I'm convinced she's disappeared. Under peculiar circumstances, at that."

Carlie's face tightened. "Are you sure you're not panicking?"

He shook his head. "She's flown the coop before, but this time I've got reasons to be worried. I'm leaving town today to look for her." The elevator arrived at Stewart's floor.

Carlie held his arm as the doors rolled open. "Kirk, I have a meeting with the fashion editor. You want to have lunch today and talk more about it?"

Stewart touched her hand briefly and stepped out of the elevator. "Love to, Carlie, but I'm leaving in an hour for the airport. The sooner I get to Houston the better."

"Kirk, call me later, okay? I want to help." She held the elevator door with one foot and kissed him on the cheek. "Don't forget!" she called, stepping back inside. The doors closed.

Stewart felt a warm glow on his face. Carlie frustrated him. He felt like putty in her hands—a frustrating, uncomfortable feeling. He ignored both the coffee machine and his own desk and went directly to the office of the city editor. Mike Murphy, as usual, was early. Never, in the three years Stewart had worked for the *Times* had he observed his boss come in later than the rest of the staff.

Stewart hesitated in the doorway, straightening his regimental stripe tie.

The city editor was a heavyweight Irishman with thick gray hair and silver-rimmed glasses. A University of Missouri journalism graduate of the early fifties, Mike Murphy was a cheerful, hardworking sort who still breathed midwestern America. Stewart had Murphy figured for the kind of man who would make wisecracks on his deathbed. The editor had already put his coffee aside, rolled up his shirtsleeves, and gone to work on a stack of papers before him. Eyes veiled, Murphy looked up as Stewart entered the office without knocking. It was one of the few privileges of a favored reporter.

"Morning, Kirk." Murphy glanced at his watch. "Your clock on the blink? This is early for you."

"Mike, I need a favor." Stewart rubbed his neck.

"Don't we all? See payroll or the credit union if you're looking for an advance. I'm just a newsman."

Without being asked, Stewart plopped down in the chrome and crimson mohair armchair facing Murphy's desk. "I need a couple of days off. Maybe three. A personal problem that just might evolve into a story."

Murphy pushed the papers before him to one side and looked at Stewart seriously. He rolled one big hand back and forth. "Which is it? Personal peccadilloes or news?"

"Nothing spicy. It involves a lady friend's safety as well as some peculiar national politics. I need to go out of town."

"Like where? And why?"

Stewart sat back in his chair and took a deep breath. "Texas, maybe Louisiana. And I don't know why. Not yet. But I'm desperate."

"You're talking in riddles." Murphy's eyes sparkled briefly, then hardened. "One of those quirky, confusing gray areas, I presume?"

Stewart nodded. "With political overtones."

"You know politics isn't your baby, Kirk. We've got the best stringers money can buy down south, not to mention the Washington bureau. If you've got a lead, take it through channels. Call Weatherby at the capital or get your ass upstairs and talk to the brass. It's their baby. Your beat is city crime and corruption, and the way I see it, that's more than enough for half a dozen shoes your size."

Stewart sat forward in his seat. "Mike, it's more than that. It's Shira, the woman I'm living with. She went after a controversial story and disappeared."

"Sure. Sure. Probably with some other stud. You'll get over it. So what's her specialty?"

"I introduced you at the Christmas party. Shira Bernstein. A free-lancer. She'd done some heavy stuff for *Penthouse* and *McCall's*."

Murphy took off his glasses and carefully began polishing the lenses. "The paper can't get involved in your personal affairs, Kirk. You know that. What the hell do you want from me?"

Stewart hesitated. Obviously, he wasn't going to sell a story on this. There was no way he would get a round-trip plane ticket out of Murphy. Quietly, he finally said, "Two days off. Personal reasons. Okay?"

Murphy eyed him keenly, finally grinned.

Stewart swiftly added, "Without pay. You can forget sick leave."

The city editor's smile hardened, but he didn't lose it. He rose from behind his desk, nudged the wastebasket aside, and walked over to the window. Looking down at the street, he said, "All right, you've got them. If you need any more time, or if you get into political hot water, you're out of my hands. The next step's the managing editor. You're a good reporter, Stewart. You've got a damned good job. So don't spoil things by getting sloppy.

Stewart suddenly felt better. Murphy was right. He was lucky, he did have a good job. His mind clicked, hastily trying to analyze the reason for his success, his good fortune in beating out a dozen others for the *Times* job. Why was he so good at crime stories? Was it the morbidity of the subject matter that made his prose so compelling? Most of his material wound up on the inside pages, concise and dispassionate; the kind of objective writing learned in Journalism 101: hard, factual, brisk, accurate. Occasionally, seldom more than twice a month, he did an in-depth feature, and then Mike Murphy would reward him with a byline. But all in all, he was a long way from a Pulitzer. He still needed something big, really big. Syndication stuff.

"You listening to me or daydreaming?" asked Murphy abruptly. "I'll get Phil and Marlene to cover for you while you're out, but there's one last thing. You can leave *after* you interview some men from the FBI."

"Dammit, Mike, My plane leaves at ten."

"You can catch a later flight. An FBI press release waits for no one. What's more, the FBI is sending your pal Tap Nelson up from Washington to conduct the briefing. If he's in town, it's an important show."

"Tap's no pal. Just a schoolmate. An eccentric one at that." Stewart got to his feet, shook his head. Look, Mike. I think—"

"No buts, how-comes, or sour faces. If our press officer's even a half-ass friend, you might get an inside track. A lead."

"Lead to what? Would you mind elucidating?"

Murphy sat back down behind his desk, lit a cigarette, and gazed up at Stewart through a blue haze of smoke. "Okay, here's what I know. Early Friday morning in the Bronx an FBI agent was shot. Assailants unknown. Damned near cut his body in half with automatic carbine fire. The police claim he was on to a huge shipment of stolen military weapons. Automatic rifles. The facts are vague. Start digging, Stewart. And give me a call after you've talked with Nelson and the FBI. *Before* leaving town." The look Murphy gave him was as explicit as a command. Stewart was obviously dismissed.

6

THE FBI PRESS conference in mid-Manhattan had come off without a hitch—or a lead, for that matter. Stewart was surprised to find that after all the journalistic huffing and puffing City Editor Mike Murphy had given the gang-style shooting in the Bronx, the Bureau—his former schoolmate Tap Nelson included—had no more to go on than Gotham's men in blue. The press conference was apparently called for one purpose, to generate leads, and to this end Press Officer Nelson had announced that the FBI was offering a reward of ten thousand dollars for information leading to the conviction of their agent's killer.

As the reporters, their notebooks mostly empty, filed out of the conference room, the short, animated press officer hurried up to Stewart and pulled him aside. "Kirk, you old scoundrel! Good to see you. Still playing golf?"

Stewart grinned. "Good to see you, Tap. No, I haven't touched a golf club since graduate school. Figure to take it up again when I retire. How's that foxy wife of yours?"

Nelson's face stiffened. "Divorced last month. Out of that bullshit."

Stewart didn't pursue the subject. He felt embarrassed, remembering that he had been unable to attend Nelson's wedding in Maryland just over a year ago. A quick affair, he thought. Too quick. Nelson was apparently still the Peter Pan type. Slam, bam, thank you, ma'am.

Several reporters, some of them Stewart's friends, hesitated beside Nelson, hoping for additional information. The FBI press officer shot them a glance of disapproval, and they moved on.

"I knew the *Times* would send you over for this story," Nelson quipped. "But damn it man, let's talk business later. Flip you for lunch? Understand a good sushi bar just opened on Fifty-second Street. Tell me. You still the bleeding-heart liberal, Kirk?"

"Only person ever thought that was you, cox. You not only ran the business end of the varsity shell, but if I recall, you aired your conservative views on the debate team as well. Which way you leaning now, Tap, or dare I ask? Still quoting Hegel and Nietzsche?"

Nelson smiled. "Politics isn't allowed among the Bureau rank and file," he said jokingly. "I've learned to keep my mouth shut over the years."

Stewart smiled, wondering if such a feat was possible. Tap Nelson had always been a motor mouth. Still, there were the more purposeful shouts in college. Nelson had been coxswain on the same crew for which Stewart had rowed stroke, but Tap had been a lone wolf, never joining a social organization. In particular he had condemned fraternities, more often than not preferring his own company, spending countless hours in the library.

"About lunch, Tap." Stewart was thinking of Shira and his trip to Houston. He glanced at his watch. "How about just coffee and a rain check? I've got fifteen, maybe twenty minutes before I catch an airport bus to Kennedy."

"Whoa! What about our story?" Nelson chided.

"I'll file it by phone. Look, I've got some heavy-duty headaches. You remember my lady, Shira. You met at Emilio's Bar down in the Village a year ago. Well, she's disappeared. I figure it's tied in with chasing Nazis down in Louisiana."

Nelson's easy manner vanished. He looked hard at Stewart.

The FBI press officer was the same age as Stewart, but he was nearly a foot shorter, a runt of a man at five feet three. He was built solidly enough, had a strong chin, thick wavy

blond hair, blue eyes, and pleasant features. Nelson pushed his
hand rapidly over the shock of hair on his forehead and chewed
his lip. Grabbing Stewart by the elbow, he gestured to an
adjoining office. "Let me get my brief and coat, and I'll share
a cab with you to Kennedy. We can pick up a corned beef at
the airport snack bar. I have to get back to Washington anyway,
so I'll just snag an earlier commuter flight." Nelson pointed
toward the door, then hesitated. "You sure Shira's not dancing
you around?"

Stewart softly retorted, "Not a chance."

"You mentioned Louisiana. Like whereabouts? And when?"

"Saturday night. She called me from an outdoor pay phone
somewhere between New Orleans and Houston. I heard highway traffic in the background."

Nelson frowned and pursed his lips. "Okay, pal, I believe
you. We just may have something in common we need to talk
about." Nelson hesitated, appeared to be contemplating. Finally, he said, "Forget the cab. I'll have one of the local office
men drive us to the airport. We'll need the privacy."

Stewart tried to read Nelson's eyes, but saw no clue to the
Bureau man's thoughts. "You have some ideas?" he asked lamely.

Nelson pointed toward the elevator. "Kirk, do me a favor.
Let's meet outside, downstairs, all right? Give me ten minutes
to round up a car in the garage, and I'll pick you up on the
street."

Stewart nodded, watched Tap disappear into a nearby office,
then idly pushed the elevator call button with his left hand. He
looked at his splinted finger and slowly shook his head. He
stood alone in the corridor.

The causes with which Shira Bernstein involved herself were
annoyingly similar, he thought. Why? Some things were difficult for a gentile to understand. Why, he wondered, were
Shira and her fellow Jewish activist friends forever scraping
away the scabs of partially healed wounds, never walking away
and letting them heal?

Once Stewart had agreed to attend one of Shira's Israeli
Defenders meetings, but at the last minute had bailed out on
the pretense of having to do some research for a newspaper
assignment. In truth he had gone to bed with an adventure
novel. Twice she had asked him to come along to anti-Nazi
rallies, and twice he had begged off. The assault by the goons
in the subway had come as a complete surprise. Had he shown

more interest in Shira's activities, the incident might not have happened. Or would it have occurred sooner? Obviously, she was in danger. He had been indifferent. Negligent. The guilt he should have felt in the past compounded itself now, stabbing at his conscience. He heard Shira's voice again, not on a long-distance telephone wire, but coming to him through a long tunnel. Her voice was distant, far away. He strained to hear, but couldn't make out what she was saying.

He took the elevator down to the lobby.

Dennis Garrett's modest Washington, D.C., apartment was located on the edge of Georgetown. As an off-and-on male model, Garrett prided himself not only on his photogenic face but also on a finely toned, lithe, muscular body. He did sit-ups daily and worked out with weights before a mirror three times a week.

Garrett put down the barbells he was sweating over and hurried to answer the door chime. The visitor's face was familiar, but he didn't smile. One hand provocatively resting on his hip, Garrett beckoned for the midmorning visitor to enter the apartment. The balding, barrel-chested CIA agent nodded and stepped swiftly inside the door, his eyes briefly scanning the entry area with its blue Persian carpet, umbrella stand filled with matching blue-dyed pampas grass, and a small plaster replica of Michelangelo's David, sans fig leaf. Immediately, from his suede jacket, he withdrew a thick envelope and thrust it forward as though further contact might contaminate him.

"It's all here? In cash?" asked Garrett, his voice quavering in anticipation.

"All there." grunted the agent. "Garrett, I've got a message for you. There's an extra thousand in the deal. Fat travel expenses, to be used today. But the rest of it, the big wad, is more than enough to set you up in style—anywhere you like. Los Angeles, San Francisco, New Orleans. Anywhere but New York or Washington."

"Really? Wait a second, please. And call me Dennis. May I fix you an eye-opener?"

The bald man squirmed and thrust out his jaw. "Look, personally I don't like you or what you've done. I just get paid to do a job, okay? But that doesn't mean I have to clink Bloody Marys with buck-hungry pricks like you."

"What's eating you? Mind your manners, Raquel baby."

"Fuck you. Inconspicuous gays I can handle. Liberated fags I'm learning to tolerate. But outright cunts, hustlers like you, make me want to puke. Your instructions are to forget the President, forget the names of the TV recording crew, forget me, and most important, get lost. The name of the game from now on is low profile, and don't forget it. We want you out of Washington and off the East Coast by seven tonight."

Dennis Garrett was only half listening. The envelope was open, and he was counting hundred dollar bills. Looking up, in a soft voice he swiftly said, "You're a thousand short."

The CIA agent nodded and half withdrew another envelope from his pocket. "It's yours, a week after the President resigns. Provided you've toed the line, nice and quiet." He handed Garrett a small card bearing nothing but a phone number. "Call me in two weeks. In the meantime, just disappear." Abruptly, he backed out of the apartment.

"Fucking *homophobe!*" sneered Garrett under his breath, as he closed the door. Time to start packing, he figured. Money talks. Los Angeles would be his ultimate destination. Seasonless, sparkling Sunset Boulevard, where who knows what lady luck might bring him? Celebrity city. But first there were debts to pay, friends to visit, a former lover to impress in New York. The hell with the CIA and its hired stooges. Shagging his ass out of the capital on time would be good enough. No way they would find him in Manhattan; besides, it would be a brief visit. Then he'd run for the Coast.

His code name was Lynx, and all anyone knew about him was that he worked for the Committee as a courier and the orders he carried were to be obeyed.

When Lynx made the call to the White House Secret Service Office and asked for Agent Fourteen he was well aware the line might be monitored. Despite this, he had to know if the videotape of Dennis Garrett had been delivered and placed in the hands of the Chief Executive. He could not let it disappear somewhere among the protective staff's bureaucracy. After talking his way past two officious secretaries running interference, Lynx heard a familiar voice on the line. "This is Marsh, Agent Fourteen."

"Lynx at this end. A public phone with no scramble. I'll be brief."

"I'm listening," came the curt reply.

"The proposal for painting the President's study. Has it been presented to the man yet? The decorator's anxious for a reaction."

"Received and being evaluated. A little shocked at the color selection. We'll get back with full particulars in a couple of days."

Lynx digested this. "No. My superiors need a report tomorrow. Meet me at the usual place."

The Manhattan noon-hour rush was on. Checking his watch, Stewart wondered if Tap Nelson had abandoned him. He debated whether to hail a cab, forget the FBI man's offer of a lift, and head for the airport on his own. The Bureau motor pool car finally arrived at the curb, and Nelson, seated beside the driver, gestured for Stewart to climb in the back. He complied, placing his overnight bag in front of his feet, but was startled to find a large hulk of a man on the far side of the seat waiting for him. Stewart had seen that empty landscape of a face too many times in news stories not to recognize Oliver Wright, director of the FBI. Stewart was surprised, and let it show. Why, he wondered, had this latest heir to the throne of J. Edgar Hoover not appeared at the news conference just minutes before?

"Pleased to have you join us, Mr. Stewart," the big, sinewy man said, a bit mildly, considering his size. He was big, very big, thought Stewart. Wright's cold eyes were set wide apart in great caves; his nose was strong, his mouth expressionless. Wright's features seemed lost on the empty lot that was his face—a face framed with neatly trimmed sideburns and iron gray hair combed straight back.

In the front seat, Stewart's friend Tap Nelson appeared nervous and distant as he introduced his superior. Stewart nodded and shook Wright's hand. The grip was firm and full of conviction.

"The chief wanted to talk to you personally," Nelson explained. Gesturing toward the man behind the wheel, he added, "and you've met Kenny Ferguson from the New York office before. His partner was the agent who was riddled with bullets Friday morning. We're all family here, so feel free to open up."

Stewart tried, unsuccessfully, to relax. He sat back as the car slid into the Broadway traffic and headed for the Midtown

Tunnel. Up front, Nelson turned toward him, watchful, waiting for Oliver Wright to speak. Like waiting for the voice of God, thought Stewart, an uncomfortable feeling inside him quickening. The FBI director definitely appeared to have something on his mind.

Oliver Wright's face remained taut as he slowly said, "Nelson vouches for you. Claims you can be trusted. God knows that's a precious commodity these days. Is Nelson correct?"

"Implicitly. Unless I'm with an attractive lady. Mind if I ask what's going on? Off the record, of course. Why all the deadpan looks?"

Wright didn't bat an eyelash. "Had any thoughts about the big civilian arms stash? Those military weapons in the Bronx, and our man eliminated?"

"Not yet. Still a shocker."

"We should have been ready for them," Wright said sourly, obviously hating himself. "Inexcusable." He pushed out his chin. "I'm told your lady friend disappeared down south over the weekend."

"Yes, sir."

"Might she have been heading over toward Lake Charles, Louisiana? Nazi hunting, possibly?"

Stewart swallowed hard. "I'm not sure, but I intend to find out."

A buzzer sounded in the briefcase at Wright's feet. The big man swiftly opened the clasps and removed a slender plastic hand set. "This is Wright," he snapped. There was a sustained silence, then he said, "Negative. I can't talk now. What? Hell, yes, I know where Singer's headed. The CIA's getting sloppy, thank God. He'll be flying back to the capital tonight on TWA." Replacing the phone in his briefcase, Wright looked out the window and grimaced at the snarled traffic.

Sitting indolently, Stewart waited for the FBI director's next parry. Had Stewart said too much to Nelson earlier, following the press conference? He didn't want his hands tied, but he needed help, help he could trust. Could he level with the Bureau?

Somber-faced, Wright asked abruptly, "This woman. Her name?"

"Shira Bernstein."

"How long has she been trying to hold Nazi tigers by the tail?"

Stewart felt as if he were being interrogated rather than

assisted. He shrugged. "I can't answer that. I've only known her for a little over two years. In that time the only reactionaries she's written about were run-of-the-mill, paranoid pussycats. Not a tiger among them, as far as I could tell."

Wright grunted. "Carnivores come in all sizes, Stewart. Never underestimate what lies in wait in the jungle."

Stewart stared at Wright but didn't respond.

The FBI man continued. Did she leave any notes around the apartment? Partially completed manuscripts? How about telephone numbers?"

"None. She keeps her current projects with her. Relies on memory, a small loose-leaf notebook, and a recorder in her purse. Self-contained."

"I'll vouch for the memory part," added Nelson quickly. "The Shira I met sounded like a walking computer. Photographic recall that would make IBM blush."

The faintest flicker passed over Oliver Wright's eyes. "Photographs. As a reporter, she takes her own pictures?"

"Often," Stewart replied. "Not bad, some of them."

"And has she shown you many of the prints?"

"We try not to talk shop all the time, but sure, I'm as curious as the next guy." Stewart shot Wright a look, then turned away, watching the crowds in the crosswalk in front of the car.

Wright withdrew from his pocket two photographs, which he kept palmed as he spoke. "The FBI would prefer that you cancel your trip, Mr. Stewart. Just a warning, you understand. It's still a free country. But I'll try to explain why, and then you decide what value you place on your life." He paused, shuffling the photographs in his hand. "You recall, of course, the national political campaigns just two years ago, the nasty rumors circulating about our divorced President's personal affairs?"

"I wasn't writing about them, but I remember the stories."

"I'm speaking of the lusty headlines in the supermarket tabloids, the insinuations that the President, before the election, had a damned ménage-à-trois, of sorts, going with a Senator Wyngate and his wife. There was other bizarre crap."

Stewart shrugged. He remembered. It was dead news, the ugly kind that goes unsubstantiated. Tabloid stuff. He hadn't given a damn about it then, and he didn't now. What did this have to do with Shira? he wondered. "I recall the incident. The senator died of a heart attack."

Wright nodded. "While the claims were being investigated by my department. Wouldn't you, under similar circumstances, welcome a coronary infarction?" Wright smiled measurably for the first time. "Thank God it all came after the election, but it's a wonder some of the President's enemies didn't start impeachment proceedings then and there."

"The charges wouldn't have stuck."

"True. But now it appears that the man in the Oval Office has another problem."

Stewart eyed the snapshots in Wright's hand. He felt irritated and impatient. "So what else is new? Recession, unemployment at an all-time high, global unrest, soaring taxes, crime in the streets." Stewart looked at his friend, who sat sideways in the front seat, but saw only an earnest, serious look. The agent behind the wheel stared stoically ahead, seemingly oblivious to the conversation.

The FBI director continued: "The President's doing as good a job as anyone, all things considered. What I feel or think, off the record, is beside the point. I'm a paid public official; I work for the attorney general, who was appointed by the President. In short, I do a job, as professionally as I can. And I get as pissed as the next person when I find a rotten egg in the carton."

"Or maybe several rotten eggs," Nelson added grimly.

Oliver Wright frowned. "That remains to be seen. But right now, there's a professionally videotaped interview in the White House that sure as hell doesn't belong there. This is strictly off the record, Stewart, and don't ever forget it. You need my help, I need yours." Wright flipped one of the photos in his hand into Stewart's lap. "You ever see this face before, either in person or in one of your girlfriend's photo collections?"

The snapshot was taken from a videotape; the scanning lines were plainly visible. "No," Stewart said firmly.

Wright proceeded. "This nineteen-year-old punk claims the President invited him, along with a couple of lesbian girlfriends, up to Camp David for a fishing trip, and then tried to seduce the lot of them."

"Christ," grunted Stewart, exhaling sharply. "What next?"

"Dates, phony autographed photos, you name it. Clever setup if I ever saw one. No name given, just the threat of releasing the tape to the press, along with a file of pertinent data—whatever the hell that means—unless the President announces his resignation during his State of the Union address on Friday. How do you like those apples that were tossed on my desk just yesterday? If I look tired, it's because I've been up all night."

Stewart shook his head in disbelief. "My sympathy for the lack of sleep, Mr. Wright, but what's this got to do with Shira Bernstein? And forgive my reporter's nosiness, but why were you in New York first thing this morning if not to participate in the press conference?"

"Easy, easy. One thing at a time," said Wright as the car stopped for another light. He copped a glance at a blonde hurrying across the street, then continued. "The President sent me here to have breakfast with his former wife. Under the crisis circumstances, I was to try to talk her into coming back to the capital for a couple of weeks, to stand by him, so to speak, during the upcoming heat."

"Mind if I ask what she said?"

"That the top man's political accomplishments spoke for themselves; he needed no defense from her."

Tap Nelson exchanged swift looks with Stewart. "Cold-hearted helpful bitch, isn't she?"

"There's a rumor she plans to run for governor of New York," said Stewart smugly.

Wright recoiled. "I didn't know that. She didn't say a word about it."

"You run in different cocktail circuits than a New York reporter, Mr. Wright." Stewart felt impatient, irritated. Where, he wondered, was all this leading? Why were they toying with him? "Look, Mr. Wright. What about Shira's trip to Louisiana?"

"That's the point—there's a direct tie between the tape and the events that occurred Saturday night near Lake Charles. The messenger who delivered the blackmail videotape to the east gate of the White House was dressed appropriately enough in a uniform, but he was also a little naive. Unknown to him, the Secret Service men routinely photograph all delivery personnel. Obviously, anyone bringing in a package on a Sunday raises more than the usual number of eyebrows. The duty men also picked up a couple of decent fingerprints, good enough to run through our computer. The messenger, it appears, was a long way from home." Wright handed a second photograph to Stewart. "Did Shira ever show you a picture of this individual?"

Stewart examined the snapshot of the messenger; it had

obviously been taken months earlier without the subject's knowledge. The photo was of a youngish, dark-haired, slender man unloading a truck in front of a gun store. American Eagle Gun Emporium. Stewart committed both the face and the sign on the gun shop to memory. "Sorry. I've never seen him before," he finally said.

Wright continued. "His name is Arnold Metz. We've traced him to Galveston, Texas. He's one of the biggest gun peddlers in the South. Legally and not so legally, it appears. Curiously, Metz was seen near Lake Charles on Friday making a delivery of automatic weapons. Our stakeout in that area observed him conducting a big transaction at a highway restaurant—the same establishment where we suspected a neo-Nazi convention to be held on Saturday night!"

Stewart leaned forward eagerly. "Where? You have the name of the place?" He suddenly felt relieved and challenged. Shira's disappearance, the possibility of real danger—it was real, very real, not his imagination after all. That this meant trouble only increased his determination.

Oliver Wright turned his head heavily and saw the excitement on Stewart's face. He pointed to the overnight bag on the floor. "Of course you have a camera in there."

"Of course," replied Stewart smugly.

"Forget the trip. I want you to stay out."

Stewart looked at Wright, decided to backwater.

"Consider it advice, fair enough?" The noncommittal tone Wright routinely used for reporters was missing now. "All I can do is ask for your cooperation. I have a gut feeling that what's happened so far is just the tip of a menacing iceberg. Whatever, it's bigger than you can handle, Stewart. And it just may be bigger than the FBI can handle."

Squirming uncomfortably, Stewart looked at Nelson, searching his features for some clue as to how Tap would react if he were probing around the surface of a similar iceberg, but he saw nothing.

Wright grimly added, "If this Shira friend of yours is involved in this, we'll find her. We have a stake in that Nazi meeting ourselves."

"Meaning?"

"The agent out of New Orleans assigned to cover that meeting—a Tyrone Jackson—is missing. And there's the New York incident you were briefed on this morning. Sorry, Stewart, but you've heard enough. We can use you here to keep your eyes open, but not down south. When we reach the airport, let our driver here take you back to the *Times* office. Take my advice. Cancel that flight, and you may live to tell your grandchildren a story to end all stories. Take off on your own, half cocked, and you'll be placing your head in a noose."

7

IT WASN'T UNTIL they had fastened their seat belts in the first-class section of the Washington-bound 727 that Oliver Wright put away his grim face. Smiling sagely, he turned to the press officer beside him. "Excellent idea, Nelson. He wasted no time shaking our man. Obviously headed for Houston. Though for a time I had my doubts your friend would take the bait."

"He *is* the bait, boss," replied Nelson, his voice an uneasy whisper.

Oliver Wright shifted his massive frame. "True. The task now is to keep him alive."

Again, an agitated, whispered response. "Mr. Wright, under the circumstances, that may not be easy."

"Agreed. And we'll be needing a favorable press. See to it that Stewart has twenty-four-hour-a-day company from the minute he steps off the plane in Houston."

The taxi lurched forward, stopped again. Traffic was moving at a snail's pace, and Carlie Chavez was seriously considering walking. Staring out at the pedestrians in front of Macy's, she suddenly found herself caught up in daydreaming. There was a Greek travel poster in one of the department store's display windows. Curious, she thought. Over three thousand years ago, according to one of the plays of Euripides, beautiful Helen of Troy lamented the suffering she endured because Paris chose to favor another with his love. But in the end, by wit and circumstance, Helen had prevailed. Illusions, Carlie thought, her thoughts doing a broad jump. Even the twentieth century was fraught with fantasy. Why, she wondered, had her disappointment at losing Kirk Stewart suddenly planted itself in her mind? The phone calls, meeting him this morning in the elevator bothered her.

Never had Carlie felt such ambivalence toward Shira Bernstein. Did Kirk really expect her to worry in the present over a woman she had damned in the past? But why had Shira disappeared?

Removing a compact from her Nina Ricci handbag, Carlie checked her makeup in the mirror. Only a part of her mind was on the reflection; the rest was mulling over her earlier conversations with Shira and their possible relevance to her disappearance. She could be in heavy trouble and needing help. Damn this awkward arrangement!

Carlie applied more lipstick to the corners of her mouth and straightened her silk scarf. By narrowing her eyes, she was able to filter out Shira and more vividly recall her fling with Kirk. Before Carlie met the good-looking *Times* reporter, she had been completedly dedicated to fulfilling her ambitions. There wasn't room for either *Playgirl* foldout hunks or enterprising and talented journalists. She simply didn't have the emotional space for them. But now that she had become a success, things were different. And Kirk Stewart was different. He was her equal. He was handsome, smart, sensitive, and polite, with a strong sense of fair play; and more important than anything else, he was fun to be with. But when they had parted, when he had returned to Shira guilt-ridden and red-faced, there had been an uncomfortable, leaden finality to his good-bye.

It was unfair, she thought, feeling a pang in her chest. How could she have allowed herself such a delusion, only to be choked off with such abruptness? But Kirk had offered, insisted on continuing an intellectual friendship. Precisely what did he mean? After all, Shira was an intellectual friend, too.

Carlie knew she couldn't have asked for a more dramatic exit, but now, inexplicably, she was being thrust back on stage

again. And willingly or unwillingly, Kirk Stewart was again
her leading man. She still wanted Kirk; there would always be
room for him in her bed, but she didn't *need* him any longer.
Walls had been built up. It was a matter of changing vulner-
abilities. Listen to the voice of reason, Carlie Chavez, not your
fluttering heart.

Carlie put away her compact, pushed herself back into the
corner of the cab, and checked her watch. The afternoon was
still young but her eyes were heavy with fatigue from hours of
scanning microfilms in the *Times* biographical library for a
story on the comeback of late twenties fashions. Trivia, mere
tinsel, compared to the in-depth, possibly dangerous investigative plunge Kirk and Shira appeared to have taken. Kirk's
worries had suddenly become contagious. Carlie had never seen
the *Times* reporter without a quick smile. This morning in the
elevator, however, the furrow between his eyebrows—a sure
sign of stress—made him look distant and alien. The wit and
charm were gone.

Her mind did another zigzag. Probing through her handbag,
she withdrew an engraved card with a miter and pastoral staff
in the corner, and once more read the address and telephone
number of Episcopal Bishop Elliott. She would call him the
minute she arrived at the studio and set up a time for his
videotape session this week, not ten days hence as planned.
Perhaps it was something Kirk Stewart had told her. Possibly,
it was her own intuition. A lawyer had to become an expert at
shopping for compatible judges and friendly jurors; a television
news reporter kept an eye open for interesting faces and col-
orful, provocative events. Bishop Elliott had a controversial
story to tell; so did that rabbi up in Yonkers who had been
badgering her. Shira Bernstein knew this. NTN News would
start probing into this Nazi intimidation business. Better late
than never.

It was three in the afternoon before Lynx could reach Arnold
Metz at the American Eagle Gun Emporium in Galveston. The
gun merchant, he had been told by the store's employees, took
long, leisurely lunches.

"I'm glad you called, Lynx," said Metz, in a hushed voice.

Lynx thought he detected a note of distress in the gun peddler's voice. "Can you talk? Is it safe?"

"Yes, yes. I'm just concerned about the untidy mess our

friends left at the restaurant. I understand you're aware of the complications, but do you also know there's an FBI agent tailing me?"

"You're clever, Metz. You'll lose him whenever necessary. No one's blaming you for what happened near Lake Charles. But there are other complications. You have a pencil?"

"Go ahead."

"A reporter is arriving at Houston's Hobby Airport, Delta Flight three-twenty-two, later this afternoon. I'll describe him. We have reason to believe he will be heading out to the restaurant to nose around and ask impertinent questions."

"You want him followed?" interjected Metz.

"He must be eliminated."

8

DESPITE SKYROCKETING SOUTHERN California land costs and encroaching high-rises, Condor Defense Industries still consumed four times as many acres as its closest neighbor, Metro-Goldwyn-Mayer. Chairman of the Board Norman Gifford had subdivided Condor's eight-thousand-foot landing strip two years earlier, accepting the inconvenience of landing his corporate jet and cargo planes at L.A. International. Most of the valuable former airport land had gone to condominium construction and a new shopping center. The rest had become Condor's two-block-square top-secret area, which employees and government officials had dubbed "the Citadel."

It was here, behind double electric fences, that Condor's advanced war planes, spy satellites, and sophisticated future weaponry were designed. Norman Gifford's company maintained another secret facility in Colorado where research was conducted on lethal nerve gases, but no facility anywhere, even those of its largest aerospace competitors, compared in number of employees, size, and importance to the Citadel. It had its own underground communications center, which doubled as a bomb shelter, a large printing plant, two photo labs, its own language school, even a basement gunnery range for its zealous security officers.

CIA Director Walter Singer loved the secrecy of the Citadel. He delighted in its elaborate security provisions, which were as good as, if not better than, those enforced at his own agency headquarters in Washington. But the Citadel didn't have government red tape to contend with. The effectiveness of such private operations had been proven a long time back by Lockheed, when aircraft designer Kelly Johnson perfected the U-2 at his top-secret "Skunk Works."

Singer knew his dreams, and the Committee's plans, could never be achieved without Condor's technical support. Musclemen, gun-wielding functionaries were a dime a dozen. What Singer was really counting on was the Fifth Estate— high technology, the super breed of computers that think like humans. Condor scientists and engineers working for Norman Gifford would make these available to the Committee. Machines would prove smarter than the cleverest men, thought Singer. To change the power structure of the nation, the key would be the proper manipulation of machines as well as men.

What especially impressed the CIA head was the Citadel's self-contained film and television department, where he now sat, rigid and diminutive, his eyes fixed on a flickering screen. With the other Committeemen, he had already sat through several one-minute TV spots, and he was now watching a half-hour film he suspected would put to shame the Third Reich's propaganda chief Joseph Goebbels.

Singer sat in a pool of darkness in one corner of the small theater, his usually alert eyes half closed in boredom. He glanced around the room, surveying his companions. Engrossed by the images on the screen, the Reverend Mr. Jimmy Hallowell sat up front. Behind him, only partially attentive, hotel man Karl Frober had spread his bulk across two chairs. Condor Chairman Gifford sat at the rear of the room behind a dimly lit console with the film's producer and editor.

Singer felt impatient. By narrowing his eyes until they were nearly closed, he could turn the film into a transparent blur, and he could see through the message itself, beyond it, into the homes of the millions of television viewers who would eventually watch it. He didn't like their reaction. Once more his special clairvoyance was shouting to him, that gifted insight into what was best for the average American. Singer listened carefully as a familiar Hollywood celebrity's voice boomed from the Dolby speakers in a style reminiscent of that of Cecil B. DeMille:

"As you ponder the startling events of the past hours, it is well to remember that the Declaration of Independence was merely an important foundation—a desperate outline for safeguards that were needed in 1776. But this is not 1776. The Republic is now over two hundred years older and wiser, and *ready for change*. We are about to embark on a true Republic, a new nation of freedom in the truest sense."

Singer pondered over the narration. On screen, the aerial shot of Mount Rushmore dissolved to a painting of the First Continental Congress. At the rear of the projection room, the editor played with the effects tracks, turning up the tape of a chorus singing "American the Beautiful." Over this, the narrator continued in more dulcet tones: "Even Thomas Jefferson, who believed strongly in democracy, said, 'No society can make a perpetual constitution, or even a perpetual law.'"

Singer shot to his feet, his silhouette a sharp outline on the screen. "No! Not that socialist." Turning in the flickering light, he called, "Stop the projector! Turn up the lights."

The Condor film production minions obeyed.

Singer shook his head. "A gripping, brilliant chiaroscuro, but the reference to Jeffersonian democracy has to go. It is inappropriate."

The film's producer looked agitated. He scribbled a few hasty notes and looked nervously from the CIA director to his employer, Norman Gifford. "I thought you wanted the wrap upbeat," the film maker offered, feebly. "Hit hard on American values, quote the sentimentalists."

Condor's board chairman slowly shook his head. "I'll defer this once to our CIA friend." Gifford paused, slowly lit his pipe. "Too much sugar-coated claptrap, Walter?"

Singer looked back at Gifford. The world's wealthiest, most powerful defense manufacturer was a relaxed, dignified man with curly gray hair parted on one side; he looked much younger than his fifty-eight years. His small hazel eyes glittered, and he waved his hands when he spoke. Singer found Gifford's disarming manner as innocent as that of a toy soldier freak or a child who collects toy guns. He once again chuckled to himself over Gifford's innocent appearance. Singer watched the Condor executive slowly climb to his feet.

"I'll tell you the uncomfortable truth, gentlemen." Gifford smiled beatifically at the men around him. "I suspect that American values are not expressed by the voices of Jefferson, Lincoln, or even the black man's beloved Martin Luther King, but more accurately by the macho pen of Ernest Hemingway."

The others chortled, but Singer felt pleased, surprised that Gifford so easily went along with him. Gifford was, after all, paying the production costs, and he was the Committee's chairman. Singer looked at each of the others, his eyes finally coming to rest on Frober. The hotel man nervously ran his fingers through his crew cut and edged his bulk sideways in his seat.

"I didn't think the film was so bad," said Frober.

From the front of the room, Hallowell added, "Seems to me its purpose is to keep the peace after we move in. If we do that, we can avoid excess bloodshed."

Singer felt an urge to laugh. "Peace? You're both dreamers. This is war, for Christ's sake. We're fighting for the future. Not the future of Worldwide Hotels, not your aerospace manufacturing outfit, Gifford, not my Central Intelligence Agency. Not even the military. We're fighting for what damned little is left of the white race and its work ethic." Singer's eyes darted from Frober to Hallowell. "It's a fight for faith. Mr. Hallowell, surely you understand that. A hellish race against the equalitarian Marxists!"

"Provocative and meaningful rhetoric, Walter," said Gifford. "I like your style." He turned to the producer and editor beside him. "Roll the last five minutes of that film again."

Stewart knew he was being tailed. Bearing down on the accelerator, he nudged the rental car quickly in and out of the suburban Houston traffic. There were plenty of vehicles on the street, but he was unable to shake the persistent green Camaro following him. Cursing to himself, Stewart turned the corner again, once more retracing his route. If he was going to learn anything at all, he needed to operate alone, and quietly. Oliver Wright should have picked up on that. When Stewart brazenly ignored the FBI chief at Kennedy Airport hours earlier and went ahead with his flight plans, instinct told him they wouldn't let it drop at that. Sure enough, the FBI director's local functionary had been at the Houston airport, watching Stewart at the Avis counter, following, hovering outside Howard Johnson's as he made an unfruitful inquiry as to Shira's whereabouts. Now that same FBI man was following, three cars back, in the off-green Chevrolet Camaro. A determined bastard, thought Stewart, accelerating again. What points the agent lost in being so damned conspicuous he regained for anticipation and skillful driving.

But Stewart had seen something else, or was it his imagination? A small station wagon was following at a distance behind the Bureau man. Another agent? Then why was he driving so covertly? Stewart looked in the rearview mirror again. The Camaro was there, but now he couldn't see the station wagon.

Darkness had fallen about a half-hour earlier. Just ahead, in a forest of neon lights and billboards, Stewart saw a huge drive-in theater marquee. Several vehicles were pulling into the driveway, lining up at the box office. Stewart joined the right-lane traffic, slowed, signaled, and followed the line of cars. He was in luck; the two cars immediately behind turned with him. He had it all figured out, a replay of a scene in a detective film. Stewart looked in the rearview mirror and saw the green Camaro nose out a pickup truck and take its place in line four cars back. Good, he thought.

At the box office he hastily tossed out a five dollar bill, ignored his change, then edged the car forward along the fence. Once inside the gate, he avoided the parking attendant with the red-sleeved flashlight and tramped on the gas. Lights out, his rented Ford shot around the rear of the lot and sped up the center driveway. Rubber squealing, fighting the asphalt for traction, he turned the wheel again, heading for the large red exit sign at one side of the screen. From somewhere behind him came the attendant's angry shout.

An instant later he was out once more on the brightly lit city street. A strange business, Stewart thought, half smiling to himself. No place for a neophyte like himself. Compulsion was replacing reason. He should have heeded Oliver Wright's advice. Still, who else would do the job? By keeping a low profile, he could find things out. He was a damn sight less conspicuous than the eager-beaver agent who had been trailing him. Stewart thought about Shira. On one hand, his reporter's instincts told him to exercise caution, but on the other, he felt that he owed it to her. He shouldn't have let her come down south. He could have at least offered to come along. Why had he been so indifferent, almost cynical, about her obsession with Nazis? True, he had tried to discourage her from this kind of probing after reading her successful story on the Knights of the White Camellia Klan. Damn her stubbornness, her fool-hardy nature! If worry over Shira Bernstein's safety didn't drive him forward, his own guilt would.

The Ford's air conditioner had sputtered out a half-hour earlier. No time now to swap cars. Fucking humidity, he thought, pulling open his shirt collar and struggling to remove his tie. He remembered the attendant at the airport car rental counter. She had been helpful, more so than she realized. A native Louisiana girl, she recalled for Stewart only two eateries on the strip of highway in question, several miles this side of Lake Charles. One was a combination all-night café, truck stop, and fleabag motel; the other a lakeside catfish restaurant called the Halfway House.

Stewart had been tempted to hole up at Howard Johnson's after making his inquiries there, but his FBI shadow prompted him to reject that plan. Besides, he wanted to get farther along the road, closer to the anticipated trouble spot. He still had a long drive ahead of him.

As the Houston traffic thinned, Stewart began monitoring his rearview mirror. Twice he rushed forward to seventy-five, then suddenly slowed to a stop beside the road, lights out, to check for pursuers. Nothing. He was on his own. The night was clear, not a cloud in the sky. Outside his rolled-down window, there was only the noise of the swamp—alien sounds that made him uncomfortable. He tried the air conditioner again. It worked. Rolling up the window, Stewart turned the compact back out on the highway. Dodging an armadillo caught in his glaring headlights, he accelerated and headed for the Louisiana state line.

The CIA director was satisfied. The others had finally agreed that he was right about the film. "One more suggestion," Singer called to the rear of the projection room. "Cut in some scenes of the capital race riots right after the blurb on the Miami alien problem."

Norman Gifford looked at Singer through a cloud of pipe smoke but kept his silence.

Frober suddenly said, "I'd feel better if George Brady were

here to review these films with us."

"An excellent idea," added Hallowell. "I still feel the general would have been a good man to have on the Committee."

"We started this group as four *civilians,* and we'll keep it that way," Singer shot back. "No military. That includes your loquacious army pal Brady."

Frober and Hallowell glared at Singer like angry dogs. There was an uncomfortable silence until Gifford coughed loudly. Placing his pipe in an ashtray and folding his arms across his chest, Gifford said, "Well, then, gentlemen? How does it feel to be so close to the wire?"

Frober grimaced. "I've missed too much sleep this week."

Jimmy Hallowell gave up another of his predictable sighs. "I'm praying we've correctly assessed the temperament of the American public, that we can effectively sway the masses."

Singer watched them all from his corner, his impatience mounting. "Sway them? The depths of human nature are dark, Reverend Hallowell, founded on aggression, violence, and repeated folly. Force is the only thing men comprehend. We'll succeed, for we all understand the dog beneath the skin." Singer squeezed off a smile, got to his feet, and began pacing the room. No one seemed to object to his taking over. He pointed to the screen. "The main body of that film defines America's problems, correct? In the conclusion, we've got to zero in on the real culprits!"

"Expand, please," said Gifford flatly.

"Jewish and Marxist prodding is what keeps the minorities pressing for more rights. The blacks and Hispanics are too indolent to organize and act on their own. The homos and feminists are ambitious enough, but they fight among themselves." Singer looked around the room. The others were listening politely. "The key to our success, gentlemen, is manipulation, absolute control of the liberal news media. Friday, following the joint session of Congress and the President's State of the Union address, we'll see these objectives realized."

"Each and every one, I trust," added Gifford coldly.

Singer gave up a condescending nod and sat down. "Sorry, Norman. I'm speaking out of turn. The chair, after all, is yours."

The defense plant executive glanced at Singer ruefully and said in measured tones, "God knows we've sweated long enough to see our intricate plans come to fruition. Our subcommittees are to be commended for their Herculean efforts. Now, with the latest Liberty Alliance contribution as well as several corporate gifts added to the six figure total from the Moral Confederation last month, we have a fourteen million dollar war chest."

Frober quickly added, "Which won't go that far. It's a piss in the bucket."

"Frober, you're a pain in the ass," grunted Singer. "Can all this loser talk. We'll have the góddamn U.S. Treasury behind us come Friday."

"Give me a half-hour on nationwide TV and I'll keep you all in loose change," added Hallowell. "Ninety thousand bucks per show, by return mail. Will that keep you satisfied?"

Gifford reached into his pocket, withdrew a business envelope, and tossed it on Frober's lap. "Another shot in the arm for you, Treasurer. Picking up the funds isn't the problem. Just takes time. I had lunch with our Oklahoma oil friend two days ago. Claims he's too old to fight with us, but the bastard's not as tight-fisted as we figured. The check's for three hundred thousand. You boys are lucky Condor's lending you the sophisticated electronics equipment you need. Even this kind of money wouldn't make a down payment on that gear."

Walter Singer drummed his fingers on the briefcase in his lap. All eyes in the room turned to him, expectant. "Gifford, your cock-a-hoop talent for fund-raising is impressive. Likewise your high-tech charity and your knack for getting things done by secret committees in proper sequence. I only trust we're not paying those recruits we solicited from *Soldier of Fortune* magazine and that lot of disgruntled Vietnam vets more than they're worth. I still say my CIA staff could handle the New York TV takeover easily enough, and on the government's tab at that."

Frober smiled thickly. "Without Uncle Sam's ubiquitous bureaucracy getting wind of it? And you're underestimating the proficiency of FBI Chief Oliver Wright."

"A definite bone in our throat," added Gifford.

Singer scowled. "He's an overgrown ox. And just as clever."

"You have enough to do, Singer. Don't overextend yourself or the CIA," said Gifford. "Returning to the task at hand. Gentlemen, I suggest we make another videotape. We need to educate the American public by focusing directly on the media masters themselves. Lay the blame for Yankee decay squarely where it belongs: with the Jewish choke-hold on American communications. Broadcasting, film, publications. Secondly, I want to go after their claims on this Holocaust thing. That event is the rock upon which modern Zionism rests. For far too long, Jews have used it as an effective crowbar to obtain whatever they want, domestically and internationally. Enough is enough."

"A second production will take time, Mr. Gifford," said the producer nervously.

"And study, to do it properly," suggested Frober. "There's not only the American Jews to consider, but the Israelis as well."

Singer shot the hotel man a scathing look. "Forget the silky diplomacy, Frober. Paul Chandler can smooth things over after we put him in the Oval Office."

Turning back to the concerned film producer and editor, Gifford snapped, "Proceed. Time and a half, double time, whatever it takes. You need additional manpower, find it outside Condor."

"There's the matter of secrecy, sir," interjected the producer.

"Precisely what do you think I'm paying my security goons for? Bring what personnel you need into the Citadel and bed them down until the job is finished. Lock them up like a jury and kick ass. You have less than a week to pull it all together. Use stock film, interviews, actors. Fabricate, if necessary. No excuses, just get the job done." Gifford rose and began pacing.

Karl Frober looked up, gently tugged on the Condor executive's sleeve. "You sure the American public is ready for the Yid phase, Norman? Questioning the reality of the Holocaust is like doubting the existence of God at a holy roller tent revival."

Jimmy Hallowell shifted uncomfortably in his seat.

Singer grinned. "We sure as hell can't eliminate the Jews without first discrediting them."

"Eliminate?" asked Hallowell, sharply raising an eyebrow.

Frober laughed. "Singer's figure of speech. Buy them out, displace, expel, what's the difference? That sound better to your thin-skinned ears, Mr. Hallowell?" Checking his watch, Frober turned to Singer. "When do we get to look over the videotape interview with that capital pansy?"

Everyone in the room sent the CIA director a skeptical look. Hallowell voiced his concern. "For your sake as well as ours, Walter, I hope this actor kid Dennis Garrett comes off halfway convincing."

Singer smiled. "He not only sounds honest, he looks it. Exceptional talent. When he's in the mood, he comes across like Mom and apple pie. The truth is, he's a first-class narcissistic prick."

Frober chortled, his fat fingers fumbling for a cigarette. "What the hell you expect? Maybe now's the time, once and for all, to discuss the fag problem."

Gifford frowned. "Later, Karl. Much later. We'll make a proper determination on what to do about the gays next week. I've got a six-man committee in Chicago working on it." Gifford turned back to Singer. "Walter, how soon will a copy of that incriminating videotape be in the Oval Office?"

"Already arrived. My people don't waste time. The President should have seen it Sunday night."

Singer was distracted by the soft, harmonic buzz of the code buttons on the lock of the projection room door. Norman Gifford's secretary—a short, matronly woman with a squashed face and a wardress's mouth—admitted herself and strode across the room. "I'm sorry to interrupt, Mr. Gifford, but you did ask me to report before I left for the day." Quietly, she began reading from a memo pad. "Vice-President Chandler called from his home in Washington; he couldn't wait and asked you to phone him. General Brady called twice from Palm Springs, says its important. And your wife is in your office, a trifle impatient." She turned toward the CIA director. "Your plane reservations for tonight are in order, Mr. Singer. There's a message for you to contact a man called Lynx at the usual telephone. He said you would understand."

Gifford impatiently waved his hand, and the woman left the room.

Hallowell looked at Singer. "About this undercover man—Lynx—you're positive he's reliable?"

Singer nodded. "Without question. He's working on a security leak that occurred at the meeting Frober chaired down in Louisiana. We may have a probing reporter on our hands." Singer decided not to elaborate.

Gifford tapped his pipe in the ashtray, refilled it. "Gentlemen, if I may continue. About that nasty little videotape."

Singer grinned. *"Contrived* videotape. Garrett has a career ahead of him in phantasmagoria."

Hallowell looked puzzled. "Phantasma-what?"

Singer replied, "Illusions, Mr. Hallowell. Rapidly changing ones at that. Like the shit hitting the fan when the President saw this Tony Award performance."

Norman Gifford smiled thinly and turned to the men at the control console. "Roll the tape of our friend Dennis Garrett."

Singer smiled and added casually, "You'll love this, I can promise."

Stewart was famished. He hadn't eaten since the quick snack at the New York airport, and it was now going on half past ten. Dora's café was divided into two wings, separated by a central area cluttered with video machines and a long, horseshoe-shaped red Formica counter. One side of the twenty-four-hour restaurant was crowded with truckers, while the other half was nearly empty, as if they purposely avoided it. The only occupants there were an older couple seated in a booth by the window and a teenaged boy nursing a milk shake at the counter.

Stewart looked over the empty tables on the quiet side of the café, but his eyes were distracted by a shapely, freckle-faced waitress who emerged from the kitchen. He smiled at her and slid onto a stool at the end of the counter.

She was in her early twenties, her long red hair in a ponytail, her legs, waist, and breasts foldout perfect, her smile infectious. "Coffee?" she asked saucily, pushing both the Silex flask and her blouse with spilling breasts toward Stewart.

"No, thanks. Make it a beer."

The waitress turned, put the coffee pot back on the warmer, then faced him again, this time both hands on her twenty-eight-inch waist.

"Somehow y'all just don't look like a tourist. Still, you're a stranger, right?"

Stewart nodded.

"Dora saves this part of the café for the religious folks—nondrinkers, nonsmokers, and minors. Want a beer, y'all have to sit on the other side with the truckers. Sally and Betty Lou wait tables in that section."

Stewart shrugged. "Forget it. Make it a French dip, with lots of fries."

The redhead tilted her head like a considering cockatoo. "Y'all haven't had one of my French dips, I can tell. Try the burgers or a Reuben."

Feeling like a college freshman at his first striptease, Stewart said softly, "Princess, I'd try *your* French dip any day. But if the house *au jus* is as bad as you imply, you can bring me a double cheeseburger."

"Son of a gun, I like the way y'all talk. Where's home? California?"

"New York. And how about me asking the questions? First, what's your name? Second, do you live around here?"

The waitress giggled, then replied, "Stella. I'm twenty-two. Unmarried. Born and raised ten miles up the road and still live with my parents, but I stay weekdays here at the motel. Now what do y'all want to drink with your burger?"

"Milk. And you have very pretty turquoise eyes."

Stella headed for the kitchen. Halfway there, she turned and said over her shoulder, "Y'all have to do better than that, lover boy. Lord, I hear folks talkin' about my eyes a dozen or more times a day!"

The teenager at the other end of the counter looked at her, then over at Stewart. He rose, shuffled over to the jukebox, and fed it a quarter.

Stewart had to shout to be heard over Willie Nelson. "Okay, then! I have a weakness for freckles!" More than a measure of truth in that one, he mused. Shira's nose was sprinkled with freckles.

She grinned. "With a shade lighter hair, I swear you'd pass for Robert Redford," she said, prancing off.

He watched her disappear into the kitchen. Folding and refolding his napkin, Stewart nervously considered his next move. Stella liked to chatter. Good. He had to start somewhere. The locals weren't going to welcome a New York reporter with open arms; even the constable, if true to form, would look upon his arrival and subsequent queries with the same enthusiasm he might afford an invasion of locusts. No matter. Right here in front of him, bouncing tits and all, was an attractive, lonely, and thus far talkative local lady. Time to pour on some of that Big Apple charm, he reasoned. No, wait. The soft, unassuming approach was in order here. Sneak in, play it roundabout, ease up slowly from the side.

Stella returned, carrying a bottle of Pearl. "Here's your beer," she said quickly. "Now y'all see a big barn of a woman with dyed black kinky hair and plucked eyebrows come prancin' through that front door, y'all hide this bottle. Or I get fired, understand? Now, what's your name?"

"Kirk," he replied eagerly. Now, time to lie. "I'm a free-lance photographer, women's fashion magazines."

"Really? Well, my God. For sure?"

"Yeah, sure. You know, Stella, it's kind of weird. An editor friend of mine suggested I check out a young gal working up the line as a waitress at a place called Halfway House. Centerfold potential, all that slick four-color jazz. But as far as I'm concerned, the real knockout's right here in front of me."

Stella blushed, adjusted her bosom, and backed away from the counter. Frowning, she said, "Damn, if I don't hear all the lines. Kirk, y'say? Anyone ever tell y'all you're full up with bullshit? I've been a waitress here for three years. Don't you think I know who that Kraut owner hires for his catfish house? All fat negras, that's who. Except for his wife, and damned if she isn't the size of a brick shithouse herself!"

"You know the owner of Halfway House?" Stewart asked cautiously.

"I don't care to know him, 'cept at a distance. He's a friend of my daddy's. 'Course Daddy knows everyone in the county." She paused, exhaled swiftly, and gave up a little pout. "So where y'all staying tonight?"

Stewart grinned and took a swift gulp of his beer. "Still haven't found a room."

"They've already turned on the No Vacancy sign out there. Next motel's ten miles beyond the Halfway House, damned near into Lake Charles." Smiling, she leaned forward and added coquettishly, "Tell y'all what, Kirk. My room's not much, but it's air-conditioned. I've got a bottle of Jim Beam in there, and I get off in a half-hour." She hesitated, giggling.

As he eyed her ample breasts, a peculiar sensation came over Stewart. He thought of another woman, miles away. And oddly enough, it wasn't Shira but Carlie Chavez a dozen hours earlier in the Times Building elevator. He could still smell her perfume and feel her pliant body against him. Stewart fought back the image, fixed his mind on Shira and the discomforting, possibly dangerous task at hand. These things he had to do now. The confusing options could come later, if they came at all.

The waitress tapped her finger impatiently on the counter. "Wake up, daydreamer." She giggled infectiously. "There's one more thing."

His mouth half open in surprise, Stewart put away his concern for Shira and gazed back at the redhead. Okay, he mused. If she talks this much while sober, who knows what might come out after she gets a couple of bourbons under her belt? "I'm game," he lied. "What is it?"

"Well," she said, winking, "I do feel kinda horny."

9

HARSH, UNCOMPROMISING SUNLIGHT streaked through the torn motel windowshade. The air conditioner was running, but the dilapidated room was still warm and reeked of stale whiskey. Stewart glanced at his watch. Already eight o'clock. He sat up slowly and looked at the sleeping figure beside him. Long red hair, stringy now and moist across her face, Stella didn't stir.

A productive but uncomfortable night, he reflected. It had been one hell of a session—pretending, just able to get it up, and when he did, barely able to follow through. His thoughts had been elsewhere—on Shira's disappearance so close by. The boozed-up waitress beside him had settled for a fast, clumsy screw then drifted off to sleep. But she had talked, thank God. Names, locations. And his ears hadn't deceived him; she had said her daddy was a deputy sheriff. Fine. Damned convenient, he thought. He wondered if he could clear out without awakening her, just dress quietly, postpone a shower and shave until later.

Easing out of bed, Stewart pulled on his tan corduroy pants, stuffed his briefs and socks in his pockets, and fumbled for his car keys on the dresser. Working swing shift, Stella apparently slept hard and late. She didn't stir. So far, so good. He grabbed his shirt and shoes and padded softly to the door.

The morning was clear, mild, and predictably humid. In the distance beyond the off-ramp, the traffic on Interstate 10 appeared light. Stewart eyed his Ford compact parked nearby, then turned his head toward the café, his nostrils savoring the aroma of bacon in the air. Bladder aching, he decided to forgo both breakfast and his car, heading instead toward the truck stop toilet.

As he strode barefoot across the asphalt, a sturdily built black man wearing dungarees, a plaid short-sleeved shirt, and a John Deere cap came out from behind the diesel pumps and extended his hand.

"Mr. Stewart? My name is Tyrone Jackson, FBI."

Walter Singer had forgotten to move his watch forward three hours from California time. He quickly made the adjustment. Singer sat at one side of the limousine, as far from the Vice-President as manners would permit. In the past month he had come to know Paul Chandler well, and in the process decided he disliked the man. No matter, he thought. Too late to do anything about such trivial annoyances.

"There's no turning back now, I suspect," said the Vice-President enthusiastically. "The fat's in the fire."

The CIA director looked at Chandler, measuring him.

The Vice-President continued, but seemed at a loss for words. "Loyalty is a fragile commodity these days, Singer. You're absolutely sure of your own CIA infrastructure?"

"I'll manage. The agency will fall in behind you. At least the people who count."

The Vice-President did not respond, continuing to gaze idly out the tinted window as the limousine passed the Washington Cathedral. Traffic on Massachusetts Avenue was light.

Singer really didn't feel like making conversation. He was tired after the night flight from Los Angeles. Chandler, eager for a report on the Committee's session at the Citadel, had insisted on the rendezvous. Meeting Chandler at his office would have been unthinkable, and for the Vice-President to visit CIA headquarters out at Langley, Virginia, might have provoked queries from the alert press. Instead, after his arrival at Dulles, Singer had been driven directly to the Naval

Observatory, just a block away from the vice-presidential mansion. There Paul Chandler had climbed into the back of the CIA limousine and begun asking one question after another. But now he was strangely quiet. As his driver turned into Rock Creek Park, Singer pointed to the fold-out bar before them. "Join me for an eye-opener, Mr. Vice-President?"

"You probably need it after that overnight hop. I'll pass. I have some tough Senate committees to face today."

Singer shrugged, mixed himself a Bloody Mary in a thermos glass with a blue CIA seal. He could sense now that something was bothering Chandler, a mounting impatience.

"About your call last night from the West Coast. Your displeasure with me for accepting the Russian invitation," the Vice-President began in a chiding tone.

"What about it?"

Chandler frowned. "You're cunning, Singer. Innovative, resolute, completely reliable. So much for the superlatives, but God, if you don't try my patience the way you play cat and mouse."

Singer sipped his drink, washed down the sourness he felt in his throat. "Forgive me, Mr. Vice-President, it's been a hectic three days, not to mention jet lag." He looked at Chandler. "Yes, I'm still concerned about this short-notice invitation to dine with the Soviet ambassador. It's my cautious nature. You're planning to accept, then?"

"Tonight at their embassy. Why not? I have the President convinced that the scope of our dialogue will not extend beyond grain and machine tool trade."

"Hardly topics for brandied conversation," grumbled Singer. "Mikhail Grotski's a devious bastard. I don't trust him."

Chandler exhaled slowly. "I know. You needn't reiterate. Half of his staff is KGB. I still say if we play our cards right, Grotski will welcome the chance to help pound nails into the coffin of the current Secretary of State."

"And the casket of the President who appointed him? Hardly. Only one way to see that happen. On taking office, the new President would have to advocate the disbanding of NATO. I suspect the Soviet's primary concern at this point is maintaining the status quo. No waves."

"We'll soon see," said Chandler, grimly. "Now then, what about communications?"

Singer shrugged. "The money boys are still out in L.A. at the Condor plant. Last-minute planning and waiting for the results of the new satellite matrix and computer runs. The next step is to set up the intercept center here in Washington."

Chandler grew silent, deep in thought.

"Why so pensive?" Singer asked abruptly.

"Cogitating. I'm still concerned about keeping the operation reasonably bloodless."

Singer wanted to say something about faint hearts and limp wrists, but thought better of it. He swilled his drink instead and sucked on an ice cube.

Chandler fixed his eyes on him, glaring. "So how long before Gifford's computer people at the Citadel give us the regional personnel and troop strength data?"

Singer nodded. "Not just printouts, Mr. Vice-President, but a feasible plan of action. Placement of key people, weapon inventories, supplies, you name it. Cracking the codes and systems technology of AT&T and the wire services hasn't been easy. We still have some security hurdles, palms that will need oiling. In the last resort, a few heads may roll."

The Vice-President shifted uncomfortably in his seat and wet his lips. "What about the communications satellites?"

Singer sighed with impatience. "A piece of cake. Inside track there. Four of them were built by Condor Defense. Three others are a joint effort by NORAD, managed by the Air Force Systems Command. A possible stickiness there, but that's why we're bringing back George Brady."

"When will the disputatious four-star arrive in Washington?"

"Already told you about Colonel Reddick. He's personally flying our retired army general from California late this afternoon."

Chandler laughed. *"Retired?* I'd say the President kicked Brady's ass out to pasture rather forcefully."

"The general may be one son of a bitch, but he's on our side, and he knows the Signal Corps inside out. Who else has the balls and the skill to command a combined assault force made up of military personnel, the Freedom Militia, Nazi shock troops, and some five hundred mercenaries?"

The Vice-President frowned. "You forgot the Klans."

"They're armed to the teeth. We'll need every man we can get. Let's hope the bullets will be few and far between."

"That's wishful thinking," prompted Chandler. "I smell violence in the wind."

"I suggest, sir, that you stop worrying about the enforcement phase of the operation. The chairman of the Joint Chiefs is loyal to you. Palmer knows where the support lies at the Pentagon."

"Yes, of course. Someone has to control the brass," Chandler replied diffidently.

Singer continued: "The Pentagon had damned well better support the cause. Rumor has it that the current administration plans to ask for the Joint Chiefs' chairman's resignation in a couple of weeks, after the NATO arms shift agreement is signed. I suspect the President finally put two and two together—all of Sandy Palmer's quiet shifting of right-wing generals and admirals to key positions. Positions, of course, favorable to you."

Chandler smiled thinly. "You mean favorable to the Committee. Spare my vanity. You're absolutely sure Admiral Palmer won't waver? He's fully committed?"

"If not, Mr. Vice-President, it's simple enough. I'll have the chairman's head along with those of any other dissenters."

"You said that a month ago about FBI Chief Wright."

"Oliver Wright's day is coming. All in time. Precise timing is imperative." Singer studied Chandler carefully, watched the Vice-President let out another sigh. The CIA head knew that despite Paul Chandler's outspoken, power-bent nature, he was still a sensitive man. Singer vainly wondered if Chandler had finally come to understand that the self-confident CIA director seated beside him was *more* than a key to the presidency; indeed, Walter Singer, with his calm, steely mind, was every bit Chandler's equal.

Swallowing with difficulty, the Vice-President finally asked, "You're not worried about the opposition? Air Force Commander Colloran? And the U.S. Army chief of staff may oppose us."

Damn Chandler, thought Singer. The onerous prick was always looking for flaws. Impulsively, Singer asked, "Do I look concerned?"

Chandler grinned. "No. To the contrary. Pour yourself another drink, Walter. But I am curious. What makes you so confident that your own clandestine activities—our cause, for that matter—haven't been penetrated? My every move watched?"

Singer looked at his glass, downed the rest of his Bloody Mary. He would indeed have another drink. Gazing back at Chandler, he said dryly, "We have been penetrated. And I'm taking appropriate measures."

10

STEWART SLOWED THE car as the Halfway House appeared directly head. The catfish restaurant was set back among the vaulted trees and woodbine just off the highway. FBI Agent Tyrone Jackson sat beside him, his lean black face cold and expressionless. Without taking his eyes off the highway, Jackson said to Stewart, "Pull over here, before we get to the restaurant."

Stewart braked and edged the Ford onto the shoulder. "What for?" he asked, as his companion jumped out, climbed in the rear seat, and slammed the door.

"They figure I'm dead," Jackson said quickly. "If I want to keep them thinking that way I can't be seen around that restaurant. So you find your chick's car. I still say it's a waste of time. That wily old swamp bird who rescued me claimed the same goons returned later, but he heard a woman's voice, too. Then a gunshot. Sorry, Stewart, I tell you she's gone. Pull out now."

"Look, Tyrone..." Stewart paused, feeling again the familiar sick emptiness in his stomach. "I know it's a long shot, but suppose she's not dead, only being held captive? Don't back out on me now. You agreed to lead the way, and that catfish house is the first stop."

"Suit yourself," grumbled Jackson, crouching on the floor behind the front seat. "Do me a favor. Park out of the way in a quiet spot? And make it fast."

Arriving in front of the restaurant, Stewart obliged Jackson by pulling up just off the road, a good distance from the main building. It was early, and the only cars out front appeared to be employees' vehicles. Almost at once Stewart saw Shira's rented Pinto with its Texas plates; it stood isolated in the center of the lot near a pay telephone booth. Reaching for his Canon F-1 under the seat, he quickly took several pictures of the restaurant, with Shira's car in the foreground. Stewart then tucked the camera away, climbed out, and walked swiftly across the parking area. The Pinto was locked. Nothing visible inside but a cardigan sweater and an envelope with several papers extending from it. He'd have to break in; the papers might be significant. He wondered if Shira had left her small notebook under the seat, as was her habit. Stewart's first impulse, stupid like most impulses, was to retrieve the tire iron from his own rental car and shatter the glass. No. Too much noise, and it was broad daylight. He could play it straight, go inside and talk to the restaurant owner, look danger right in the face.

Before he could make up his mind, a blue and white sheriff's car crept into the parking lot, and behind it, a forest of chrome CB antennas and chromed wheels gleaming in the sun, came a large tow truck. The patrol car circled, came up beside him, and stopped, the uniformed driver eyeing both Shira's Pinto and Stewart with consuming interest. The plump deputy who finally oozed out of the vehicle like spilled custard was in his middle forties, had ruddy cheeks, a pockmarked chin, and close-set brown eyes. His shirt was wrinkled and soaked with sweat, but his badge, belt buckle, and Wellington boots were polished like mirrors.

"This your automobile?" he asked casually, in a slight drawl.

Stewart shook his head. "A friend's. Rented at the Houston airport."

A careless smile playing about his mouth, the deputy took his time withdrawing a folded paper from his shirt pocket, then read its contents. He walked slowly around the Pinto, checked the license, then returned to confront Stewart. The driver of the tow truck sat silently, puffing on a cigarette.

"This vehicle's been parked here since Saturday. Apparently

abandoned, 'cording to the owner of the restaurant. Illegal,
just leaving it. Unless y'all can rustle up a driver, we're towing
it in."

Stewart glanced over his shoulder. A fat, owlish-faced man
with wiry red hair and beard swaggered toward them from the
restaurant.

The deputy looked up. "Mornin', Willy. This the automobile
you want towed out of here?"

"Yes, yes." The Halfway House proprietor waved a liver-
spotted hand toward the car, then turned his transparent blue
eyes on Stewart. "And who might this be?"

"He claims to know the driver. Whatever, the wheels still
go to Abernathy's Garage at Vinton. I'll notify the rental folks,
and they can claim it."

Stewart shifted uneasily on his feet. "Look, Sheriff, you
can check with the Avis office in Houston. I've already made
inquiries there. The Pinto was rented by my girl; she's disappeared. I'm trying to track her down." He pointed to the front
seat. "I want to get inside. Her belongings are in there. And
possibly a clue."

The deputy scratched his rear, glanced at the restaurant
owner, then at Stewart. "Can't do that. Not unless y'all can
prove it's your rental, or else next of kin. Y'all want to file a
missing persons report?"

"Yes." Stewart thought twice. "No. I mean later. I'm pressed
for time." He saw the man with the red hair and beard gazing
into the front seat of the Pinto. "You're the owner of this place?"
The man looked like a retired German U-boat captain, thought
Stewart.

"Yes, that is right," he grunted, in a coarse, guttural German-
accented voice, neatly confirming Stewart's impression.

"The name Shira Bernstein mean anything to you?"

The restaurant man shrugged. Spreading his hands, he rasped,
"Absolutely nothing. Should it?"

The deputy was busy writing up a tow ticket. Stewart looked
across the parking lot toward his own rental car, expecting to
see Tyrone Jackson curiously peering over the top of the rear
seat, but no one stirred within the vehicle. Jackson was playing
it smart.

Stewart started to say something, but stopped. More questions would get him nowhere. Sticking around would be not
only unproductive but possibly dangerous. Still, he couldn't

resist asking the obvious; it would be expected. "You have a meeting here last Saturday? Large banquet with delegates from all over the country?"

The German-American's face was suddenly friendly. "We cater dinners all the time. Especially busy on the weekends."

"My girlfriend is a reporter. Came down to sit in on some kind of Nazi or Klan convention."

The restaurant owner's stomach shook as he laughed. "Who was she looking for? Martin Bormann? Not here, my friend. The Southern Nurserymen's Association rented my banquet hall Saturday last. You are mistaken. Tell me, are you a reporter, too?"

Stewart's entire body stiffened. "Yes. How did you know that?"

"I'm an excellent judge of ethnicity, character, and profession. New York?"

"If I'm the newsman, how about letting me ask the questions?"

The man shrugged, shoved his hands in his pockets, and ignoring Stewart, slowly walked around the car, watching the tow truck operator attach his rig to the Pinto.

A dead end, Stewart thought. He was about to dig into his wallet, pull out his *Times* I.D. card, and ask the men to call him if anything on Shira should turn up. No, he thought quickly. Thus far, no one in the area knew his last name. Stella, back at the truck stop, knew his first name. Good God, with a pack of problems already, he had almost forgotten. Might the deputy in the sweat-stained uniform be Stella's father?

Stewart scanned the faces before him, decided it was time to shove off. "Thanks for your help. I'll make some inquiries up the line," he said calmly. "How far along the highway is the turnoff to Calcasieu Lake?"

The restaurant man's left eyebrow arched slightly. "Four miles. Take State Twenty-seven south."

Stewart nodded, turned, and was less than ten yards away when the German-accented voice called out to him.

"Just in case," he shouted, "what was the young woman's name again? Sharon Bernstein?"

Flinching, Stewart replied, *"Shira.* Shira Bernstein."

"That's a Jewish name, yes?"

"Very much so. Make a difference?"

The man rubbed his beard and slowly shook his head. His

watchful eyes seemed to ponder for a moment. "You have lodging nearby, a place where I can call you?"

"No." Stewart said two more sentences, his voice very tight, and very hard. "But I'll keep in touch. You can count on it." Turning away, Stewart quickly strode across the lot to his own car, climbed behind the wheel, and turned the key. "Lying bastards," he said quietly. "They both know something."

"Relax, pal," came the low voice from behind the seat. "Precisely what I was trying to tell you. This is a waste of time."

Stewart hesitated. He reached into his accessory bag, withdrew the 200mm telephoto lens, and screwed it onto his camera. Leaning out the window, he quickly focused on the men by the tow truck. *Click, click*. Behind him, Jackson snarled, "Will you kindly shag ass out of here?"

Stewart put his camera away and angrily tramped on the accelerator. As the Ford compact shot back out onto the access road he thought he heard the sound of shattering glass. Glancing in the rearview mirror, he saw the restaurant owner reach inside Shira's Pinto and retrieve the white envelope. Stewart cursed softly to himself.

A mile farther down the road, Tyrone Jackson climbed out of the rear seat, joined him up front, and lit a cigarette.

Stewart looked at his companion askance. "Look, Jackson, you help me, I'll return the favor. How'd you fall into all this?"

"I didn't start out big. Couple months back we traced a dozen threatening letters sent to the heads of a couple TV networks in New York. Turned out three of them came from that Kraut back there."

"Which networks?"

"I was only told about NTN, but I suspect ABC and CBS were hit, too."

"What became of it?"

"I joined the Halfway House staff as a waiter. Nothing happened until the day before the banquet when the owner told me to take a walk."

"He fired you?"

"No. Just said to take a couple of days off. Naturally, I was suspicious. You sure all this is off the record?"

"Until you give the green light. You've got my word. I went into a holding pattern the minute Oliver Wright asked me to share his cab to the airport."

"Still, it'll make a helluva story when you get the green light."

"Yeah. Provided I live that long," Stewart replied grimly. "So what happened? You took a walk from the restaurant, and then?"

Jackson's eyes sparkled. "Walk? Hell, no, I hid. That's when this unmarked delivery truck—I traced the Texas plates later—showed up and unloaded cartons. Figured it was canned food or similar restaurant crap until I overheard some conversation. Guns! MAC Nine automatic carbines."

Stewart looked away from the highway, staring at Jackson and thinking about his words. There had been a Nazi meeting, a banquet room filled with paramilitary loudmouths. Suddenly the idea that there was far more to it than that flooded over him. The realization that Shira had stumbled into a conspiracy, and that he had done likewise, suddenly chilled his spine. Stewart's eyes snapped back to the road and he kept them there.

Jackson continued. "Strange exchange of conversation. While the driver—twenty-five at the oldest—was delivering these guns the Kraut asked, 'How's business?' I could barely hear the conversation, but I did pick up part of the reply. The gun peddler said, 'Fine. We just sent another four dozen MAC Nines up to New York to replace the ones we lost in the FBI raid. And we've got plenty more where those came from.' I couldn't make out the rest. Then they went inside the restaurant office."

A wave of weakness coursed sluggishly over Stewart. "God, what next?" he said quietly.

Aboard the Delta jet circling over Lake Pontchartrain, the Fasten Seat Belt sign blinked on. Lynx put aside his copy of *Soldier of Fortune* magazine and complied. The sky over the New Orleans airport, he noted, was clear, with only scattered white clouds. Lynx was relieved. In his haste to depart the winter weather of the capital he'd forgotten his raincoat.

Lynx hadn't counted on an FBI agent from New Orleans muddying up the waters that combined the Nazi–Freedom Militia fish fry. Nor had anyone expected a free-lance woman reporter to come probing, or the situation to be further compounded by a determined staff man from the *New York Times*. He wondered if Arnold Metz had already closed in on Kirk Stewart. Lynx swore to himself at the snooping reporter and at the Committee itself. He was becoming more and more deeply involved. Why was Walter Singer pushing him, risking his possible discovery? He couldn't possibly be everywhere at once. Since the FBI had a twenty-four-hour watch on the Houston airport, he couldn't chance an arrival there—too much possibility of recognition. Putting down in New Orleans he would pick up a car and drive to Galveston for his rendezvous.

Lynx thought about Arnold Metz. Doing business with the gun merchant was like hiring a messenger of the devil. This trip he would do much more than discuss weapons deployment with the Texan. Lynx could be thankful for one thing; Metz wasn't the least bit squeamish about dirty work. And the new task that Lynx was about to assign the gun peddler—a specific deployment of the new EMR weapon—was anything but clean.

After a twenty-minute drive, Stewart and Jackson neared their destination. The air conditioner was still defective, working half the time. Swamp on both sides, the narrow trace wound east along a levee. Stewart cursed and sweated behind the wheel. It seemed more of a wagon trail than a modern road, though the Ford's wheels bounced easily along the ruts as he followed Tyrone Jackson's directions without question. Stewart had never been good at navigating. He knew that without Jackson he would be hopelessly lost. Only once had the FBI agent consulted the map in the glove compartment; he knew the area. According to Jackson, they were now heading directly toward Calcasieu Lake.

They had made two stops: one at a pay phone along the main highway before entering the swamp, the other at the cabin of the old black fisherman who had saved Jackson's life. The old man was fearful, refusing to accompany them back into the marshland, but he had drawn a map for Jackson, indicating the specific area where he had heard the men's shouts, the protesting woman's voice, and the gunfire.

The route Stewart now followed—hemmed in on all sides by murky water, saw grass, and liana, muffled by cascading masses of laurel—grew increasingly ominous in appearance. In places the thick, muddy water beside the levee bubbled—a sure sign of quicksand.

"Stop here," Jackson said, his voice shattering Stewart's daydreaming.

Braking and turning his head, he studied the FBI agent's hard, perspiring face.

"Listen," Jackson said, cocking his ear.

"What? I don't hear anything."

"I thought I heard an engine—small airplane, maybe. It's gone now."

Stewart frowned. "The hell with it. I'm driving on."

"No." Tyrone Jackson smiled. "We're here."

Stewart looked around the morass, shaking his head. "She must have tried to get away," He hesitated. "You're convinced they killed her?" He regretted the question before he had finished asking it.

"Yes, I'm afraid so."

"But what about motive? The Nazis have been in the news before."

Jackson sighed impatiently. "You tell me. Too many unanswered questions. Like why fly that mysterious German in from Paraguay?"

Stewart turned, distracted by a movement beside the road. A feral dog leaped out of the thicket, a frog clamped in his jaws. The animal gave an appraising glance at the car, decided it was neither threatening nor edible, then ran off down the road and disappeared over the levee.

Stewart's thoughts returned to Shira's phone call the night of her disappearance, her questioning him about hunted Nazis retired in South America. The sudden, frightened edge in her voice came back to him. He looked at Jackson and asked, "Any thoughts on the bigwig's identity?"

Jackson slowly shook his head. "Can't say for sure. Probably one of those former SS butchers from Hitler's death camps. Or a crony of that quack doctor, Mengele."

"Retired exterminators," Stewart remarked. "Jackson, it's not just the Jews. These people would just as soon kill a black as bat an eye at them."

"I knew that when my bureau supervisor sent me into the fire. But he didn't order me out on this one. I volunteered."

"From what I've been reading in their literature, these reactionaries have some distorted, bizarre ideas, Jackson. They claim it's *your world* now, that the balance of power has shifted from the whites to the minorities. These racists are afraid, filled with panic. They're convinced that the bastardization of the Aryan race is at hand."

Jackson nodded, obviously aware. Melancholy settled on his face, but deep in his expressive brown eyes there were small sparks of resolve. He pointed off to the side of the levee. "The ground's stable enough over there. They dragged me out past a small fisherman's storage shed and dock. Let's go, and I'll show you the area."

Jackson was so nimble at ducking liana and laurel that Stewart, the camera around his neck catching on the branches, had trouble following him, but at last they came upon a small, dilapidated dock. Secured to it was a long square-stern punt. Jackson gestured for Stewart to climb aboard. "We'll save time by taking the boat out to that point. Our friends took me by land on Saturday."

"There are no oars," said Stewart.

"We don't need them. Some of the water's too shallow for rowing. We can pole instead. There's more quicksand around here than water. Mind your balance."

"How far we going?"

Jackson finished untying the punt, grabbed the long pole, and balanced himself in the stern. "Just out past those tall cypresses."

The sun was higher in the sky. It was going to be hot, thought Stewart, regretting not having worn a hat. He looked around him, considering the staggering, primeval swamp. The smooth, flat bottom of the boat skimmed over the grass and shallow pools of the soggy marshland.

"Muck, misery, and moccasins," said Jackson, his face grim.

"And quicksand," added Stewart. "So why didn't they just drop you off right out here in the mud? The same with Shira?"

"The two musclemen may not have known about my fisherman friend's boat. More important, at night, with only a lantern, if you don't know what's best, you stay on the trails. They figured it was good enough to let the 'gators take care of me. I suspect they took the woman to the same place."

Two ravens took flight from a tree overhead, their cries shattering the suffocating stillness of the bog. Suddenly, a rifle shot rang out.

Stewart's heart skipped a beat. Spinning his head, he saw Jackson drop his pole, clutch at his side. Stewart reached out, too late. Eyes pinched in pain, breath hissing through his flattened nostrils, as if in slow motion Jackson arched backwards into the murky yellow water.

A second and third rifle shot rang out.

Stewart flung himself flat on his stomach, hugging the floor of the punt. A hole appeared in the hull near his hand. Then he felt a searing pain as a bullet grazed his shoulder. He winced, feeling both astonishment and pain. Did he dare raise his head, look up? Fear had caught him in its jaws, holding him, pressing his face to the bottom of the boat, his lungs heaving against his camera, his heart racing.

From another quarter came the staccato blast of an automatic weapon. A loud, guttural cry, followed by the sounds of a body—no, two bodies—splashing into the mire.

"Jackson!" Stewart shouted, cautiously raising his head. Looking back, he saw the FBI agent and heard him wail in terror. Tyrone Jackson was alive, but sinking rapidly; only his head and chest were above the surface of the bubbling ocher mud. His eyes stared back at Stewart, wide with panic. The area reeked of marsh gas. The boat had slid some ten yards away from Jackson's body. Had the gunfire ended?

Frantic, obsessed with fear, Stewart lay flat in the punt, trying desperately to paddle toward Jackson with his hands. The muck oozed through his fingers. The punt slid forward several feet, then caught on an underwater obstacle. He clawed the water uselessly. The black man called out to him, his last words a series of gasps: "You're in it, too, Stewart—up to your fucking ears." The warning was barely comprehensible, but Stewart understood. He'd remember that helpless face forever. Then Tyrone Jackson's head disappeared beneath the surface, nothing remaining to mark his grave but intermittent bubbles.

"*Olev Shalom*—may he go in peace." The voice came from behind Stewart, somewhere off to the left. "He's gone, and there's nothing either of us can do about it." The voice had a strong accent, one Stewart couldn't immediately identify. "Sit up in the boat, my friend—very carefully—and I'll throw you a pole."

Cautiously turning, gazing toward the edge of the bog, Stewart saw a short, medium-set man in his thirties. He had a weathered face, receding curly brown hair, a neatly trimmed mustache, and piercing blue eyes. The interloper wore a thin silver chain under an open khaki shirt, bush shorts, and lug-soled hiking boots. In his hand was a smoking Uzi automatic carbine.

"My name is Motti Barak," he called. The staff he had improvised and now held in readiness was little more than a stripped, gnarled branch. "I should like to assist you, Mr. Stewart. But I will expect you to help me in return. Can we strike a bargain? I come from the Middle East, where bargaining is often a way of life."

Stewart pulled a handkerchief from his pocket and held it against his bleeding shoulder. Steadying himself, he tried to climb to his feet. "Whatever you say," he called back.

"Stay on your knees, if you are unfamiliar with swamp flatboats. Can I expect your cooperation, then, if I lend you a hand?"

"You're the one with the arsenal. Do I look like the argumentative type?" asked Stewart.

Motti Barak grinned. "Use this." He tossed the long branch.

Stewart let go of his painful shoulder and caught it. Immediately, he began probing the mud for leverage. Too deep.

The man on the bank shook his head. "You won't find bottom there. Probe for underwater roots and use them for leverage."

The ploy worked. Stewart felt the punt slide forward in the ooze. Less than a minute later, skimming through the saw grass, it struck firm soil. As he scrambled up the bank, his rescuer smiled effusively and stepped forward.

"Come quickly. We have important work to do," Barak instructed. He quickly examined Stewart's shoulder wound. "You'll survive until we get back to town. A very slight surface wound."

Bewildered, Stewart stared at his resolute rescuer. "Mind if I ask who you are?"

"Not at all. Major Motti Barak. In order of importance: soldier of fortune, jet pilot, and former air attaché for the Israeli embassy in Washington."

"Former attaché?" Stewart eyed Barak sharply, but saw only innocent hospitality in his face. "What are you doing now?"

Barak shrugged. "What else? I'm rescuing a foolish newspaper reporter from deep trouble." Adjusting the strap on his automatic carbine, he slung it over his shoulder and extended his right hand. There were long scars on his fingers and forearm. "We will shake on it, all right?"

Stewart extended his own hand and relaxed a little. "How did you get here?"

"I followed you. It was quite simple. My car is parked behind yours on the levee trail."

"Who shot my companion?"

"Tyrone Jackson, yes. And would have killed you as well, had I not happened on the scene when I did. I'll show you, come." The small man beckoned for Stewart to follow him down a muddy, narrow path. Barak, his gun slung over his shoulder, seemed satisfied that the danger had passed, and Stewart didn't question him. He had little choice in the matter; even finding his own way back to the car would be a problem if he were left to his own devices.

Overhead, the Gulf Coast sun was huge, unremitting. Stewart heard a rustling in the weeds off to one side. Barak strode on, unperturbed.

"A wild pig or an alligator," he said flatly.

Stewart shuddered.

Abruptly, they came upon the two bodies, partially in the bog. Like a game hunter beside his prize trophies, Motti Barak hovered over the still forms, smiling. Hesitantly, Stewart stepped forward. His mouth parted, refused to close. One of the men wore a familiar chocolate brown uniform. The sheriff's deputy! *Stella's father?* The second man—his puffy face staring blankly at the sky, his red beard caked with mud and already crawling with insects—was the restaurant owner.

Swiftly, wordlessly, devoid of the slightest sign of emotion, Barak went through the dead men's pockets. Sifting through their wallets, he examined identification, personal mementos, photographs. When he came upon the picture of a young woman in the deputy's wallet, he looked up at Stewart, flashed the snapshot, and said, "The sheriff's daughter. This kind of trouble you don't need, my friend."

Stella. Barak knew all about her. But how? He watched silently as the Israeli continued to search the bodies, stopping twice to make notes in a small leather-bound booklet. Here was a clever, ruthless man, an individual who thought clearly, measured his opposition shrewdly.

The 9mm automatic carbine had made an abstract painting of the restaurant man's shirt, but from a shredded pocket Barak withdrew a folded envelope. Wiping off the blood and gore, he glanced at it briefly, then came up to Stewart. He held it out. "This belonged to your woman?"

Turning the sticky envelope over in his hands, Stewart saw that it was addressed to Sally Brudde, at his own address in New York. *Sally Brudde?* The return address read Association for White Rights, with a post office box number in Tallahassee. It meant nothing to him, but it had been in Shira's car—that alone was significant. Why had she been using another name? Her involvement apparently went far deeper than just a muck-raking story.

Stewart carefully removed a sheet of paper from the envelope; it, too, was perforated by a bloody bullet hole. An invitation to attend a Ku Klux Klan rally in Jamestown, Virginia. Stewart noted the date: *tomorrow*. He idly turned it over and was about to crumple the invitation and fling it away when his eyes caught something in the bright sunlight. A slight impression—two sets of digits, possibly telephone numbers or street addresses—indentations from a ball-point pen on an overlaying document. One of the numbers was obscured by a 9mm bullet hole.

Barak was watching him, so Stewart refolded the paper, tucked it inside his shirt pocket. He looked at the Israeli. "Major Barak, I have a question."

"Only one? I'm lucky. Call me Motti, please."

"You seem to know why I'm here. You must know about Shira Bernstein. You've met her?"

Barak nodded, and his expression hardened. He came up to Stewart. "Yes, the girl is important, and I'm sorry for you. The Nazis are important to me. But there's more at stake at this moment."

"I'm listening."

Barak sighed softly. "Your democratic government, for a starter."

Stewart felt giddy. He held up his hand and slowly shook his head. "Hold it, Major, please. That's heavy, but let's take one thing at a time. Tell me about Shira first."

Barak looked away, avoiding his eyes. "She's dead. I was too late. I'm sorry. Unfortunately, I cannot be everywhere at once."

Stewart swallowed hard, an empty feeling shooting up from his gut. His head hurt. He felt sick, paralyzed by a new kind of loathing. He was silent for a long time. Finally, he was able to choke out, "Motti, I'm indebted. I owe you one for saving my life back there. But what in *hell's* going on?" He pointed to the dead men. "What am I caught up in here? Some kind of anti-Nazi vendetta? Everybody's armed to the teeth. Machine guns! What next? Is this the big finish or just a beginning?

Give, Major Barak. Who's declaring war on whom?"

"Only men like this pair can answer that question." Barak's voice had an indignant ring.

Stewart persisted. "It's madness. Murderers belong behind bars. Fighting them like this is as bad as what the Nazis themselves do. Do you presume to act for all Jews?"

Barak kicked the deputy's body over and replaced the dead man's wallet. "I act for myself, but I am far from alone. Retribution, Mr. Stewart. Do you mind if I call you Kirk? Retribution, nothing more, nothing less. Eichmann had his day in court. It proved little. Why bother with extradition, kidnapping, and arrest? I have learned to strike more swiftly. We must kill, eliminate, rid society of this ugly cancer once and for all."

Stewart felt thirsty and confused. Wiping the sweat from his forehead, he said swiftly, "Seems to me, the good book says, 'Vengeance is mine, saith the Lord.'"

"That's your Bible, not mine."

"Forget religion, then, and consider modern law."

Motti Barak's face was expressionless, but his voice was hard and sharp. "Save me from idealists. You put them in jail for a period, take away their dangerous toys, yes? Then they return to haunt you worse than before."

Stewart felt confused, increasingly broken. "I never understood Shira's zeal. I'm still not sure I understand yours."

"You will understand, and much sooner than you think. We Israelis can no longer afford to be like you Americans—smug, fat, indifferent, looking out for only our own interests. Perhaps Adolf Hitler was God's punishment for our past complacency."

Stewart looked irritably at Barak. "But in America there's still a measure of benevolence and charity."

Barak laughed, a deep, unsettling chortle. "There's no such thing as a humane Nazi, Mr. Stewart." He spat in the direction of the two corpses, turned, and silently trudged off toward the levee.

Stewart shrugged and started to follow, but Barak suddenly turned. "No. You wait here. They arrived in an air boat. I'll retrieve it and we'll flip it near the quicksand, then drop the bodies in the mud. There must be no evidence of our encounter." He gestured toward the camera around Stewart's neck. "And that means no pictures."

"Quicksand always gives up its dead," Stewart shot back, remembering a jungle book he had read as a child.

"True," replied Barak, grinning. "But it will take several days for internal gases to float the bodies. When they do surface, the FBI agent will be with them. While I'll regret leaving my automatic carbine behind, it will confirm to any investigating authorities how the gun battle took place: a both-sides-lose, swamp shoot-out that you and I, from this moment on, know nothing, *absolutely nothing* about."

"Whose payroll are you on, Major? You wanted to bargain. You asked for my help. How?"

"Patience. I'll return. The bodies, watch them." He pointed to the sky, then disappeared into the thicket.

Stewart immediately brought his Canon into focus on the bodies. As a reporter, he took the phrase "no pictures" with a grain of salt. When he was finished, he gazed up and saw the first of the broad-winged buzzards circling overhead. Stewart was tired, but there was no place to sit, only mud, water, and saw grass. First the splinted finger, then the grazed shoulder, he thought. What next? A Purple Heart or a gold star for his mother? The wound beneath his compressed handkerchief had stopped bleeding, but it still throbbed. He was anxious for Motti Barak to get this ugly business over with so he could get back to civilization. Good God, but then what?

Watching the carrion birds circle overhead in the sun, Stewart felt a peculiar uneasiness come over him, tightening up on his nervous system. He suddenly felt unbearably, miserably hot. The sun seemed to be coming closer, ever closer, and he felt consumed by its searing flames. Then out of the monster sun he saw a vision of Shira. She was calling to him, crying for help. Tears slowly formed in his eyes, ran down his cheeks.

Abruptly, the image faded, the heat subsided, and all he felt was anger. Stewart thought for a long time about what the Israeli had said: retribution.

11

CARLIE CHAVEZ GLANCED at her watch, then once more flipped through the script the feature writers had rushed down to her an hour earlier. She was running late. Carlie liked her network job, her royal blue carpeted office, her white Herman Miller desk, the view of Rockefeller Plaza. Despite an occasional bizarre assignment, she enjoyed being a TV personality known to millions, took pride in her worldly perspective. Celebrity status had its disadvantages—among them a certain loneliness—but she'd learned to cope.

The phone on Carlie's desk buzzed softly. She picked it up, said her name, and listened. "You forgetful bastard," she finally said, twirling in her chair and rolling it to the window. "Damn you, Kirk Stewart. You were supposed to call me yesterday while I was at the *Times* "

Kirk's voice was strange, taut and cold. "I'm sorry, Carlie. This Shira thing got out of hand. I've run up against a blank wall and I'm bushed."

"Bushed? You sound like death warmed over."

"You've got that right. I'm afraid Shira—" Stewart paused, then said bluntly, "I suspect she's dead, dammit."

Carlie sat bolt upright. She swallowed hard before continuing. "How? My God!"

"I don't know everything. So far, it's hearsay. I'm miserable, and I need your help."

"Sure, Kirk. I'm sorry. Look, what can I say? Where are you calling from, for God's sake? It sounds like one of those bad connections from Nantucket."

"Try State Route Thirty, Louisiana. Listen, what I have to tell you is more bad news, but it may develop into one hell of a news story. Trust me and you can be the one to break it on the tube." There was a moment's silence, then Stewart's weary voice continued. "When I return I'll expect to get together for some scotch and sympathy, and you'll get the details. But right now, I need fast assistance, no questions asked. Are you alone in your office?"

"Just a minute." She rose, closed the glass door separating her from the secretarial pool, and returned to the phone. "Okay, proceed."

"Do you have access to Daniel Ruben's office?"

Carlie stared at the telephone in bewilderment. "Kirk, kindly get serious, will you? Ruben is NTN's chairman of the board. I've seen him three times in an elevator and politely said hello. I had my picture taken with him at the Christmas party. A TV reporter I am, a network vice-president with access to the penthouse I'm not. So why do you ask?"

"So you break a few rules. Use your initiative. I need to know about some letters Ruben received recently from Nazi or Klan groups. Threatening letters. They might contain some reference to a forcible takeover of the network."

"Are you serious, Kirk?"

"Couldn't be more so. Remember that FBI raid a few days back—the weapons stash in the Bronx? Take my word for it. There's a tie-in."

Carlie pursed her lips and exhaled slowly. "Good God, Kirk. How do I walk in and drop this on Ruben's lap without being put on the griddle in return?"

"You're a professional, Carlotta. A reporter always finds a way. Start probing, and dig deep. But keep it to yourself."

"I'll have to tell my immediate boss, Alan Simon. I'll need his help to get upstairs."

"*No*. Not yet. Too risky. Go right to the board chairman.

And tell Ruben to keep the FBI out of this until I tell you otherwise."

Carlie ran nervous fingers through her long black hair. "How soon do I get back to you?"

"Uh-uh. You don't. I'll call tomorrow, after lunch."

"Kirk, be reasonable. That's not enough time."

"Baby, if I told you over the phone you'd never believe the reason. Take my word for it, we haven't got many more hours. I need everything you can get, on the phone, tomorrow."

Carlie nodded, once more gazing at her watch. Time to head down to the makeup room. She thought for a long moment.

"Carlotta? You still there? Wake up."

"Yes. I'm sorry. When will you be back in New York?"

There was a long pause. "I'm not sure. I'll shoot for Thursday." Stewart's voice became tense. "Good luck, Carlie, and good-bye."

She frowned, turning over Kirk's words in her thoughts, combining them with what she had heard from the bishop and the rabbi. She hung up slowly, then started to dial Alan Simon's office. Changing her mind, she slammed the telephone down, grabbed her purse, and headed for the door. The hell with protocol. She would burst right in on NTN's chairman, talk to him in person. There wouldn't be time for her makeup session; her viewers would have to take her as she was—in the flesh, without the pancake.

Hurrying to the elevator Carlie worried over the odd tone she had heard in Kirk's voice. The reporter she knew so well was known for his restraint; he was a digger of facts, not fancies. Kirk had never crawled out on a limb. He had done well, exceptionally well, at the *Times*. Her instinct told her there was risk here, and that she should follow his instructions to the letter. Her emotions told her she very much wanted to get together with Kirk Stewart again.

While Carlie Chavez diligently went about Stewart's bidding, Oliver Wright sat glumly in his Washington, D.C., office wrestling with uncomfortable thoughts. Leaning back in his swivel chair, the FBI director stared at the wood inlaid ceiling and slowly puffed on a fresh panatela. Wright was big-built, a burly man, but he was neither slow nor lacking in intelligence. All his life he had been a collector of information; he was fascinated by facts of all kinds, savored them, collected them like some old men collect string. But many questions still continued to baffle him about the character assassination attempt that was being made on the President. He needed more facts. Foremost in his mind was why the administration's enemies didn't go for the jugular. Wright was aware that the President of the United States was the most skillfully guarded man in the world. The Secret Service had made strides, big ones, since the Dallas sniper shot Kennedy, the attempted assassinations of Ford and Reagan. But still, if a brilliant assassin—mad or otherwise—set his or her mind to it, the job was not impossible.

So far, what he did know was sketchy. The President's foes, from all appearances, were highly organized, intelligent, and cunning. On the debit side, the FBI definitely needed more men. There were the security leaks—God knows how many—at the White House and the Pentagon. There was the conflict between the two intelligence agency heads, although the feud was not of his making; it was, in fact, as old as the agencies themselves. But why had certain longtime friends of his in the CIA suddenly begun to shun him?

On the credit side, the men he did have were steadfast, loyal. The Secret Service and other Treasury officers would rally to his side when the chips were down. The New York Police were determined to get to the bottom of the arms warehouse incident. And he did have the cover of the *Times* reporter working for him. A stroke of luck there, but would it last? Kirk Stewart could conceivably wind up as a Judas goat or a sacrificial lamb.

Wright thought for a long time about the press—often an annoyance to him. But suddenly its importance, the crucial part it played in the system of checks and balances—became clearer to him than it had ever been before. An insidious disease had taken root in America and had spread rapidly since he had been heading the FBI, but until this last month, he had always looked upon the neo-Nazis, the various Klans, the Freedom Militia, and the Liberty Alliance as highly fragmented groups. Never had it occurred to him that they might one day merge into one strong militant force, as well organized as their sworn enemy, the Communist party. Was it, in fact, possible?

Wright's intelligence sources, including some highly incriminating computer data, pointed to a mysterious Committee. But who and how many were on the Committee remained a riddle. He suspected Walter Singer was involved in some way, but he had no proof. And why had the head of the CIA just concluded a mysterious meeting in Los Angeles with a group of ultraconservative businessmen? Perhaps the Committee was not military but civilian. The possibilities were endless, the implications stirred the imagination; still, at this point, no laws had been broken, and he had no hard evidence.

Wright knew his limitations. He knew his world was law enforcement. Admittedly, political campaigning and jawboning turned him off. He had never really considered internal Communism a threat to the nation, not as long as his staff kept a finger on each troublemaking cell. There had been far more activity in the sixties and seventies than in the current decade. Nor had he worried that reactionary hot air was dangerous to the national security and welfare. But increased distribution and stockpiling of automatic weapons was another, more frightening matter, and now a known gun runner also appeared to be a conspirator in a blackmail threat to the President of the United States.

Before this latest incident, Wright's men had methodically tightened their net around Arnold Metz and his associates down in Galveston. The FBI could no longer afford the luxury of waiting, standing by, watching the trap, hoping to uncover more of the coast-to-coast conspiracy that apparently existed. The threat to the President was too immediate. *Friday!* Enough evidence on Metz was there. He would have to be arrested on a lesser charge and brought in for questioning immediately.

Wright reached for his telephone. Bypassing his secretary, he direct-dialed the three digits that would connect him instantly with his bureau chief in Houston.

Stewart cursed the stifling heat, reached over, and rolled down the window on the passenger's side of the rented car. His shirt was soaked with sweat. The Ford's air conditioning had finally given up the ghost just outside Port Bolivar.

Stewart had been warned long ago that crime reporting would sometimes be a grisly job, and the hours were unpredictable, particularly during full moons. He had accepted that fact and adjusted to it, but there were times when the mean streets, the ugliness, the middle-of-the night intrusions on his sleep became damn near insupportable. Like now, he thought, considering the narrow margin by which he had just escaped death.

Finding a service station just outside Port Bolivar, Stewart pulled over, determined to clean himself up. Motti Barak, following behind in his own car, remained outside, refueling and talking with the attendant.

Stewart glimpsed himself in the dirty mirror of the rest room. He scrubbed, applied to his shoulder the Bacitracin the Vinton pharmacist had supplied him, then quickly covered the wound with an oversized Band-Aid. Pulling on a clean navy blue sports shirt with the silk-screened emblem of the Central Park Jogging Club on its pocket, he straightened the collar and combed his hair. He stared at himself for several seconds, thinking, oddly enough, after what had happened, of Carlie Chavez and his phone call earlier. He suddenly realized he not only wanted but urgently needed a woman's company. Stewart closed his eyes tight, trying to squeeze the thoughts of his first and last date with Carlie Chavez out of his mind, cram it back into the dead business file where it belonged. But the image remained vivid and uncomfortably warm. Shira had gone for a week to visit her sister in Ohio. He and Carlie had gone to a beach near Provincetown. She lay beside him, her soft forest green cotton blouse open, her contrasting ivory breasts glowing in the moonlight. He had teased them with his tongue while she moaned with pleasure and anticipation. Slipping his hand between her legs, along her thighs, he'd felt warmth through her Dolphin shorts. But when his fingers probed beneath the elastic waistband, Carlie had abruptly dismissed him. Despite the fact they were both aroused, a conversational battle had begun, with Shira Bernstein the primary subject. Confused, but stubborn and a little angry with desire, Stewart had won the tryst, but by the time it was over, Carlie Chavez had defeated him, more than once kindling his guilt. He felt that same discomfort again. There was something he had to do for Shira, even now, after death. He wasn't entirely sure what it was, but he would do it, come whatever. He had failed Shira miserably. Despite her secretive nature, her stubbornness and dedication to her causes, he should have taken control. Stewart felt his neck prickling. How could he possibly have thought of Carlie at a time like this? Was it Shira's death that was tearing him apart or was it Carlie?

Swallowing hard, Stewart looked away from the mirror and slipped out of the rest room. He headed toward the car where Motti Barak would be waiting. Stewart felt a measure of relief;

not good, just better. Whatever their relationship, he and Carlie
had some tough work cut out for them and there wouldn't be
time to resurrect the past or fantasize on the future. The way
events were slamming into place, he would barely have time
for a good cry on her shoulder.

Engines howling in a thundering blast, the F-15 wasted no time
showing its disdain for the ground. The Palm Springs airport
runway disappeared in a fast blur beneath the two-seat, trainer
version of the Fighting Falcon. Seated at the jet's controls, the
pilot adjusted the flaps and increased the rate of climb into the
California sky. Colonel Pete Reddick enjoyed flight time, looked
forward to it. His desk work, the scepter of command he carried
on the ground as a newly appointed squadron commander at
Langley Air Force Base, Virginia, paled in comparison to the
power he felt in a fighter cockpit.

With or without his glossy black flying helmet, Pete Reddick
was a hard-featured man—square chin, curly brown hair, blaz-
ing hazel eyes beneath beetle brows. At forty-two he had flown
more than three hundred hours in the U-2, and a hundred plus
in the more advanced SR-71 super secret research jet. He had
put in ten years of highly sophisticated, hush-hush work, and
Reddick was accustomed to clandestine, odd-hour departures,
the kind of secrecy that prevented him from discussing his
work with his wife and family. The extra pay was worth the
effort, and the danger was negligible; American spy plane operations had become more sagacious since the infamous
overflight of Francis Gary Powers. Secret missions had become
routine for Reddick. But this one—ferrying the garrulous, outspoken General George Brady from Palm Springs to Andrews
Air Force Base—was unique. Reddick was under orders to
keep quiet about their arrival in Washington, D.C. His annoying
telephone contact, a man he had never met called Lynx, had
twice warned him of the need for secrecy.

Reddick thought about what lay ahead. He knew his career
had a lot going for it, but there were also some black marks
against it. If he had it to do over again, he would have become
an astronaut; he wouldn't have known the satisfaction of killing
and spying on Commies, but the adulation would have been
rewarding. Not much fanfare in U-2 and SR-71 assignments.
And now that his updated physical exam report was in, the
Blackbirds were history for Reddick.

His new fighter command was a lateral transfer, with no boost in rank. Reddick still felt bitterness at having been by-passed for a brigadier's star at his last promotional review. The word was out that he was a maverick; some of his enemies at the Pentagon were accusing him of stubbornness, arrogance, and political fanaticism. Well, Patrick Henry was a fanatic too, he thought. To hell with their spurious complaints; after all, he was a born leader, a good one at that. He had a definite way with the men he commanded. Morale was high, his crews were confident, highly skilled, and disciplined; they toed the line.

Reddick once more consulted the folded map strapped to his knee, then glanced out of the perplex canopy as Mount San Jacinto slipped by.

"Colonel Reddick?" The intercom voice from the rear cockpit was slightly slurred and metallic.

"Go ahead, General," Reddick replied.

"What's our ETA at Langley Field?"

"I'm taking you directly to Andrews, General. Closer to the capital. The CIA director's sending a car to meet us."

"Good, good. But the time?"

Reddick checked his watch. "We should make it by twenty-two thirty eastern time if we don't pick up a headwind."

"I'm curious, Colonel. How many men in your fighter squadron can we count on? I mean, have you got a grip on their sentiments yet?"

"All hand-picked, sir. Any fence straddlers were transferred out."

"Excellent. And your sentiments?"

Reddick thought for a moment. "Begging your pardon, sir. I don't understand."

There was a long silence; then the intercom crackled again. "The men who met in Los Angeles—Singer, Gifford, Frober, and Hallowell. They tell me you're one of our best shots. The Committee seems to feel you're the hardest son of a bitch to come along since Patton."

"Patton was a general, sir."

"Don't worry, Reddick. We'll soon fix that. But how fanatic a bastard are you when it comes to patriotism, what's right for the country?"

"Tell me where you want the flag, General, and I'll put it there."

"And keep it there?"

"You've got that right. I play to win."

"Good. So do I. We're not going to lose the next one, Colonel. When I evacuated my troops out of South Vietnam, we had to leave behind eight hundred thousand M-16 rifles, six hundred tanks, some seventy fighter aircraft, many still in their goddamn shipping crates. Incompetence. Cowardice. I felt like dropping a bomb on Capitol Hill then, and I still do."

Reddick eased up slightly on his turn. There were scattered high cumulus clouds in the area, but the weather was clear and cloudless to the east.

"You with me, Colonel?"

"I'm listening, General. I was with you back in 'Nam, but I was flying U-2 recon missions at fifty thousand feet over the Chinese border."

"I like your style, Reddick. But with the rest of the Air Force apparently lined up against us, we'll have our work cut out for us next week."

"We'll be ready for anything they throw our way."

"Don't mind me if I nod off, Colonel. I just came in from eighteen holes of golf."

"Sure. Just let me know if you change your mind and want to make a pit stop en route to Washington."

Reddick completed his long, banking turn, eased back on the throttle, and set a course due east. He felt a familiar tightness in the back of his neck. Tension. Suddenly, he imagined orders being given, military shouts, his own voice, but it seemed to belong to someone else. It's time for action, the voice snapped. Are you listening, Reddick? The entire military system had gone to seed. Mediocrity has replaced excellence. Indifference prevails, not ambition. The Communists could walk all over us tomorrow. Break some heads, Reddick; don't mind that quartet pulling the strings. Don't be afraid to spill a little blood for Christ's sake; this is your big chance, so don't blow it. Nothing wrong with the feeling of power; those who can handle it should never hold back.

The Pentagon inner sanctum, a brigadier's star to replace the chicken on his collar—they were close, tantalizingly close. Colonel Pete Reddick, with his love of fast airplanes, with his private dreams of command, with his unfulfilled need to fight a war—the entire reflection was there, staring back at him from the side of the F-15's perplex. The profile of an ambitious officer on a dangerous course? No! Come what may, he thought, this was the right course. Even according to that moralist and spiritual leader the Reverend Jimmy Hallowell, this was the only cause left for America.

Stewart wanted to drive straight through to Galveston, but Motti Barak objected. The Israeli insisted he wasn't about to help Stewart on an empty stomach. Now they lingered at a Port Bolivar café over platters of bayou crayfish and bottles of beer, trying—not too successfully—to get to know each other. Stewart found his companion annoyingly elusive and secretive; the only subject Barak seemed willing to discuss at length was the infinite number of fighter aircraft he had flown in his lifetime. Stewart was surprised to discover that Barak knew so much about the weapons dealer in Galveston. Despite this, he decided to remain closemouthed about his knowledge of the gun peddler's videotape delivery to the White House. He also decided not to tell the Israeli of his own meeting with the FBI director the day before.

After a short ferry ride across the bay, they arrived in downtown Galveston. Stewart was having a difficult time adjusting to the staggering humidity. He parked his own car on a side street and climbed into Barak's cool Mercury Bobcat. It, too, appeared to be an airport rental. Stopping at a corner phone booth, Stewart found the address of the American Eagle Gun Emporium in the Yellow Pages. It turned out to be an incongruous building on a modern, glass-tower-lined street. Painted red and white and resembling an old barn, it bore an old-fashioned sign with raised, ornate gold letters.

Considering the hour, traffic was light. At Stewart's urging, Barak drove slowly past without stopping, for parked nearby was a green Camaro with a familiar face behind the wheel: the FBI agent from Houston. Stewart managed to raise his camera inconspicuously and get a quick shot of the building.

"The green car," said Stewart quietly. "The man with the newspaper."

Barak grinned as he turned the corner. "I saw him. He paid no attention to us. But we'll stay off a bit."

Stewart looked at his watch. "It's a little after five. The phone book ad says Metz closes at five-thirty. I suggest we make sure there's no rear entrance."

"And then?"

"Park down the street and wait. When our man closes shop, we follow him."

Barak nodded.

Stewart put his camera back under his seat. "But stay behind the FBI agent."

"You're positive he's FBI? I'm beginning to suspect you know much more than you've let on to Motti, yes?"

"Pure speculation," Stewart replied calmly.

12

THE SMILE ON the face behind the locked glass gun counter had the sort of ruthless charm that only the genuinely insincere possess. Slender, in his mid-twenties, with frizzy black hair, Arnold Metz had a narrow, cadaverous face on which a smile seemed out of place. More often his fierce, charcoal eyes with their premature crow's feet cleverly masked his inner hate and anger with a curious frigidity. His customers seldom knew what he was really thinking, and his two employees tolerated his discomforting coldness. They were paid well. It never mattered what his friends thought, for Metz had no close friends. He enjoyed being a loner.

Though he had not yet succeeded in his assignment—to eliminate the meddlesome news reporter—Metz was unconcerned. There was still time, and Stewart had left a trail a mile wide. All this he had just explained on the telephone to Lynx. Metz was now alone, having sent his assistants home early. Business was light on Tuesdays, and he would be locking up in twenty minutes. Behind him, in glass cases lining the wall, were not only rifles and handguns from all over the world but also a fine assortment of collectors' weapons. Once a month he put these antiques up for sale. He had found them at auctions in Houston and Dallas. Nowhere in the country, he reasoned, was there a gun dealer who took such pride in his inventory. The dollar value of his stock had soared beyond his wildest dreams; business had prospered in the last two years. It seemed like only yesterday that his father had passed away and left him this thriving business. If Arnold Metz was not the largest gun dealer in the United States, he was indisputably the youngest.

And the shrewdest, he thought, gazing out the front door before he began the ten-minute procedural lock-up of the display cabinets. The green Camaro was down the street, parked at the corner again. When would the FBI give up? Hadn't he proven in the two weeks they had shadowed him that he was—on the surface—arrow straight? It had been child's play to shake the tail and deliver the truckload of guns to the Halfway House in Louisiana. He had been clever, planned carefully. Little did the Feds realize that he was far more than a mere gun merchant, that he was also an accomplished, highly paid master assassin. The *New York Times* reporter would soon find this out. As would the President of the United States.

Twirling the dials of the automatic sensor alarm, Metz set the digital code to manual, allowing him access to the store for another hour. He could now return later on and activate the formidable array of locks at the door without inadvertently summoning a squad car. The lieutenant heading the precinct burglary detail, whose palm he occasionally greased, disliked false alarms at gun stores.

Tonight, Metz reminded himself, he needed to be especially careful. He had to shake the FBI agent, and planned to do so at his nearby home. Metz would then slip back to the store for his secret meeting. Lynx was arriving, bringing additional orders from the Committee. Most important, he was bringing in one of the most sophisticated field weapons Condor Defense Industries had yet devised. The EMR—electro magnetic rocket. Metz had long looked forward to getting his hands on this deadly, electronically controlled weapon, which could be fired from an ordinary Springfield rifle, but had the homing mechanism and the destructive power of an anti-tank shell.

Metz was excited. He thought about the liberals' death-choke on America, and he recalled what the hotel executive

Karl Frober had told him just before the banquet. He remembered vividly the man from Paraguay's speech. No, he thought. It wouldn't come to that. No goddamn niggers would gain power. Not now, not a year hence during the nominations. Never would a Negro be elected President of the United States! Not nominated! Not elected! The liberals, including the current President, claimed that Governor Freeman of California was more than qualified. Impossible! How could a black be qualified? And shit, the two conservative Supreme Court justices were retiring, and the President was hinting that he would nominate a couple of pinko women to the court! Christ, what was it all coming to? Well, Metz, he told himself, you'll show them. You'll send those motherfucking Commies where they belong. You'll blast them to hell and back. This EMR device is just the weapon to do the job.

Arnold Metz turned off all the overheads except the night light, grabbed his black leather biker's jacket, and strode toward the front door.

From their vantage point over a block away, Stewart and Barak watched the gun store owner close shop and swagger up the street; they then turned their eyes to the green Camaro. The FBI man in it hesitated, then slowly pulled away from the curb.

"I suggest we keep our distance, Major," said Stewart. "Let the Camaro maintain visual contact."

Barak gave Stewart a hard, sour look. "You've done this before?"

"Only as an enterprising reporter."

Ahead, the FBI vehicle slowed, then stopped. Barak frowned. "Our man from the gun store doesn't drive a car. He walks."

Stewart checked his watch again. "Must live nearby."

For several minutes they played a game of cat and mouse, until finally some five blocks away, Arnold Metz approached an inconspicuous two-story white house and ascended the steps. Stewart watched the FBI shadow park his car, predictably, a block away. From the relaxed manner with which the agent was handling the situation, Stewart suspected that the watch on the gun merchant was a casual one; perhaps it had gone on for some time. Still, he and Barak couldn't remain where they were. The residential street was virtually devoid of traffic, and they would be easily spotted. The ball of fire that was the late afternoon sun disappeared beyond the horizon. Darkness would set in fast.

Stewart said swiftly, "Leave the front door to our buddy in the Camaro. Let's nose around back."

Barak seemed to be thinking along the same lines. He wheeled the car around the corner and headed for a narrow alley that appeared to run the length of the block.

Stewart saw that all the buildings had small enclosed court-yards on each side each of which had access to the alley. No garages were in evidence, only look-alike houses and monot-onous white picket fences. Barak was only partway into the alley when he braked, startled.

Stewart was surprised to see Metz suddenly emerge from a wooden gate half a dozen houses away. Barak saw him, too, and didn't hesitate; he immediately backed off, as if he were using the alley only to turn around. Stewart watched in the rearview mirror as their quarry paused, looked their way briefly, then strode off in the opposite direction.

Stewart looked at Barak and asked, "Why did he come out the back door? Think he's going back to the store?"

"He might be headed anywhere, now that he's shaken that Bureau tail." The Israeli shook his head, stopped the car, and slid quickly from behind the wheel. Reaching in the back seat, he probed through a canvas overnight bag and withdrew a small pistol and a folded envelope-sized tool packet. "Take the car and shadow this character. Stay on top of him, Kirk, but in-conspicuously. I'll check the house."

Stewart slid across the seat, "Where do we reconnoiter?"

"At the corner by the gun shop. Half an hour. If one of us doesn't show, the other is to check into that Hyatt motel we passed on the way from the ferry. Questions?"

"None. Child's play."

"Don't we wish. Be careful."

Quick-stepped and confident, Barak set off into the alley.

The Israeli, thought Stewart, was almost too perfect. Barak thought clearly, measured his chances shrewdly, seldom made a mistake. There had to be a flaw somewhere. Was Motti Barak the man he claimed to be? Stewart couldn't put his finger on what was bothering him, but it was there, a lingering, uncom-fortable uneasiness.

•   •   •

Barak felt confident as he surveyed the area. Behind Metz's house a strip of garden had been dug out, and marigolds and nasturtiums struggled through the picket fence bordering the alley. The neighbors' houses were in a tumble-down condition, the one on the left abandoned, its windows boarded up. The alley smelled of uncollected garbage. Somewhere, a neighbor's dinner had overcooked; the scent of scorched cabbage was heavy in the air. No one saw him pass through the gate. The back door stood at the top of a narrow flight of stairs, inside an enclosed porch. Good, Barak thought. He wouldn't be seen by passersby as he forced the entry. Beside the door was a pushbutton, soiled with years of grime. The back entrance had been used often by visitors, he concluded. Barak rang the bell and heard a raucous jangle somewhere within. He waited patiently and pushed the button again.

Excellent. He really didn't want to be confronted by a wife, lover, roommate, or housekeeper. An untended house was more rewarding than one whose occupants were untalkative or uncooperative. The doorbell was loud enough, but he had to make sure. Barak hesitated, then rattled the door softly. Apparently no dogs. *Good.* Why did every home in the United States seem to have a dog? Was it another capitalist luxury or some deep-seated need of the Americans?

Barak looked through the window at the inside of the door. He was in luck. A deadbolt, not keyed from within. But still, it was too simple, he calculated. A gun merchant wouldn't be so nonchalant about security. Carefully, slowly, Barak ran his practiced, sensitive fingers around the doorjamb. Three inches above the threshold, just below one of the hinge pins, he found the edge of the concealed copper circuit.

From his tool kit he withdrew pliers, a length of wire, and tape. He quickly secured each end of the wire to the copper leads on the doorjamb. He could now swing open the door without breaking the alarm circuit. Swiftly, with a carbide cutter, he made a six-inch hole in the window, reached inside, and turned the deadbolt. Then he swiftly folded his tool kit, shoved it in his back pocket, withdrew his Beretta automatic, and stepped inside the house, gently closing the door behind him. With experienced stealth and the grace of a leopard on the stalk, Barak slipped quietly through the cluttered kitchen. From all appearances, the house's occupant was a bachelor—

a not too tidy one at that. Dirty dishes and pots everywhere, even on the floor.

Barak stepped into the dining area, made his way into a magazine-strewn living room. His every movement was unhurried, deliberate, easy. Despite the circumstances, he felt no fear or urgency whatsoever. Breaking and entering was one of the more pedestrian skills the KGB had taught him.

Stewart cruised around the neighborhood until he spotted Metz. The gun merchant appeared to be headed back to his store. Stewart drove slowly, finally pulling up to the curb and killing the engine. He watched with interest as Metz joined a man standing in front of a Seven-Eleven store and conversed briefly, then walked swiftly a few doors down the street to the American Eagle Gun Emporium. Stewart watched Metz use several keys to unlock the door, then escort his companion inside.

Climbing out of Barak's Bobcat, Stewart hurried along the sidewalk, anxious to get a better view of what was taking place inside the gun store. He crossed the street. Cautiously approaching the chest-high windows—which were framed by white shutters and covered with an expandable steel gate—he looked inside. There was no one in the showroom, but a light burned in a back room.

Stewart glanced up the street, distracted by the siren of a patrol car in the distance that sounded as if it was headed his way. Opting for discretion, he headed back to his car and climbed inside. He could do nothing now but continue his vigilance, wait for Metz.

Motti Barak slowly and methodically examined Metz's living room. Barak liked to work alone. Indeed, Laurenti Baroski, as he was known in Russia, was an extremely successful sleeper for the KGB *because* of his solitary nature. He had achieved all of his spectacular accomplishments with few, if any, accomplices. Teamwork was fine for others—especially the Israelis and their notorious Mossad—but it had never worked for him. Although he was a product of Communist education and upbringing, something in his blood made him a loner; he had a stubborn bourgeois streak that he had never been fully able to explain.

It had been a long and difficult road to the United States

and this small house in Galveston that was suddenly so important. When he had first come to America he had looked on the Stars and Stripes as the ugliest flag in the world. Now, a year later, he had mellowed. Out of necessity he had made friends in Washington and several other cities, and had spent a short five-day vacation in the American West. But only once, while fishing in a trout pool along the Fryingpan River in Colorado, had he thought about defecting, seeking political asylum in the United States. *Defection.* Such an act would be like consigning his parents to prison, or at the least to a mental institution. A death warrant was not beyond the realm of possibility. Few people knew the actual fate of the state's enemies—the KGB knew how to keep and bury its secrets.

Barak could never desert his parents; their commitment to Israel was his own. His wife back in Ivanovo had divorced him ten years earlier when he agreed to become an overseas *shpik* for the KGB. She had not understood his motivations, but that had been her surface explanation; down deep, they had really never understood each other. The woman he had met and cared for in Jerusalem while in Israeli flight training was a different story. But that affair had been abruptly, tragically terminated by an Arab rocket shell. Berta had been moving large bags of sand around the kibbutz doors and windows at the time. She was trying to keep the Arabs out. Everyone in Israel was trying to keep the Arabs out, Barak thought. It was like pushing back the desert sand.

Barak had been cautious about making good friends in Israel, but often he could not avoid companionship. The KGB's primary interest in sending him to the Holy Land was not so much to spy on the Israelis as to prepare his cover for later assignment to the West. But still, Barak had made and lost friends. Two of his close acquaintances in fighter pilot school had been killed in Golan, another in the Sinai.

It had been a long time since anyone called him Laurenti Baroski. He liked the Hebrew name he had taken for himself in Israel. Motti Barak. Barak meant lightning. He had even painted the symbol on the side of his first assigned fighter. Flying had come easily to him, as had language skills. Though there was a slight accent to his English, his French and Hebrew were flawless. As a warrior he had cut his teeth fighting the Egyptians in Sinai; he had flown more Mirage fighter missions than he could remember against Arab terrorist enclaves in Syria and Lebanon. It had especially pleased his KGB superiors when Moshe Dayan himself presented Barak with an Award of Combat Merit. Curious, he thought. In the Soviet Union no Jew would be permitted to fly a military jet, but in Israel he had flown three different types of fighters, including American.

Barak missed Ivanovo, his parents' small but comfortable apartment on Novo Sayidovsky Street. But more than Mother Russia, he longed for the calmness he had always felt in Jerusalem. At dawn and sunset the Holy City, sprawled lazily over the hills, was tinted in a soft pinkish glow; at midday it sparkled, bathed in brilliant yellows. Jerusalem was a sanctuary, a place where time was suspended, where at night the stars were closer, brighter, than they were in Russia. After Berta's death, he had gone from the fighter base to the city, sat in the chapel with the Chagall windows, and prayed. He had also made promises to himself. Whether the oaths were retribution or simply renewed determination, he wasn't sure, but from that time forth he had committed himself. The moment his parents were out of the Soviet Union, away from the clutches of the KGB, he would defect and fight for Israel. To date he had dealt halfheartedly in espionage. But soon he would fight with every inch of his soul.

Barak put his rememberings away and applied himself to the present. Disturbing events were happening in the United States. He could empathize with the American moderates; he understood their fears and frustrations. And he knew why the Israelis were interested in the U.S. Nazi movement. But why had his superiors in the KGB expressed so much interest in this soft underbelly of American society?

Going over to the window, Barak surveyed the street out in front through the sheer curtains. Quiet. The FBI agent was still parked a short distance away. Barak wondered if Kirk Stewart was having any luck. Complications, this young capitalist reporter had brought him. Perhaps it was time to leave the congenial but troublesome American behind.

Inside the American Eagle Gun Emporium, Arnold Metz ran his fingers carefully over the smooth, twelve-inch long casing of the EMR, at the same time listening to his visitor's lengthy instructions for the weapon. The man known as Lynx wasted no time getting down to specifics. "You have until Friday to practice with the projectile, Metz. Absolute secrecy, of course, is in order. I trust you have access to isolated test facilities?"

Metz nodded. His eyes were glued to the EMR.

Lynx's cold, even voice continued: "You will be hidden in the rear of a canvas-back army truck just off Constitution Avenue, the route the President's limousine will take after he leaves the Capitol Building rotunda. We will provide you with a small portable TV on which to monitor his State of the Union message. From it, you will take your cue." He paused, waiting for Metz to look up and give him his undivided attention.

The gun store owner looked at him gravely.

Lynx continued: "If the President resigns—the Committee still hopes your little videotape will be effective—there will be no need for your additional services in Washington. If he does not, you will fire the EMR at the presidential limousine. In either event, you will be paid the agreed sum."

Metz picked up a matchbox-sized stainless-steel container and turned it over in his hands. "And this is the homing beacon your men must plant in the President's car?"

"It will be there. That's the least of your worries. Your helicopter escape, likewise, has been arranged by insiders in Washington. But the weapon, if it is necessary to use it, must not fail. Can we trust in your proficiency?"

"You wish to see my sharpshooting awards, my hunting trophies?"

"Unnecessary," Lynx replied curtly. "But as I said earlier, I trust this hunting expertise will prove beneficial in finding and eliminating the New York reporter."

"I won't have to work hard. From what you say, I suspect Stewart will find me." Metz ran his palm over the death's-head tattoo on his left forearm as if it were a token of strength. "The assignment, matter of fact, is hardly sporting. Like shooting fish in a barrel."

Lynx nodded. "Good."

Metz smiled with twisted lips. Suddenly, a shrill buzzing sound emanated from his jacket pocket. He quickly withdrew a small receiver and switched off the alarm. Grim-faced, Metz strode for the exit. "Wait here. Lock the door when I leave. I'll return as soon as possible."

Lynx looked puzzled.

"An electronic light beam crosses the living room of my house. It's been broken."

The other man shrugged. "Perhaps a false alarm. That dog of yours. Or your temperamental bird?"

Metz hesitated in the open doorway. "The beam is set five feet off the floor. And the falcon is locked in the bedroom."

Motti Barak idly kicked through several magazines on the floor, pursed his lips, and shook his head. All the magazines were the graphic kind emphasizing sultry-eyed musclemen, most clad in black leather or cowboy garb. Scanning the room, he saw no desk, no papers, correspondence, or address books— items he wanted to examine at length. The only decoration was a grouping of old movie posters on one wall. Barak had half expected to see an old musket or powder horn in evidence, but the room had a Spartan look. No gun collection anywhere to be seen. Moments later, Barak understood why. The hallway led to a large den, or more properly, thought Barak, a dungeonlike chamber that would have done credit to the Marquis de Sade. The room was dim, without windows, the only light coming in from the hall. He flipped the light switch, and his eyes took in a bizarre collection of medieval weaponry, leather thongs, chains, and studded restraining apparatus. Tacked to the ceiling was a five-by-seven-foot Nazi flag, and lining one wall were pictures of men and women in an infinite variety of bondage costumes.

And there were other photographs. A likeness of Bismarck; a picture of Charles Lindbergh arriving in Paris; von Richthofen—the Red Baron—posing beside a World War I Rokker. There was an aerial shot of the Hindenburg over the Manhattan skyline. Barak paused for a long time at a fairly recent framed photo of a pilot standing next to a U-2 spy plane. Barak read the autographed inscription with more than casual interest: "To Arnold, best regards, Pete Reddick."

Barak's eyes drifted back to the Nazi flag on the ceiling, the torture toys on the walls. He got a sudden, sick feeling in the bottom of his stomach; his hand felt clammy as it gripped the Beretta. There was another feeling, too. A distinct uneasiness, an impression that he was not alone. Suddenly he heard a low, menacing growl from behind him. At the same instant his mind flashed back to the kitchen, the metal pan on the floor by the sink—not a small cooking utensil but a large one, and filled with water! He turned, feeling adrenaline coursing through his body. His gun hand was only halfway around before the snarling black and brown blur shot through the air and grabbed his arm. The gun flew from his hand, sliding under the leather couch in the corner.

Barak reeled, trying to shake the Doberman's tenacious grip on his forearm. The dog's jaws grappled lower, tightening around his wrist, pulling, dragging. Barak swung as hard as he could with his free arm, driving his fist into the animal's chest. The dog backed off with a sharp grunt, ribs heaving. Barak swore softly in Russian. Catching his breath, heart in his throat, he watched the snarling animal slowly circle him, its ears ramrod stiff, teeth bared and salivating, eyes savage.

Pain stabbed at Barak's bleeding wrist; he tried to edge toward the door, but the Doberman, smelling his fear and reading his mind, stationed itself in the hallway. Growling deep in its throat as it prepared to spring again, the dog dug its forepaws into the carpet.

Barak winced and glanced around the room. The dog hurtled toward him, this time aiming for the throat. Barak was a small man, but his arms and hands were strong; still, he was no match for the writhing, snapping creature that was clawing, burrowing toward his neck. Barak's hands gripped the animal's throat as they fell to the floor, but he couldn't hold on. Scratching, pawing with fury, the dog leaped to one side. Fangs bared, eyes flashing and still fixed on Barak's throat, the Doberman drove in again. Barak kicked with both feet and rolled to one side. The dog hesitated.

Motti Barak gasped his lungs full of air. At the same moment his eyes caught sight of the medieval spiked ball and chain hanging from the wall. Frantically, he reached up, his bloodied fingers closing tightly around the heavy chain. Tearing it from the wall, he slowly climbed to his feet, the dog watching his every move. It, too, appeared to be catching a fast second breath. But Barak was no sooner standing than the animal, with a terrible roar, leaped at him again. Barak swung. The sharp spiked ball was halfway through its arc when it slammed with a sickening thud into the Doberman's skull.

Barak fell backward, carried by the force of the animal's lunge. But the dog slid limply off his chest, emitting a low whimper. Then it lay at his feet, blood oozing from its nose, brown and black chest heaving. Finally, it was still.

The room's terrifying silence was broken by a shuffling sound in the hall. His breath still rasping in his throat, Barak lifted his eyes away from the dead Doberman and looked toward the doorway.

"An expensive, valuable animal," said Arnold Metz ominously, from behind a Luger pistol. Cautiously, measuring his steps, he entered the room. His hate-filled eyes fixed on Barak, he reached into his pocket and withdrew a long, slender silencer.

Barak stood his ground, didn't move.

A look of anticipation and sheer pleasure covered Metz's face as he slowly screwed the sound suppressor over the barrel of the Luger.

"Surely a man condemned to death has earned one last cigarette and a final statement?" asked Barak drearily, hands spread in a helpless gesture. Nodding toward the steamer trunk beside him, he asked, "May I sit?"

Metz nodded and waved his gun. Barak sat down.

"No one smokes in my house," snapped the gun merchant, his dark eyes spewing venom. "And words, under the circumstances, are useless."

Motti Barak's jaw clenched. "I understand that here in Texas you have an old saying: 'String a man up, kill him without his final say, and his spirit will dog you seven times seventy years.'"

"Don't make me laugh." Metz's red-sparked, homicidal eyes were cold and speculative. "Bullshit. You're not a Texan; you're not even an American."

Barak sighed. "Quite correct. What is your point? I'm less human?"

Metz sneered. "That accent—"

"Israeli. And you naturally dislike Jews. From the curious memorabilia on your wall, I suspect you are an ardent admirer of Adolf Hitler and his friends." Barak's eyes darted briefly to the hallway. Had he seen a shadow near the front door?

Metz raised the Luger, menacing his captive with relish. "I had my doubts you were a run-of-the-mill housebreaker. A fucking Israeli spy, then. Interesting. For your information, Jew, I am not an admirer of the Fuehrer. Adolf Hitler had the right idea, but he was too weak."

Metz edged a few steps closer. His words set a funeral bell tolling in Barak's head.

"Otherwise his Reich would have survived to this day. The Fuehrer was too sympathetic. Now things will be different. In less than a week history will be rewritten in the world. And when we are finished with America, the Germany of World War Two will appear to be a Jewish vacation resort."

"You were not even born at the time. What do you know of the Holocaust but what you have read?"

"Yes, I have read. All your Zionist bullshit propaganda."

Barak shook his head. "You are like the others. You work so hard to bury the truth."

"The truth is our cause itself."

"*Our* cause? You and who else?" asked Barak calmly, buying time.

Metz didn't respond. He slowly raised the Luger, pointed it at Barak's head.

The Israeli didn't flinch. In the hallway there was a sudden sound. His gun wavered only slightly, as Metz turned his body, his eyes flashing sideways. His movement was enough to offset the trajectory of the heavy tire iron. Instead of striking Metz on the back of the head, it tore flesh and drew blood as it clipped the side of his face, then bounced off his gun hand. Metz cried out in pain. At the same time the Luger went off, then flew across the room.

Barak leaped for the gun.

Cursing, one hand on his face, Metz glanced down the hall. Barak followed his surprised stare. Kirk Stewart was standing in the front doorway. Barak frantically probed under the couch, trying to wrap his fingers around the Luger. Assessing the odds, Metz ran down the hallway in the opposite direction, swiftly entered the bedroom, closed the locked the door.

Stewart repressed the urge to smile. He knew the tire iron was a dangerous ploy, but the distraction had been Barak's only chance. Stewart would have put Metz out for the count had the gun peddler not suddenly turned. Stewart waited until Barak had retrieved the Texan's Luger, then said firmly, "I owed you one."

"*Baruch haba,*" Barak replied. "Blessed is he who comes." He gestured to the hallway, indicating that Stewart was to follow him quietly.

Together, pressed against the wall, they approached the bedroom door. Stewart listened, reached gingerly for the handle, found it secured. Barak pulled him back and, aiming for the lock, fired the Luger. The silenced gun went off with a sharp click. Brass and wood shattered. Stewart kicked the door open and stood back. No one blew their heads off, but Stewart felt a strong draft. The bedroom window was open, curtains fluttering in the breeze. Cautiously, Stewart looked into the room. Barak sent him a knowing look and dashed for the window. "I'll follow Metz," Barak said swiftly. "I suggest you leave quietly by the same way you came in: by the front door. Then lose that FBI agent."

Before Stewart could respond, the Israeli leaped through the window and disappeared. Barak was as elusive as quicksilver, Stewart thought, shaking his head in annoyance. He pulled the window closed, secured it, and glanced nervously around the room. The king-sized bed was covered with a custommade black leather spread. Above the bed, a *King Kong* poster; on one side, a press bench with weights. The closet was open, dirty clothes on the floor. In the corner, above a bureau on a perch, a large peregrine ruffled its wings. Its sinister eyes were on Stewart, cold and menacing. Damn Metz and his unfriendly menagerie, Stewart thought. Then he saw the address book.

With a sense of foreboding, he eased across the room. Stewart paused halfway, reconsidering. A falcon isn't dangerous; it's a bird of prey, he told himself, but it's harmless to humans. Even before he could put the thought away, the bird came at him, neck feathers ruffled, talons extended. He ducked as it raked his head. It emitted no shriek, no call; the only terrible sound was the furious beating of the falcon's wings against Stewart's head and arms. The bird threw itself repeatedly against him, rose in the air, fluttered back, tearing, clawing, with its talons, probing and slashing with its sharp beak.

Stewart ducked, trying to shield his head, face, and throat with his arms. My eyes, he flashed, I have to protect my eyes. The peregrine swept down on him repeatedly. With his arms over his face, Stewart stumbled across the room. Where was the door? A knob! He found the opening, passed through. Oh, God, it was the closet. Ripping a shirt from a hanger, he swung it desperately at the bird, but it stubbornly came at him again. Blood was running down his fingers and arms. The peregrine was the largest he had ever seen, strong of wing with razor-sharp claws. Protecting his eyes with one hand, he pulled the closet door shut with the other. The falcon struck repeatedly with its beak against the wood paneling. Then suddenly all was quiet.

Stewart's throat felt dry. The closet was pitch dark and smelled of mothballs and dirty socks. Groping overhead for a light and finding none, he felt helpless and foolish. What now? Opening the door just a crack, he saw the bird. Stewart's own blood now streaked its brown and white feathers as it rested on its perch, meeting his gaze with piercing, lusting eyes. Without warning, the falcon swooped toward the crack in the door, its beak and talons prying at the jamb. Stewart pulled the door completely closed, slumped down against the closet wall, and swore softly.

He sat there for a long time, thinking. Calculating the distance to the front door, he tried to decide on his next move. He felt for a heavy jacket on the rack above him, but found none. Only a few lightweight shirts. The bird seemed to sense his slightest move, but there had to be a way out. Stewart reached above him again, found a wire clothes hanger. A chance.

There was the sound of a chair falling over in the bedroom. Again the pounding of the falcon's powerful wings. An alarmed shout. Had the Israeli returned? A gunshot, deafeningly loud.

Stewart opened the door again, a crack no more than an inch wide. He was surprised to see the angry bird come at him again. Quickly, he thrust the coat hanger through the narrow opening as far as he could. The falcon ignored it, continuing to tear at the wood, trying to squeeze through the opening. Twice Stewart tried to hook the wire over the bird's head, once snagging a foot. No, not the talons, he thought, probing again. Suddenly, in a flurry of feathers, the hanger caught behind the peregrine's neck. Stewart instantly pulled it tight. Wincing, sweat pouring off his face, he held the closet door tight with one hand and twisted the clothes hanger with the other.

Watching the beautiful bird's death throes, he felt sickened. Had Kirk Stewart, the environmentalist, come to this? In all his life he'd never so much as wrung the neck of a chicken for Sunday dinner. Expecting to find Barak outside, Stewart pushed open the closet door and dropped the falcon.

For several seconds the two men shared a strained silence.

The FBI agent, blood streaking down the side of his youthful face, stood numbly in the doorway, his service pistol still smoking. For a long time he stared in bewilderment at the dead falcon; then he looked up.

But he had glanced up too late to see Stewart lift a small address book off a nearby bureau and slip it into a back pocket.

Stewart wiped the sweat from his face and smiled benignly at the agent.

He didn't smile back.

The FBI man was around Stewart's age, tall, well-built, with high cheekbones and darting hazel eyes. He was still visibly shaken by the onslaught of the peregrine. Tucking his gun away with a rueful look, he said, "Mr. Stewart, you've suddenly become one major pain in the ass for the Houston office. My name's O'Laughlin. Local bureau chief. The top banana in Washington, D.C., has taken a protective interest in you. This time you won't get away."

"Enjoy the drive-in movie?" asked Stewart glibly.

"I'd seen it before. The same for your little escape act." O'Laughlin mopped the blood from his cheek and neck with a handkerchief. "What happened to Metz?"

Stewart jerked his head toward the window.

"The dog? You did that?"

"Wasn't easy," Stewart lied.

"I'm impressed, but right now let's get the hell out of here."

Ignoring the FBI agent, Stewart's eyes were taking in, one by one, a group of framed photographs over the dressing table. They were of sparsely clad women and men. Posed pictures taken at a gymnasium. One photo in particular caught and held his attention. The handsome face and impish eyes were the same as those in the photo Oliver Wright had shown him in New York—the young gay, the would-be actor in the blackmailing videotape! The enlarged photograph, like the others on the wall, was autographed. Stewart bent closer, squinting to read the cursive script. "Sincerely, Dennis Garrett," it said simply. Garrett, Stewart thought, storing the name away for future reference. He turned back to face O'Laughlin. "In a hurry?" he asked.

The FBI agent blotted the blood on his neck. He looked irritated. "You want to stick around this dump and maybe go for number three? Make it a strikeout? A dead Doberman. This goddamn sadistic love bird. Jesus. The dude who lives here not only has weird politics but a weirder lifestyle. Want to bet there's an alligator or cobra in the cellar? I've already radioed for reinforcements."

Stewart stiffened. "I could use some fresh air. Where are we going?"

O'Laughlin pointed toward the door. He said sternly, "The Houston airport. You go willingly, friendly like, or we put you in cuffs. I'm booking you on the first flight to New York."

"You think you can work any faster with me out of the picture?"

O'Laughlin exhaled slowly, glancing around the room. "It may take time, but we'll clean house here, get to the bottom of this. Amazing what modern crime computers can accomplish."

Stewart grimaced. "That's all you're going to do? Feed it into a processor at the capital? The FBI plays video games while schizos like Metz run loose. Obviously Oliver Wright told you about my lady friend's disappearance. What makes you think Metz wasn't directly involved?"

The agent stared myopically back at Stewart. "Maybe so. Maybe not. Speculations and assumptions don't add up to a conviction."

"Come off it, O'Laughlin. What's the FBI waiting for? Does Death have to appear in center stage before Oliver Wright realizes this is grand tragedy and not a musical comedy?"

O'Laughlin headed for the door. "Let's go, Stewart. Back to your typewriter before you get your fingers blown off."

Stewart wanted to say something, to tell the agent about his friend Motti Barak, but his throat closed on his thoughts. No, he reasoned; he'd given his word to the Israeli. The charade would continue until he could squeeze more information out of Barak.

Stewart quickly mulled over his position, thinking of a half-dozen ways he still might find some answers here in Texas. Arnold Metz was more than a weapons dealer, Stewart calculated. He had to know something about Shira. But now he'd disappeared, as had the Israeli. Stewart fingered the small address book in his pocket and wondered about its possible value to Oliver Wright back in the nation's capital. Then he thought about Carlie Chavez waiting for his call at NTN. Finally, he remembered that Mike Murphy expected him back at his *Times* desk no later than noon tomorrow. Rapidly adding it all together he suddenly remembered that he had paid for the trip out of his own pocket. Stewart wanted to stay in the house a while longer, alone, to search for additional clues, but the FBI agent was waiting impatiently at the door.

"One question, O'Laughlin. Is the Bureau picking up the plane fare?"

"Yeah. If you're out of Texas by tonight."

Stewart smiled. "You've got yourself a deal." He put away his flip mood and walked outside, trying to stay a step ahead of the ugly premonitions rising like a flash flood in his head.

13

"THANK YOU FOR watching the six o'clock news. On behalf of the rest of the crew, I wish you a pleasant evening." Carlie Chavez smiled her usual wrap-up grin, then shuffled through several papers in front of her, waiting for the music tag to be fed into the studio and the red light on camera one to go out. She was tired, suddenly anxious to go home and slide into her Jacuzzi-equipped bathtub. When the floor director gave her the high sign, she rose from her place at the news console, unplugged her lapel mike, and headed for the studio door. "Don't let the macho goons wear you down, girls," she called jokingly to the two female members of the technical crew.

Two women coiling up cables smiled back and winked. Otto, the nearest cameraman, gave Carlie a half-ass Bronx cheer.

Carlie's producer met her at the door. He seldom came into the control room, let alone the studio itself, and seeing the dour look on his face she prepared herself for bad news.

"Sorry, Carlie. We're forced to change the program for to morrow afternoon's featurette. Your key guest refuses to come down from Yonkers."

"Rabbi Marks? Uncooperative? Since when?" she asked,

with disbelief. "He's a jewel."

The producer looked at her, shrugging. "Someone took his anti-Nazi remarks on your first show as anti-patriotic. They've painted his synagogue with swastikas and planted those little Fourth of July flags—you know, the kind kids wave at parades—all around the building in the flower beds."

Carlie recoiled and let out a sharp sigh. "So what do I do now? Run away from a story?" She started for her office. "I'll call him."

The producer grabbed her arm. "Forget it, Carlie. He's scared shitless. That isn't all. They threatened him—phone calls and notes. If he appears on any more talk shows, his family will get roughed up."

Carlie tasted a sudden bitterness in her throat. "So much for all the reports we did on the New York melting pot."

"Wishful thinking. The only bumper stickers you're apt to find with red hearts and melting pots are in steel towns still lucky enough to keep the furnace stoked." The producer pushed his gold-rimmed glasses higher on his nose. "Pardon my *steely* skepticism—and the pun—but why all the sudden reshuffling of program priorities on behalf of pseudo-Nazis and all these other paramilitary cretins? We did an overkill on the subject six months ago for chrissake."

Carlie impatiently ran a hand through her long, dark hair. She wasn't in the mood to defend her position or argue. Not now. One day a week the show's format was hers to arrange and she could select the guests; it was all there in her contract, and the rest of the news crew knew this. Carlie felt more determined than ever. She would proceed with the panel show tomorrow, rabbi or no rabbi. The Roman Catholic monsignor would still be there, as well as the Methodist and Episcopal bishops.

Damn, she thought, If only an outspoken free-lance journalist like Shira Bernstein were available to complete the panel. Carlie's thoughts went to Kirk Stewart nosing around in the South, his telephone request for her to snoop through the NTN board chairman's mail. Was it all connected? The producer's lips were moving as in a silent movie, for Carlie wasn't listening. She was worrying over Kirk's safety.

Outside his limousine, the CIA director impatiently paced the tarmac, waiting for Colonel Reddick's F-15 to complete its taxi over the darkened Andrews airbase apron. Walter Singer had deliberately chosen this isolated location away from the main military terminal; here no one would see him pick up the pilot and his passenger, General Brady. They would be able to leave the field and slip into Washington quietly. Singer was all too aware that the forced retirement of the crusty four-star was still big news; the recent *Newsweek* coverage of his grating speeches in California had caused an international uproar. The CIA head was determined, at any cost, to avoid additional publicity. The general's assignment would be kept secret and his movements would go unreported, at least until Friday noon. Singer wanted Brady's military expertise, his inside track at the Pentagon, his ability to cut through red tape and move men and matériel fast—*not* his infamous grandstanding.

When the jet turbines finally wound down, two men crawled out of the Falcon and came toward Singer, their flight helmets cradled in their arms. Introductions were unnecessary. Everyone had met three weeks earlier at a planning session.

General Brady, feisty and impatient as ever, asked the CIA head, "Where to, Singer? Wherever, it's past my cocktail time. I could use a stiff touch."

Singer gestured toward his limousine. "The Vice-President is waiting at his residence, General." Turning to the beetle-browed pilot at Brady's side, Singer added dully, "You're to come along as well, Reddick."

The long drive from Galveston to Houston's Intercontinental Airport had been an uncomfortable one for Stewart. The FBI agent's equanimity annoyed him. There was also that familiar hollowness in his stomach. Begrudgingly, Stewart led O'Laughlin into the passenger terminal, paused, and asked, "You're planning on sticking around until takeoff time?"

The Houston bureau man didn't smile. "You've figured that right. If we're paying the fare, I see you to the door of the plane and stand by until it clears the ramp."

Stewart bought the point. "Thanks."

"Now that the matter's settled, let's pick up your damned ticket and get something to eat. I'm famished."

Stewart nodded. He wasn't hungry, but he'd keep O'Laughlin company with a good stiff drink. After the encounter with Metz and his fearsome peregrine, he needed it. It had been a frustrating, though not entirely useless day. Tomorrow, when he joined forces with Carlie in New York, he would be more productive.

In Los Angeles a large group of black pickets straggled back and forth in front of the imposing facade of the Metropolitan Tabernacle. They were waiting for the Reverend Jimmy Hallowell to leave the building after a guest speaking engagement. Horn trumpeting, a fire red Maserati Bora took the driveway loop too rapidly, nearly bowling over one of the marchers. A woman in the picket line shouted and waved her fist. Hotel magnate Karl Frober indolently waved back from behind the wheel of the sports car.

Frober rolled down his window, his puffy, questing eyes examining the white marble steps and facade of the church, at the same time nervously taking in the agitated protesters. Two doormen hastened down the steps to confront Frober.

"Has the Reverend Mr. Hallowell finished yet? I'm to pick him up."

"Yes, sir. He's waiting in the reception area."

"I'm Karl Frober. Tell him to hurry."

The two men nodded and hurried up the steps. Several restless blacks strolled closer, examining the car and glaring at Frober hatefully. He looked away, avoiding their stares.

Minutes passed. Frober checked his watch, wondering what was keeping Hallowell. He wiped the perspiration from his forehead, suddenly wishing he were elsewhere. Sighing, he quickly rolled the car window back up. The pickets, for lack of anything more promising, had apparently decided that his Bora was fair game. One of the women came forward and tapped her sign on the polished hood of the car. Frober read it: "Hallowell Is a Racist." Behind her, he saw an even larger banner with a message scrawled in red paint: "Screw the KKK."

The woman before him, almost as overweight as Frober, was clad in blue-striped shorts and a tight-fitting sweater. She swaggered up to the window on the driver's side. "Well, lookee the fat boy. You're a little late for the service, Bozo. Church let out twenty minutes ago."

"Then why don't you quietly go home?" asked Frober bravely, managing a measure of politeness.

A burly, sneering man came up behind the woman and started to shout something, but was distracted by activity at the top of the marble steps.

Frober looked up and saw Jimmy Hallowell in the doorway, his arms around two frail old women. One of them handed him an envelope. Convenient, Frober mused, smiling to himself. Tidy way to make a tax-free buck; ersatz religion, as usual, was big money. All it took was a gimmick. Hallowell had a personality and style uniquely his own. He relied on modern electronics media, souped-up special effects, conservative but expensive clothing, untimely arrivals, and secret leave-takings. Again taking in the angry pickets, Frober suspected the Reverend James Hallowell wasn't about to make an inconspicuous departure tonight.

Clad in a gray alpaca suit and dark blue paisley tie, Jimmy Hallowell shook hands with several tabernacle officials, nodded effusively, then hastened down the steps to Frober's waiting Maserati. "Let's go. *Now!*" he shouted, climbing in and slamming the door.

The pickets closed in, menacing the car, but Frober tramped on the gas. The Maserati's V-8 instantly responded with a mellow roar. "Admirers?" Frober asked grimly. "Forgot you were a celebrity, Reverend. I should have picked you up in one of those armored half-tracks Condor builds back in Detroit."

"Lovely city, Los Angeles," Hallowell sneered, gesturing toward the tabernacle. "Inside, a crowd of little old ladies— fanatical zombies. Outside, everywhere I look, the infamous southern California cereal bowl: flakes, nuts, and fruits."

Frober wasn't amused; he kept his eyes on the road. "How much time do you have before returning to the East?"

"I'm leaving in the morning. That's another eight or nine hours too many to spend in your modern Babylon."

Frober frowned. "Testy, testy. You're not finding your hotel accommodations comfortable and homelike? The Centurion's the flagship of all my facilities."

"Your hotel's adequate. It's the city. Too many souls to save, so short a time."

"Forget your job tonight. We're going to dine in style at Chasen's."

Hallowell smoothed the sides of his silver hair. "You missed a fine sermon. I tell you, Karl, your money and your political machine may save this sick country, but it's time you and Norman Gifford both thought about saving your own souls."

Taking the Hollywood Freeway on-ramp, Frober quickly

accelerated. The Maserati's engine burst into a deep-throated rumble. Frober glanced sideways at Hallowell and smiled. "Religion may be the common cause, the opiate of your mob, Jimmy, but I prefer to keep my own mind uncluttered. Alert, free to reason."

"Good," said Hallowell, with obvious relish. "Then perhaps you'll listen to a little reason." He paused, kneading his hands. "I'm concerned over a few rumors I'm hearing, about a window of vulnerability at the subcommittee level. There are certain issues a Christian man has to stand up to."

"Like what?" Frober nursed the car up to sixty. It felt like forty-five.

"Like this Klan doctor arguing before our Civil Unrest Committee in Chicago. I never did like the name we gave that group, incidentally. This quack insists that welfare people are useless parasites who will never work and —"

"Quack's a strong word. You're being judgmental, Reverend." Frober felt annoyed. He tightened his grip on the wheel. The speedometer read seventy-five.

Hallowell frowned. "I read his irresponsible report. Clever euphemisms on paper, but in the flesh, he claims, these so-called parasites will be excess baggage in the new order of things. He's been quoted as saying they should be disposed of, the quicker the better. Terms like 'evacuated,' even 'eliminated.' We can't condone his sick rhetoric."

"I agree. Most unpleasant, the *offal* truth."

Hallowell glared at him irritably. "I dislike your get-it-done-but-don't-tell-me-about-it mentality. What's going on, Karl? Even the minorities are children of God and have certain rights."

Frober grunted and raised his voice slightly. "Like homosexuals, who want to exploit their political cohesiveness and take over San Francisco? Like blacks, who thrive on crime? And, to use the Klan doctor's term, these 'welfare parasites' who rob the government blind?"

Wooden-faced, Hallowell snorted, "And what final solution do you suggest?" He glanced nervously at the speedometer.

"We listened to the bleeding hearts during the Carter period. We very nearly met our goals during the Reagan years. Now the pendulum has swung in the opposite direction, too quickly. Our enemy in the White House and his liberal supporters in Congress have pumped millions into jobs and rehab programs that don't work. And I hear what you're saying. I've heard

some of these psychotic extremists who propose that if the
flakes can't or won't work, we should take them out to the
local stadium, seal the exits, and shoot them. Then feed their
useless bodies to the steam plants for energy production. Or
possibly fertilizer." Frober shrugged and leaned back against
the Maserati's contour seat. "Outlandish concepts, I agree. But
there has to be a morally acceptable hard-line solution. We
must set some examples if we want to regain productivity."

Hallowell shook his head. "Productivity or sick entertainment? Why not throw them to the lions? Some of our supporters
appear to be as degenerate as the Romans."

"Nonsense," retorted Frober. "They'll find a humanitarian
way. We're dealing with practical economic reality. We've got
to let the subcommittees do what is necessary and expedient."

"Catchwords, Karl. You haven't changed since we first met.
At times you frighten me. Tolerate but don't advocate. Is that
it? And do you have to drive so fast?"

A sudden feeling of trouble hovered invisibly between the
two men. The Maserati slowed marginally. Frober finally broke
the silence. "Sometimes, under the burden of command, I
frighten myself, Reverend. But what the hell? It's not our
decision. That's why we have subcommittees and chairmen. I
like you, Jimmy. You have an absolutely free rein with religion,
and that's as it should be. We'll give the Chicago group a free
hand with welfare reform. And that is also as it should be."

"And yet you acknowledge that some of the subcommittee
members are Nazis or Klansmen?" Hallowell asked quickly.

"Just keep the lines open to heaven, Jimmy. That's enough
for one man."

"I know how to do my job. I pray every night that with
God's help Friday's events will be peaceable, that there will
be no loss of life."

"If all goes well, that will be the case, but were the Crusades
peaceable, Padre?"

Hallowell's close-set eyes stared ahead, out the windshield.
"Nice car," he said, running his fingers slowly over the black
suede dashboard. "Something's on your mind besides dinner,
Karl. Let's have it."

Frober tapped on the accelerator and veered out into the fast
lane. Thickly, he said, "Before Singer left for Washington, he
insisted I get through to you on a few points. Videotaped
sermons won't suffice. Gifford and I agree. Television ap-

pearances on Friday and Saturday night would be token perfor-mances. Like I said, Jimmy, religion is the opiate of the people, and you're their fix. You'll have to appear on the network live every day for the first week. We need an anchorman we can trust, someone who'll be a dedicated member of the team. Hard telling how long it will take to convert the media elite, if we can accomplish it at all."

Hallowell looked at him severely. "Save your breath. Be-sides being the national tranquilizer, as you so cynically phrase it, I have other commitments."

"Break them. Walter Singer's already sold the Vice-President on the idea. Chandler will appear with you at the initial press conference. Pack your bags for a week's stay in New York."

Hallowell replied emptily, "I have no other options?"

"None."

"Is this my first taste of freedom under the new govern-ment?"

"Freedom is earned in the next book, Reverend. You think you can sell that concept to your little following?"

"Little?" Hallowell seemed to brighten. "Last month the Moral Confederation's rolls swelled by another hundred and ten thousand. That's a total of over four million followers."

Frober laughed, sliding his fingers up and down the steering wheel. "No one ever said we weren't beholden to you, Jimmy. But you've got fifty times that number of people to tranquilize starting Friday." Frober thought for a moment, then seriously added, "We can expect trouble from the Jews, Roman Cath-olics, and liberal Protestants."

"You underestimate God, Mr. Frober. And *me*. I'll have four million new souls in my hand tomorrow, three times that number by next, and the rest will follow out of confusion. What's good for the goose is good for the gander."

Frober couldn't respond to that. He turned the Maserati off the freeway at Highland, circled down to Sunset Boulevard. "How long since you were last in Hollywood?" he asked blandly.

"Two years," replied Hallowell, somewhat sourly. His eyes surveyed the glitter pacing the sidewalks, men and women alike hovering on dimly lit street corners. "There's moral decay everywhere, but it's just a little worse here," he slowly added, shaking his head.

"Oldest profession in the world. As the situation is now, the ladies no longer have a corner on it," grumbled Frober.

Hallowell didn't respond. His eyes were glazed; he appeared to be mesmerized by all the street action. He turned and smiled at Frober. "Doing the Lord's work, I meet them all," he intoned. "I have two former call girls in the Crusade Choir. Another, born again just last month, works in our Richmond headquarters mail room."

"Charming," replied Frober, stopping the Maserati at a red light.

On the corner Hallowell spotted an attractive, heavy-breasted redhead in a gold lamé jacket and minishorts. The girl winked at him.

"Drive around the block," Hallowell said firmly.

Five minutes later, after a terse conversation on the sidewalk, which Frober couldn't hear, the Reverend Mr. Jimmy Hallowell scribbled something on a piece of paper and handed it, along with a twenty dollar bill, to the nodding redhead. She winked, jacked up her breasts, and strutted off. Hallowell climbed back in the car, his face softly flushed. "Most challenging. You never know," he said. "Some accept my invitations, others laugh in my face. Very difficult. If I can get them to a service just one time—"

Frober drove back out into traffic. "Service? What service, for crying out loud?"

"Outreach. The most difficult part of revival. The hardest part." Hallowell pushed out his chin, fingering his tight shirt collar.

"Yeah. Of course," quipped Frober. "The hardest part?"

Hallowell was about to speak again when Frober, grinning from ear to ear, hushed him with a raised hand. "Since we're going out to dinner in style, Reverend, I'll try to be elegant. In France, what you've just told me would properly be called *merde*. In Texas, it comes out *bullshit*. But here in Hollywood, eyeballing that little scenario, most folks would say a charlatan's just paid a cute cocksucker to meet him later in his hotel room."

14

SEEKING REFUGE AT the home of a friendly neighbor, Arnold Metz had eluded his pursuer and called a doctor—a local Galveston gun club member and a patron of his store—to mend his torn face. The wound took five stitches. Following treatment, Metz had returned home to determine what was missing. One room at a time, he had examined the house. The shot the doctor had given him to ease the pain made him lethargic, but not sleepy enough to mollify the rage he felt over the two intruders who had killed his dog and hunting falcon. He wondered how much they knew. The enterprising reporter Stewart would surely put the pilfered address book to good use.

Metz had been lucky; the Israeli had returned and unwittingly led him to Intercontinental Airport and Kirk Stewart. Finding a telephone booth, Metz dropped in a quarter and called the Houston Marriott. He expected Lynx to be eager to hear from him, but the voice at the other end sounded irritated. "You took too long with the doctor, Metz. What about the weapon? After what's happened, is it safe at your store?"

"Absolutely." He didn't tell Lynx that the EMR was not there, but with him at Houston's airport. Nor would he reveal that he planned to practice with it tonight if need be. Proficiency, that's what they wanted. Bullshit. He was a sharp-shooter and had the medals to prove it. His first EMR target, he decided, would be a big one—a particular passenger jet soon to depart for New York. He paused in his conversation with Lynx, waiting for a jet to pass by.

"Where are you, Metz? The airport?" came the sharp query.

"Yes. I've found Stewart. He's inside the passenger ter-minal, and that FBI agent is hovering over him like a mother hen. A curious development. Neither of them realize it, but they're being followed by the Israeli."

"Fine mess," grumbled Lynx. "How do you know which man has the address book?"

Metz pulled himself together, put more authority into his voice. "Does it make a difference? Ali three know too much. I'll take care of them. One at a time if necessary." He felt confident. Very confident.

Lynx's voice sharpened. "We can't allow the entire project to be threatened by your incompetence and the curiosity of the *Times* reporter—not to mention the implications of the Israeli's involvement. You'll take care of this tonight, understand?"

"I'll do my best."

"You'll succeed or we'll have no reason to talk tomorrow." Abruptly, there was a click and the line went dead.

Unable to fight off hs frustration and anger, he slammed the receiver on the hook. Quickly, he assessed the situation. There was no way he could pass through the metal detectors to the passenger lounge with his handgun, but he had to make sure his quarry boarded the DC-10 for New York.

Metz hovered inside the phone booth, looking through the glass to the main lobby. He watched the short man with the canvas overnight bag rise from his seat and proceed to the Transcon passenger counter. Paying cash, the Israeli purchased a ticket, selected a seat from the same wall diagram the reporter Stewart had used earlier, then proceeded down the D Con-course.

Metz removed his leather jacket, carefully folded it over his Walther PPK pistol, and entered the terminal. He quickly stowed the bundle in a nearby metal locker, glanced up at the video screen that carried the Transcon Departure Schedule, then hur-ried after the Israeli. Excellent, he thought. Two birds with one stone. He hadn't expected the Jew to follow the reporter aboard the plane. Once more reviewing his plans, Metz walked faster, heading toward the metal detector at the end of the concourse. Earlier he had observed the FBI agent and Stewart disappear into the airport restaurant—the section that served leisurely meals, not quickie pre-flight snacks. That had given him plenty of time to plan carefully. While the two men were enjoying their beef tenderloin, Metz had proceeded down the utility staircase, sapped a night custodian with the butt of his Walther, and locked him in a plumbing closet. Taking the employee's keys and panel-back motor scooter, he had sped across the jet taxi apron to the soft, grassy place just inside the wire fence, where he had earlier tossed the EMR, rifle, and homing device. The secluded spot was in the shadow of an air freight shed, and it had taken him several minutes to find the weapons in the darkness. In a matter of minutes, the maintenance scooter, a canvas noose drawn tight over the weapons in the rear, was back in its parking place beneath the passenger satellite, right beside Gate 43 and Transcon Flight 312. Using the stolen pass key, Metz hurried back up the stairs into the terminal.

Metz sat, his head buried behind a day-old newspaper, observing, waiting, amused by the similar behavior of the Israeli seated at the far end of the lounge. The Jew was watching Stewart and O'Laughlin, but made no effort to join them.

Metz heard a soft chime on the P.A., followed by "Flight three-twelve to New York, Newark Airport, is now ready for boarding. Ticketed passengers may now proceed to Gate Forty-three."

Amusing, thought Metz. The Israeli was wearing a hat, and now he put on eyeglasses with heavy tortoiseshell frames, apparently hoping the FBI agent wouldn't recognize him. Very amusing. The hunter, the hunted, and he in turn was after them both. Metz put out his cigarette and slowly climbed to his feet. The reporter, he noted, was one of the first to board the plane, but his FBI companion did not immediately leave; instead he crossed the broad carpeted lobby, took a seat in the main concourse, and lit a cigarette.

Feeling the perspiration on his face and beneath his shirt, Metz kept his back to the FBI agent as he headed for the throng gathering at the boarding gate. The New York–bound jet—one of the wide-bodies—wouldn't be filled, he noted. Judging from the passengers he had seen in the waiting area, it would depart with half its capacity. Metz edged closer, elbowing his way into the center of the crowd. Ahead he saw the Israeli show his ticket to the attendant and disappear into the red-carpeted tunnel leading to the plane. Metz smiled. So far, so good. Beside him a dark-haired, overweight woman was towing a small boy and wrestling with a shopping bag. *"Vamos!"* she said, jerking the straggling child forward. Behind Metz was a young couple with a sleeping baby. *Children,* he thought, with a slight grimace.

Sentiment simply hadn't entered his mind before. He suddenly remembered reading about Mussolini's infamous remark when the Italian dictator's motorcade had struck down a small girl. "What is one small child in the will of the state?" Il Duce had been quoted. Hard words, thought Metz. Incomprehensible to many, but he understood. There hadn't been time for sentiment then. And there wasn't time for it now.

The Chicano woman prodded her child to hurry along. Metz deliberately dropped his newspaper. As he bent to retrieve it, it was a simple matter to slip the small, stainless-steel box into the fat woman's shopping bag.

Metz was satisfied. His incriminating address book, the New York reporter, the Jew, the EMR homing device—in a matter of seconds all would be aboard the DC-10. Nothing more to do here, he thought, excusing himself and stepping out of the boarding line. Keeping the remaining passengers between himself and the FBI agent sitting in the main concourse, he headed for the nearby service stairway he had used earlier. The soft music from the overhead speakers soothed him.

Kirk Stewart had a window seat in a row by himself near the front of the plane. A brunette stewardess with signal-red lips and pretty teeth hovered over him, offering him a pillow. Her eyes twinkled. Stewart winked back, thanked her, and watched her promenade down the aisle. He glanced at his watch. All he needed now was to get airborne, lean back, and catch some sleep. Six years as a reporter had given Stewart a deep-rooted dislike for waiting. Waiting for editors, waiting for interviews, waiting for commuter trains, waiting for airplanes. Thank God for competition, he thought, thinking about airline service in general, cheerful flight attendants with pretty legs in particular. If he was guilty of hating right-wing extremists—either now or in the past—his contempt could hardly be worse than his festering annoyance with Communist bureaucracy.

Stewart glanced up as a second stewardess flashed by. No,

he thought. Not in a thousand years could he be a Communist. But then he couldn't be a fascist, either, so what did that leave him? People can't function at extremes, he reasoned. There always had to be a middle road. A moderate. The word itself had a nebulous, dull ring to it. Color me gray, he mused. A face in the crowd.

He thought once more of the Galveston gun merchant who had escaped and would easily recognize him if they were to meet again. He remembered the man's eyes most of all, their intensity, the hint of desperation, the red-sparked frenzy. He wondered if Arnold Metz would open his gun store tomorrow, buy another guard dog, and replace the hunting falcon. Or would he disappear, go underground completely, begin a vengeful manhunt for him?

A hand tapped Stewart on the shoulder and he turned to look up.

"*Shalom.* May I join you?" The voice was Motti Barak's, but Stewart didn't recognize the Israeli until he removed his hat and horn-rimmed glasses. Barak sighed. "Dobermans, that I didn't need," he said, sliding into the vacant seat.

Stewart put away his surprised look. "Good to see you again, Major."

"Our visit to Galveston was unproductive, I'm afraid. I think we'll both do better in New York."

A fat woman and her small boy slipped into the row across the aisle from them. The wide-eyed youth stared at Stewart and grinned. His mother pulled a teddy bear from a shopping bag, handed it to the boy. She also withdrew a small, shiny stainless-steel box from the bag and gave it a perplexed look. Turning it over in her hands, eyebrows knitting, she shrugged and placed it in the elastic pouch on the seat before her.

Stewart smiled at the woman, turned back to Barak, and lowered his voice. "You're persistent, Major, but I suspect you're bound for the wrong destination."

"Hardly," Barak whispered. "You seem to be headed there."

Stewart laughed. "Number one, I'm supposed to report back to work tomorrow. Two, I was forced to board this plane. There's a Bureau man outside."

"I know. I've been watching from a distance."

Stewart glanced over his shoulder, making sure the seats behind them were still unoccupied. Reaching into his pocket, he withdrew Arnold Metz's leather-covered address book. He said thoughtfully, "According to this little document, the men who killed Shira Bernstein—and who knows how many others—are probably in the nation's capital."

Barak started to reach for the booklet, but Stewart jerked it back a few inches. Stewart chose his words carefully, knowing that later he might have to justify them. "Easy, easy. I'm still debating about how far I should trust you. This goes to the FBI in a couple of days, but only after I've finished with it."

Barak shrugged. "As my grandmother would say, 'With sense you're loaded.' Please give it to me, Kirk."

"I want Shira's killer, Motti. And I need an exclusive story, and I intend to get it, with or without your assistance. Give me a hand and I'll keep your mission secret. Compromise me and you'll see your picture on the front page of the *Times*."

"Trust is reciprocal, I agree. Have I disappointed you yet?" Quickly, Barak seized the address book out of Stewart's hand and began leafing through the pages.

"There's more," whispered Stewart. "There was a photograph on Metz's bedroom wall of a young homosexual who lives in Washington."

"So?" Motti Barak rubbed his chin thoughtfully. "That makes two photographs of interest to us in the Galveston house. Was the one you observed autographed also?"

Stewart nodded. "Two photos? What did you find?"

"There isn't time. I'll explain later." Barak shoved the address book into Stewart's pocket and stepped into the aisle. "Come," he said quickly. "I had planned to double back to the capital *after* New York. I can't wait. Do you wish to join me or remain here? There is another departure a half-hour from now on Eastern. A direct flight to Dulles."

Stewart sat in his seat, frozen. He wasn't sure what to do next. "Okay, so how do I get out of here? That agent's no fool. He'll sit it out until the plane leaves."

Barak smiled. "And we will wait also. Just outside the aircraft, in the loading vestibule at the end of the tunnel. Trust me, I've done this before."

Stewart grabbed his camera and followed the Israeli. For Shira's sake, he'd be tempted to follow the clever major to the end of the earth; for a Press Club writing award or a Pulitzer, he wasn't so sure. "Appears I'm indispensable," he whispered.

Barak turned. "That's debatable. But I do need that address book."

From his hip pocket Metz withdrew a small sterling-silver flask, unscrewed the top, and finished off his Myers's Rum. A strong, warm excitement filled his body as he thought of what was going to happen in the next few minutes. He would not only test, and prove, the effectiveness of the new EMR, but he would have the satisfaction of killing two enemies—ugly flies contaminating the ointment. The method he had chosen, the dramatic finality of it all, was deeply satisfying.

The airport taxi apron was wet from the intermittent showers that had blown in from the Gulf just after dark. The night was warm. Metz looked skyward, but saw no moon. Once more a light, drizzling rain began to fall from the scattered thunderclouds overhead. He had carefully observed the flight pattern, was satisfied that Transcon Flight 312 would take off, as the other departures before it had done, on Runway 3, heading north. He had positioned himself less than three hundred feet from the end of that runway, hidden in the shadow of an overhaul hangar.

Metz waited, poised, as the DC-10 roared, gathered speed, and hurtled down the runway. Metz squinted through the telescopic sight of the Springfield, held his breath. The aircraft was light and lifted quickly, soaring past him. His hands, steadier than ever since arriving at the airport, gripped the rifle comfortably, tracking slightly ahead of the big jet. Slowly, he pulled the trigger.

The projectile roared toward the climbing DC-10, moving faster than the plane itself. The sharp polished-steel nose of the EMR, with the mindless precision of an automaton, sped the shortest distance between the firing source and the small impulse beacon in the homing box aboard the plane. The trajectory should have terminated in a twelfth-row seat in the plane's tourist section, but it first had to pass directly through the starboard wing. The wing was filled with high-octane jet fuel.

For five long seconds the sky above the Houston airport was turned from night into high noon by the blinding, roaring flash.

Inside the passenger lounge, Kirk Stewart and Motti Barak ran to the window. Stewart's mouth fell open as he stared. From somewhere behind him came a woman's loud wail. Outside, just below on the flight apron, Transcon's ground crew fell to the ground, eyes fixed on the rain of debris at the end of the runway.

Stewart felt sick to his stomach. His entire body was shaking, both knees jerking galvanically like fresh shark meat in a skillet. He had to sit down. Staring out at the flames at the end of the field he felt numbed by a defeat that was beyond comprehension. Could this have been a coincidence?

Speechless, struggling with his own private agony, Motti Barak finally edged away from the window. He looked at Stewart and shook his head, speaking slowly and thoughtfully: "You still feel like an airplane ride tonight?"

"We don't have a choice, Major. We have more reason than ever to get to Washington." Stewart held up his bandaged finger. "I've got four good fingers on this hand. Nine are as good as ten when it comes to choking a man to death. First, I'm going to file a story, and for that, I'll need your help." Stewart paused, took in a deep breath. His body felt numb. Gesturing toward the burning plane, he added, "The second job I do alone. Throttling this bastard Metz by the neck. Pushing my fingers into his pharynx until he turns blue, green, purple. The same goes for any other individual responsible for Shira's death. Or that crash."

"If they don't get you first," Barak replied solemnly. "No, Kirk, leave it alone. You're talking like a heroic fool."

Stewart didn't hear, didn't want to hear. "When the time comes, stay out of it, Motti."

15

THE LONG CHARCOAL-GRAY Chrysler was parked in the shadows across the street and a few doors down the hill from the Soviet embassy. The capital policeman assigned to keep watch on the Russian legation had come by a half-hour earlier to check the driver's credentials. Flashing his light into the limousine, he hadn't lingered long, for in the back seat, sitting next to a young technician with a tape recorder, was a man well known to most Washington lawmen. CIA Director Walter Singer's popularity with the local police was, in fact, deep-rooted. To a man they liked his conservative background, his isolationist philosophy, and especially his hard-line ideas on crime prevention.

Singer adjusted his earphones. Thus far the bugged dialogue had been uneventful, at best a tedious vigil. The CIA head was still annoyed that Vice President Chandler had accepted the Soviet ambassador's dinner invitation. But for that, Singer thought, he could be elsewhere. Damn Chandler anyway; the man was suffering from a fatal combination of mediocre intelligence and an egocentric personality. The Vice-President, as usual, was taxing Singer's patience. Nevertheless, he had been the convention's choice to carry the ultraconservative banner. There was a popular following to consider. Chandler would have to suffice.

The bond between the Vice-President and the Committee would be fragile, but Singer was determined to make the alliance work, see the events through precisely as planned. Singer wasn't really worried. After all, most of the military was going along with him like wheat in a strong wind.

Though Singer enjoyed acclaim at the Pentagon, he knew his popularity no longer extended to the White House. The schism had begun months earlier, compounded itself with vicious momentum, and now had reached the point where at any time he could expect his exclusive parking place at CIA headquarters to be painted over with a new name.

No matter, Singer thought, looking out the rear window of the car, up the hill toward the lights burning in the Soviet embassy windows. The President, he reasoned, out of customary courtesy alone, would give him several days to tender his resignation and conclude his affairs. This was Tuesday night. Singer only needed to hold out, stall if need be, until Friday noon. Perhaps during hs State of the Union message the President would announce, among other important revelations, the CIA director's dismissal.

It no longer mattered. In a few days Singer's position would be secure, and he would be able to conduct this affair as he saw fit. That, after all, was part of his agreement with the other members of the Committee. Gifford, Frober, and Hallowell had assured him that Paul Chandler would be little more than a figurehead after being sworn in. Chandler would occupy the Oval Office, preside over all of the ceremonies, but the Committee would run the country. Singer, of course, would manipulate the Committee. Moreover, if he continued to play his cards shrewdly, he would also run the military.

Singer relished his newfound power. His popularity, expectedly, did not include an open-door welcome at the Soviet embassy compound. Tonight's candlelit supper between Ambassador Mikhail Grotski and Paul Chandler was off limits to him. Despite this, Singer had insisted on personally escorting the Vice-President and his wife to and from the embassy.

The cigarette-box-sized transmitter inside Paul Chandler's jacket and the minimicrophone concealed in one of his gold cuff links provided a record of the dialogue at the Soviet ambassador's dining table. The subject matter of that conversation, the CIA director felt, could not wait until morning when his recording crew would provide a transcript. Nor could he rely solely on the Vice-President's memory.

The Soviet legation's dining room was modest in size, with a parquet floor covered by a Turkoman carpet of the best quality. On one wall hung a Gobelin tapestry; on the opposite wall hung two elaborately framed pictures—one of Lenin, the other of the Moscow River, with the Kremlin and Saint Basil's in the background. There were four place settings at the candlelit, damask-covered table, but only two men sat facing each other, lingering over coffee and cognac. The ambassador's wife had escorted Mrs. Chandler into the library.

Mikhail Grotski's clean-shaven skull and carefully manicured, varnished fingernails glistened in the candlelight. The ambassador wore a striped black tie and gray suit with two ribbons and a small gold star on the lapel. Above his tight collar, his face was full and round with thick rolls of skin under protruding eyes.

The Vice-President was dressed in a navy-blue pinstripe with a somber Pierre Cardin tie and button-down collar. Paul Chandler's eyes were red-lined and tired. Nervously, he fidgeted with the ornate sterling coffee spoon. "Now do you understand the meaning of a hard-soft policy?" he asked the man across from him anxiously.

Grotski smiled thinly. "I understand that your views differ remarkably from those of your National Security Council and the Cabinet." He paused to take a sip of water. "You have voiced some interesting concepts, Mr. Vice-President. Perhaps 'intriguing' is a better word for them. You ask what we Soviets would do if the United States were to withdraw from NATO and pull back into the confines of the Western Hemisphere."

"American weapons on American soil," Chandler offered quickly.

"Yes, I understand. But in exchange, you would accelerate weapons production and increase your inventory of armaments, true?"

"Only to close the gap, Mr. Ambassador."

Grotski pursed his thick lips. "I find it most curious that these concepts are divergent from those expressed by the secretary of state. And certainly the President must have . . ." Grotski thought for a moment. "May I speak freely, Mr. Vice-

President?" He paused, gesturing with a fat finger to the waiter standing attentively in the doorway. The slender, grim-faced Tartar came up behind Chandler, leaned over his shoulder, and replenished his snifter with Napoleon cognac. At the same time, unseen by the Vice-President, the waiter sent a private nod to Grotski.

"By all means, speak freely," urged Chandler.

The two polished marbles that were the ambassador's eyes shone greedily. "Good. But first, I suggest we dispense with formalities." He raised his glass. "Are you enjoying the cognac?"

"Very good indeed, Mr. Ambassador."

Grotski sighed. "You will note I stay with the vodka, yes? Easier on my digestion. But I propose a toast, to *informality.* Feel free to call me Mikhail." Grotski polished off his drink in the Russian manner.

Chandler raised his glass and followed suit. His gold-nugget cuff links eased out of his sleeves and glistened in the candle-light. "To informality," he feebly offered, feeling the cognac ignite in his stomach. Chandler studied the man across from him. The overweight, heavy-drinking Grotski was usually dour and didn't talk much; when he did, was prone—like other Russians Chandler had known—to exaggerate. He had met Mikhail Grotski four times before: twice on business at the State Department, once at a White House luncheon, and once at a reception for foreign legates at his own vice-presidential mansion. The gulf between their temperaments had suggested that they would be unlikely dinner partners, but now, at Grotski's request, they had come to face each other at opposite ends of the table. If the conversation was not mutually rewarding from a political or intellectual standpoint, it was at least amicable. But Chandler saw something else. Grotski was hiding something. And now the Russian's eyes were on his cuff links. Damn Walter Singer for insisting that he wear the mike!

"Forgive me for staring," said Grotski slowly. "As a youth in the Urals, I worked in a gold mine. I have never seen such splendid nuggets." Grotski paused, sipped his vodka and patted his thick lips with his napkin. "Tell me, Paul. May I hold one and examine it?"

Chandler squirmed, seeking a throwaway remark. None came. Smiling, he reached for the left cuff link—the one with no microphone.

"No. Not that one," Grotski said. "It's quite ordinary. The link on the right, please."

Chandler tensed and swallowed with difficulty. He had rehearsed his next move several times, on each occasion praying he would never have to make it. Not since the Nixon days had government recording been so sophisticated, so invisible, but still? A tiny wire led from his sleeve down to the back of the cuff link. The inconspicuous connection looked like part of the clasp, and the mike itself was buried inside the folds and facets of the nugget, detectable only under the closest scrutiny with a magnifier. Masking his concern, Chandler carefully detached the wire, removed the cuff link, and extended it toward Grotski, conjuring up a smile. "An expensive souvenir of a trip to the Colorado Rockies," he quipped.

Chandler watched the Russian slowly turn the nugget around in his hand, flip it over, continue to admire and examine it.

The Russian was lost in brooding silence for a long while. He finally spoke. "Beautiful. An exceptional piece of jewelry." Pondering a moment, Grotski reached out and dropped the cuff link into his water goblet. "Do you mind? There is an old Kurd proverb: 'A man who drinks from a stream bearing gold will never thirst for wealth.'"

Chandler stared quizzically at the Russian, then down at the crystal water goblet, trying, not too successfully, to appear nonchalant.

Grotski ignored the cuff link and met his eyes. "Now, Paul, my friend. We both can talk candidly. 'Off the record,' as you Americans put it."

Trying not to flush, Chandler straightened in his chair. "As you wish."

"Tell me. Is it true you are bringing General George Brady out of retirement?"

Chandler evaded the question, "Why do you ask?"

Grotski chortled and reached into his pocket for a cigarette. Flicking his wafer-thin, brushed gold lighter, he lit an American filter tip with ceremony. "You strike me as an individual who can handle any hypothesis."

"I'm flattered. Please continue," Chandler said, curious to the core.

"Supposing, Mr. Vice-President—ah, I forget so soon— Paul. Supposing a reactionary movement, one of significant measure, were suddenly to come into *de facto* power in the

United States? What do you think the Soviet position would be?"

Chandler tried to hide his grimace. The Russians knew more than Walter Singer and the Committee realized. "I don't understand your question, Mikhail. Please elaborate. Are you referring to the next election?"

Grotski smiled, sipped his vodka, and leaned forward eagerly. "No. Not power assumed by legal means. More complicated. And ruthless. A more specific word for it would be 'conspiracy.'"

Chandler folded his napkin, placed it on the table. Shifting uncomfortably, he asked, as calmly as he could, "You speak of a military coup d'etat?"

Grotski shrugged. "I believe we both know better than that. A partial one, possibly. Tin-hat juntas work only in Third World countries."

"You have me at a distinct disadvantage, Mikhail," Chandler stiffened, feeling slightly angry. "There are things you know, hidden information to which I am not privileged."

"Some of your countrymen work toward a quasi-isolationist America, an end to democracy, the formation of an elitist republic, it appears. You are not aware of this? Such a government, I suspect, would be at best similar to Napoleon's France. At worst it would be as great a menace as the German Third Reich."

Chandler frowned and said, "A strange hypothesis. But if it were true, the Russian bear would surely not be frightened?"

Grotski smiled. "Never. The proper word is 'anxious.' We are still talking off the record?"

Chandler nodded. "Absolutely."

"The Soviet Union would take a dim view of any drastic modification in the U.S. Constitution. That is, unless the new isolationist, conservative government was willing to make certain international concessions."

Biting his lip, Chandler exhaled. "What type of concessions?"

The Russian blew a long column of smoke toward the ceiling, leaned back, and laughed. "It is not possible for me to speak on behalf of the High Presidium, but, my friend, I can tell you this. Our intelligence agents have been aware of your unorthodox relationship with the chairman of the Joint Chiefs and the head of the CIA. We also know about certain secret meetings that were held within the confines of Condor Defense Industries in California."

Chandler digested the news. "We underestimate the ability of your moles and sleepers."

Grotski quickly polished off the rest of his vodka. "You must do what you must do, yes? With the capitalists, it's always divide and conquer, conquer and divide. Beware, my friend. It's a vicious self-destructive circle."

The ambassador didn't say that grimly, thought Chandler, but the words had an ominous ring to them. He wanted to disagree vehemently, but thought better of it. Finally, he said quietly, "Yes. We've heard it all before. Give capitalism enough rope and it will hang itself."

The Russian folded his hands in front of him. "I had not intended to quote Lenin, nor to lecture to a dinner guest. We are not impulsive like Americans, so we must wait and see, yes? Our reaction might depend entirely on who would lead this new government and on how many weapons were removed from Europe. We want NATO disbanded. What would your new President want? Who will be at the helm?"

"Supposing, Mikhail, for the sake of discussion, that I were at the helm?"

Grotski smiled thinly, shrugged, and reached into the water goblet. He tossed the gold cuff link back to Chandler and rose from the table. "Then in the future we must know each other better, yes? Shall we join the ladies?" he asked, wrapping an arm around Chandler's shoulder.

16

IT WAS STILL dark when the telephone jarred Carlie Chavez awake. She had been dreaming about Kirk, a deep, satisfying, romantic dream. Sleepily, she looked at her clock radio. Two minutes after six. The alarm was set for seven-thirty. Still groggy, she let the princess phone ring one more time before hesitantly picking it up.

"Hello."

Intense breathing greeted her, followed by a series of clicks. God, not an obscene phone call at this hour of the morning, she thought. Then an operator's intercept, followed by the metallic thunks of quarters being deposited. Carlie started to count the coins, then lost track.

"Ms. Chavez?" The male voice sounded muffled, as if speaking through thick gauze or a handkerchief.

"Yes. Who is this?"

"You may call me Lynx."

Carlie sighed wearily. "And you can call me Mink. Better yet, Russian Sable. So what do you want?"

A short silence. "I'm not amused. Your prying friend Kirk Stewart, the newspaperman."

"Go on. I'm listening. What about him?"

"And you knew a Shira Bernstein, correct?"

Carlie stiffened, raised herself to one elbow. "You use the past tense. You have some information about Shira?"

Again, a disconcerting silence. Carlie's heart quickened.

"Your reporter friend is in imminent danger. You will be also. But you both will be unharmed if you return certain documents and cease meddling."

"What documents?"

"Didn't Mr. Stewart tell you about the address book?"

"He hasn't even called. I don't know what you're talking about."

"Stewart will contact you soon. When he does, get him out of Washington, D.C., and back to New York. Place that address book in safekeeping and show it to no one. No one at the *Times* or at the network. Do you understand? I'll contact you tomorrow night."

Carlie shook the hair out of her face, gripped the phone tighter. "I'm a reporter, Mr. Lynx, and I take my orders from no—"

"There are other stories for both of you to pursue," he snapped, cutting her off. "Leave us alone, Ms. Chavez. This is a warning. No more interference."

Carlie felt confused. She decided to keep her tone noncommittal, but she was running an unfamiliar obstacle course, and she was still only half awake. The voice—was it vaguely familiar? Out of the past? God, how many voices had she heard as a TV newscaster? "I'm sorry, but I think—"

He cut her off again. "I'm sorry also. I have no more quarters, so this must be brief. The two of you keep digging, and we will dig as well. Kirk Stewart's grave, Carlotta. And yours."

Stewart had been unable to sleep on the plane, and he was tired. The high-rise Merrimont-Arlington near the capital's Key Bridge was booked to capacity, but Stewart had talked fast, finally managing to wangle a room from the desk clerk. Despite the early hour, the hotel lobby was crowded. Motti Barak had gone to the Israeli legation's compound and would meet him later.

Not only was Stewart still sickened by the plane crash and weary from the red-eye flight to Dulles Airport, but he now had a new worry—a gnawing concern over a fellow plane passenger who was now registering at the same hotel. Again Stewart studied the curly-haired stocky individual standing before the reception desk. He had a round, pinched face, large ears, and staring out from behind tinted eyeglasses were moist, downward slanted eyes that reminded Stewart of small clams. The face was vaguely familiar; he was sure he had seen it before the scene at the Houston airport. Possibly in a news photograph? Memorable mugs were common stock to a reporter, but the familiarity of this face wasn't the only thing that disturbed him. Ringing an alarm in his head was the Polaroid photograph this stranger had taken just before boarding the plane at Houston. Ostensibly it was a snapshot of two stewardesses. But Stewart knew that he and Barak had both been caught in the background of the picture. Barak, too, had commented on the incident, feeling that it was more than a coincidence.

This individual had just finished registering at the desk and joined a loud group of acquaintances at one corner of the lobby. Stewart suddenly noted that most of the people in the reception area wore lapel buttons. He had seen the buttons before: the circle and cross executed in gold, the drop of blood fired in red cloisonné. The Klan. Several others wore lapel ribbons that read, "Give me liberty or give me death—KKK."

Stewart looked at the men with distaste and started for the elevator, but then he paused. He was anxious to get to his room, but his reporter's instincts overcame his fatigue. Was this a Klan convention? One of the men wearing a ribbon stepped over to a cigarette machine and fumbled for coins. Stewart thought fast. He dug in his pockets, found a couple of quarters, and joined him. "Need some change?" he asked.

"Yeah. It's rejecting dimes and nickels." The man's rubicund face glowed with annoyance. "You got a quarter?"

Stewart quickly swapped coins.

"Thanks, pal." He eyed Stewart's camera narrowly.

"What's happening? You boys having a klavern meeting nearby?"

The man punched a button and grabbed his pack of Camels. He looked at Stewart, grinned, and cocked his head. "Don't you read the local paper, Mac? We're having a recruitment rally out in Jamesboro at noon today. Hell, it's the biggest Klan function since the march on the capital in the thirties." Abruptly, he dismissed Stewart and returned to his friends.

Overhead the Caribbean sky was cobalt blue with puffs of white clouds. The sinewy young Haitian had led the Russian overland, crossing the mountains at night from the Dominican Republic. They had then traveled by outrigger pirogue the final short distance to Gonave Island. Not once had the Haitian questioned his mysterious client's consuming need for secrecy, for he was being paid well. Moreover, the guide himself could not be seen in the larger villages or Port-au-Prince, where he was wanted by Haiti's president-for-life and hunted by the Tonton Macoutes.

The Haitian was doing a job. It wasn't difficult, and money talked in these poverty-stricken latitudes. Still, he might have come alone anyway, for he was curious. He had heard rumors that a new, as yet unoccupied resort hotel was to be turned into a prison, and this news bothered him. A political prison for his fellow blacks? If not, who would be placed there? What kind of prison could be made from a hotel? A comfortable one, from what he and the Russian had seen thus far.

The guide didn't understand what was happening, and his Soviet client was strangely uncommunicative. They had moved only at night, skirting the numerous army patrols and the dreaded National Police lookouts. Approaching the new landing strip, he and the Russian had watched as one unmarked olive-drab cargo plane after another landed and unloaded supplies. They had gone in close to the field and heard voices. American voices. Two nights in a row they had watched, fascinated, as tons of food, clothing, medical supplies, and filing cabinets were off-loaded. They had both counted, written all this information down. One aircraft carried a bulldozer, another a monstrous generator and jeeps. Then three more jet transports landed, and from them emerged a full company of U.S. infantrymen. The Haitian guide and the Russian had followed the men and equipment four miles down the road to the great hotel. And now, hidden in the green blind, they watched as Haitian workmen and U.S. Army personnel toiled to erect around the resort a high chain-link fence topped with barbed wire. The silent Russian repeatedly used his binoculars and made endless notes and drawings.

The guide, too, picked up his glasses and studied the rising barrier closely. It was a stout fence set deep in concrete. The insulators along the top meant there would be electricity. He smiled as he saw a long line of black workmen cultivate the ground along the inside perimeter of the fence. They were planting fire lilies and birds of paradise. The Haitian swung his binoculars seaward, beyond the huge, sparkling swimming pool, the tile deck with its lush landscaping and brightly colored cabanas. There was no sandy beach, only picturesque cliffs, a jagged shoreline with raging surf pounding against the rocks. On the farthest outcropping of land, men were constructing what appeared to be a concrete-block guard tower.

The guide lowered his binoculars. His ears had picked up the sound of engines approaching. Swiftly, he signaled his client to lower his head and fade into the undergrowth.

Two large trucks came roaring down the road. They were open-back Haitian army personnel carriers, but they carried American soldiers in combat gear.

Stewart wondered what urgent business had taken Motti Barak to the Israeli embassy, but puzzled as he was, he had not pursued the question. Barak had promised to return to the hotel at eleven, in time for them to get to the Klan rally at Jamesboro.

Stewart stood in the shower, taking his time, letting the water course down his face and back. Never before had hot suds felt so good. Stewart thought again about Barak. The inquisitive Israeli both annoyed and pleased him. Stewart needed help badly; he would be a fool to go a step farther alone. The *Times*, with all its resources, was a comfortable backstop, and his boss Mike Murphy knew how to catch. But Stewart was pitching to a dangerous opposition he knew absolutely nothing about—an enemy team that made up its own ground rules.

Stewart had seen the man with the Polaroid shaking hands with Klan members in the lobby. They had welcomed him as though he were a special luminary. Perhaps he was an Exalted Cyclops, Grand Dragon, or Wizard of Wizards. Stewart had always been amused by the Klan's names for its leaders.

Turning off the water, Stewart toweled himself dry and pulled on his last pair of clean shorts. They were the bikini briefs with the small red hearts, the ones Shira had given him for Valentine's Day. He remembered how she'd teased him, patted his ass, accusing him of being too macho to wear them.

Quickly, he went to one of the beds, fell back, and grabbed the telephone. Now, he thought. It was a matter of priorities. He had three phone calls to make: to his old schoolmate Tap Nelson at FBI headquarters, to Carlie Chavez at the network, and to Mike Murphy at the *Times*.

Stewart hesitated. No, he had agreed to give Carlie twenty-four hours to do her burrowing and come up with pay dirt. He would wait until late afternoon to call her. If he phoned Nelson now, the FBI probably wouldn't let Stewart grab a couple of hours' sleep, let alone go wandering out to the Klan rally at noon. He'd call Tap Nelson on his return from Jamesboro. Mike Murphy, on the other hand, expected him back at his desk at midday, which was impossible. An explanatory call might save his job.

After putting up with one disconnect and a long wait at the the *Times* switchboard, Stewart at last had Murphy on the line. His boss sounded busy and impatient, but his tone softened as he heard Stewart's story; not all of it, only the salient points he had chosen to bait the editor.

"Look," Murphy snarled. "I'm sorry about your lady friend. Damned sorry. But this other thing, Christ! The goddamn plane crash had to be a coincidence."

Stewart exhaled and said swiftly, "I need another day, Mike. I'll be back tomorrow and explain it all. I'm going to bring in a story."

"Come off it, Kirk. What kind of war you fighting? A personal one?" The words fell dully in Stewart's ear.

"You amaze me, boss. Dammit, it's not my war. It's the news media's war. And it's against misinformation. Not to mention some other crap, like ignorance, intolerance, and, worst of all, violence."

There was silence for a moment; then Murphy said, "Yeah. Sure. And not necessarily in that order. It's not only a mouthful, but a separate edition. I'll save feature space for you in Sunday's editorial section. So get your ass into the office tomorrow."

"Thanks Mike. But this story won't wait until Sunday. I'll have something for you in twenty, thirty hours."

"Bullshit."

"Get off my back and take me seriously, will you? My neck's stretched out a furlong and a half!"

Murphy laughed. "What do you want from me, Stewart? Pity and a pat? Things are tough all over. My brother's a cop on a tough Brooklyn beat, and he plays ostrich every day."

"Sure, Mike. See you *mañana*." Stewart slowly replaced the receiver on the hook and sprawled across the bed, staring at the ceiling. Silently, he cursed Murphy. The editor had his soft spots; it was all a matter of getting to them. *Later*.

Despite his exhaustion, Stewart's mind remained a merry-go-round. He phoned the hotel desk, asking to be buzzed at a quarter to eleven, then pulled back the sheets and tried to drift off. It took several minutes, but the revolving, painted horses finally slowed to a pace, then stopped. Stewart slept soundly for nearly two and half hours.

Motti Barak had forgotten Kirk Stewart's room number. Now as he ambled up to the reception counter he once more came upon the stocky man from the airplane, the one who appeared to be a ranking Klan officer. He stood in front of Barak at the desk and did not turn around. Barak could easily overhear his words to the room clerk.

"You have a Mr. Stewart registered here. Kirk Stewart. He's a member of our party, and I'd like him to receive this." The man handed the hotel employee a copy of *Southern Partisan* magazine, waiting to observe which box the clerk placed it in.

Noting that the room numbers on the letter boxes were plainly visible from the counter, Barak flinched. Supposedly, no one yet knew that Stewart was registered here. The man must have lifted his name from the Eastern Airlines flight manifest when they boarded in Houston. Barak turned, hiding his face as the Klansman stepped away from the desk and proceeded across the lobby. Barak watched him pause near the tobacco shop and whisper to a tall, swarthy man with a pock-marked face who held a cellophane-covered bowl of fruit. The two conversed briefly; then the man with the gift-wrapped fruit stepped into a nearby elevator.

Barak hurried to the house telephone in the foyer.

Stewart checked his watch. It was a quarter after eleven, and he was dressed and waiting for the Israeli's return to the hotel. In the meantime, he would polish off some important home-work.

Finding a pencil in the desk drawer, he carefully spread out Shira's Klan invitation, the back of which bore faint ball-point pen impressions. Holding the pencil on its side, he slowly rubbed the soft lead back and forth over the depressions. Numbers emerged. Phone numbers with area codes.

The telephone rang, interrupting him. Stewart took his time going over to the night stand to answer it.

"Hello."

"It's Motti."

"Where are you?"

"In the lobby. I want to meet you here. Get out of the room quickly. And take the stairs, not the elevator."

"Hold it. Relax, Motti. I just woke up. What's the rush?"

"Kirk, there's no time to explain. I want you downstairs immediately."

"You crazy? Why?"

"Shut up and listen, you empty-headed *goy*. You're in trouble. If you stay in that room, you're going to get an unauthorized delivery. A bowl of fruit. And the way I see it, the redneck delivery man is out to bust your ass—or mine. Now move, please!"

The line went dead. Stewart hung up the phone. For a moment he was beyond any movement. But only for a moment. His puzzlement quickly turned to fear, and it occurred to him he had not yet committed himself irretrievably to this undertaking. He never went into anything on a permanent basis. If he got out of this one, perhaps he should play it smart and disappear. Grabbing his jacket, he bolted for the door, but his hand was no sooner on the handle than he heard a sharp rap.

Stewart edged back along the wall. "Yeah? Who is it?" he called unevenly.

"A gift, sir! Compliments of the management."

Damn Barak. The man was a clairvoyant. Stewart debated what to do next. A few feet away was an electric shoe polisher, a red and black buffer unit with a long chromium handle. Stewart picked it up, hefted it over his shoulder, and stood behind the door.

"The door's open. Come in!" he shouted, away from the entry.

The door slowly opened. A tall man slipped inside immediately, started to close the door behind him. He carried a bowl

of fruit. Before the stranger could turn and fully survey the
room, Stewart struck, letting the weight of the shoe polisher
come down violently on the man's skull. The stranger's head
and shoulders thudded against the wall, and his arms and legs
flailed uselessly. Apples, bananas, and grapes spilled across
the carpet, and something else. Catching Stewart's eye was a
silenced Luger pistol. The man had been concealing it, ready
for use, behind the bowl of fruit.

Stewart's mind flashed. He started for the weapon, thought
better of it. His would-be attacker was out for the count. A
silencer-equipped gun that size felt good in some men's hands,
but not Stewart's. Wait, he flashed. Empty the cartridge! He
did so, pocketing the bullets and tossing the gun under the bed.
He suddenly wondered if the man had come upstairs alone.

Stewart had to think fast and clearly. Barak was waiting for
him downstairs. Safety in numbers. Snatching up the invitation
with the graphite-covered phone numbers, Stewart scrambled
out of the room, locking the door behind him.

Only when he was in the elevator alone did his breathing
return to an even pace. Calmer now, he again thought of the
gun. He should have taken it, passed it on to the Israeli. A bad
decision, considering the danger confronting them.

When the elevator doors opened at the lobby level, Barak
was there, grim-faced and waiting. Without saying a word, he
led Stewart rapidly out of the hotel into the street.

Stewart paused and swore to himself, suddenly remembering
he had left his camera in the room. He turned, starting back,
but Barak grabbed his arm, holding him.

"If we are to be outnumbered, we're better off outside, with
the public," the Israeli said swiftly.

In the foyer near the hotel's house phones, a sullen, crimson-
faced man straightened the convention label on his double-
breasted blue blazer and cursed. "Shit!" Pulling the telephone
he had been using off the narrow counter, in uncontrolled anger
he hurled it into a nearby trash receptacle. He watched the
Israeli and the newspaper reporter pass safely out of the hotel,
then turned to the two men beside him and snarled, "A royal
slip-up. The motherfuckers both got away from our man. Get
up there and find out what happened."

•   •   •

Colonel Pete Reddick knitted his heavy brows in a scowl. He had tried to ignore the amorous, apricot-colored poodle, twice nudging it away, but again it was wantonly humping at his bare leg. A blue satin bow on its ear fell askew, then dropped to the floor.

"Frieda! Damn it to hell, get in here and take care of your dog!"

Reddick rolled up the *Playboy* magazine he had been perusing and whapped the poodle on the nose. It yelped and backed away. From the distance it gave him one last contemptuous sniff, then trotted under the dressing room curtains and disappeared down the massage parlor hallway.

A sliding door next to Reddick opened.

"It's about time," he grunted.

Clad in a white smock, a tall, bosomy girl with wavy platinum-blond hair smiled provocatively and chirped, "Sorry to keep you waiting, Colonel." Her cornflower-blue eyes twinkled as she gave him an appraising look from head to toe. "Mmmmm. You've lost some weight since your last visit."

Reddick tucked in his gut and tightened the pink towel around his waist. "Your goddamn dog likes men. Why don't you keep him in your office?"

Again, the provocative smile, the heavy Swedish accent. "Raphael doesn't like all men. Only the ones I prefer." She wiggled Reddick's earlobe.

Reddick sat down on a stool, put his arms around Frieda's waist, and pulled her onto his knee. She struggled to rise, but only halfheartedly.

"Colonel, you're a married man. I'm embarrassed."

Reddick liked to hear Frieda make small talk. Her voice had a breathless quality that reminded him of Marilyn Monroe's. Sliding his hand underneath her smock, moving it slowly up her leg, Reddick felt a strong pull of excitement, and something more. She wasn't wearing a slip or underpants.

"My marital status didn't bother you last time," he soothed.

"Ah! I didn't know." Pulling away and tossing her long hair out of her face, she continued, somewhat peevishly. "That was before I discovered that my favorite Air Force squadron commander had a wife and family." She winked and giggled softly. "I have my standards, Colonel. Now come, I have a new device to show you."

"What kind of a device?"

"Come along," she insisted, waving a scolding finger and pulling him into an adjoining room.

"A mechanical robot with an electronic dildo, no doubt," he said sarcastically.

"Silly man. Look what I have for you. A computerized exercise machine." She smiled and gently pinched the spare tire around his stomach. "You come up from Langley twice a month for massage, but this would be much better for you, yes?"

It took Frieda ten minutes to convince Pete Reddick that the device was, in fact, the latest rage, that electromuscular stimulation was the lazy man's way to a trim and healthy body. He would try anything once, he thought, letting her apply the conductive rubber pads to his waist, chest, and buttocks.

"We'll bypass your legs," she stressed. "They look trim and muscular enough. We don't want to turn a skilled pilot into a plow horse."

"Wouldn't mind being hung like one. This contraption do anything for the cock?"

"No. But I can."

"I thought you avoided family men."

"Perhaps I'll weaken by the time you finish this treatment."

"How long will that be?"

"Forty minutes." She finished strapping him to the table, made several adjustments to the nearby control console, then started for the door. "A magazine, Petey? *Playboy* or *Playgirl*? Which do you prefer?"

Reddick shot her a peeved look. "Purple words coming from a lady in white. Keep the erotica and hand me the *Aviation Week* in my jacket pocket."

Frieda complied, wiggled out of the doorway, then poked her blond head through the curtains. "You want Raphael back here to keep you company, perhaps?" She disappeared, not waiting for his answer.

Odd feeling, Reddick thought, as the machine began stimulating muscles, contracting and relaxing at the rate of forty times a minute. The device took him some time to get used to.

Reddick was usually a fast reader, but he had a habit of taking his time with *Aviation Week*. He always wondered how its editorial staff consistently managed to report on aircraft configurations, performance data, and new weapons—both domestic and foreign—releasing such information to the public long before it was declassified. *Leaks*. Too many security leaks, he concluded. Time to tighten ship at the Pentagon. Even the Vice-President concurred on that. Or rather the President-to-be. Reddick still hadn't decided what he thought of Paul Chandler. His recent meetings with the Vice-President, along with the chairman of the Joint Chiefs, the head of the CIA, and the retired general he had flown from Palm Springs, had proven amicable, interesting enough. But they had hedged when asked about Reddick's specific role on Friday. Twenty-four fighters to be kept on alert over a twenty-four-hour period, no more details until later.

Reddick heard a telephone ring in the hallway. A moment later Frieda came into his room with a cradle phone. "For you," she said, plugging it into a jack beside his contoured couch.

Reddick waited until she left, then picked it up. "Colonel Reddick."

"This is Lynx."

"You're calling me here?" Reddick's face tightened. "This is a breach of protocol."

"Protocol means nothing to me. I take instructions and pass them on, whenever, wherever. You doubt my authority?"

"No, of course not." Lowering his voice, Reddick added, "I can't talk now."

Lynx's voice hardened. "Obviously. Just remain silent and listen carefully. I tried to get back to Washington late last night but couldn't risk being spotted by certain adversaries who were on the plane."

"What adversaries?" Reddick whispered.

"That and other business is what we must discuss immediately. At the Klan rally in Jamesboro. Civic Square at noon. Be there, Colonel. I'll find you." The line went dead.

Reddick put the telephone aside and gritted his teeth. The electronic exerciser continued to squeeze his stomach at forty impulses a minute. In the doorway, his head protruding under the curtains and his tongue lolling, Raphael waited.

17

IT WAS NEARING noon. Beside Stewart in the taxi, Barak remained uncommunicative. Stewart pushed himself into the corner of the seat and stared out at the suburban expressway traffic, cursing softly again at the loss of his 35mm Canon and the pictures he'd taken down south. He checked his watch. Jamesboro was still twelve miles away. He wondered again if Shira had planned to attend this rally.

"You're hungry, perhaps?" asked Barak calmly.

Stewart looked at him. "We can eat after the rally." The Israeli was always thinking about food. It was hard for Stewart to think of anything but the attempt on his life minutes before in the hotel room. Stewart usually wasn't the reflective type, seldom had a spare moment for heavy-duty philosophy. He met day-to-day challenges as he would probably meet the grim reaper—open-mindedly, with a measure of cynicism and a shrug. But now it bothered him that someone was manipulating masks of death, shoving them in his face before his time. And now he was helping his adversaries; attending the Klan rally would be leaping out of the frying pan and into the fire. No, not quite. Barak had reminded him that if past performance was a measure, there would be police around. Plenty of them.

If he stayed up front, out in the open, he would be safe. To a degree. Whatever, he needed the Klan part of the story. Stewart pulled the Arnold Metz address book from his pocket, deciding to go through it again. Now not only the gun merchant, but individuals here in Washington as well wanted him dead. The attempts on his life were obviously connected. But why was he so important? So far he knew little, damned little, and he had nothing of substance to build a news story on. He and Barak had just scratched the surface. It had to be this address book that they wanted.

Thumbing through the pages, Stewart found several names with Washington addresses and telephone numbers. Had Arnold Metz lived here previously? Was this booklet Metz's own little Odessa file?

The only entry Stewart recognized was Dennis Garrett, the President's would-be blackmailer. He had also seen the name on the autographed muscle photo in the gun peddler's bedroom.

Barak edged closer to Stewart, looking over his shoulder. He, too, was examining the address book. The Israeli withdrew from his pocket a small pad and pen, copying down a number that interested him.

Stewart noted the name: Colonel Pete Reddick, Langley Air Force Base. "What's Reddick's involvement?" he asked Barak.

"I'm not sure, but as a fellow pilot, I'm curious. His photo was on Metz's wall."

Stewart turned to the last page of the address book. "Look at these. A list of code names, all with corresponding numbers and cities."

Barak scratched his nose. "Strange. Animal names—Badger, Fox, Panther, Lynx."

Stewart tapped the page. "I suspect that these numbers are post office boxes." He put the book away and looked out at the side of the road. They were passing the Quantico Marine Corps reservation. Jamesboro, he knew, would not be far ahead. Stewart made up his mind that after the Klan rally he would have the address book copied, page by page, and send the duplicate to Carlie in New York for safekeeping.

Ten minutes later the taxi dropped Stewart and Barak in front of the Jamesboro Town Hall. Police patrol cars were parked everywhere. Across the street in the center of a small park, several white-robed Klansmen were setting up public address equipment on a white latticed bandstand. In back of the portable podium a banner read "Save Our Land—Join the Klan." Surrounding the area in a semicircle was a phalanx of some two dozen Virginia State Police wearing visored helmets and carrying riot clubs. An equal number of local officers and sheriff's deputies wandered at random through the gathering crowds. Good, thought Stewart. There's safety in numbers.

Stewart nudged Barak, and together they ascended the Town Hall steps to get a better view of the scene. Stewart watched, fascinated, as the first of the visiting Klansmen began to appear, arriving separately in a ragtag procession of passenger cars and pickup trucks. Most of the licenses, he noted, were from out of state. One bumper sticker read "God, Guts, and Guns Made America."

Many of the Klansmen had brought their families, and several children waved American and Confederate flags from the vehicle windows.

Stewart heard a chorus of heckling as the men in the cars put on their tall, white, peaked hats and shuffled to the bandstand. None wore hoods over their faces.

"The conehead Klan!" crowed a teenager from his perch in a tree. An angry black woman standing near Motti Barak yelled, "You're in the wrong town if you're going to spread this shit!"

Stewart went back down the steps, urging Barak to follow him to the end of the motorcade. A white Mercedes-Benz drove up as close as it could to the park's grassy knoll. Several police formed a line between the car and the bandstand as a robed Klansman with five red bands on each sleeve climbed briskly out of the back seat and waved to the gathering. A small percentage of the crowd clapped; several jeered. Most were silent.

"Motti, is that face familiar enough?" asked Stewart quickly.

Barak nodded. "He's the one who sent the bowl of fruit."

"And the same asshole who took our picture as we boarded that plane."

The public address system crackled to life as one of the Klansmen on the bandstand sonorously announced, "Jamesboro friends, we members of the Central Virginia Dragons, Klavern Six, are proud to introduce our national leader, the Exalted Archon, Bobby Harrington, of the Knights of the Invisible Society."

Stewart grimaced. The day was cool, a brisk breeze wafting through the trees in the park, but the very idea of attending a

Klan rally caused little drops of sweat to tingle on his back. Stewart watched as Bobby Harrington climbed swiftly up on the gazebolike speakers' platform, looked over the increasingly agitated crowd, then bowed his head in prayer. His words were mumbled, barely audible over the loudspeaker system. Gesturing for Barak to keep close by, Stewart tried to move in closer. They passed through the police ring, approaching to within fifty feet of Harrington. Before the Exalted Archon's prayer could be concluded, a teenager hurled a firecracker into the crowd.

Stewart cringed. He turned in time to see the youth swiftly apprehended by a U.S. marshal standing nearby.

Stewart quickly stepped aside as a dozen children passed him, heading for the bandstand. Each wore a white T-shirt trimmed in red, emblazoned with a blue eagle over the words "American Youth Corps." They were singing, albeit off key, a verse that seemed to profoundly agitate Motti Barak.

The Israeli shook his head. "Just like the Hitler Youth," he whispered. "History is repeating itself."

"The wrong kind of history," added Stewart, looking away from the children to study the crowd's reaction. Most eyes were guarded, watchful; some were red-lined and angry. Beside the podium, two Klansmen opened a wire mesh cage, releasing a dozen white doves.

The children, mostly young teenagers, climbed the steps of the bandstand and fell in behind the smug-faced Harrington. Stewart listened closely as their high-pitched voices rang out across the park:

> Will you rally to your children?
>   Won't you lend a helping hand
> To preserve the white child's future
>   In a free and happy land?
> Now we folks can band together;
>   At last we've found a way,
> For the Aryan knights are marching.
>   Thank God they're here to stay.

At the song's conclusion, there was a scattering of applause and a few catcalls. Bobby Harrington waved a hand toward the youth group behind him. "The Invisible Klan Society is first and foremost a family organization," he shouted. "Dedicated to the proposition of live and let live, love and compassion! I see some sour faces out there, some expected black ones that are angry, but I also see some happy people. How many Christians are out there in the crowd?"

An old man standing near the bandstand shouted, "Nazi scum! Go back where you belong!"

Harrington surveyed the crowd with an even stare, his eyes finally settling on the old man. "The Klan doesn't hate the black race, or any other race. And we don't hate so-called liberal religions, but we do believe the mixing of races is evil, sinful, and contrary to God's will. It is destroying the integrity and productivity of America! You want to know why we've come to Jamesboro today? To recruit new members."

Stewart cocked his head, listening carefully. Barak had his arms folded in front of him.

"The Klan is growing, my friends. Day by day our numbers increase. We want more God-fearing men, women, and children to rally beneath the fiery cross. And we need them this week."

Two young black men passing by in a car shouted, "Death to the Klan, you fuckers!" The vehicle moved slowly on without stopping.

Exalted Archon Harrington continued. "There's a sampling of your liberated Negro. The new Commies among us, brainwashed by books and dishonest television shows like 'Roots.' The works of dishonest black writers are proliferating in your local schools and libraries. And it's time to do something about it! I don't know about your children out there, but I sure as hell would never permit my kids to read the filth of devious-minded, semiliterate black writers!"

Stewart bit back his anger. The blatant racism and arrogance were almost more than he could handle, but he kept his silence.

Suddenly a neatly dressed young black in a suit and tie, standing with several TV news cameramen at the edge of the crowd shouted, "Imperial Magician, or Exalted Dragon, or whatever you call yourself! Are you accepting pertinent questions from the crowd?"

Harrington looked up, angry and affronted, but he quickly conjured up a smile. "That's what we're here for. To enlighten reasonable people. Speak up!"

"I'm a reporter. *Washington Post.* My older sister is a speech writer for the White House. Maybe you'd like to expand on your loose comment about semiliterate black scribes."

One of the Klansmen behind Harrington suddenly cupped his hands around his mouth and shouted, "Go back to Georgetown, you pinko fag!"

Stewart winced and slowly shook his head. He watched Harrington leer back at the black reporter. Small beads of perspiration were visible on the Klan leader's forehead, and his jowls sagged noticeably. Pushing his eyeglasses higher on the bridge of his nose, Harrington said softly into the microphone, "God save us from the liberal press! I didn't come here to discuss genetics or compare the intellectual and creative capacity of blacks to that of whites. There isn't time." He focused on the young reporter. "If you'd like to take some of our literature with you, boy, I'm sure you'd find it enlightening."

Stewart felt his stomach tighten as he watched the reporter shake his head. Near the black, a white college student in a leather-sleeved letterman's jacket shouted, "Harrington! You're full of horse shit. Maybe you should read a few articles by high-caliber black journalists. Or can't you read?"

Some of the crowd laughed. Two Klansmen came up behind Harrington and whispered in his ear, but he motioned them away. To the expectant audience, he snapped, "Did you hear what Joe College said about watermelon-eating writers? He said a *few*. That's the key. Coincidence, not consistency! Julian Huxley once postulated that if six monkeys sat at six typewriters and banged away at random until infinity, they would eventually write all the classics of literature in correct order. Talent, my friends, or biological coincidence?"

Several feet away from Stewart a gangly farmer in an abused straw hat raised an arm. "This isn't no college campus, Harrington. Talk straight and make some sense!"

Burning with anger, Stewart turned, tapped Barak's shoulder, and gestured away from the crowd. Together, they walked outside the perimeter of helmeted police. Stewart didn't want to believe what he was witnessing. It didn't seem possible. The man was a maniac. But the scene was real, very real. He looked back. The wind picked up, blowing across the park and fluttering the Klansmen's robes. The Exalted Archon continued to raise his fist and wave it. The catcalls became less frequent. If the crowd wasn't captivated, it was at least listening, thought Stewart.

Barak shrugged. "Some will follow, yes. The easily manipulated rabble always does. There's nothing more we can learn here. Harrington's flanks are well protected."

"What are you saying? That we should try to nab him? And *then what?*"

Barak lifted Stewart's hand and gently tapped his splinted finger. "You have so short a memory? Persuasion works. Gentle or otherwise, we must force him to talk. I suggest we follow him back to the hotel."

"Not the hotel," replied Stewart. "We'll need reinforcements."

Barak thought for a moment. "I suspect you're right. You claim to have a contact at FBI headquarters. Can you trust him? Possibly, at this point, you should tell the bureau chief himself what you know. It's a risk, but then—"

"I'll talk to my friend, but I'm still not sure about Oliver Wright. I need to think about it."

Barak shrugged. "Go into town, then, and I'll merge into the background here and follow the Exalted Archon."

"Exalted *psychopath,*" Stewart prompted.

Stewart wasn't at all anxious to hightail it to the FBI. What he really wanted was to get away from Barak, to be alone somewhere, to work on the mysterious telephone numbers, the impressions on Shira's invitation, which was still in his pocket. Now he had the opportunity. "Major, be careful. Where do we meet later?"

Barak thought briefly, then said, "Take a room somewhere. Use a false name. Leave word for me at the Israeli embassy where you can be reached. And, Kirk, do not bring up my name when you talk with the FBI."

Barak glanced up the street. "That taxi just arriving. By the diamond-shaped light on the roof you can see it's from downtown Washington. Take it back to the city. The ride will be cheaper than a local cab."

Stewart nodded, took off at a trot. Bobby Harrington's abrasive words still clanged in his mind like cymbals.

Motti Barak turned back toward the bandstand and watched Harrington raise both arms high in the air, attempting to quiet the crowd. The full white sleeves with their five red stripes fluttered in the wind as the Klansman frowned, shook a clenched fist, and rasped into the PA system, "The Jew Communists say integrate! And by the love of God, I don't have to tell you out there what that means. 'Integrate' translates into 'rob, rape, riot, and kill.'"

Barak ground his teeth and swore softly to himself in his native Russian. *Jew Communists!* Bobby Harrington—regardless of which side he was on—like most Americans, was grandly ignorant about Communism. He would know even less about what it meant to be a Jew in Russia. Barak shook his head.

Harrington began pounding the lectern. "Join us! The Klan is Christ's way for white men." He turned, plucked a flower from the hair of one of the small girls on the platform. "Behold," he shouted, "the purity of the White Camellia! The Klan has a simple solution!"

Simple solution, Barak thought irritably. Right this instant he wished he had a simple solution of sulfuric acid to pour down this demagogue's throat.

Standing next to the Diamond Cab, Colonel Pete Reddick was in the process of paying his fare from the capital when he was nearly bowled over by the tall, shaggy-haired man hurrying to claim the rear seat.

"What's the hurry?" Reddick asked irritably. The driver handed him change for a twenty.

The individual in the back of the taxi didn't respond, his attention still riveted on the Klan rally across the street. The cab made a U-turn and took off in the direction from which it had come. Impetuous bastard, Reddick thought. Another former hippie who'd never served, never undergone the spit, polish, and discipline of the military. No manners. Obviously upset with the rally. Probably a fucking liberal.

Reddick looked around him, surveying the crowd. A policeman eyed him warily. He smiled back. Walking across the square, Reddick took a seat on a park bench, away from the rest of the throng. He was glad he had changed into civilian clothing, the Izod shirt, wool blazer, and the comfortable stretch slacks he had kept in a locker at Frieda's Massage Salon. He felt comfortable and relaxed; Air Force blues, under the circumstances, would be conspicuously out of place. He waited patiently for the rally to end, his eyes watchful. Uncomfortable, waiting for the approach of a man he had never seen before. Lynx knew what he looked like. So much for piss-ant security files.

Reddick glanced briefly toward the bandstand, where the

white-robed men stood. The national leader of the Invisible Society made sense, he mused, even though Bobby Harrington often sounded like a broken record. He had met the Exalted Archon three times. Once at the Officers' Club at Andrews Air Force Base, again at the American Eagle Gun Emporium in Galveston, and then at a post–Super Bowl party in New Orleans. Harrington wasn't a close friend, but he was generous with expensive booze and held his liquor well. If nothing else, thought Reddick, Bobby was a convivial drinking companion. Reddick pulled out a Marlboro and lit it.

Twenty minutes passed uneventfully. The Klan members ended their meeting with a pledge of allegiance to the flag, punctuated by two water-filled condoms hurled at the bandstand. Then the crowd began to withdraw, urged on by baton-wielding police.

Reddick put out his cigarette and followed Bobby Harrington to the white Mercedes-Benz. He called out the Klansman's name. The Exalted Archon turned, pulled off his peaked headpiece, and smiled.

"Enjoy the speech, Colonel? Welcome aboard." Clasping Reddick's hand, he gestured toward the open rear door of his car. Together, they climbed inside. Up front, a driver started the engine and accelerated slowly through a path cleared by the police. Harrington pointed to the patrol cars, gleefully counting them out loud. "Ten, eleven, twelve. Hell, there's over a dozen. Amazing what a federal court order will do for the right of free assembly, Colonel. Never could I personally afford a security force like this."

Reddick smiled, but felt distinctly uncomfortable; faces were staring into the car at him. Many faces, and not all were friendly. From out of nowhere a beer can struck the windshield. Then swiftly the Mercedes moved away from the crowd, past the Town Hall, down a side street. The inside of the vehicle became whisper quiet.

"Why the confused expression?" asked Harrington, as he unzipped his white robe.

Reddick hunched his shoulders. "Something's gone wrong. I was supposed to meet Lynx at that rally."

Harrington laughed as he pulled away the rest of the voluminous overgarment. "We had certain enemies in attendance at the rally. Lynx couldn't afford to be seen. His identity, for good reasons, must be kept secret. Don't worry, our undercover friend is waiting for us."

"You still delight in mystery, I see. Bobby the goddamned wizard," sniped Reddick.

"No. Archon. *Exalted* Archon. The distinction will be important in the days ahead." Harrington nudged the shoulder of the man at the wheel and pointed to a Shell service station on an opposite corner. The driver crossed the street, pulled the Mercedes up to the pumps, and stopped. While the attendant pumped gas, Harrington led Reddick to the rest room around in back. The Klansman quickly checked the men's room to make sure it was unoccupied, then held the door open.

"You're to go in alone, Colonel. Sit in the stall, close and lock the door. Do not stand or attempt to see out. Remain seated until I open this outer door again and summon you."

"What kind of crap is this?" asked Reddick irritably. "I've already got my work cut out for me, Harrington. This cloak-and-dagger bullshit I don't need. Nor do I have the time for it."

"You're a military man, Colonel. And smart military men follow orders to the letter. Or have you forgotten? If Lynx is paranoid about being recognized, that's his privilege. Or his problem. Your job is to listen to whatever he has to say. Mine is to wait outside, making sure you aren't interrupted."

"Holy Mother of God," grunted Reddick, shuffling into the rest room and entering the toilet cubicle. The outer door closed firmly behind him. U-2 and Blackbird duty had never subjected him to this kind of hush-hush bull, he thought. Reluctantly, cursing in monosyllables, he sat down.

Almost immediately he heard the outer door to the rest room open and close; then he heard soft whistling. Under the stall he saw two polished wingtips proceed to a nearby urinal.

"Colonel?" the even voice asked.

"You got it. Cut the social proprieties. Get to the specifics, Lynx. What the hell you take me for, a tea room fairy?"

The voice that came back to Reddick was uncompromising. "I have something for you." A hand appeared beneath the partition; in it was a Polaroid snapshot. Reddick took the photo and held it up to the light. Examining it, he said, "Quality merchandise."

"Not the flight attendants, Colonel. Behind them, the two men."

"Go on."

"The one at the left. He's purportedly a former Israeli fighter pilot, trained to fly U.S. jets; he's now a legation aide in the capital. We think he's either linked to the Mossad or working for the FBI."

Reddick heard urine begin to flow in the urinal on the other side of the stall. He studied the faces in the photograph, but they meant nothing to him. The stewardesses, on the other hand, were knockouts. "Sorry, I can't help you," he said. "Who's the tall bastard? A cop?"

"No. A *New York Times* reporter."

Reddick looked closer. "Hold it. His face is vaguely familiar. I'm not sure, but he may have climbed into my taxi after I arrived at the Klan rally. Still, both men are absolute strangers to me."

"They may not be for long. Both were in Arnold Metz's house, where your photograph, unfortunately, was hanging on the wall. Also your name and phone number appeared in Metz's address book, which is in their possession. Are you listening, Colonel?"

Swallowing hard, Reddick was at a loss for words. He needed to think. Only one question came to his mind, and even as he asked it he doubted whether it would earn a straight answer. "Who the hell do you work for?"

"Let's say internal intelligence and let it drop at that."

"Don't mince words with me. I'll ask Singer myself."

"I work for him and others. But I'm the one who should be asking questions and giving orders today, Colonel. I suggest that, starting immediately, you carry a gun at all times. Just a precaution. If either of the men in the photograph confronts you, do not hesitate to use it immediately."

"Thanks for the advice."

"One more thing. We may have another job for you. The CIA director's still working on the details."

Reddick waited impatiently. The toilet seat was getting uncomfortable, probably wrinkling his slacks. "Go ahead. I'm listening, dammit."

"Later," Lynx said abruptly. "Our man Metz will contact you. Thanks for coming by, Colonel."

Reddick exhaled sharply. He heard the urinal flush, saw the polished shoes turn, then listened to Lynx's footsteps withdraw outside. As the outer door closed, he heard voices raised in anger, but Reddick couldn't quite make out what was being said.

The national leader of the Klan didn't like to be ordered around, by Lynx or anyone else. Bobby Harrington stood face to face with Lynx, unflinching, despite the flurry of epithets being hurled at him.

"That's what I said, Harrington; you're an asshole. No more fuck-ups. No more impulsive acts. What you attempted at the hotel was just as stupid as Arnold Metz's blunder with the airplane. What good would it do to kill the reporter if the address book isn't on him? We have to get our hands on it first, then—"

"Stewart's a bone in my throat," retorted Harrington. "A spy is a spy. I say he goes now."

"Agreed. But you have more important tasks than to play hit man, Exalted Archon. Let our specialist Metz handle this work. He has not only the dirty hands of experience, but the pathological mind for it as well. He'll arrive in Washington at any time."

"What about the colonel in there?"

"Take him back to the capital. And see to it that he returns to the officers' billet at Andrews, not to that Swedish broad's bordello."

Following Barak's advice, Stewart checked into the Rhode Island Avenue YMCA. He now sat in a phone booth behind closed doors, in one hand his credit calling card and the mysterious paper with the telephone impressions, and in the other several dimes. His ball-point pen was clutched between his teeth.

Stewart went over the graphite-enhanced impressions again. There were three sets of numerals. The first was patently clear, easy to read. Punching the number, Stewart was surprised to find it was a Washington, D.C., massage parlor called Frieda's. The second number had a 213 area code—Los Angeles. Stewart charged the call and listened carefully as a throaty female voice came on the line. After several seconds of confused dialogue with Stewart, she identified herself as executive secretary to Norman Gifford. Condor Defense Industries, concluded Stewart; the board chairman himself.

At a loss for words, Stewart hung up. He made a brief notation beside the number, and turned his attention to the last set of digits, which was partially obliterated by a .22 bullet hole. This would be more difficult.

Stewart looked more closely at the graphite-covered paper. The number carried a Washington exchange. The missing digit wasn't entirely effaced, he noted. There was a trace left of the top and bottom of a noncursive numeral. That eliminated 2, 3, 5, 6, 8, 9, and 0. Easy enough thus far. The bullet hole obscured the middle of a 1, 4, or 7. Wait. Possibly even a sloppy 9. Too many combinations, he thought. It would be a wild guess, but he had to try. Picking up the phone, he dropped in a coin and began pushing buttons.

18

ARNOLD METZ GLANCED up at the clock on the Dulles passenger terminal wall. It was two-thirty. He was annoyed by the sudden change of plans that had been forced upon him. Had everything gone according to schedule, he would have remained in Galveston, practiced at leisure with the impressive new weapon Lynx had delivered to him, then taken an early flight to the capital on Friday morning. Events had accelerated, however, and so would he. The probing newsman and the interfering Israeli had necessitated a quick change in plans.

Metz arranged for a rental car and hurried out of the terminal. He had not taken a chance on carrying weapons in his flight baggage. He would pick up the crate containing the EMR device along with three handguns at the Delta air freight facility, then proceed to Frieda's Massage Parlor, where he would store his little arsenal until he needed it. All except the silenced Luger and a box of shells, which he planned to put to immediate good use.

Metz felt a sudden exhilaration, pleased that there would be no more closet work. He was keenly aware that his covenant was at last beginning. And such a fine start! With the plane explosion he had finally put on the spiked gauntlets, and they felt good. The movement would swallow and digest many important people before the week ended. Shooting down the jet in Houston was merely practice, excellent practice; it had definitely steeled him for what lay ahead. Lynx had told him the disappointing news that Kirk Stewart was not aboard the plane. A pity so many had died needlessly, he mused. This time he wouldn't fail to eliminate the meddlesome reporter. He would be more cautious and more thorough.

The FBI director sat alone in his office.

Oliver Wright spread the letters of inquiry, the PSQ and the federal clearances, the family biographical sketch, several news clippings, and some dozen photographs across his desk, arranging the material in order of importance. The dossier on the head of the Central Intelligence Agency had been two years in the making, and it was impressive. Walter Singer was an interesting man.

Wright was satisfied; his FBI staff had done a thorough job. Little about his adversary's background had been left to conjecture.

Walter Hobart Singer—also known by the code names Warren Backer and Rook and his unofficial nickname among the agency rank and file, King Lear—was born October 23, 1940, in Cleveland. A Scorpio, Wright mused, remembering his wife's extrapolations on astrology. He thought for a moment: 1940, the Year of the Dragon. He couldn't remember more, not that he wanted to.

Wright perused the documents before him. Walter Singer was definitely an overachiever, but what else? Narcissism, ingratitude, a propensity for heady daydreaming—these were the negative traits Singer had inherited from his divorced father, a man he had seldom seen since the age of seven. His mother had never remarried. Singer had openly admitted being spoiled as a child by his mother's doting and a comfortable family inheritance. Neighbors remembered him as a clever child with a yeasty mind and a talent for mischief. Elementary school teachers claimed he was a hard worker but a rebel, and one recalled he had several times been disciplined for insubordination and unruly conduct. Wright read a notation from a former classmate who asserted that Singer hated school.

According to the information before Wright, Singer made no close friends in the seventh and eighth grades. His mother dropped him off at school and picked him up after class. He was at the top of the rolls scholastically, and had been overheard calling his classmates mediocre, admitting that mediocre people bored him.

The loner instinct so soon, thought Wright, holding up an enlarged black-and-white photograph. It was a picture of the CIA director's high school football team. A much younger Walter Singer stood somber-faced in sharp contrast to the smiling player beside him who held a shiny brass trophy.

Wright studied the photograph thoughtfully, turned it over, read the notes on the back: Singer had been upset when his teammates voted another man most valuable player, despite the fact Singer had been the leading scorer all season.

Wright picked up the personnel security questionnaire again, double-checked several dates, then went back to the biographical profile. Singer had graduated with honors from the University of Maryland; during a four-year hitch as a Navy officer he had won a medal for rescuing a trapped pilot from a fire aboard the carrier *Ranger*. Indeed, his dossier was replete with commendations. Soon after he was recruited by the CIA, he had picked up a presidential citation for his undercover work in Southeast Asia. A year later Singer was promoted to head the London office of the CIA, the youngest regional administrator in the agency's history.

Wright noted a personal point, entered by a CIA psychologist at the start of Singer's agency career. Singer apparently had no problem attracting women, though more often than not his affairs were short-lived. Favoring variety and going for numbers, he'd never married, never came close. Wright turned over in his hands several photographs of women recently seen with Singer. Young, attractive, bosomy, they looked like models or stewardesses. No frumpy middle-aged types for Singer; he demanded elegance and youth, and apparently got them.

Instinct told him that Singer had his finger in more than one cookie jar, but the file entry that bothered Wright the most was the report of the CIA director personally driving the Vice-President to the Soviet embassy, then waiting patiently outside during Paul Chandler's visit there. Wright withdrew a fresh cigar from his humidor, sat back in his chair, and bit off the wrapper. He lit it and stared for a long time at the material spread across his desk. It was time, he reasoned, to have a no-holds-barred talk with the reporter, Kirk Stewart.

• • •

The YMCA phone booth was getting muggy. Stewart wiped his forehead and cracked the door. So far he had eliminated three telephone exchange possibilities: The number ending in 1 was the city library; 4 was out of service; 7 was a noisy pizza house. Stewart made some notes, dropped in a coin, and tried the last combination, the grouping ending in 9.

"Mr. Backer's office," came a brusque female voice.

Stewart was momentarily confused. "What firm is this?" he asked quickly.

"Firm? This is Warren Backer's private line," the woman irritably shot back. "Who's calling, please?"

"I'm sorry. Wrong number," assuaged Stewart. Knitting his brows, he slowly replaced the receiver on the hook. Who was Warren Backer? His mind flashed on something he had picked up in an early writing class: In the classic detective novel, the hero requires patience and persistence, and eventually all the pieces fit into place. Stewart had all the patience in the world, and he had just picked up another interesting piece to the puzzle. Three new pieces in all, including the contacts with Condor Industries and the Washington massage parlor.

He had found the phone numbers in Shira's car. Had she jotted them down or had they belonged to someone she knew, or was on to? Stewart exhaled sharply. He desperately needed more time. Reaching into his pocket, he pulled out Arnold Metz's address book.

Walter Singer sat at his desk and cogitated. The morning's intelligence reports from overseas lay neatly stacked on the right side of his desk. Directly before him was the two-page computer printout of proprietary domestic information that had been sent out on the Committee's scrambler from California. The news from Condor's Norman Gifford at the Citadel was far more favorable than the international CIA dispatches. Across the nation, everything was moving like clockwork; the Committee's intricate provisions for secrecy had thus far functioned without a flaw.

The CIA director squared his shoulders and tapped both hands on his desk. He had read all the reports carefully, and he was satisfied. He leaned back in his leather chair, thoughtful. He'd covered all his bets, and his hands were still scrupulously clean. Excellent. Only two more days to go, and the alchemy was working. The nation's health depended on strong preventive medicine, and he was fully prepared to administer it.

The other members of the Committee underestimated him. Hallowell, Gifford, and Frober were little more than greedy jackals; who was greediest was a moot point. Singer suspected that if his back were to the wall he would trust his CIA minions before any of the Committeemen. There were a dozen shop men in particular he could count on, come whatever. They were intensely loyal and productive as well; bonuses at the end of the month made them more productive. And for special assignments, the necessary forays into the enemy camp, there was his undercover man, Lynx. Thank God for Lynx the go-between, Singer reflected, who afforded him the pleasure of being insulated from men like Arnold Metz. Singer had never met the infamous Texan and didn't intend to. The prick actually went so far as to shoot down a passenger jet! How could they continue to use him but at the same time control his madness? The hit man probably sat in a grimy basement poring over campaign photographs of Rommel's Afrika Korps, all the while pulling his pud.

Keeping trigger-happy types like General Brady and Colonel Reddick simmering on a back burner took effort enough. Metz had to be kept at a distance. From now on, Singer decided, he would make a concerted effort to keep his hands even cleaner, stay farther back in the wings. Others could prompt the performers; he had to think of himself as a master choreographer. Stage managers were a dime a dozen. Dancers, no matter how talented, were basically cattle, born to be prodded.

His private telephone—the line for his Warren Backer cover—buzzed insistently. Singer picked it up. "Yes? Not another hang-up call, I trust."

"No, sir." His secretary put through the board chairman of Condor Defense.

Norman Gifford sounded agitated. "Sorry, Singer. There's been a setback. A problem with Argonaut Twelve."

"There isn't time for problems," Singer shot back impatiently.

"We're concerned over the satellite's jamming device— whether the Pac-33 Interface and rebound amplifiers will function properly over the Midwest."

Singer winced. "Don't give me your Citadel think tank gobbledygook, Gifford. Elucidate."

"It's possible some three hundred FM radio stations will still be able to broadcast without interference."

Singer swallowed hard, made a slight strangled noise into the phone, and slapped his palm on the desk.

"Walter?" asked Gifford. "You hear me? The jamming—"

"Jam failure up your ass!" Singer felt the first pangs of a super headache coming on. Never had he talked so roughly to the nation's most powerful aerospace executive. On top of that, Gifford was the chairman of the Committee. The hell with it, Singer decided, zeroing in again with all the tact of a panzer. "Damn it to hell, Gifford. Bust ass out there if necessary. We need to kill both the AM and FM signals. All of them. You have a little over forty hours to pull your quality-control team together. Either that, or you can personally round up the extra brawn required to forceably close down those stations."

Stewart hesitated, once more checked the Georgetown address with the one in Metz's address book, then crossed the street and entered the two-story brick apartment building. The paint was peeling from the mailboxes in the lobby, and they bore only numbers, no names. Spotting a door marked Manager, Stewart pushed the buzzer but heard no ring. He knocked. A dog inside barked. After several seconds the door opened, revealing a disheveled gray-haired woman in a muumuu. Her flowered dress was dirty, and she reeked of gin.

"Afternoon," Stewart offered cordially. "I'm looking for Dennis Garrett. May I have his apartment number?"

A slender young man with longish black hair and a satiny face swung through the doorway from the street, a bag of groceries in one hand, a bouquet of red carnations and a mailbox key in the other. The woman ingored the tenant, her red-tinged eyes fixed on Stewart.

"Not here any longer. Moved out two or three days ago." Looking Stewart up and down, scratching her bosom, she added, "What's it to you?"

"I'm a friend. Did he leave a forwarding address? It's important that I find him immediately."

The woman wiped her slavering lips on the sleeve of her dress. "I never meddle in my tenants' affairs. Especially that one's affairs. Try the goddamn post office." Unsteadily, she edged away, nudging a mangy Pomeranian back inside and closing the door before Stewart could protest.

The young man in the turtleneck sweater started to climb the stairs but suddenly hesitated. Cocking his head, he eyed Stewart speculatively. "You a friend of Dennis Garrett?"

Stewart straightened. "Depends. Why do you ask?"

"Clever, clever. Answer a question with another question. I was his roommate. The bitch left owing me money."

Feeling relieved, Stewart quickly said, "Owes me, too." Go for the resentment, he thought. Resentment and sympathy often opened an otherwise mum mouth.

The youth looked back at him. "I see. Are you one of his gay friends?"

Stewart bit his lip. "Do I look gay?" He couldn't resist the query.

"*Que signifie ce mot-là,* 'gay'?" the young man replied with a disappointed look. "By your definition, probably not. Can you determine the shape of an iceberg just by looking at its tip? You straights are a pain in the ass."

"Yeah, sure. How about some help? Where did he go?"

"You're probably a bill collector." Twirling his keys, he started up the stairs. "I thought you might be a friend of his who got the shaft. He's good at that."

"Wait!" Stewart shouted. "Look, I'll level with you. I'm not a damned bill collector. I haven't even paid last month's phone bill myself, and they're threatening cut-off." Thinking fast, Stewart added, "I'm a starving Greenwich Village writer. Porno novels. Okay? I still need your help."

"Interesting. Well, in that case, go ahead."

"This Garrett—I don't care one iota if he was a bedroom buddy or not—he's blackmailing a friend of mine. Some lives have been lost and more are on the line. Your former lover, roommate, whatever, is a rotten apple, pal."

The young man's eyes left Stewart, focused on the floor as if to burn it with pain. Angrily, he said, "I hate that cheap bastard. Especially now, when he's come into a few bucks and could pay back what he owes me."

"Money? From where?" asked Stewart.

"I don't know. But he appears to have plenty of it. He probably got it from some rich sugar daddy he met at the gym. All Dennis ever thought about was weight lifting in front of a mirror. I called him Grunt. What else do you want to know?"

"Relax. You're doing fine. What's your name?"

"Tim."

"Mine's Kirk," Stewart said warmly, extending his hand. "Don't stop now, please. It's important. Where did he go?"

Tim's eyes took on a damp, depressed look. He thought for a moment, then said, "He left me a note, addressing it *'Mon Cher,'* mind you. Said he was headed for Los Angeles. That's a laugh. I know better. He's gone to New York to see Freighter."

"Freighter?" Stewart already had a pen in hand, Metz's address book open to a blank page.

"That's his name. They're ex-lovers. He owns a biker bar off Second Avenue called Le Brute."

Stewart finished writing, looked up, and asked, "Tim, tell me. You ever hear Garrett mention the name Metz? Arnold Metz?"

"I don't remember."

"Does the name Warren Backer mean anything to you?"

"No."

"Any calls from Texas that you know of? How about TV producers, cameramen friends?"

"Sorry, but Dennis was secretive, almost led two lives. A Gemini. I'm not much help."

Stewart tucked the address book and pen away and started for the door. "On the contrary. Thanks."

"These TV production types. If you find them, send them my way. I'm studying drama at the Shaw Conservatory. Contacts, you know."

"Sure, Tim. I'll work on it."

"Oh, Kirk? Being from out of town, you have a place to stay?" The question had a coquettish tone.

"Yeah. Don't worry about it."

"Just thinking, if Garrett should call or if I remember something else."

Stewart tightened. "I'll be working out at the Rhode Island Avenue YMCA around dinnertime. Call and leave word, have them post the message on the bulletin board. My first name's good enough." He smiled at Tim. "Thanks for the help." Stewart strode out of the building.

He heard Tim's fluted voice trail off. *"À bientôt, mon ami."*

The telephones hurriedly being installed in the thirtieth-floor penthouse suite at the Potomac Plaza Hotel were not the ordinary type. The five technicians placing them were microwave relay engineers. Three worked for Condor Defense Industries

out of the Hartford Electronics Division; the other two came
from Condor's Citadel facility in California. The busy quintet
had not only top secret military clearance but CIA credentials
as well. The man in charge was Sam Wadislow. A lean, balding
engineer who had worked for Condor since earning his doctoral
degree at M.I.T., Wadislow had thin gray hair combed over
his crown and a gaunt face as white as a cadaver. His teeth
were uneven, and he wore steel-rimmed glasses that had been
mended with black electrical tape.

For the past half-hour the Potomac Plaza's owner, Karl
Frober, had tried to avoid Wadislow's morguelike face. The
studious, shy electronics genius, Frober thought, could easily
have been mistaken for New York's mad bomber of the sixties.

"Excuse me, Mr. Frober, I need you," Wadislow said, looking up from his intense perusal of a wiring diagram on his
work table.

Frober sighed and maneuvered his paunch away from the
window. He had been staring aimlessly across the Potomac
toward Roosevelt Island and, beyond it, the Virginia suburbs.
"Yes, Wadislow?"

"You'll have two direct ties to American Tel's Long Lines
Center in New Jersey. And we've given you three additional
circuits to each of the major TV networks in New York. There's
another line to Singer's office at CIA headquarters in Virginia.
But if you want the Pentagon feed as well, we'll have to lose
one of those pirated relays at AT&T's Bedminster Control Center—possibly the international circuit to Haiti."

Frober frowned. "The direct link with the Haiti operation
is imperative. And so is the Pentagon. Eliminate one of the
New York circuits and substitute."

"Good," replied Wadislow. "There's no time to add another
tie."

"Tell me, how many undercover men can we count on at
the Bedminster Long Lines Center?" asked Frober.

"Four. All members of the Freedom Militia. Over a dozen
other key AT&T technicians will require someone riding shotgun over their shoulder. I'm still working on it."

"Reinforce your crew with those Nazi cadres in Newark."

Frober turned away from Wadislow, examining the wiring
diagrams on the work table until he found the blueprint of the
United States, Alaska, and Hawaii. Once more he carefully
traced the colored tapes that formed a chromatic spiderweb

from city to city—the all-important auxiliary communication network that would be activated, along with the satellite systems, on Friday. He looked at it, satisfied. Norman Gifford had been right: Sam Wadislow was brilliant. He and his men had done a magnificent job. Frober knew that at a given signal, thousands of circuits—both domestic and international—would be cut including the entire Washington, D.C., switchboard, for a twenty-four-hour period, perhaps longer. Only the Committee's emergency network, along with military and CIA radio traffic, would be permitted to function during that time.

Sam Wadislow returned to supervise his assistants in a far corner of the room. Frober sat down before the diagrams and made several notations. Running his fingers repeatedly through his crew cut, he exhaled slowly. He thought about the Committee's headquarters arrangements. Their temporary command office was supposed to have been informal, simple, but already technical complications had made the site look like a Red Cross disaster center. The one-year-old Potomac Plaza was not the most exclusive of Frober's international chain of hotels, but it was the newest, and by sheer height alone, commanded the most beautiful view in Washington. The Committee had chosen it for a headquarters, not only because his price was right—gratis—but for its easy access to Fort Myers, the Pentagon, and the expressway leading to CIA headquarters in Virginia.

Frober and Jimmy Hallowell had taken rooms down the hall from the Committee office after arriving in Washington several hours earlier by commercial jet. Norman Gifford had remained behind in southern California to attend to last-minute satellite communications problems at the Citadel. Gifford intended to fly to the capital later that night in Condor's corporate jet.

To Frober's disappointment, Jimmy Hallowell had shown no interest in the elaborately equipped penthouse command center. After checking into his own suite, he had gone directly to meet with his friend, Vice-President Chandler.

Frober took off his tie and put it in his pocket. The room was warm and he was perspiring. It wouldn't do any good to check the thermostat; he was always warm when others were comfortable. It wasn't the flab, he reasoned. It had to be his metabolism.

One of the telephones in the room rang shrilly, surprising Frober. The system wasn't scheduled to become operative for another twenty-four hours. Then he saw it wasn't one of the red, blue, or green phones, but the black instrument beside the sofa—the hotel switchboard line. He picked it up.

"Frober here."

"This is Lynx."

"We can't talk; this is an open line. I'll meet you in thirty minutes. Wednesday's RP, understood?" Frober hoped that Lynx would not forget their arrangements. RP meant "rendezvous point." Any emergency meeting on Wednesday was to take place at the Lincoln Memorial. On Thursday the location was to be the Lee Mansion at Arlington.

"I remember perfectly," said Lynx. "I have a tight schedule, so please be on time."

19

"Look, Stewart. I need your cooperation. Metz has disappeared. And you could be next on his hit list."

Stewart looked at Oliver Wright, cautiously measuring him. "I'm already aware of that."

Smelling of furniture wax and stale cigar smoke, the FBI chief's sumptuous office was too large for Stewart's taste. The high wood-inlay ceiling, nine-foot glass-enclosed bookcases, a fireplace big enough to thaw a castle, combined with the sheer size of Oliver Wright himself, made Stewart feel small and inconsequential. On the far wall, a portrait of J. Edgar Hoover glared down at him disapprovingly. Without Motti Barak at his side, Stewart felt eerily alone.

"Where's my old classmate, Nelson?" he asked, abruptly changing the subject.

Wright sat back in his chair and propped his feet up on an open desk drawer. "Tap took three days' vacation time to extend the upcoming weekend. Ski trip up to Stowe."

"This week—*now?*" Stewart asked, making no effort to hide his incredulity.

"Nelson's a press agent, not a cop. His office is covered. What's the problem?"

"Nothing. Just that, if it hadn't been for him, I damned well wouldn't be here in the first place."

Wright smiled. "Correction. If it weren't for the FBI, you probably would have remained in that closet long enough for Arnold Metz to return. The damned peregrine might not have killed you, but Metz would have." Wright paused. "I'll be talking with Nelson later on the phone. I'll give him your condolences."

Stewart winced. He sat for a moment. "You seem to have all the particulars on Galveston." He glanced at his watch. The FBI chief's interrogation had been going on for a half-hour, and he was tired of questions. His bandaged finger and shoulder were bothering him again.

Wright looked at him. "O'Laughlin in Houston is one of my best men, but not *quite* as sharp as I hoped. Up until the minute you walked into my office, we were convinced you were one of the charred remains aboard that jumbo jet."

Stewart smiled. Now, he reasoned, was the time. Reaching into his pocket, he withdrew two folded pices of paper. The Xerox copies contained only the addresses of Dennis Garrett and Colonel Pete Reddick, plus the animal code names from the last page in Metz's address book. Stewart knew that if he wanted to strengthen his own or Barak's hand, he couldn't turn over the entire booklet and the mysterious phone numbers on the invitation. He wanted to check a few things out before the FBI clamped an iron hand on him. He tossed the papers across the desk.

"What's this?" asked Wright, sourly. "A feeding list from a zoo? And who are Garrett and Reddick?"

"Garrett's the gay blade who's been threatening the President. Don't bother with that address. As might be expected, he's skipped town. Who the colonel might be is anyone's guess, but his autographed picture was on Arnold Metz's wall. As was Garrett's."

Wright looked at Stewart shrewdly. "These are copies. Where's the original?"

"A confidential source has it," lied Stewart effortlessly. "It's an entire address book, but the sampling you have there should keep the Bureau occupied. Metz isn't the only one who wants the book."

"I don't like being jacked around, Stewart. Who wants these names *besides* Metz? Your suspect?"

"I don't *suspect,* and I'm not second-guessing. I *know.* The Klan's Exalted Archon, Bobby Harrington. The question is, who are he and Metz working for?"

Stewart felt disappointed; even the mention of Harrington's name did not seem to move Wright. Stolidly, the big man continued to study the documents.

Stewart wanted to help, but he wasn't sure about Wright. He wasn't sure any longer about anyone in the government. Withdrawing from his pocket the paper that bore the pencil-shaded phone numbers, he held it in his lap and unobtrusively tore off the bottom set of digits and his accompanying notation. He tossed it on Wright's desk. Stewart waited, then asked. "You want to help? Why did Shira Bernstein have this unlisted capital number in her possession?"

Oliver Wright looked at Stewart stonily. "Warren Backer is an alias of the head of the CIA. You might as well know. It's time somebody blew Singer's goddamn useless cover."

Stewart was stunned.

Wright calmly continued. "Singer is cunning. His fingers are everywhere, like a horny octopus. But he doesn't have access to the megabucks. I'm looking for the money men. There's a hidden chain of command out there. Somebody hired Garrett and Metz. Whoever the bastards are, they're also stirring up the Klans and the recruiting mercenaries for some nefarious purpose. I've got my own sleepers over at CIA, and their communications are clean. The top money man can't be Singer." Wright held up Stewart's notes, shook them, and growled, "You toss me crumbs I've already tasted, and for this I'm supposed to be grateful? I want it all."

Stewart's neck muscles stiffened. Was the FBI chief lying through his teeth? Stewart had to stall. He watched Wright once more run his finger down the list of animal names, considering them individually, along with the numbers that followed.

"Interesting," Wright said. "One of these names is familiar. And the post office boxes are a start."

"I'm surprised you didn't have observers at that Klan rally. And what about the attempt on my life at the hotel?"

Wright scratched his nose and smiled. "We're not as inefficient as you think. We had a man assigned to Jamesboro. He had his eye on Harrington but had no reason to know of you. Quite frankly, I wish I'd never heard of you. You've suddenly become a superdome headache, Stewart. As for the character you bopped on the head at the hotel, that's still a civil matter. The police first have to ask for Bureau help."

"Have they?"

Wright nodded. "Two men from our local office are on the way out to the Merrimont-Arlington now. Stewart, we need that entire address book."

"And so do I." Leaning forward, Stewart said eagerly, "Mr. Wright, I obviously made a mistake getting involved in all this, but that's beside the point now. Shira Bernstein was involved up to her pretty neck, and she's been killed. I want to know why. And the public has the right to several answers as well." Stewart paused, watching Wright gather up his thoughts, then continued, "Now I'm on a damned hit list. I'm a reporter, Mr. Wright, and I smell a sour wind. A conspiracy, a cabal, you name it. You're the professional investigator. To me, it's become more than a story. If some kind of cataclysmic event is about to hit the country in the solar plexus, John Q. Public needs to be warned. What's the CIA director up to? That list— codes, whatever it is—should be worth some information in return. Say a reasonable explanation, a hint of what you're after? And don't give me one of those shrugs and need-to-know excuses. If I'm on a shit list, doomed to die, I have a right to know why."

Oliver Wright placed the material Stewart had given him in his center drawer, closed it, then straightened his regimental stripe tie and pushed out his chin. Soberly he said, "You're not going to die, my friend, if you continue to cooperate. Who is this Motti Barak you mentioned earlier and what's his involvement?"

Stewart felt trapped. He thought for a moment. "He saved my life. I promised I'd say nothing about him."

Wright frowned. "You've already told me he traveled with you."

"Information you'd have routinely discovered in a matter of hours from the hotel's registration clerk or airline records."

"Come off it, Stewart. Don't pitch me this reporter-not-revealing-his-source bullshit. Start at the top."

Stewart rose to his feet and calmly walked over to the window. Already the rush-hour traffic on Pennsylvania Avenue had begun. "Sorry, Mr. Wright. Placing my own safety on the edge or otherwise, my word still carries a little weight."

"Jesus Christ!" grumbled Wright, his fingers drumming the desk. Brows furrowing, he said, "You're holding out on us, Stewart, and that's a mistake. A big one."

"So what else is new? The damned Bureau's holding out on the press, Mr. Director. You're perched right on top of a powder keg, and you're scared shitless. Well, who isn't? Obviously, you don't want the *New York Times* or any other paper to know your worst suspicions. Not yet, at least. And so you're depriving the American people of important facts—facts that could affect their immediate welfare."

"Listen, my friend. Lay off the platitudes. I may be sitting on a powder keg, but you're on a soapbox. Get off before you fall off. Cooperate and I'll make another deal with you."

"What kind of deal?" Stewart asked glumly.

"Go find this associate of yours—this Israeli. What's his name?"

"Barak. Motti Barak."

Wright scribbled a notation on a pad before him. "Return here with Barak first thing in the morning, and you'll get the full story."

Stewart didn't immediately respond. Careful, he thought. A trap? "That's up to the major. Barak's strange. I'm not sure he's interested in the FBI's help."

Wright pulled the cellophane off a cigar and bit off the end. "Possibly, maybe so. But a good reporter needs an inside track, Stewart. And you're a good reporter. What's the slant on your story now? Should you go ahead and file it? A twisted, convoluted bucket of tripe, that's what it is. There's danger in dealing with things as you would like them to be, rather than as they are." Wright paused, tapping his desk with a pencil. "What, for example, do you know about the STOL press preview tomorrow at Andrews Air Force Base?"

Stewart shrugged. "The announcement of a new military transport?" He came away from the window, closer to Wright's desk. "Not my department. I'm sure our Washington bureau or our aviation editor is on top of it."

Lighting the cigar, Wright blew a cloud of smoke across his desk toward the small framed picture of his wife and children, over the manila file folder with Stewart's name on the tab. There was a secret smile on his face as he said, "Perhaps, Stewart, *you* should cover that story."

"I'll think about it, Mr. Director." He started for the door.

"If you want to save the taxpayers some money, forget about having me followed. I'll tell you where I'm going. I'm heading for the Y to work out, take a swim, and hit the spa. I'll call Barak from a pay phone. If he's had a change of heart, we'll touch base with you first thing in the morning. If not, I'll grab the first available flight to New York. I'll be back at my *Times* desk by noon tomorrow."

"If you're smart, anywhere you stay in Washington you'll use a false name."

Stewart looked at Wright. "I'm ahead of you. Already registered under the name of Allan Baker."

Wright nodded. "You feel safe walking out of here alone?"

"Emphatically. I had an FBI agent in tow when I played great white hunter in that swamp, and look what happened to my shoulder. Thanks for your time."

Stewart left the room and closed the heavy walnut door behind him. He felt better, but still he cursed his old classmate Tap Nelson for having left him to face the Bureau wolves alone. Hastening out of the building, Stewart considered Oliver Wright's proposal as well as the alternatives. Once more he cursed his fevered imagination and tried to shut out the image of a hired killer relentlessly stalking him. The vision wouldn't go away.

At CIA headquarters in Virginia, Walter Singer sat at his desk and cracked his knuckles. It had been quiet since Norman Gifford's dismal call from Los Angeles, he thought. Too quiet. His spacious contemporary office with its chrome and glass furnishings had suddenly begun to close in on him. Usually the phone would be ringing off the hook, his appointment schedule would be jammed, and he'd be running late. This afternoon's solitude was his own doing; he needed several hours to think and plan, and his secretary was holding all calls. Those who needed to reach him had his unlisted number.

Singer nervously checked his watch. Nearing quitting time and still no word from the chairman of the Joint Chiefs on whether he had been able to postpone the SAC practice alert at Omaha on Friday. General Brady, too, was due to report in, let Singer know if the Committee could count on the support of U.S. Marine helicopter squadrons based at Oceana, Maryland, and Santa Ana, California.

The CIA director's eyes wandered to the trophy wall on one

side of his office. The large bronze commendation from the American Legion was tilted to one side. Singer frowned. Damn the sloppy night crew and their feather dusters. Rising from his desk, he strode across the room and straightened the plaque. Once more he scanned the inscription on the award, pleased with what he saw: "For Tireless Speaking Engagements on Behalf of Vietnam MIA Personnel." Singer strolled back to his desk and sat, but his focus remained on the cluster of commendations.

Singer had long been aware of his strengths, and he took pleasure from them. His hatred of liberals had grown several-fold since being appointed head of the CIA. Now, once again, his seething contempt for collectivism in general, big government and the current President in particular, penetrated his consciousness. His falling-out with the Oval Office had festered for a year, and now it was an open, terrible wound. Secretly, he hoped the President would refuse to be intimidated by the Committee's blackmail attempt. Then Arnold Metz could do his job.

Singer grimaced at the thought of Dennis Garrett. *Playgirl* foldout material or not, Garrett was a pansy, and Singer detested homosexuals. The plan had been Karl Frober's, and Singer had only reluctantly gone along with it. The EMR weapon would be a much better solution. Singer again considered the instructions he would send to Metz. The gun merchant—assassin, with his veins full of ice water, was a necessary member of the team, but like a dangerous, caustic substance, he had to be kept at arm's length. Thank God there was Lynx.

Singer exhaled wearily, spun in his chair, and picked the silver-framed photo enlargement of his mother from the credenza. It was dusty, as was the polished bronze bust of actor John Wayne beside it. Turning the portrait over in his hands and wiping the gloss on his sleeve, he thought of Angela Mae Singer over at the exclusive Seaview Rest Home in Baltimore. On impulse, he kissed the portrait. He'd neglected to send her flowers on the first of the week, as was his custom. Singer decided to take along yellow roses when he visited her to-morrow. He returned the picture to its place of prominence and ran his handkerchief quickly over the Wayne bust, at the same time cursing the janitorial staff.

Rubbing his reddish-blond mustache, Singer sat forward. His mind clicked and changed gears. Withdrawing from his desk drawer a large pad of tracing paper, a compass, and a calculator, he went to work. Singer unfolded a map of the East Coast and neatly taped a sheet of transparent paper over the area where Chesapeake Bay entered the Atlantic. He found several latitude and longitude notations he had jotted down on the side of the map, and picked up his calculator and a sharp pencil. He would now resolve several questions, the foremost of which was the time it would take two 747 passenger jets departing Washington, D.C., to reach the Bermuda Triangle.

Stewart hesitated outside a pay phone in the YMCA lobby. He knew he couldn't reach Carlie Chavez until after six-thirty when she finished her taping. He decided to place the call at a quarter to seven and in the meantime get some exercise.

The gym was crowded with businessmen and government employees seeking after-five workouts, and Stewart had no difficulty finding a racquetball partner. His opponent, a wiry assistant curator at the Smithsonian, was good, and after only one set Stewart had to beg off. The shoulder and finger were giving him a bad time, and he was outclassed. Dripping with sweat, he padded down to the gym and checked out a basketball. For a half-hour he practiced lay-ins with his good arm. Stewart knew he had to keep moving. Keep the body in gear, the mind idling. Events had accelerated beyond belief. The time had come to think ahead, not back to Shira. He had to be on guard, plan carefully, let go of retribution. Smoldering revenge would only keep him off balance.

Stewart had the court to himself. At the foul line he sank three shots in a row, missed the fourth and fifth. Unable to concentrate, he glanced nervously at every new face that entered the gym. Relax, he thought. Metz may be out there, but it was a big city. Damn this sociopath who felt no guilt, simply didn't understand remorse. And the others! Misdirected paranoids. Conventional wisdom wouldn't work against men of this mold, he reasoned. They were all as mad as hatters.

Another ball went through the hoop with a clean swoosh. Stewart shook his head. God Almighty, why was he labeling everyone else a Freudian delight, when he himself was learning the real meaning of fear and panic?

Leaving the gym, Stewart went into the weight room, tried some sit-ups, but found them impossible. His shoulder still bothered him. He disliked the area anyway, the closed-in stuf-

finess, the sour smell of dirty socks and sweat. After ten minutes in the bubbling spa and an equal time in the shower, he
felt invigorated. No time for a swim tonight. Dressing quickly,
he headed for the front desk. There might be a message from
Motti. Nothing in his box, but he spotted a memo bearing the
name Kirk tacked to the cork bulletin board behind the counter.
The clerk handed Stewart the note, and he read it quickly. Not
from Major Barak, but a Timothy Harris. A number to call,
as soon as possible. Then Stewart remembered. Tim. Dennis
Garrett's former roommate in Georgetown.

Stewart retreated inside one of the lobby phone booths,
inserted a coin, and dialed the number on the note.

"Hello." The voice at the other end sounded agitated.

"This is Kirk Stewart, the writer, remember?"

"I remember. Can you talk? Are you alone?"

"You've got it."

Stewart heard a heavy sigh. Tim's epicene voice began
slowly. "It's like—well, like this. After you left, I did some
thinking. I remembered what Dennis said about this fascist,
right-wing congressman he knows. The dude's the biggest per-
vert on Capitol Hill, bar none. The prick is also a first-class,
two-faced hypocrite."

"Hold it, Harris. Who you talking about?"

"I'm getting to that. This congressman's palsy-walsy with
Jimmy Hallowell and the Moral Confederation, condemning
us as fags and dykes on one hand, then patronizing us on the
other, as long as we bring him a few lines of premium coke.
A two-face. You get the picture?"

"All ears, pal, but what's the connection?" The booth was
warm, and Stewart had to partially open the door. He glanced
around outside. No one nearby.

Tim's voice continued. "Okay. I called this friend of mine,
Karen. She used to be pretty thick with Garrett. Platonic, you
know? She likes to talk. I may have struck pay dirt for you.
She reminded me of a party we all attended at the congressman's
house in Virginia when his wife was out of town. Karen and
her girlfriend were a part of the floor show."

"Yeah, I follow. So Karen's kinky. Go back, Tim. What
congressman?"

"Schmidt. Hank Schmidt of Nevada."

Stewart's breath caught in his throat. Schmidt's bigoted remarks to the press were nothing new, and there had been a few

tabloid tales about the notorious partygoing member of the House, but they all paled in comparison to this story. "Go on, Tim," he said, anticipating the worst.

"These two women overheard Schmidt talking to Garrett off to one side, by the Jacuzzi. Something about making a TV clip, a commercial for some defense plant out west. Condor Industries, I think. Karen also told me the name Metz rang a bell. Possibly an acquaintance of Congressman Schmidt, or they met him through Garrett.

Stewart felt a clutch in his stomach. His mind whirled. "This Karen and the other girl who heard this. Can I meet them?"

There was a pause, a short laugh. "Sure, why not? You're in luck. Karen and Wanda hate Schmidt's guts. But they're broke and money talks. Remember the golden rule: those that have the gold make the rules. They're putting on another little show for him tonight. You game for going out to Falls Church and dropping in on them unannounced? The ladies could care less. The more the merrier."

Stewart swallowed hard. Convenient, he thought. Another damned seamy corruption story, his for the asking. "What time?"

"Between seven and eight. You want me to pick you up?"

"You're on, friend."

"Be out front in an hour. I'll be in a red Fiat Spyder." Tim hung up.

Congressman Hank Schmidt, you sly bastard, thought Stewart, smiling, staring at the phone. Stewart glanced at his watch. *Carlie!* He'd almost forgotten. Reaching for his wallet, he found the long-distance credit card and Carlie's office number.

Seconds later he heard her not-so-cheerful voice.

"Hi, Carlie," Stewart said quickly. "Go ahead. I'm prepared for the worst. What's going on?"

"Kirk, you were right. There's double trouble here. I'm frightened. I want you to get out of this and return home now."

"That sounds like an order."

"Take it any way you like. I received a warning call about you this morning. From some goon calling himself Lynx. And the network isn't alone in receiving those threatening letters. A prominent rabbi was threatened—the same letter format—and told not to appear on my show today. What's more—"

"Slow down, Carlie. Better yet, stop. You're talking in circles. What happened?"

"More than I can explain now. I can't talk, Kirk. Alan Simon

and my producer are with me. An emergency meeting. We
need to hash this out before I can give you any more details.
I need another hour. Trust me."

"Always have, baby, but how much do they know?"

"Look, do me a favor and call back later? Make it at home,
okay?"

Stewart thought quickly. "Forget the phone, Carlie. I'll catch
the ten-thirty Eastern commuter flight. Be a sweetheart and
wait up? I'll grab a cab in from La Guardia. We'll talk when
I get there."

Her voice grew increasingly nervous. "Fine. Eat light and
I'll fix a midnight supper. Bye, Kirk."

He replaced the phone on the hook and exhaled sharply.
Stewart made one more call, this time to the Israeli embassy.
He asked for the military attaché's office and then Major Motti
Barak, but was surprised to hear that they had not seen Barak
for several weeks. They assumed the major was in London.
Stewart replaced the receiver and swore.

At Dulles International Airport, the United flight operations
manager strode up to the dispatch counter where one of the
airline's senior pilots impatiently waited for him.

"Well, Chief?" the pilot asked irritably. "Were you able to
clear the air or not? I know the length of that Haiti airfield.
But how thick is the macadam?"

The operations executive shook his head. "Here's all I have.
Don't waste your time with it. There's still no additional data."
He flipped the aeronautical chart across the counter.

The pilot looked at him, grabbed the document, and stuffed
it inside his bulging briefcase. "I asked for specific runway
conditions for the new field at Gonave Island two weeks ago.
I've sent three teletypes since and gotten nothing but 'Details
forthcoming' in return."

The man behind the counter shrugged. "You ever try to get
anything but French and Pidgin English out of Haiti?"

"Fine. What the hell's going on down there? They still
pouring concrete? I'll tell you one thing, pal. I can't speak for
the pilot of the second plane, but *I'm* not setting a 747 down
on a two-bit strip that hasn't been certified for jumbos."

"Agreed. Relax, Captain. You'll have the necessary information by Friday morning."

"If not, your special passengers will land at Port-au-Prince, and they'll have to swim across. Goddamn island, I never heard of it before. When do we find out who we're working for on this one?"

The operations manager paused to light a cigarette, then shook his head. "You know military charters. Stamp 'Classified' on a purchase order and nobody dares ask questions."

"Except the pilot. When the hell is this party to Haiti coming back? It's a one-way charter!"

"Search me. I was told they'd make other return arrangements. Sharing the wealth with Pan Am or TWA, probably."

Leaning forward across the counter, the pilot crooked his finger. Softly he said, "Just between you and me, I'll wager a day's wages we're sending six or seven hundred of those illegal aliens back to Haiti."

"Get your smart ass out of here, Captain. I'll see you Friday."

The pilot wagged his finger like a metronome. "I still say we're ferrying unemployed Haitains home." He started for the door, but the operations manager called him back.

"Maybe so," he said slowly, his eyes scanning Friday's work sheet. "But they're sure as hell dining in elegance. These passengers get the red carpet menu—Strasbourg paté, a choice of butterfly steak or poached salmon, truffles, Paul Masson cabernet sauvignon 1979, and a full selection of after-dinner liqueurs."

20

STEWART FELT THE sports car shudder as Tim Harris raced through the gears, maneuvering the Fiat out into the Route 50 traffic. The top was down and it was noisy, the wind tearing through his hair and biting at his ears. Stewart didn't feel like shouting, so he kept to himself. Above him, the Washington sky was gray and baleful, hiding the moon. The night was cool, but not the usual cold of January.

Harris had a heavy foot, Stewart mused, thinking of his own VW Rabbit convertible, which he kept in storage eighty percent of the time in Manhattan. It had plenty of get up and go, too, and Stewart drove it fast. But not this fast. Stewart's knuckles whitened against the dash as Harris careened in and out of the fast lane, intimidating slower traffic.

Stewart pressed back in the bucket seat. He'd subjected himself to far worse than a good story. And this was far more than a story. Tim Harris's two women friends appeared to be a good lead, possibly a critical one.

At Seven Corners, Harris turned off the Leesburg Pike, then drove less than a mile into Falls Church and turned right again. After a third and fourth right, the Spyder's left signal light blinked on, and they pulled into a quiet residential street that ran slightly uphill. The suburban homes were spacious, with large, neatly landscaped lawns. Harris braked and parked behind a Toyota Corolla with D.C. plates.

"This is it," he said.

Stewart nodded, climbed out of the car, and inspected the house as best he could in the darkness. It was a two-story Greek Revival structure with black shutters and colonnaded portico. The only lights inside came from a large window at ground level. As they proceeded up the walk Stewart could see through the translucent draperies into a long, narrow living room decorated in Early American. The room appeared to be unoccupied. Harris pushed the button beside the front door, and they heard a harmonic chime that sounded like "How Dry I Am."

Stewart smiled. "What makes you think they'll invite us in, Harris?"

"Should have brought a bottle for the ladies, I suppose. Don't worry. Congressman Schmidt likes me—or seemed to, last time we met. You have some kind of cover worked up? The porno writer jazz might not play so well with a House member. And please call me Tim."

"Yeah. About the cover. How about a Hollywood stunt man? My brother's the legit thing, and I've heard his lines often enough to quote from memory."

"Suit yourself," Tim replied, grinning.

Stewart pushed the button this time. They waited, but there was no response.

Tim looked at his watch. "We're early. Probably they're out back in the Jacuzzi." Gesturing toward the side of the house, he led Stewart across a path of flagstones to a tall, latticed gate. From somewhere on the other side came the sound of music.

Stewart shook his head, pointing to the Guard Dog on Duty sign nailed to the gate. "Hold it, pal. You know the pooch well enough to make a proper introduction?"

"Relax," said Tim. "It's a scam. The congressman's wife has a silly Afghan that pisses at the sight of its own shadow. If she's gone, the dog's with her. Tim opened the gate and proceeded down the side walkway. Stewart followed. The side and rear yards of the house were hidden from neighbors' prying eyes by tall Italian cypresses growing so close together they formed a hedge.

Rounding the corner, Stewart saw a Roman-style swimming

pool, nude statuary, a cabana that looked like a guest house for a Jean Harlow movie, and beside it, a steaming spa. A kaleidoscope of Malibu garden lights lent a carnivallike atmosphere to the scene. Whoever planned the yard had not consulted with the original architect, Stewart mused. It was a southern California dream exported to the East. The large swimming pool, lined with garish red and blue tiles, had been drained for the winter.

From beside the spa, a portable cassette player blared Carly Simon's "You're so Vain." Tim pointed to the vapor-clouded Jacuzzi and what looked to be two heads resting against the coping. Behind them on the deck was a decanter of white wine, a trio of half-filled glasses, and a neat stack of bath towels.

"Surprise company," Tim called out musically.

The heads didn't turn toward them. They didn't hear; the stereo was too loud, thought Stewart. He wondered why the neighbors weren't complaining.

Tim moved in closer, this time shouting, "Karen! Wanda!"

Still no response. Stewart was getting edgy. As they approached the octagonal spa, the steam took on a nightmarish pink glow. Stewart saw why. The water was a bright crimson.

Stewart felt stunned, fixed to the deck like the surrounding statues. It was a scene from Dante's *Inferno,* with a sticky sweet smell of blood in the air. He watched Tim Harris slowly circle the bubbling pool, pause, and spasmodically stoop to turn off the cassette player. He gazed dumbly back at Stewart, his mouth half open, his hands visibly trembling. "Jesus Christ," he whispered. "Holy Jesus Christ."

Stewart felt a numbness entirely new to him. Without the music, the drone of the pump and gurgling water seemed louder, more insistent. The two women, bullet holes in their throats and chests, stared into nothingness with the blank look of glazed dolls on the shelf of a carnival arcade.

"My God," moaned Tim.

"Listen to me. Keep your voice down," Stewart ordered, his eyes on the house. A light burned in an upstairs rear room. "Tell me, Tim," he whispered. "Did the women know you were bringing me out here?"

"Uh, sure. I said something about this guy Metz, that you and Garrett knew in common. That you were curious about my ex-roommate's TV clip."

"What else?"

"That you were a mutual friend, that's all."

Stewart stiffened. "My *name*. Did you tell these people my name?" He had to struggle to keep his voice low.

"Well, yes. What was wrong with that?"

"Where did you call them from?" Stewart asked quickly.

"My place, where else? Don't you think we should call the police? I mean, Christ—"

Stewart turned away from the spa, grinding his fist into his other hand. He pulled it away, cursing. He'd forgotten the splinted finger. Stewart looked across the yard, back toward the house and the light upstairs, but his eyes hesitated as they swept by the lighted, drained swimming pool. There was something there.

Stepping over to the edge of the coping, he looked down. His heart caught in his throat as he stared at the slightly obese nude body lying face down on the bottom of the pool. Sprawled in a lake of congealed blood, his head canted grotesquely to one side and a bullet hole in his back, was Congressman Hank Schmidt.

Stewart swallowed back his bile. The end of a long-handled pool vacuum had been thrust into the victim's rectum in a sick punctuation.

Tim shuffled over to the edge of the pool, gave up a strangled gasp of his own. He backed away in shock. Stewart gently shook his shoulder. "Let's move out. I don't feel like being the only life of the party."

"Ditto on that," Tim replied, tearfully.

"We'll call the police later, from town. Right now I want to put some time and distance between us and these corpses."

They ran around the side of the house. Tim paused to open the gate. "What happened?" he whispered. "Was it drug-related? Karen and Wanda were a little kinky, maybe, but they never hurt anybody. How about the neighbors? Didn't anyone hear?"

Stewart cut across the front lawn, pulled open the car door, and slumped into the black leather seat. "The music. And maybe a silencer. Dammit, Harris. Get this bucket of bolts started!"

Tim threw himself behind the wheel, gunned the engine to life, and pulled out from the curb.

Staring back at the house, Stewart was surprised to see the light go out in the living room.

The Spyder made a swift U-turn, tore down the dark residential block, turned at the corner. Seconds later, eight blocks down the arterial, Stewart looked around and saw lights sweep out from Congressman Schmidt's street, hesitate, then head in their direction.

"We're being followed," he shouted to Harris. "Ever done any rally driving?"

"No, but I know how to handle this baby."

"Then move it." Stewart felt the car shudder as Tim hunched forward, shifted back into third, and tromped on the gas. Their lead on the car behind them had shortened, perhaps a third of a mile.

Stewart's heart began to thump. He instructed Tim to make several turns, circle around a large Falls Church supermarket. Tim's eyes flickered from the road ahead to the mirror and back to the road.

"Concentrate on the driving," Stewart admonished. "I'll keep watch behind." His heart sank when he saw the persistent sedan was still behind them, coming on fast.

Tim turned off the city street and headed for the expressway. "You paying for the ticket?" he asked, accelerating again.

Stewart nodded. "Just lose our friend before we get back to Washington."

There wasn't any question that Tim Harris made up his mind to do just that. Twice he suddenly swerved across lanes, ducking between large semi-trucks, then rocketing ahead in the slow lane, only to brake, slip sideways, and dodge through slower traffic to get ahead. Stewart tightened his seat belt. He sniffed the brisk wind to get the smell of death out of his nose. He felt like pushing his feet right through the floorboards. Either luck was with Tim, he thought, or the highway patrol was on its coffee break. No red lights appeared.

Stewart tried to piece together what had happened, but nothing made sense. Congressman Schmidt knew Arnold Metz; that had been established. They both were involved in, or knew about, the incriminating videotape. But they were both ultra-conservatives. Why would Metz kill Schmidt? To punish him for his betrayal? The two women had obviously talked; that gory scene made a small degree of sense. Apparently Metz and his friends would stop at nothing.

The Fiat's tires squealed as Harris once more dodged into the fast lane and accelerated. It wasn't until they had reached the Potomac and crossed the Rochambeau Bridge that Tim relaxed his grip on the wheel and slowed to the speed limit. Entering the tunnel under the Capitol Mall, he slowed the sports car even more, glanced at Stewart, and grinned. "We lost him. I think I need a drink."

Stewart did not return the smile. He was thinking about Tim's phone call earlier to his two women friends. "Look, buddy," he said seriously, "we've got a problem. I don't think it's safe for you to go back to your apartment. Don't ask me why. There isn't time to explain now. You'd better play it safe and spend the night elsewhere. Come to think of it, take my room at the Y. It's paid for, and I won't need it. I've had a sudden change of plans. I have to leave town tonight."

Tim looked frightened. 'The police. Can't we go to them now?"

"No, not the local gendarmes. I have my reasons." Stewart reached into his pocket and withdrew Arnold Metz's address book. "Take this. And here's the key to my room. You'll be safe there. Don't bother registering. I used a fake name anyway. Lock yourself in for the night. First thing in the morning take that booklet to Oliver Wright, head of the FBI. *No one else*, okay? Go to the reception desk, tell them you have to see the director, and don't let them put you down. Use my name and you'll get to him."

Tim looked at him askance. "Sure, referred by a porno writer. The Bureau's going to be impressed."

"Forget that crap. I'm a reporter, and he knows it. Give him the address book and explain what happened at Falls Church. Tell him about everything, your phone calls, the works. But *only* Oliver Wright. Understood?"

Tim nodded.

"Don't forget the details. Your life may depend on it."

The Fiat stopped at Constitution Avenue for a light. Eyes moist, Tim let out a quick sigh, turned, gave Stewart a bewildered look. "And you?"

"Take me back to the YMCA for my suitcase. I'll catch a cab out to National."

"I'll drive you."

"No, you won't. I don't want your face to be seen anywhere in Washington tonight. Sit tight and sleep soundly until Wright takes you under his wing tomorrow."

• • •

Arnold Metz reported to Lynx on the dot at ten-thirty, as requested. For some minutes he listened intently to instructions being given at the other end of the line. Then he began responding to the questions, one at a time. Almost all of his answers were in the affirmative.

"What name is he registered under?" Metz asked coolly.

"Allan Baker. Don't forget. Do you have enough money?" asked Lynx.

"Yes. Frober gave me more today. Expenses are the least of my concerns tonight," replied Metz, his eyes on the rental car he had left parked outside the telephone booth. Three black youths had ambled up beside it.

"And should be," came the voice of Lynx in the receiver. "We've come too far, too much has been accomplished for our work to be jeopardized by less than half a dozen people. Pull all the weeds out of the flower bed, Metz, or you will be treated like one of them."

"I'm doing what I can, but I'll need a few hours more. This isn't easy. We're leaving a trail of blood."

Lynx laughed, a tinny, uncomfortable sound in the receiver. "You're a hunter, Metz. A professional hunter. Don't sound so squeamish. I know better. Be imaginative and put that hunter's lust to work for us. Good-bye."

Metz replaced the receiver, exhaled slowly, and turned— to be confronted by a shiny switchblade held to his throat by a bearded black who had slipped up beside the booth.

"The keys to the car, baby. Quick and silent like if you're a smart dude. How much you got in your wallet? Anybody brave enough to stop and use a street phone in this neck of town can't have more than a couple of bucks on him. And maybe no brains either, huh, Bozo?"

Metz looked back into the uncompromising bloodshot eyes, saw the other two youths already in the front seat of his rented Fairlane, then looked up and down the street. Deserted, except for a cab waiting on the opposite corner for a light to change. The car keys were on the ledge beneath the pay phone. Slowly, Metz slid them off and extended them at arm's length.

The young man grinned, grabbed them away, and slowly backed off. "Easy come, easy go," he jived, bouncing back to the curb and tossing the keys to his friends inside the car. "Hey, man," he added, "almost forgot. Toss your wallet out here, okay? Let's just check out how much you got in there.

Got a little bet goin' with my buddies here, classifyin' and declassifyin' honky types."

Arnold Metz felt a familiar surge of pleasure as he reached inside his jacket, toward his hip, for the Luger pistol tucked in his waistband. He wasn't in the slightest hurry as he withdrew it, aimed carefully, and pulled the trigger. The gun roared, and blew a hole in the startled black man's chest. Moving the barrel a few degrees he aimed the gun at the open mouth staring at him from the car's passenger seat. Glass and blood exploded as the Luger went off again. Tires screeched in protest as the car tore away, the panic-stricken driver narrowly missing a fire plug as he wheeled around the corner and out of sight.

Metz swore. Not only were his personal belongings in the vehicle's trunk but his silencer was under the front seat. A silencer he had an immediate need for!

The taxi across the street drew swiftly up beside Metz. The driver already had the window rolled down. "Jesus!" he said. "I saw it all. Thought for sure you were going to get your throat slit. My radio dispatcher's already called the cops."

The gun barrel was too hot to tuck back in his waistband. Metz crammed it in his jacket pocket, unconcerned over the protruding handle. "You available for hire, cabbie?" he asked.

"If it's a local trip, you've earned yourself a free ride, pal."

Metz didn't thank him. Pondering a moment, checking his watch, he asked, "So how far is the YMCA?"

"Nine, maybe ten blocks."

"I'll ride. Take me there," Metz hissed impatiently. Silencer or no, he would still do the job, he reasoned. He was fully determined; his mind was calm now, as cool as a reptile's blood.

The night attendant at the Y's reception desk was an old man in his seventies with glasses and glistening white hair combed in an old-fashioned part far down one side. He glanced up from a copy of the *National Enquirer* as Metz approached the counter.

"You have an Allan Baker registered here?" Metz asked politely.

With a bored look, the old man flipped through the tab cards beside him, finally replied, "Yes. Room five-twenty. But you can't go up. No visitors after ten o'clock. I can buzz if you want him to come down to the lobby."

Metz thought for a moment, then quickly replied, "No, you're right. It's late. I'll come back tomorrow."

The old man turned back to his tabloid. Abruptly, Metz leaned across the counter and brought the full force of his Luger handle down on the clerk's head. Leaping over the counter, he was surprised to find the old man slumped in a wheelchair. Fuck! he thought. Piss-pot invalids! What next? Would the next obstruction be a helpless old blind lady? Swearing repeatedly to himself, he swiftly wheeled the bent-over form into an adjoining office. Removing the ring of pass keys attached to the clerk's waist, he withdrew, closed the door and locked it. Calmly, he walked out from behind the counter and proceeded across the foyer to the elevator. Once more he cursed softly at the loss of his silencer.

The fifth floor was quiet except for a shower running in the rest room at the end of the hall. As the elevator door closed behind him, Metz paused, considering his plan of attack. Across the hallway a janitor's closet door was slightly ajar. Metz opened it, surveying the contents. Utility sink, dust mops, broom, a floor waxer; on the shelf above, paper towels, toilet paper, and several cans of spray paint—no, not paint. Looking closer, he saw that the aerosol containers were insecticide bombs. Taking three of the canisters, Metz proceeded down the hallway until he found room 520.

Examining the three keys on the ring, he found one that was stamped "Master." Quietly, he slipped it into the lock, gently turned it, and eased the door open. Moving swiftly inside, he closed the door but didn't turn on the lights. The room was narrow; both the blinds and the window were open, admitting a chill breeze and the reflected gray light of the city. On the bed, a dark-haired man, breathing heavily, was sound asleep. Clothes were neatly folded over the back of a chair; a wallet, keys, and a Gideon bible lay on top of the chest of drawers. And something else. A small, very familiar leather-bound address book.

Metz scooped it up, thrust it in his pocket, then turned his attention to the form on the bed. He had initially planned to use the pillow, but flailing arms and thrashing kicks left something to be desired. It would be grotesque—an unpleasant way to kill, Metz reasoned. Pistol-whipping was equally gruesome, and there was a chance the man might survive. Metz couldn't afford to make a mistake. Why not be tidy for a change? He had something infinitely better. His mind drifted back to his dead Doberman and falcon, and his face hardened with renewed determination. Just a tap on Stewart's head would be enough to put his delicious little plan into effect.

The weapon caught the sleeping form just behind the ear. Metz tossed off the bedding and quickly dragged the limp body across the room to the small closet by the door. Within seconds he had crammed his victim inside the closet. Metz gathered the three aerosol cans with the skull and crossbones on their labels, placed them next to the body, and broke the release tabs. He swiftly closed the door. Piling sheets and blankets against the crack along the bottom, he stood back, completely satisfied. Then he left the room, locking the door behind him.

21

FOR THE MOMENT, Stewart felt reasonably safe. He was certain no one had spotted him at the Washington airport boarding the New York commuter plane. It was already after eleven. The taxi from La Guardia Airport dropped Stewart off at the liquor store on East Fifty-ninth Street, one he knew was open late. He paid and dismissed the driver, knowing the shop was only three blocks from Carlie's apartment on Sixty-first, just off Madison. Two bottles of Rothschild Mouton Cadet wouldn't add much weight to his flight bag and the walk in the invigorating night air would do him good, possibly revive his spirits.

Leaving the liquor store, Stewart glanced up at the sky. It was clearer here than in the capital, with a tawny full moon poking through the scattered clouds over Central Park. The neighborhood was busy enough to venture the walk to Carlie's and yet quiet enough to give Stewart several minutes to think. Grappling with his feelings, he thought of the missing persons report he had to file in the morning and the sad cable he would compose and send to Shira Bernstein's parents in Tel Aviv. He winced, remembering the tearful scene at the airport two years before as they had seen her father and mother off when the pair had emigrated to Israel. Shira had promised faithfully to fly over and see them during the summer. It swiftly came back to Stewart how she'd scraped and scrimped for the fare, and good-naturedly complained that he spent money like so much tap water. Free-lancing had just begun to pay off for Shira. Stewart remembered the banquet four months back, the Outstanding Writer Award presented to her by Columbia University's Journalism Club, how happy she'd been. Then her excitement over the expense-paid weekend for two she won in an Anti-Defamation League news article contest. Stewart had gone with her to Grossinger's Resort in the Catskills and had returned home three pounds heavier from too much sour cream, lox, and matzo ball soup. For two weeks after that, he'd done twice his usual number of monkey drills.

Now that Shira was gone, he was forced to face something he'd been avoiding, a latent feeling that her talents and causes had triggered. A secret envy? How long would the damned pall hang over him, the growing question of whether he'd given her his best part?

Stewart crossed Park Avenue and headed across Sixty-first toward Carlie's apartment building.

A young girl smiled as she passed by. Stewart smiled back. Her infectious grin reminded him of Carlie's. He suddenly wondered what it was about Carlotta Chavez that still fascinated, captivated him. Good looks, intelligence, plenty of it to spare, but many women had those qualities. Stewart knew it wasn't Carlie's success, her celebrity status that drew him. He'd never enjoyed showing off ornaments. If anything, a date on the town with the popular TV newswoman had its disadvantages. Privacy had always been important to him.

The building doorman recognized Stewart. He was expected. The elevator door slammed shut, the closeness tightening around his thoughts, suffocating him. It had to be Carlie's drive, as well as her talent. Not intellect alone, but her restless, volatile energy. No other woman he'd known had such overflowing vitality and expressed it so well. Small wonder her TV image moved millions from coast to coast. Carlie's good cheer, independence, and heady stubbornness were much like Shira's, but the similarity, Stewart knew, ended there.

Shira had described herself as a Marian the Librarian type. His lovable, calculating librarian, however, had brought home books like *The Joy of Sex, Occult Orgasm,* and other titillating volumes they had read together. As a couple they had tried their damnedest to discover the difference between concupiscent and benevolent love. He remembered Shira's peculiar sense of humor, how she'd once suggested a large mirror over their bed and a surrounding moat of baby alligators. Stewart had installed the mirror, but the rest of the design was thankfully impractical. She'd been forced to make do with two small rubber alligators he found at a novelty shop. Stewart could still see her laughing.

The elevator door slid open. Time to turn off the past, force Shira Bernstein completely out of his mind, and start thinking of Carlie Chavez. Worry about the business at hand, Stewart! Carlie was different, a world apart from Shira. With her, life was a matter of brandy stingers, Mantovani records, and satin sheets in alternating colors—all this depending on her mood or the position of the zodiac. Strange things, daydreams, Stewart reflected, as he stepped briskly down the hallway. When he gave himself up to a dream, it was difficult for him to snap out of it. He pushed the buzzer to Carlie's apartment, satisfied that she would have him back to reality in no time flat.

Carlie didn't come to the door; instead the latch buzzed. Stewart shoved the door open and went inside. The stereo was playing low, but he recognized the record: Rodrigo's *Fantasia para un gentilhombre for Guitar*. The music came back to Stewart quickly, the Andrés Segovia concert at Lincoln Center to which he had taken Carlie some time back, long before he had become so thick with Shira.

"Kirk? I'm in the kitchen!"

Stewart dropped his duffel by the door, withdrew the bottles of wine, and ambled along a long, parchment-white hallway lined with Sister Corita posters. He paused in the kitchen doorway, leaning against the jamb. "Do you always admit unseen strangers at this hour?"

Carlie was tossing a salad. She smiled, wiped her hands on her apron, and came up to Stewart. "I trust the doorman's judgment. He hasn't let me down yet."

"Good way for a sexy lady to get in trouble."

Softly, she said, "You were expected." She gave him a peck on the cheek, then stood back, carefully surveying him. "I'm sorry, Kirk. What can I say about Shira? The entire scene is unbelievable. For the last hour I've been mulling over just how to begin."

"Same here. My problem is deciding where to begin. A

helluva lot's happened since we talked on the phone." Stewart gestured over his shoulder. "The concert guitar. You being nostalgic for my sake?"

Carlie gave him a brief, sultry look, then quickly put it away. "It is a bit heavy, considering the time and topics at hand. What would you prefer?"

"Let it play." He pointed to the oven. "I smell roast beef." Stewart inhaled deeply, noticing another distinct odor: pipe smoke.

Carlie smiled, took his hand. "I forgot." Leading him into the small dining room, past the table set for two, she whispered, "I suspect you're starved, but the prime rib will keep in the warmer. We have an important guest whom I can't talk into joining us at the table."

They entered the living room. Stewart was surprised to see a white clerical collar, gray tweed suit, congenial middle-aged face, and a gangly frame of a man gather themselves together and rise from the sofa. The man with the gray curly hair, blue eyes, and briar pipe looked distinctly familiar.

Carlie made the introduction. "Kirk, this is a friend of mine. The Right Reverend Burgess Elliott, Episcopal bishop of New York."

The bishop smiled and extended his hand. He was a match for Stewart in height.

Carlie quickly added, "Bishop Elliott was being taped tonight, a panel forum at the network studio. I insisted he come over here afterward to meet you. Now maybe you can convince him to join us at the table."

Stewart grinned. "Carlie's a fine newscaster but a better cook, Bishop Elliott."

Elliott shook his head; he looked nervous and agitated. "I'll try to be quick and to the point."

"What he has to tell you isn't pleasant," Carlie warned Kirk.

"Relax, please," said Stewart, nodding to the sofa and taking a seat in a nearby stuffed chair. He glanced up at Carlie.

"The usual?" she asked. "Bombay on the rocks?"

Stewart nodded. Her voice was velvety soft, and he liked it. He watched her leave the room to fix his drink. As always, Carlie's walk was a subtle sexual dance. She was wearing a dark green slit-skirt lounging dress of velvet with elbow-length sleeves. Elegant, he thought. Carlotta Chavez was always elegant. Stewart exhaled wearily. The bishop's eyes were on him, noting his fatigue. Above the clergyman, a numbered serigraph of Philippe Noyer's *White Rolls-Royce* was the focal point of the room. The artist's subject matter—a young huntress in a pith helmet, accompanied by a bottle of Vat 69, a pet leopard, a cockatoo, a limousine, and a kimono-clad Oriental maiden— was too much for Stewart. Especially now, he mused, in contrast to the dignified figure of the bishop of the Episcopal diocese of New York, who sat quietly beneath it on the white satin sofa.

"I'm sorry, Bishop Elliott. Carlie's bizarre artwork distracted me."

Smiling, Elliott glanced over his shoulder. "Yes, engrossing to say the least." As he turned back to Stewart, his eyes lost their sparkle. "The program we taped tonight—a roundtable discussion group from Citizens for the American Way. I'm one of the co-chairmen, Rabbi Marks is the other. The remaining two board members are the Reverend Dr. Higgins of the United Methodist Church and Monsignor McGraw, president of Cleveland Catholic University. We all received threatening letters containing a warning about not appearing on the program."

Carlie reentered the room and quickly interjected, "Those letters were identical in format to the mail received by the network's board chairman, Kirk. That's why I felt you should talk with Bishop Elliott."

Stewart took the drink from her hand and ran the lemon wedge around the rim of the glass. "I've read about your organization's work, Bishop Elliott. Being a moderate, I'm impressed. It takes courage to form a counterforce to the self-righteous Jimmy Hallowell and his so-called Moral Confederation."

Burgess Elliott nodded gravely and sipped his brandy. "Carlotta, please. Before I proceed, show him that short TV interview you did with Hallowell—the videotape you played for me earlier."

Carlie went to the VCR unit in the corner, inserted a cassette, and turned on the television set. Seconds later, her own image appeared.

Stewart watched with interest as she asked Jimmy Hallowell why he believed that the fundamentalist ethic was the wisest course for America. The preacher thought for several seconds, smiled, and vigorously responded: "I stand by the penned words of our forefathers. The Mayflower Compact proclaims that 'We have come to these shores for the glory of God.' Are the news media aware of the Mayflower Compact?"

The camera cut to Carlie Chavez, who nodded. "Yes, Mr. Hallowell. We too have studied history and political science. Go on, please."

"'The glory of God,' it proclaimed. A born-again person understands when I shout, sing, yes—some of us even speak in tongues—about the glory of God. Not the glory of atheism, abortion, adultery, and so-called humanism. I'm tired of the liberals, the Commies, the perverts parading their pride. It's time for God's people to come out of the closet and change America!"

"But with belligerence? With sticks and stones?" Carlie asked.

"Whatever is necessary to do God's work," Hallowell answered, smiling.

Carlie turned off the videotape, came over and sat across from Stewart on the zebra skin and chrome chair, where the light of the table lamp fell softly on her face. Stewart studied her, impressed, as usual. He knew he could never intimidate Carlie with journalistic expertise. She was his equal. The bishop was speaking in a faraway voice, but Stewart wasn't listening.

Carlie frowned at Stewart, ending his mesmerized stare. He straightened in his seat and listened attentively as she said, "Hallowell sincerely believes he's trying to save America." She slowly shook her head. "He's only encouraging bellicosity, making people afraid."

"And fear is the fuel of the fanatic," Elliott added swiftly. The clergyman sipped his brandy. "Interesting, but sad. Throughout history, from the caveman to medieval times into modern history, the extremist has always looked over his shoulder, behind him, under the carpet. Superstition and paranoia are the worst manipulators of men's minds."

Stewart was tired. He had to force himself to respond. "Some people need to be manipulated; others don't. It's simple, in a way. They can blame it all on Satan. To quote one of my favorite comedians, 'The devil made me do it.'"

Elliott managed a weak smile. Eyebrows knitting, he leaned forward, "Bigotry in capital letters, I'm afraid. But Hallowell and his fanatic friends aren't alone. There are others."

"I'm frightened," interjected Carlie. "Tell Kirk what happened."

Elliott picked up his pipe, sucked on the stem, decided not to relight it. Tucking it in his pocket, he said, "One of the choir members at Saint John the Divine—a young man of German extraction who lives in Yorkville—defected from the congregation several months ago. He claimed, in an emotionally charged meeting with the cathedral canon and choirmaster, that he was joining a fundamentalist, born-again congregation and that he intended to sing with Jimmy Hallowell's Television Crusade. Of course we sorely missed his talent but wished him Godspeed." Elliott paused, studying Stewart and gathering his thoughts.

All Stewart could do was nod solemnly. He was hungry, and he found it difficult to concentrate. He wished the bishop would get to the point.

Burgess Elliott smiled mechanically. "The young man was a bit of a rebel before he came to us, it appears. He said his parents were backsliding Lutherans; they run a rowdy rathskeller on Eighty-sixth Street. To be brief, our young friend unexpectedly returned to the folds of Saint John the Divine last week. He was extremely agitated, and he told a frightening story. The Cathedral canon referred him to me. It appears that after he left us, he joined the Moral Confederation and also a secret Bund in Yorkville with American Nazi sympathies. He wouldn't admit it, of course, but I suspect the members in some way were linked to the Odessa."

Stewart was wide awake now, listening intently.

Elliott continued. "After initiation and comprehensive indoctrination by the Bund, he evidently came to realize his mistake."

"I have a question," said Carlie, interrupting. "Doesn't this kind of extremist passion run deeper than this? I mean, is it possible for a person to have only a casual flirtation with such a movement?"

Stewart held up his hand. "Slow down, Carlie. I'm fascinated, but you're both turning the prism too fast."

The bishop smiled thinly. "Hate can be learned, but it can also be *unlearned*. Any of us can join the rot, become participants in the lurking cruelty of the world. Learning to loathe is all too easy." Elliott shrugged and slowly exhaled. "Learning to love is more difficult, requiring patience and tolerance. These extremist groups ignore compassion, forget intellectual curiosity, cannot tolerate the splendor of innocence. Perhaps our young choir member's esoteric thinking was too strong for them. When he returned to us, he appeared to be in a maelstrom of revulsion."

Stewart leaned forward. "Over personalities or policies?"

"Over what the Bund had planned for his former church, and for me, I suspect." Elliott paused, studying Stewart. "Like the proposal to burn a fiery twenty-foot cross in front of the cathedral. I assume this is a reaction against my humanist statements, my attitude toward minorities. As you know, Saint John the Divine is on the edge of Harlem." Elliott turned from Stewart to Carlie. "Thank God we have people like Carlotta Chavez to help us on television. She's opened eyes with her investigative reporting." He looked at Stewart again, smiling wanly. "Now perhaps you will do likewise in the *Times*. May God give you both the perseverance and strength to see this through, to comprehend what I tell you in all its dimensions."

Stewart took a big sip from his glass. "Continue, please."

Elliott leaned forward. "The young man told me that if Citizens for the American Way was not disbanded, trouble would come to the officers and board members . . . and it did come. Rabbi Marks was the first. His splendid synagogue in Yonkers was desecrated with swastikas and signs denouncing the rabbi. Methodist Bishop Higgins received three phone calls warning him to resign from the board. Last night a fire bomb was thrown into the Methodist bookstore in Newark. Monsignor McGraw was attacked by hoodlums on his way to the taping this evening; they poured red paint over his car. He was so shaken he was unable to appear with us on the panel."

Stewart shuddered, his breathing coming out in a rush. His mouth felt dry. Swirling the ice cubes in his drink, he finished it off. He felt its warmth, but it did nothing to lift his spirits.

Elliott looked at him. "Let me finish. I must go, and your dinner is waiting. What really bothers me, what Carlie insisted I pass on to you, is something our prodigal baritone told me would occur on Friday—the day after tomorrow."

"Unfortunately, Friday the thirteenth," added Stewart, smiling.

The bishop continued. "The Bund to which he belonged is under the command of an unknown and very powerful Committee. Or so he claimed."

Stewart felt a shiver of excitement. Progress. He was intrigued, but decided to play it hard. "What kind of orders has the Bund received?"

"He didn't know all the details, only that he and several others were to be on forty-eight-hour call—or alert, as he put it—starting just before the President's State of the Union speech on Friday. He also said there were rumors that the Bund would close down the *New York Times* for the entire weekend."

Stewart felt stunned. "God Almighty," he muttered. His mind started spinning again. He fought back the impulse to ask Carlie for another drink; it would only add to his alarm. Instead, he stared at the empty glass before him. The bishop was silent now, letting his words sink in.

Carlie tapped Stewart gently on the arm. A shadow of doubt fell across his face. "Kirk, I'm afraid that's only the beginning." Her voice suddenly became controlled and careful, as if she were talking to a business associate, not an old friend. "Tomorrow I think you should take a look at those letters to the network brass. They also seemed to be tied in with the plans for Friday."

Burgess Elliott set his brandy snifter aside and stood up. "I must be leaving." He shook his head. "I would prefer to believe the young man in question was grossly exaggerating, but one can only go by instinct, and my instincts tell me he spoke the truth."

Carlie got up to follow the bishop to the door. "I'll get your coat. Please be careful, Burgess. Have the doorman hail a cab for you."

Stewart rose and accompanied the clergyman into the hall. "Bishop Elliott, I'd like very much to interview this young informant tomorrow morning if you can arrange it."

Elliott gazed at Stewart solemnly. "Sorry, I was getting to that. It will be quite impossible." His face looked like a clay mask as he added, "His body was found yesterday morning, floating in the East River."

22

IT WAS AFTER midnight, and the FBI chief was in a grim mood. Wright's problems were escalating by the hour, and he had an annoying headache. The President was concerned over a possible disloyal faction in the Secret Service. The press had been badgering the New York office for progress reports on the killing of the agent at the Bronx armory. O'Laughlin, his bureau head in Houston, was asking for more men to handle the plane crash investigation and the disappearance of Arnold Metz. Now even the network TV news people were bugging Wright. His headache had intensified after calling Stowe, Vermont, only to learn that Tap Nelson couldn't be reached at his rented condominium. It had been six hours, and Nelson had still not returned the call. There was no indication he had received Wright's message to return immediately to the capital.

Chucking two aspirins into his mouth, Wright took a swig from a bottle of Perrier and surveyed the three men who waited across from his desk. Two of his agents stood attentively, one on each side of the short, dark, curly-haired man in the leather wing chair. "You look tired, Mr. Barak," Wright said sharply.

"I am tired, Mr. Director. And I am also bored. When will you be convinced that this is a waste of time for both of us?

It is late." Barak stifled a yawn, exhaling slowly instead.

"Which points up the importance of my attendance at this meeting."

Motti Barak glanced up at the two men hovering over him like obedient watchdogs. "Meeting? You use the term loosely, of course. *Interrogation,* I believe, is the proper word, yes?"

Wright did not respond, offering him only a ghost of a smile.

Barak continued, "Mr. Wright, I can do absolutely nothing for you while I am sitting here in this office. Left to my own devices, however—"

"Why were you following the head of the CIA?" Wright asked, interrupting. "And why were you waiting outside the Chinese restaurant where he was dining with General Brady and Chairman Palmer?"

Barak shrugged. "Tell me your own reasons, Mr. Wright, for *also* following Mr. Singer. We have similar business, apparently. You'll agree that it's unusual for men of their stature to meet secretly in a private upstairs dining room at the Shanghai Trader restaurant? Particularly at eleven-thirty, after the establishment had closed, true?"

"I'm not at liberty to discuss proprietary FBI business. But your activities, on the other hand, are of interest to the U.S. government." Wright leafed through Barak's Israeli passport, noted the visa stamps, then picked up a 9mm Browning automatic from the corner of his desk, thoughtfully patting it and turning it over in his hand. "Your gun permit is in order, Major Barak. We've established that you were an assistant to the military air attaché as well as a courier for the Israeli Air Force. But according to your diplomatic immunity stamps, your visa expired four days ago."

"I have applied for an extension," said Barak dryly.

"We called the Israeli embassy, Major. They told us that your mission to Washington ended three weeks ago, that you are on leave, awaiting reassignment."

Barak straightened. "Surely a man is entitled to a vacation prior to taking a new position?"

"Without informing your employer? I think you're lying. A hot-shot jet pilot doesn't spend his vacation attending Ku Klux Klan rallies, visiting Louisiana swamps, and provoking madmen to plant bombs on airplanes."

Wright watched Barak's eyebrows arch slightly. Leaning forward, pushing the gun and passport aside, he snapped, "You had business in Texas? Louisiana?"

"You're quite positive I was there?"

"Come off it, Barak. You think the Bureau's in a coma? You made flight reservations in and out of Houston. You rented cars. You returned with a *New York Times* reporter in tow and registered at the Merrimont-Arlington. Now what the hell's going on? And don't tell me you work for the *Jerusalem Post*. The Mossad, I might halfway believe."

Barak smiled. "How sinister, Mr. Wright. Try the KGB."

"Get off my back, Major. Now what about Kirk Stewart? What do you know about his dead girlfriend? And how about my missing agent in Louisiana? And the dead agent in New York? Turn on the light, Barak, and we can both stop stumbling around in the dark. Whose side are you on, for chrissake?"

Barak smiled again, then said thoughtfully, "How do I know whose side *you* are on, Mr. Wright? Perhaps, since the young reporter seems to have taken you into his confidence, you should be talking to him."

Wright sat back in his chair, glanced at his assistants, then once again to the Israeli. Barak's eyes were hooded now, carefully studying him. He was playing a confidence game, Wright thought, and thus far the FBI was losing. What now? Detain this Motti Barak on some spurious charge, interrogate him in the morning, when he could bring Kirk Stewart in at the same time? No, keeping him in the tank would rile the Israeli legation, cause an incident; besides, Stewart was leaving for New York first thing in the morning. He needed the reporter now. Wright glanced at his watch and swore softly. He would continue, despite the hour. Both Stewart and Barak knew more, far more than they had let on. Wright picked up the phone. Immediately, he had the information operator on the line and a second later the phone number of the YMCA on Rhode Island Avenue. Watching the Israeli's face slacken noticeably, Wright pushed the buttons on his phone, waited through several rings. He silently thanked the agent who had learned the fake name under which Kirk Stewart had registered.

A gruff man's voice answered, "YMCA."

"You have an Allan Baker registered? Ring his room, please."

A long pause. "Sorry, we've got a problem here. The switchboard is closed."

"Well, open it. This is important FBI business and can't wait until morning."

"Who's this?"

"FBI Headquarters."

"Sorry, just a minute. I'll let you talk to the lieutenant in charge."

Wright took in a breath, let it out quickly. Now what the hell? A cop answering the phone? Several seconds later, a new voice in the receiver.

"This is Lieutenant Kelsey. What room you want? And who's calling?"

The name was familiar; Wright's aides had worked with Kelsey before. "Lieutenant, this is Oliver Wright, FBI. You need a call-back verification, or are you interested in saving time?"

"Both, maybe. Depends on what's on your mind."

Insubordinate bastard, thought Wright. "I want to talk to Kirk Stewart. He checked in there under the name Allan Baker. It's important to a case we're working on."

"At this hour? It must be." There was a long pause at the other end of the line, a commotion in the background, several agitated voices. The lieutenant came back on the line. "I think you may want to hustle on over here, Mr. Wright. The night desk man is still a little groggy, but I gathered that he was clobbered by some character asking for Kirk Stewart's room. The clerk's pass key was taken. My men just came back from the fifth floor, and they claim we have a homicide on our hands. Stewart's dead."

The troop carriers were empty, except for their drivers. One hundred forty-four trucks had rolled out of the gate at Fort Bragg, North Carolina, and headed north. In the center of the base near the armory, the light still burned in the Motor Pool Dispatch Office. An army colonel, cigarette suspended from his lips, withdrew a dozen red map tacks from a box in his desk and carefully divided them between three Washington, D.C., area locations on the wall map beside him. He placed four tacks at Fort Myers, four at Andrews Air Force Base, the last four at the Quantico Marine Barracks. Each red tack represented a dozen vehicles, a total of forty-eight trucks to each base. Enough to transport a thousand men. But where the hell were they going? And at this ungodly hour? The more the colonel thought about the Navy and Marines borrowing a fleet of trucks on short notice, the more curious he became, and with the irregularities in command procedure that had occurred, he was irritated as well. Wearily picking up his phone, he dialed. After several rings, a tired voice answered; the brigadier general who was his superior didn't sound pleased at being disturbed. "What's up, Colonel?" came a gruffy query. "A problem?"

"Sorry, sir, but there seems to be a peculiar communications problem. I still haven't received orders for that fleet of personnel carriers. I've tried twice to call Washington for a clarification, but I've had no response."

"It's almost two in the morning, Colonel. What's the goddamn problem?"

"Just following regulations, sir. I was told to expect written confirmation, a Teletype authorizing the mobilization and transfer. Orders were supposed to have been cut at the Pentagon by the Marine Corps chief of staff, but nothing has arrived."

The voice at the other end of the line grunted, "You sent the trucks out just as I instructed?"

"Yes, General. But isn't this highly irregular?"

"Yes and no. Colonel, I gave up trying to outguess my superiors ten years back. A damned phone call from a four-star of George Brady's stature was good enough for me. Especially so when he has the blessing of the chief of staff. You want to check it out, okay with me, but I've been told the paperwork's been cut and sent on its way. Worry about it in the morning, Colonel. Hell, from what I hear, those personnel carriers are a drop in the bucket. The Pentagon's asked for two battalions of Fort Bragg's airborne troops and a dozen Chinook choppers as well. All to go to Andrews Air Force Base."

"Mind if I ask what gives, Colonel?"

"Damned if I know. A classified, joint Navy-Marine maneuver, from appearances. Why they're bleeding Army facilities dry for a practice alert, I can't figure. Stop worrying, Colonel. Close up shop and get some sleep. Good night."

23

LIVE AND LET live, Stewart reasoned, as he ignored the tiny ant investigating his dessert dish. The music floating into Carlie's dining room was loud, much too loud: "Blue moon, you knew just what I was there for, you heard me saying a prayer for someone I really could care for, and there suddenly appeared before me—"

Stewart put down his snifter of Grand Marnier, rose from the softly lit table, and strolled wearily to the stereo deck in the living room. Lowering the volume, he returned to the dining room doorway, paused, and studied Carlie as she spooned down the last of her pineapple sherbet.

Her veiled eyes looked up inquiringly. "Depression era nostalgia a bit heavy for you?" Her voice had a definite sultry ring to it.

Stewart smiled. "On the contrary. Not enough memorabilia in my life in the fast-lanc life-style. But the record's either vintage or shopworn. Who's the vocalist?"

"Connie Boswell. Sit down and finish your coffee."

Stewart watch her light a thin brown cigarette with a gold tip.

She puffed without inhaling, her hand trembling slightly.

"This entire day's been incredible. Look. I'm nervous as you are. I feel like one of those moving penguin targets in a shooting arcade."

"Ducks, Carlie." Stewart plunked down opposite her, gazing past the flickering, nearly spent candle in the center of the table. He searched her eyes. "You've got to unwind. There's nothing we can do until morning."

"Tell me, Kirk. How can these people be so blind to their own prejudices?" She slowly shook her head.

There was a short silence. Stewart tried to gather up his thoughts, but nothing serious wanted to come out. Frustrated, he offered her his best W.C. Fields imitation: "'I am free of all prejudices,'" he said in a drawling voice. "'I hate every one equally.'"

"You're getting drunk."

Stewart couldn't put the role away, not yet. Mockingly, he sneered and raised his glass. "'A woman drove me to drink, and I never even had the courtesy to thank her.'"

They both laughed. He leaned forward and she looked at him wistfully. Too wistfully, thought Stewart. He tried to avoid her searching eyes, pretending to study the brandy snifter.

They both listened to the music drifting in from the other room: "And there suddenly appeared before me the only one my arms would ever hold—"

Carlie giggled, breaking Stewart's reverie. "I'm not only an old-film buff, but I collect old records, too. You've probably never heard of Connie Boswell. She made 'Blue Moon' work where others failed."

Stewart didn't care an iota, but felt obliged to ask why. "How so?" He took another sip of his brandy. His mind was beginning to feel woolly, but at least he had begun to relax.

Smiling, Carlie puffed her cigarette and then snuffed it out. "Rodgers and Hart wrote it in 1933 for Jean Harlow, for a proposed film, *Hollywood Revue*. It never made it to the theater. They tried again, once more unsuccessfully, to have Shirley Ross introduce it in *Manhattan Melodrama*. Finally, the song became a hit on the radio with Connie Boswell. That's the recording you're hearing." She looked at him. "Kirk, you're not listening!"

"Whatever, Carlie. Sorry, I'm having trouble fixing my mind on the thirties."

"Well, then, try fixing it on me. There are two of us at this table, remember? That glazed look on your face is hardly becoming."

"Sorry." Stewart let out a short breath. "I was preoccupied. Busy counting my blessings that I'm still alive."

There was an uncomfortable silence, and then she blurted, "Kirk, I'm worried. I'm not trying to put the make on you, but after what you've told me, I don't think you should go back to your apartment. You're safer staying here."

"Convenient," Stewart replied warmly.

Carlie smiled, reached over, took his drink. She took a small sip, looking at him through the glass balloon. She handed the snifter back to him. "Well?" she asked softly.

Stewart didn't respond. He polished off his brandy and looked at her, savoring the invitation. Carlie's brown eyes were like small polished stones, warm, waiting, expectant. His past, both distant and recent, seemed to belong to someone else, in another time and place. The present belonged to Carlie Chavez. Or did it? Her restless eyes continued to search his soul.

"You usually notice the little things," she said quietly. "My outfit. The new dress. I bought it today, to wear tonight, for you."

"I'm sorry. I did notice it. Stunning," he said sincerely. "My mind's miles away tonight." He suddenly felt a pang, remembering Shira's evening dress; it was green also. The one she had worn to three consecutive concerts at Lincoln Center, the best dress she had. Once more the image of Shira had imprinted itself on his consciousness. How could he possibly wrap himself in Carlie's affection?

"I hope your lengthy silence is more interesting than mine," she quipped.

"You want to talk about our strategy for tomorrow?" Stewart asked, almost apologetically.

"We had an agreement, remember? No unpleasant conversation at the table. We're both tired. It's late. I suggest we get a good night's sleep so we can run the course tomorrow in fighting shape."

"You serious about my staying over?" he asked blandly.

"If you're shy, you can sleep on the sofa." She pushed her chair away from the table.

"Carlie, I need a friend now more than ever before. Other than that . . ." He slowly shook his head, waiting for some sign of approbation or a hint of displeasure, but she only looked at him vacantly. A clever woman, he thought. Maybe he wanted her after all.

"Sympathy, a warm bed, and an alarm clock I'm prepared to dispense," she said, blowing out the candle. "But I assume you've toted along your razor and toothbrush?" Flinging her hair over her shoulder, she smiled, walked smoothly out of the dining room, and padded toward the bedroom.

Stewart sat in the darkness, warmed by the quality booze and intoxicated by Carlie Chavez. Pull yourself together, Stewart, he mused. Are you mourning or not? No! Only old crones in black with whiskers on their chins continued to wail forever. Wasn't he a crime reporter, sophisticated enough to understand death in all its dimensions? Here today, gone tomorrow, the simple facts of life. All the tears in the world weren't going to bring Shira Bernstein back. He looked at the empty place at the table, the candle, then down the hallway. Did he dare climb in bed again with Carlie? Could he erase his lost affair from his mind for ten, fifteen minutes? An entire night, if necessary?

A quarter of an hour later, bathed, stripped, and stretched out on the king-sized bed beneath blue satin sheets—a color Carlie had selected because the moon was in Aquarius—Stewart looked around the room. She had redone what he remembered as an already stunning bedroom. The walls were a deep midnight blue with shutters, spread, and a thick fur rug all in white. Giant lamps on either side of the bed, shiny chrome, with silver shades, were turned down low. Stewart felt a familiar shiver of excitement as Carlie emerged from the bathroom in a thin, clinging nightgown. Shira had alway preferred to sleep in the nude. He watched Carlie turn off the lights, silently slide into the other side of the bed. She smelled faintly of talcum powder and light perfume. Setting the radio alarm, she whispered softly, "Good night, Kirk," then turned her back to him.

Hesitantly, he rolled toward her, kissed her lightly on the shoulder under the nightgown and said, "Thanks, Carlie, for taking me in." but as he edged back, flattening himself against the silky sheets, he thought he heard a distant, alien voice. Shira? Was she calling to him? The voice faded away.

His intense needs, the closeness of Carlie's body, erased all else from his mind. Stewart suddenly felt powerless, unable to fight off the compelling attraction; there was a familiar swelling, a twinge of excitement, impending pleasure, in his groin. He felt both confused and helpless.

Stewart rolled over to the side of the bed, turned on the lamp. Carlie stirred, turned, and gazed at him curiously. He wanted to talk, but words under the circumstances, seemed totally superfluous. He searched her eyes to see if she shared his concern and anguish but the thoughtful, distant smile on her lips revealed she was in her own dream world—hers was a special kind of female privacy that wasn't about to be explained. Her eyes closed, then opened. They were filled with want, frightened with their own definition of love, but definitely guarded. Her lips were moist. Wordlessly, he extended his hand. She quickly burrowed into his arms, warm and protected.

Carlie angled her mouth against his, then hesitated. She leaned back, cocked her head to one side, and focused on his face. "You're trembling," she whispered.

Stewart did not reply. All he could do was pull her closer, thrust his tongue deep inside her mouth; his hands gripped her smooth buttocks and gently pulled her up, over his hips. After a long kiss, she sat up, her long black hair sweeping across his chest. Her eyes, wanton and hungry now, bore down into his own, penetrating his thoughts. Small beads of perspiration formed on the clean planes of her face as her limbs flexed, riding him slowly at first, then more passionately.

They changed positions, and gently kissed in a lotus stance. Her body now had a warm, animal tang that excited him. With the tip of his tongue Stewart probed Carlie's breasts, her navel, the inner folds of her swollen mound. He licked passionately at her body as if he were savoring a delicious peach. Then once more her legs entwined, their bodies joined in frenzied, wild thrusts. Stewart could feel her feverish clitoris; it was strained and swollen, like a hard pecan. Seconds apart, they both shuddered in ecstatic pleasure as he detonated within her.

No sooner had their act been consummated than Stewart began to feel the guilt. No, let it go, he flashed. Not now. This was no time to stew over past affairs. This, obviously, was spontaneous relief from loneliness, a two-way street of mutual need. He had proven that he could have her, but could he still keep his shattered, confused soul to himself? The quick, piercing pleasure was a two-edged sword, and now his heart ached. But for whom? The orgasm was completely uninhibited, one of the most satisfying he had experienced, but he also felt the loneliness gushing out of him. All he could do now was gently lie on top of her, matching her breathing with his own until she, too, was emotionally sated.

Stewart continued to hold Carlie for several minutes, silently stroking her shoulder. He felt confused. Finally, he rolled over on his back and stared at the ceiling. A small tear rolled down his cheek, uncontrolled.

"Troubled?" she asked nervously.

He didn't respond, and she tried again. "It's typical when Leo is squared with Scorpio. It's all in the ascendant."

Stewart looked over at her, unimpressed by the words. "You think I'm too much of a romantic for the times?"

Carlie smiled warmly. "You can't let go, can you?"

"Forget it. It's over." He hesitated, looking into her wide eyes. "I'm with you, and I like it." Something was happening to him, something he couldn't quite understand.

"Kirk, you didn't answer my question."

He squirmed uncomfortably. "I need time. I'll try to put it away. Looking back, maybe the relationship wasn't so casual after all. Sorry to be such a downer, Carlie." He looked at her and saw the feverish glimmer for him in her eyes slowly fade and nearly go out. Almost, but not quite.

24

THEIR VOICES HUSHED, the two men sat over breakfast in a quiet corner of the Andrews Air Force Base Officers' Club. Colonel Pete Reddick was immaculately attired in his dress blues; his heavy eyebrows furrowed as he forked, without enthusiasm, at a Denver omelet. He scowled at the man across from him. "I've learned that our operation has been penetrated. Lynx told me about the reporter and the Israeli agent."

Arnold Metz smiled conspiratorially. "I leave for New York when our breakfast is concluded. The reporter won't trouble us much longer. And I'll eliminate this brazen Major Barak as well. I suspect, however, that the Israeli may try to contact and question you."

"It's getting risky," snapped Reddick. "I don't like it, Metz. Morever, I don't like you. Truth of the matter, I haven't forgotten our falling out. I wouldn't have met you, but Lynx insisted on it."

"Come, come, Colonel. It's been three years. So I took the gold medal at the National Rifleman's shoot, and you took the silver. Still the pouting loser?"

"You were a cheating cocksucker then, and I suspect you still are." Reddick bit into a piece of raisin toast, chewed it quickly. "Get it all out, Metz. Arrive at your point."

"Walter Singer, General Brady, Lynx, you, and myself. The five of us have much in common. Unlike the others." Metz paused, sipped his coffee, wiped his curled lips on his wrist. "Courage, determination, guts if you prefer plain language."

"What are you driving at, Metz? You're baiting me, and I dislike it. You preparing to speak out of line?"

"I always speak out of line, Reddick. That's my nature. And yours, from what I understand."

"That's supposed to mean what?"

Metz paused, rolling his yellow eyes. He waited for a passing busboy to move out of earshot. "Every man has his price. What do you want out of all this? Truthfully, Colonel."

Reddick thought for a moment, trying to get his annoyance with Metz out of his mind, direct his thinking back to the rational plane where it belonged. Why did he still detest the gun peddler so fiercely after all these years? There was something evil about Metz, something damnably perverse and reptilian. "I have both political and personal reasons for being involved," he finally answered, figuring to end it there.

"An evasive reply. And you don't strike me as a vague, simple man," said Metz swiftly.

Simple, thought Reddick. The insulting bastard. Quickly fingering the eagle on his collar, he snarled at Metz. "I've been twice passed over for a brigadier's star. I want it, and *more* that's coming to me. My record deserves it. Secondly, the nation's military strength sucks. Among nations, we've grown soft. Like the weak wolf in the pack, we're cowering, belly up. I'll tell you something, Metz. What happens to animals in nature applies to men among nations. The country's sliding down the goddamn sewer. I don't pretend to be the Dutch kid with his finger in the dike, but yes, I'm willing to stick my neck out to save the tattered remains of Old Glory."

Metz nodded. "Fine, then you'll agree that it's results that count. The Committee insists that the takeover be civilian, with only minimal military assistance. Do you concur?"

Reddick grimaced. "No, I do not. Civilians, armed or otherwise, lack not only clout but organization and discipline. If you must know—"

Metz waved his hand. "The head of the CIA agrees. Walter Singer's shrewd. The other men on the Committee have money, spiritual influence, and technological expertise. Without it, we'd be nowhere today. But let me tell you this." Metz leaned forward over the table and lowered his voice. "Vice-President Chandler will be no fucking better than that prick who's in the White House now. He'll be a temporary replacement. Singer will take over when the time is ripe. As for the Committee, their days of power will be numbered, once they've served their high-minded purpose." Metz paused, studying Reddick, obviously trying to gauge the state of his nerves. Slowly, he continued. "Hallowell and Frober are Milquetoasts. Gifford has some strong ideas, but he's a walking computer and completely fucked over by his defense manufacturing business." Metz tapped a hairy finger next to Reddick's plate. "That Committee may see to it you get your star, but they're no fools. They'll sure as shit make sure you never get the slot you want at the Pentagon. You're not their type, Colonel. Only Singer appreciates your talents."

Reddick squirmed, looked back across the table in a crouching silence. Jesus, he thought, a plot within a plot was the one thing he didn't need. Not now, not less than thirty hours from the time he would activate his squadron, place his men on station. Damn Metz and his inside information! Again General Brady's words hammered away in Reddick's ears: "This is not a military takeover, but the enforcement responsibility cannot be denied."

A waitress approached and warmed their coffee. Reddick waited until she was out of earshot, then said defiantly, "Continue, Metz. I'm listening."

Glancing nervously around the room with the eyes of a lizard, the Texan leaned forward. "You've been assigned to fly escort for the two 747s carrying members of Congress to their *extended vacation* in Haiti. You are to ensure that they arrive as planned, without interference."

Reddick nodded. "Riding shotgun to the Gulag. You know more than I figured. Go on."

"Supposing, Colonel, those two planes never arrive at their destination? Say they're lost at sea. Victims of the Bermuda Triangle?"

Pete Reddick felt a clutch in his stomach. "Christ. What are you saying?"

"That we simply end, once and for all, the possibility of liberals or moderates reassuming power in this country at a later date."

"You're mad, Metz. It's rotten enough that we're stashing them for a year or two in a fucking detention camp." Reddick felt numb.

Metz stared at him with a crooked smile. "Perhaps, Colonel, I was wrong about you. Lynx led me to believe you were a dedicated hard-liner, that you understood the meaning of the term 'enlightened depotism.'"

"I am committed. But this?"

Metz quickly replied, "Walter Singer suggests you use Sparrow air-to-air missiles. All our enemies will be aboard those planes, except the President."

Reddick nodded glumly. "Who you trust will resign."

Metz chortled. "That's the Committee's pipe dream. I have other instructions."

"Odd that you receive instructions from Lynx and Singer, and I receive vague suggestions." Reddick was losing ground and wanted to regain it.

Metz slowly savored his coffee, studying him through hooded eyes. Several seconds passed. "If it were up to me, Reddick, you'd receive unalterable orders. I'm hardly the considerate type. But Singer obviously has a misplaced humanitarian streak or a guilty conscience. Whatever, he can't order a pilot to shoot down over seven hundred of his countrymen. The CIA head only suggests you consider the idea, weigh its possibilities and advantages. Your conscience will tell you what is best for America."

Reddick exhaled sharply. "I already know what's best for America."

"Don't be naive, Colonel. You know as well as I do that the Committee's plans can never work if we simply displace the present government. Slapping them in cold storage isn't the solution. Our enemies have to be eliminated, and it has to look sudden and accidental. When the people hear that their government has been wiped out, they'll be numb with shock, vulnerable and easy prey. They'll do what they're told, without rebelling."

"Fine," grunted Reddick. "If Singer, Admiral Palmer, and General Brady feel the same way, let them tell me as a group."

"Brady and Palmer know nothing of this. They will never concur. It's Singer's concept, but your show. The CIA head picked you because you're tough. You're the only flyboy who can handle what has to be done and the only one with brains enough to understand why. If I could handle an F-15, I'd do the job myself."

Reddick rubbed his jaw. "Singer's asking me to weigh the lives of seven hundred against the welfare of two hundred million—in all objectivity, of course. It's fucking political assassination."

"Stop wavering, Reddick. Think of the world's great revolutions. Progress is written in blood, not ink. Our country's got to be rescued from malaise and decay, and quickly. You know that." Metz's eyes flashed wildly. "We're a confused population, Colonel. Half Judaized, half Negrified! The future of America depends on enlightened military leaders like you. Colonels—or should I say generals?—who will—"

"Stop, you fool!" interrupted Reddick. "What about foreign reaction and the press?"

"The crash will be reported as a midair collision between the two planes. I'll show you Singer's projections on paper; a simple maneuver will convince the most attentive air space radar controller." Metz shrugged. "In any event, we will control the press."

Reddick eased back in his seat, flexing his knuckles. Metz was going too fast for him, much too fast. "And the President?"

Slowly and unflinchingly, Metz said, "His speech to Congress tomorrow will be his last. His epitaph. It's time for a public demonstration of the new homing weapon. The EMR is a most ingenious, destructive device."

In New York City it was half past eight in the morning, and Stewart was hungry. Unfortunately, Carlie's prowess in the kitchen didn't include stick-to-the-ribs breakfasts. Coffee, period, was the eye-opener bill of fare she had offered him, along with the promise of hot rolls when they arrived at her NTN office at Rockefeller Center. Stewart had decided to go there first, check over the hate mail the network board chairman had received, then report in to his desk at the *Times*. He wanted to talk with his boss as soon as possible; he needed Mike Murphy's help. Stewart would also call Oliver Wright in the capital within the hour, make sure that Tim Harris had relayed the information about the homicides at Congressman Schmidt's house. Most important, there was the matter of the address book. He also had the missing persons report to file on Shira. It would be a busy morning.

Stewart stood next to the building's doorman, waiting. Carlie had dashed back upstairs for a forgotten briefcase. Stewart thought about the day ahead. If Murphy at the *Times* agreed, he would continue to keep a low profile, running underground like a mole for several more hours. There were leads to investigate, knots to unravel before tomorrow's presidential speech. If he stayed under cover, his work would be not only easier but safer as well. He and Carlie had made an agreement. They would combine forces, pool their energies, and break the story on TV and in print as soon as possible, late tonight or in the morning; they could only pray and cross their fingers that it wouldn't be too late. But several mysteries remained unsolved. Who controlled the conspiracy? Where was it headquartered? To what extent was Walter Singer involved? He and Carlie needed the missing pieces to the puzzle and needed them fast. Time was working against them.

"Go ahead," he said to the doorman. "Flag us a cab. She'll be down in a second."

"You won't need a taxi," he replied. "Ms. Chavez has a driver waiting." The doorman pointed to a dark blue sedan that was waiting at the curb. A stocky man with the grim face of a pit bull terrier behind the wheel. He looked at Stewart expectantly.

Carlie emerged from the elevator lugging an alligator-hide briefcase. Her long hair was tied back with a silver silk scarf that matched the one at her neck; her business suit was dove gray, tailored, elegant. Stewart smiled fondly, touched her arm. Carlie, as usual, radiated self-confidence in every step, he reflected. There were times when his feeling of closeness to her equaled and in different ways even surpassed his closeness to Shira. It was crazy. Unexplainable. What was love anyway? With Shira he had found a sordid happiness in bickering; with Carlie, there had never been an argument, hardly ever a difference of opinion.

Together they left the building and hurried to the curb.

"Sorry to take so long upstairs. The phone rang when I went back into the apartment."

Stewart's eyes were on the waiting BMW sedan. "Who's the goon? He looks like a private eye."

The driver climbed out of the car, circled to the curb, silently opened the back door. Carlie nodded to him, darted inside. Stewart slid in beside her.

"Not my idea," she said. "My boss insists I have a bodyguard for a couple of weeks. This I need yet?"

Stewart shrugged. "The wheels you should complain over? Saves the cab fare."

Carlie smiled. "The studio pays for my transportation. That's in my contract. Kirk, you didn't ask what the phone call was about."

Stewart felt a familiar qualm, tried to stifle it. "Do I look like the nosy type?" He smiled, gave her a quick peck on the cheek. "Strike the question. I'm a news hound, remember? Fire away, I'm all ears."

The driver headed out into the traffic on Park Avenue. Carlie let out an uncomfortable sigh. "It was the news desk at the network. One of my story editors thought I would want to know. The remote crew brought in a videotape from uptown. Sometime after midnight, they burned a sixteen-foot-high, gasoline-soaked cross in front of the Cathedral of Saint John the Divine."

25

THE AIR POLICE guard at the gate noted the diplomatic credentials and promptly waved Motti Barak through. Barak had visited Washington's Andrews Air Force Base before—often, in his role as assistant to the Israeli military attaché.

Once inside, Barak followed the remote van of a local television news crew. Ahead he could see the flags and bunting around the area set aside for the C-11 press preview. Beyond the hospitality tent, on the airfield taxi apron, were parked two of the new short-takeoff and landing transports. Barak glanced in the rearview mirror, noting the cars filtering onto the airbase. The FBI had finally released him in the small hours of the morning, but he suspected they were far from finished with him. Oliver Wright's men were probably following at a discreet distance, monitoring his every move. Barak smiled in self-satisfaction. It didn't matter. He had worked everything out in precise detail.

He chose a parking place carefully, away from the other press vehicles, and once more reviewed his plan. Carefully, he checked his equipment: the papers he needed in order to obtain the all-important press badge, his microphone and tape recorder, a clipboard, and finally the dozen brushed gold ball-point pens imprinted with the words "Fly El-Al Israeli Airlines." One by one he examined the pens, noting which two had silver pocket clips instead of gold. All the writing instruments had handsome, fluted tops, but the ones with the silver clips contained miniature microphones. Because of the minitransmitter, the ink cartridges were small—so small that the pens would write only a few dozen lines before running dry. This didn't concern Barak. His needs were immediate. If his selected recipients tossed away their gifts before the day was over, so much the better.

Barak tucked the pens in his jacket pocket and flipped open the tape recorder to test the batteries. Good. He put a clean tape in the cassette deck, closed the lid, turned the unit upside down, and with a small Allen wrench removed the plastic back cover. He smiled to himself as he once more checked the hidden receiver; the two additional cassettes concealed inside the machine would record any conversation in the immediate area of the pens with the silver clips. One tape for each microphone; two opportunities, he reasoned, to pick up proprietary conversations. His own hand microphone and the visible cassette would be a journalist's prop, nothing more. Barak closed and secured the lid. Gathering his equipment together, he climbed out of the car and headed for the press tent.

Walter Singer had decided to remain outside his CIA limousine until after the C-11 flight demonstration. From where he was parked he could hear Air Force General Colloran's speech to the assembled press. Bernard Colloran praised the aircraft's builder, Condor Defense Industries, apologizing for last-minute business that kept that corporation's chairman, Norman Gifford, from attending the press preview. Singer smiled, all too aware of the nature of that last-minute business. He listened as the Air Force Commander assured the two hundred correspondents that there would be a lengthy question-and-answer session immediately following the demonstration.

Singer watched Colloran raise his hand, signaling to the flight crew in the C-11 cockpit.

Less than five minutes later, the STOL was poised, not at the end of the runway, but in the middle, just opposite Singer's limousine. With its oversize flaps extended almost to the ground, it looked like a giant predatory bird. The CIA head had to roll up his window as the roar of its four-bladed turboprops rose to a banshee scream. Brakes clamped, power up full, the flight crew shot the bolt, and the trembling aircraft leaped forward. In the length of a football field the C-11's pilot let its wind up, and the plane clawed its way into the sky at an impossible angle. The gathered reporters stared up in amazement, looked at each other, and clapped.

Singer, too, was impressed. He climbed out of his limo and watched for over thirty minutes as Condor's new transport went through its paces. When the C-11 pilot returned the plane to the field, settled it into its place on the apron, and silenced its engines, the wide-eyed reporters congregated around the clam-shell doors behind the tail. An authoritative voice over the PA announced that a cargo-loading demonstration would now begin.

In the distance across the tarmac, Singer saw General Brady talking to Colloran. Singer walked toward them, edging through the crowd of reporters. Two armed aides accompanied him, one slightly ahead like a pilot fish, the other trailing behind.

The CIA director looked at the shiny new C-11, pondering. Men like Norman Gifford felt a sense of accomplishment in designing and building a better airplane, Singer thought. For himself, the satisfaction would come from perfecting, perhaps someday heading, the world's most efficient government. A government capable of devising absolute solutions.

Singer came up beside George Brady, nudged him gently, then politely nodded to General Colloran. The reporters were closing ranks on them. "The new bird performed well," Singer said quietly in the retired army general's ear. He was surprised to find Brady in civilian clothing, even more surprised to find him in the company of Bernard Colloran, an Air Force four-star who was definitely in the enemy camp. Singer spoke again in a whisper. "I suggest, Brady, we go off where we can talk with the others."

Brady nodded and looked for a path through the crowd, but a woman reporter stood before him, blocking his way.

"Gentlemen," she said, "I'm from the *Atlanta Constitution*. What effect will this new aircraft have on Georgia's Dobbins Air Force Base. Will the C-11 eventually phase out the C-130s stationed there?"

George Brady turned, deferring to the man in the blue uniform behind him.

"There's no substance to that rumor," General Colloran replied brusquely. "I suggest you talk to my staff officers for more details on deployment." Colloran led her off to a nearby contingent of Air Force brass.

Singer felt relieved. But he and Brady weren't alone long. A teenage boy in an Air Explorer Scout's uniform tapped the general on the arm. "Pardon me, sir. My father was the pilot on the demonstration flight. He said you might autograph this picture." He held up a press photo of the C-11. George Brady was in it, smiling along with the flight crew.

Brady nodded, groped in his pockets for a pen. Singer was about to reach inside his own jacket when he saw the handsome ball-point being thrust through the crowd toward Brady. More than one pen; one for the general, another for the expectant teenager.

"Compliments of El Al and my newspaper," said the small, eager man with the microphone and tape recorder.

Singer squinted at his press badge. An Israeli journalist. The *Jerusalem Post*.

George Brady noted the inscription on the pen, thanked its donor, and quickly signed the photo. The youth smiled and backed off. The general kept the pen. Another reporter, a heavy jowled, oafish man wearing horn-rimmed glasses and a wrinkled corduroy suit, tried to burrow in between Singer and Brady. The CIA assistants pushed him back, only to have his place taken by the Israeli and his outthrust microphone.

Singer frowned. The assertive reporter was still handing out ball-point pens like candy at an orphanage. The disappointed fat man received one, too, staring at it with a perplexed, annoyed look. Shrugging, Singer slid a pen into his jacket pocket, elbowed the reporters aside, and forcibly pushed Brady before him to the edge of the throng.

The Israeli called after them. "General Brady, is it true you're being called back to active service, and if so, by whom?"

Brady glanced over his shoulder. "No comment."

"Are you still on the board of directors at Condor Defense?"

Tugging at Singer's sleeve, Brady whispered, "Fucking, noddy-nosed Jew! Let's get out of here and leave these hungry birds to the Air Force. It's their goddamn show, not mine. Where's Reddick?"

"Follow me," Singer said, leading Brady out of the crowd. Singer pointed over to the edge of the flight apron where the Air Force colonel stood alone, away from the press, a short distance from the C-11's wingtip.

Singer was pleased at the location Reddick had chosen. Ten minutes of privacy was all they needed. Singer had been surprised to find that Brady was not wearing his four-star Army uniform; the hot-shot F-15 squadron commander, on the other hand, looked resplendent in his closely tailored blues. Singer liked uniforms. The lack of one was the only thing he disliked about his agency position.

The men shook hands. Brady was the first to speak. "Your end of it shaping up, Colonel?"

"Flawlessly, sir."

Singer wanted to ask Reddick about his visit with Metz, but he knew this wasn't the time. He turned to Brady. "What's the picture at Strategic Army Corps?"

The general's eyebrows arched slightly. His eyes went hesitantly to Reddick, then back to Singer. "Some of my old pals aren't as talkative or friendly as they used to be. Either I've got bad breath or my shitty retirement status is putting them off. I'm getting a cold shoulder at staff level, but don't sweat it. I'll beat the sons of bitches at their own game."

Singer shot Brady a swift look of disapproval. "Promises aren't good enough."

The general smiled, waved a conciliatory hand. "Unwind, Walter. I don't need their cooperation. If the old guard closes the front door, we'll slip around back. STRAC is now under direct control of the Air Force Strike Command. When my men neutralize underground command center in Virginia, STRICOM will have its hands full merely regrouping. They won't have time to get a full grip on what I'm doing at Sixteenth and Ninth Army. All I need is a two-hour lead. Two fucking hours, that's all. Without backup communications, they're dead in the water." Brady's ruddy face furrowed as he turned to Reddick. "Do you concur with the timing, Colonel? Sorry I can't wangle more Air Force support for you. I realize your two fighter squadrons aren't much more than a piss in a bucket."

The colonel looked back stolidly. "It's not the quantity that matters with men of the caliber I have under my wing. We're not talking about air control of the continental United States, sir. Only a three-hundred-mile perimeter around the capital."

"You're smugly confident, Reddick," interjected Singer. "Good. We need that kind of spirit."

Reddick smiled. "My people are under complete control.

Each plane will be at the right place at the precise time. You can count on it."

Singer turned, zeroing in on Brady again. "How about those Chinook and Huey helicopters?"

Brady nodded. "General Garlock's cooperating with that specially trained Marine force of his. I have Army Airborne at Fort Bragg on provisional alert as well." Brady hunched his shoulders, squinted at Singer. "It's not the jarheads and the backup paratroopers that worry me, Walter. You want the mother-fucking truth, I'm concerned about the talking birds. All we need is for the Seventeenth Air Force to set up one of its C-135 Airborne Command Posts, with General Colloran personally in charge." Brady turned, leveled a finger at Reddick. "Your Air Force commander-in-chief has his suitcases and mobility kits packed. All he and the President need is the slightest hint of what we've planned."

A navy admiral with too many stripes on his sleeve to count stepped rapidly up to the group. "Let me worry about the Air Force," Sandy Palmer said bluntly. "And it's Singer's job to keep an eye on the President."

Singer was pleased that the chairman of the Joint Chiefs had finally joined them.

Reddick saluted. Singer extended his hand, and Brady, out of uniform, did likewise. Admiral Palmer looked at them and gruffly said, "Sorry I'm late, gentlemen. Let's dispense with civilities and get down to business. This meeting should be terminated as quickly as possible. Don't stare conspicuously, but behind me, off to the right, are two men posing as reporters—the two scribbling on clipboards. I've seen them before. They're FBI agents. My own security people tell me they've been following you, Walter, since your arrival at Andrews an hour ago."

Singer shrugged. "Admiral, your astuteness is commendable, but I'm already aware of their presence. What's more, my own men—several of them, to be sure—have the situation under complete control. The two Bureau men in question will not reach a telephone or the radio in their car, nor for that matter will they be permitted to leave the base until tomorrow night." Singer smiled. "At ease, Admiral. The CIA employs finesse. Oliver Wright is a blunderer; he merely amuses me. You can feel free to speak. We're safe enough here."

Palmer's eyes slipped from Singer to each of the others in

turn. "This operation isn't easy for me," he said stiffly.

"Not easy for any of us," added Singer.

Palmer looked at the CIA director speculatively. "The Andrews base commander wants to know why we're spotting two civilian passenger jets on the apron tomorrow."

"You replied tactfully, of course?" asked Brady.

"Not exactly. Told him it was privileged information—a D.O.D. proprietary maneuver, and to mind his own business."

"Good," said Singer, grinning. "If he has any more doubts, have him call my office." Rubbing his palms together, he swiftly added, Gentlemen, finish quickly with your coordinating. I have an important call to make to our ubiquitous friend Lynx and it can't wait."

Singer backed away and headed across the tarmac toward the string of phone booths that had been set up next to the press tent. He walked rapidly, ignoring the two FBI men who watched him pass. Singer felt calm and relaxed. At the telephone booths, he paused, turned, and once more considered each of the men he had just left.

Admiral Palmer, the chairman of the Joint Chiefs, was important to him, a vital cog; without his validating signature, the movement would have foundered in a sea of Pentagon red tape. And Palmer was the only one who could outmaneuver the President's fair-haired boy, the Secretary of Defense. Tomorrow, thankfully, the secretary would still be in a hospital recovering from surgery.

The only thing that bothered Singer about the Chairman of the Joint Chiefs was that Palmer was a nervous Nellie, all too often a pain in the ass. Still, the admiral was the only one who could bargain with the heads of the individual services. He had the rank, if not the respect.

On the other hand, Singer liked George Brady. The still energetic, retired Army general, his face carved with lines, was in his mid-sixties, but there wasn't the slightest slump to his frame. His firm voice, his intense gaze—his Irish eyes had a piercing quality—made Singer forget the four-star's age. Brady could move people as well as tanks.

Singer looked at the third man, the Air Force colonel with the carved-marble face, threatening eyebrows, and outthrust Mussolini chin. What Pete Reddick lacked in congeniality, he seemed to make up for in military discipline, spit and polish. He looked mean, determined, almost frightening. Reddick had

a lean, compact body, and Singer guessed that here was a man
like himself, who considered physical fitness paramount.

Singer wasn't concerned about the career generals and admirals down the line who would soon be asked to support the
Committee. The intelligence he had gathered told him that high-
ranking career officers looking forward to comfortable retirement in Palm Beach, Indian Wells, and La Jolla did not make
waves. Most but not all of them. Air Force General Colloran,
who was rumored to be next in line for the top job at the
Pentagon, filling Palmer's shoes, was a staunch supporter of
the President. General Pilling, head of the Strategic Air Command, had a brother who was a liberal senator from Illinois.
Both were good friends of the man in the Oval Office. A couple
of other vacillating Army generals might constitute a problem
at staff level. A few ranking Navy officers had also concerned
Singer until the chairman of the Joint Chiefs had promoted
them to foreign duty. Letting them sweat over the seething
Middle East powder keg had effectively taken care of that
problem. This had thus far gone much more smoothly than
Singer had expected. And still there had been no leaks. Not a
hint, thank God, in the press.

Singer was pleased with the military phase. The civilian
aspect looked even more favorable. With a little less than twenty-
four hours to go, he knew it was all a matter now of striking
swiftly. From Maine to Hawaii and from Florida to Alaska,
the key element would be high-tech communication and surprise. Deploy the right people at the precise time to the proper
place. Stab swiftly and rely on the narcotic effect.

After viewing the cross-burning videotapes, Stewart took a cab
from Rockefeller Center to the New York Times Building on
Forty-third Street. Entering the lobby he nodded to the security
guard, showed his I.D., and was about to step into the elevator
when one of the copyboys from the newsroom grabbed his
elbow and whispered, "Kirk! Hold it."

Stewart stopped, puzzled. He recognized the face. It was
Jeff Donaldson, a part-timer in the newsroom and a journalism
student at NYU. Stewart looked back at the youth curiously.
"What's up, Jeff?"

Donaldson's hand still gripped his arm tightly. "Look, you
can't go up to your desk or to the city editor's office. Not right
now."

"Why not? What's wrong?"

The copyboy pulled him off to one side, out of the elevator foot traffic. "Murphy sent me down to intercept and warn you. There are two FBI agents and a New York City detective up there anxious to collar you. Been there almost an hour, waiting. From the sound of it, they're squabbling over who should drag you in. What gives back at the capital?"

Stewart exhaled sharply. His spirits sagged. "Long story, Jeff. I'll tell you later. So what does Mike want me to do? Disappear? Get lost?"

Donaldson pointed toward the elevators. "Hell, no. He wants to meet you in the basement. Suggested the furnace room. I'll go back up and slip him the high sign that you've arrived."

Stewart cocked his ear, wondering if something was hidden here. He needed Murphy's help, but was it safe? Stewart hated snap decisions.

"Don't worry," the copyboy urged. "He'll find an excuse to get away from the cops. You sure everything's okay, man?"

"Yeah, sure," Stewart replied unevenly. He headed for the elevator under the blinking red arrow, watched Donaldson step into an up car.

Inside the elevator, several thoughts flashed through Stewart's head. All right, Mr. Big-Time Reporter, he told himself. Now's your big chance. Don't muff it. Keep away from the police. You're privy to the greatest yarn of the century. You have some leads, a few names—like Norman Gifford and Walter Singer. Some dates. And holes, too many of them. You need more time. Prefatory matters first: You've got to take Mike Murphy into your confidence. Supposing, God forbid, you and Carlie are both snuffed?

Carlie intended to go for a news feature, convince the network brass to preempt scheduled programming if necessary. You need a banner headline, Stewart, and at least three columns in a morning edition. You also need staff help for follow-up articles and sidebars. You have to sell it now, not later. But what was happening upstairs?

Less than ten minutes later, his tie askew and face wrapped in a scowl, Mike Murphy swung through the heavy steel door of the furnace room.

Stewart sat on one corner of the building engineer's desk, scanning the morning edition. He looked up, but didn't bother to rise as the burly editor approached. Murphy's scowl slowly turned into a leprechaun smile as he extended his hand.

"Welcome back." Murphy glanced around him. "Don't laugh. Maybe I'll have maintenance set you up with a desk and phone down here. A wastebasket, too, which I'd like to cram over your head."

"Forget all that and just get me another camera. If the first one wasn't insured, take it out of my pay."

Murphy scowled. "You've got it. Kirk, for chrissake, what's going on?"

Stewart fired back his best impish grin. "How much do you know already?"

Murphy's hand shot out to both sides. "Carlotta Chavez did some hinting on her newscast last night. I talked to her on the phone afterward. What she didn't tell me, this morning our Washington bureau did. Then a half-hour ago, I got more bad news over the wire service; Congressman Schmidt and two girlfriends were murdered, and some character who knew this— a Tim Harris—was killed in *your* YMCA room."

Stewart's heart plummeted. He suddenly felt sick. Tim Harris! How? The Bureau knew Stewart had planned to stay in Washington and hole up at the Rhode Island Avenue Y. Had Wright engineered the murder? How deep was the conspiracy? And how did the police trace it all back to the massacre at the Congressman's suburban home so quickly? All he could do was gaze numbly at Murphy.

The city editor continued. "Your office phone upstairs has been buzzing off the hook. I took all the calls at first, but now the Bureau and the extradition specialists from New York Homicide are monitoring everything that comes in." Murphy shook his head, grabbed a chair, and straddled it, arms folded across its back. "What's going on, Stewart? Maybe just a tiny hint for the boss before the damned roof caves in on his head? And what have you got on that plane crash in Houston? From the way you talked on the phone from Washington, I gathered that the country's about to change its underwear in front of the whole goddamn world."

Stewart held up his hand. "Relax, Mike. You'll have a coronary. I'll take it a step at a time. First, I need to know about those phone calls. They're important."

Murphy shrugged. "Only three callers identified themselves. My girl took the others. She said they all sounded like the same guy; asked when you were expected back in New York. Didn't identify himself."

"Okay. What about the others?"

Pulling a note from his pocket, Murphy put on his glasses and read from it. "The first call was from Oliver Wright, FBI chief." Murphy looked up at Stewart and smiled. "At least you're not playing in the farm league. The second caller was Tap Nelson, Wright's press aide. Number three was some dude named Major Barak. Spoke with an accent. He was the most insistent, asking me to keep his call absolutely confidential. You're to buzz him back, the exact time and the Washington phone number indicated here." Murphy handed Stewart the scrap of paper. "So who's Barak?"

Stewart didn't respond. He glanced at the message, noting that the return call was set for 1:00 P.M. Good, plenty of time, he reasoned. "Okay, Mike, where do I begin?"

"Jesus. You're asking me?" Murphy's face turned grim and purposeful. He waited.

The editor's expectant gaze had a cathartic effect on Stewart. "Mike, listen. I should be dead right now, but I'm not. I'm going to hand you a story to end all stories. We've got to give it a news service feed tonight, come out with our own break in the morning edition. It's our only chance to stop these madmen in their tracks."

Murphy looked up at Stewart, eyes hooded, his jaw steady as stone. "I know what you're going to tell me. I've been doing a little digging myself. There are some religious groups out there wheeling and dealing to take over the networks and a few influential papers, the *Times* included. They'll try to force some shuffling of directorships, maybe a little arm twisting on stockholder proxies."

Stewart gave up a long, exasperated sigh and slowly shook his head. "It's not the fundamentalists we have to worry about. It's their camp following of Nazis and so-called patriots. And they're ruthless. Nothing will stop them. God, I'd give up my right arm tomorrow if stockholder battles were all we had to panic over." Stewart paused, looked at Murphy, saw a puzzled frown. "Look, Mike. What I need from you is immediate help. Keep the police and FBI diverted, off my trail. And I need three people to do some research, come up with sidebars. That camera—send it over to Carlie Chavez at the network. I'll get it from her. I have to go back on the street for several more hours. Cover me."

"Hours for what?" asked Murphy, for the first time a trace of concerned doubt in his voice.

"You and your bosses want to keep the presses rolling all weekend?"

"What's that supposed to mean?"

Stewart frowned, got to his feet. "Tomorrow, after the President's speech, the networks will be closed down and major newspapers around the country as well."

Groaning, Murphy looked at Stewart with a sour face. "Impossible, inconceivable."

"The operation's been planned for months, and they're ready to move. Counting on the element of surprise. I figure some startling headlines might pull the plug, maybe stop them before they blow the whole dam."

"Stewart, your naiveté amazes me," chided Murphy. He smiled uncertainly and shook his head. "New York could go blackout for twenty-hours—hell even longer—and we'd still publish. Ever hear of satellite communications and air freight? You forget our printing plants in Carlstadt, New Jersey; Lakeland, Florida; Torrance, California? The competition has similar alternatives."

Stewart wasn't convinced. "I'm aware of these facilities, but so are the extremists. I'm telling you these people are well organized, armed, and ruthless. And they're only one part of a well-oiled coast-to-coast machine. It's headed by a damned *committee,* a cabal, of sorts. We've got to find out who's in charge."

Murphy nervously pulled out a cigarette, lit it, looked up hesitantly through a pall of smoke. "A cabal to accomplish what?"

"Force the President to resign. Eliminate the Supreme Court liberals. Install a new reactionary cabinet. Overhaul the nation's media. They sent threatening letters to the chairman of NTN. Carlie let me read them."

"Cranks. All cranks. The network took them seriously?"

"No, but I do, Mike. What I've been trying to tell you is just a starter. The American Nazis, the Klan, the Freedom Militia, the Moral Confederation, along with possible military help—"

"Hold it!" Murphy shot to his feet, snorting smoke through

both nostrils like a bull. "A military coup in the United States is about as likely as a snowman in Death Valley in July."

"Mike, do me a favor? Sit your ass back down and just listen. The country's about to be given a Tabasco enema it doesn't need. I'll start from the beginning."

26

ARNOLD METZ DROVE out of the Holland Tunnel, arriving in Manhattan at half past two. He headed for Kirk Stewart's apartment building on Sixth Street. Metz was irritated, his nerves frazzled by the uncomfortable compact rental car, the city traffic, the maze of one-way streets. He had been on the road for over four hours, driving almost steadily since his breakfast meeting with Colonel Reddick at Andrews Air Force Base. His only stops had been at turnpike toll stations and telephone booths. Repeatedly, he had called the *New York Times* office, but all his attempts to discover Stewart's whereabouts had been unproductive. No matter. He would find him.

Metz thought about the reporter and the woman as well. This was all-out war, and they were a threat, an enemy that had to be nullified. He had made a mistake at the YMCA in Washington. He should have been less dramatic, used the stiletto, blood or no blood. Had he turned on the light, he would have known. This time, he would be careful; there would be no slip-ups.

Finding a garage, Metz parked the rented Plymouth, withdrew from the trunk the small satchel that served as his portable arsenal, and walked swiftly toward Stewart's apartment building. Metz paused at the corner. While waiting for the traffic to clear, he popped a capsule into his mouth. The red devil was his own concoction, a fifty-fifty blend of speed and digitalis.

He was still undecided as to which tool he would employ to kill Stewart. Metz was hungry, but food, at the moment, was only a minor consideration. The reporter had to be found and disposed of quickly.

The lobby door was open, and a cleaning woman with greasy, tied-back hair was scrubbing the quarry tile floor. Metz pushed the buzzer below Stewart's mailbox and got no response. He pondered whether to call from a pay phone nearby to see if Stewart would pick up the ring. No, he thought, surprising the reporter would be better. The building superintendent might be of help. Stepping around the cleaning woman, Metz proceeded down the hallway. He tapped sharply on a door marked *Concierge* in ornate, cursive gold leaf.

Almost immediately, the door opened. An older woman primped at her upswept, nearly white hair and surveyed Metz through jeweled bifocals. "Yes? May I help you?"

"I'm looking for Kirk Stewart, the newspaper reporter," he replied quickly. "It's important; I'm a friend of his from Texas." Metz twitched his nose. The room smelled of cats and rosewater.

She studied him. "Young man, I do happen to be the superintendent's wife, but keeping track of tenants isn't my job."

Metz briefly considered reaching in his pocket for a twenty dollar bill to refresh the woman's memory, but seeing her jewelry and gazing the expensively furnished apartment, he thought better of it. This broad simply wasn't the type to be bribed, he figured. "You haven't seen him at all? What time does he usually come home from work?"

The woman looked irritated. She picked up a blue-point Siamese and began stroking its neck. "If you must know, I don't expect him back until Monday." The cat looked at him and purred.

Metz silently ground his teeth. "Not until after the weekend?"

"Yes. That's the message he sent over by his friend."

Metz tensed. His hand shot out, grasping her forearm. The cat jumped to the floor. "That's not enough. What friend? When?"

"Let go of my arm! You're hurting me!" She turned, looking back over her shoulder for assistance. "Willard!"

Metz propelled the woman into the apartment, kicked the door closed behind him. An older man rose stiffly from his chair, hesitated, then proceeded across the room. Metz drew his gun, pointed it. The man and woman froze.

"Now listen carefully, Grandma. *Who* came by and *what* was the message? Where's Stewart?"

Nervously fingering her gold necklaces as though they were a rosary, the woman looked back at Metz tearfully. But she kept her silence.

The old man in the tweed jacket and ascot, the one she had called Willard, took off his glasses. They trembled in his hand, fell to the floor. "Madie, don't you think—"

"Quiet. I'm not afraid of this predaceous ruffian," she snapped.

Metz roughly slammed the woman against the wall and twisted her arm. He watched her drawn face suddenly turn from red to off-white. Her male companion eased forward, wringing his hands. "I took the call," he said despairingly. "Mr. Stewart said he was sending over a staff car from the NTN office to pick up some personal items. When the driver arrived, I took him upstairs." Willard lowered his eyes in self-contempt.

"Where did this errand boy go when he left?" barked Metz. "And what did he take?"

"Stop!" the woman cried. "You're hurting my arm."

Willard continued, "We don't know where the driver went. He took clothing. But he telephoned the newswoman Carlotta Chavez when I let him in the apartment."

Metz released his hold on the woman, eased her away from the wall, then let her go. "Either of you call the police, I'll return. That's an ironclad promise. No matter when, and I'll break her arm." Halfway out the door, he turned back to the old man and hissed, "Or worse, Willard. Maybe both of your legs. Play it safe and live to collect your Social Security."

The wind, salt-smelling and brisk, swept over Battery Park. Kirk Stewart looked out through the dirty window of the phone booth. He watched Carlie Chavez tighten the collar of her coat and munch unenthusiastically on the hot dog she had just purchased from the sidewalk vendor's cart. She ate only half, tossed the rest to the pigeons, then looked back at Stewart and waved. He hung up the phone, rattled the door open, and went up to her.

Carlie straightened her silk scarf with a fussy gesture Stewart liked. He grinned. Carlie was a meticulous dresser, and she looked good in her business suit and matching coat; she was one of the few women he knew who looked feminine in any kind of clothing.

She looked at him with a faint smile. "Good or bad news from Washington?"

Stewart shrugged, gestured toward the promenade running along the waterfront. "Let's walk. The news depends on how you look at it. My Israeli friend didn't tell me anything I didn't already know. He claims there's a leak at FBI headquarters or in the Secret Service. Might even be Oliver Wright himself, although God knows he hates Singer."

They walked slowly along the sea wall. Carlie pondered, then asked, "Oliver Wright? That seems hard to believe. He's been a friend of the President for years."

Stewart paused, staring across the gray expanse of water as though looking for a bottle with a message in it—some secret, scribbled bit of advice, some wisdom from afar that would provide all the answers. He inhaled the clean, stiff breeze off the bay, looked back at Carlie. "Precisely what I told Motti Barak. He's not convinced. He insists I stay away from the Bureau people for the time being. That doesn't leave us much."

"What else did the Israeli say?"

"That's the clincher. He had some direct quotes, supposedly from the chairman of the Joint Chiefs, the CIA director himself, and some renegade Army general. Barak has a tape recording he claims will set me back on my ass. Sorry, Carlie. Forgot we were a team. Toss *both* of us back on our asses."

Carlie smiled. "He played the tapes on the phone?"

"I wasn't that lucky. He said an assistant had it and that it was being copied. Barak gave me the impression he was stalling. Peculiar. I'm to call him at the Israeli embassy later tonight."

"I thought you said he couldn't be reached there?"

"He claims everyone's dirty laundry is on the line now, and that his cover is blown. All I know is that he promised to play the entire recording for me tonight."

They both moved to one side of the walk as an old woman passed by, somewhat unsteadily, on her bicycle. Carlie stopped walking and sent Stewart a scornful look. "Kirk, you know that tonight will be too late. We need more time to prepare the story. Dammit, my TV crew is fast, but not that fast."

"Sorry, Carlie. I couldn't agree more; that's what I told Barak. He threatened to cut us off if we didn't play ball his way. Claimed he had his own problems and was being watched, that it was bad enough I wouldn't oblige him by going back to Washington on the first available flight. He needs another hand."

"Not a bad idea," she said softly. "If that's where the main action seems to be, I think we should both go. Might be a problem pulling my staff together for a remote out of the Washington studio on short notice, but still—"

"No. You stay here. I'll go first thing in the morning. Our Washington bureau chief's already at work, trying to set up a meeting for me with three key senators known to be friendly with the President."

"Why should I remain here?" Her eyes were on him.

Stewart sighed. "According to Barak, this mysterious committee—whoever they are—will be coming to New York immediately following the President's speech, if not before."

"For what purpose?" Carlie asked incredulously.

"To appear on their own TV special. Cutting into all four networks simultaneously."

"Oh, my God. And where will this farce originate?"

Stewart shrugged. "Barak didn't know. Could be at CBS or ABC, but after reading those letters to your big boss, I'm betting on NTN. There's work cut out for you right here in Manhattan."

Carlie's face turned dismal. "Kirk, who are we fighting?"

"I'm going to find out. We have some leads, remember?"

Carlie paused by the rail, letting her gaze shift out past Governors Island. She watched a sleek white cruise ship slowly move outward through the Narrows. "I'm worried," she said finally. "And frightened." Turning back to Stewart, she lifted her eyes, gazing into his. The wind blew several long strands of hair across her cheeks and lips.

Stewart liked what he saw. Carlie was beautiful even when her hair was a windblown mess, he thought. Softly, he said, "You look cold."

"I am. Hold me, Kirk."

Placing his arm around her shoulder, Stewart drew her closer. He lowered his head and kissed her ear. Getting too comfortable again, he thought, feeling a familiar surge in his pulse. He was startled as she suddenly looked up and kissed him, leaning into him with warm suggestion. Then slowly, she pulled back, smiling thoughtfully.

"Well?" he asked.

"That wasn't what you thought it was for," she said quickly. "Please. It's to be careful, Kirk. You tall, foxy hunk, I've come to like you."

"After what's happened thus far I couldn't be anything but cautious. Paranoid's a better word."

"I think you should carry a gun. When we get back to the apartment I want you to take mine."

Stewart laughed. "I wouldn't know how to use it. I'm better off dragging out my college karate." Wishful, sloppy thinking, he mused. He hadn't practiced it in half a dozen years.

Carlie frowned. "You really think this is worth all the risks?"

He looked at her. "Don't give up on me now, Carlotta Chavez. You're as famous as Jimmy Hallowell and just as respected. If ever I needed a celebrity, the time is now."

"Celebrity?" Carlie asked seriously. "What's that got to do with it?"

"Americans are hooked on expertise, credentials, and celebrities. Folk heroes, Carlie." Taking her hand, he led her around a puddle. "Hallowell's one variety, you're another. Instead of believing in themselves—reading, experiencing, learning, whatever—Americans listen to celebrities and take their advice." He paused and looked at her. "They feel empty when their heroes—political leaders, actors, sports stars, whoever—turn out to be fragile after all. Like when they run to religion, drugs, booze, even suicide."

Carlie dropped Stewart's hand and stared at him. "And I'm one of these celebrities—these heroes you're describing."

Stewart turned, smiling. "Not that kind. If you were, I wouldn't need your help—or your company. You work on your audience's mind, not its emotions," he replied, somewhat lamely. "I'm trying to focus on idolatry. I'm convinced hero worship is corrupting."

"Come off it, Kirk. The public is wiser now. P. T. Barnum's notion that there's a sucker born every minute no longer holds true. Television's made the difference."

Stewart pondered for a moment, looked back at her. "For good or bad?"

"Why aren't you among the adoring throngs? Who are your heroes? What makes Kirk Stewart such a unique face in the crowd?" she asked.

"Fair question." Stewart went over to the guard rail, gesturing for Carlie to come up beside him. He looked up toward the Hudson, across the harbor toward Staten Island. "Sometimes I get to thinking, Carlie. I see the a damned dope, the crime in the street, the confused, screwed-up American value system. Conspicuous consumption and fucking waste. Selfishness. Even the chickenshit graffiti on the subway cars can gnaw away at a man's sensibility, his pride in his city, his politics. I get pissed off, like the worst of the extremists." Stewart pointed to the ferry that had just pulled away from the Whitehall Street terminal. "Then I come down here. Sometimes I jog. Other times I walk. Occasionally I need a boat ride to pick up my spirits, so I walk the decks of the Staten Island ferry. Reminds me of the cross-sound trips I used to make as a kid in Seattle. There are ferries all over the Pacific Northwest. You know what I do out there in New York Harbor, Carlie?"

She looked at him expectantly, but kept her silence.

"I turn up my collar against the cold, stand by the rail, and play tourist, gazing at the Statue of Liberty. I also check out Ellis Island, and I think about the millions of immigrants who came through there, including my own grandfather. Looking back this way, I see the promise of the impressive Manhattan skyline. And if all that's not enough to boost my spirits, I go back to my apartment in the Village and read over the journal I scribbled when I was fresh out of college—the story of my second-class trip across Russia on the Trans-Siberian Railroad." Stewart paused, shaking his head and savoring the recollection. "When a man's seen all the vacant, joyless faces in the Soviet Union, he's better equipped to handle the empty, demanding stomachs in America. Compromise isn't comfortable, but that's what it's all about, Carlie. Compromise isn't bad or good, but God in heaven, it's capitalism's chance for the future." He took her hand and they walked on in silence.

When the taxi dropped them off at the lower Second Avenue address the driver looked from Carlie to Stewart, pointed to the bar doorway, and said impassively, "Buddy, I got news for you. You may get the lady inside the door, but she'll die of thirst before they serve her."

Stewart winked, tipped the driver, and dismissed him. Le Brute, he noted, didn't appear to be an ordinary homosexual hangout. The outside of the bar—painted a somber black with only one small, almost apologetic sign above the door—gave no indication that the establishment catered to the S-and-M motorcycle crowd. Carlie, however, had set Stewart straight on the way over in the taxi, telling him she had done a TV news clip on this and similar haunts several years back.

Together, they went inside. It was midafternoon, and the dim interior was almost deserted. On one side of the room a long bar, constructed of varnished, cigarette-burned railroad ties, ran the length of the wall. Attached to the bar at random intervals were oval urinals containing matchbooks. The inside of Le Brute, like the exterior, was painted black. There were crude chalk drawings on the walls, some of them obscene. The place reeked of stale beer. Behind the counter, a man filling the cooler with beer bottles looked up as Carlie and Stewart approached.

"I'm looking for the owner, a guy named Freighter," Stewart said boldly.

The man grunted. Stewart waited for him to put aside his case of beer and answer. He was a tall, rather gaunt man in his late thirties, wearing a brown bomber jacket and tired Levi pants. His head was shaven, and he had a red bandanna tied around one sleeve, a yellow one on the other. Despite the early hour, his red-lined eyes had a dull, liquored gaze. He gave Stewart a hard look and said, "I'm Freighter. So what do you want?"

"A couple of questions, a minute of your time."

The bar owner raised an eyebrow. "If you're from the Health Department, checking out my sinks and toilets, be my guest." He gestured toward the rear of the room. Three other men at the bar, engaged in jocular conversation and swilling beer, looked up only briefly.

Stewart smiled. "Look, we need to find Dennis Garrett. I understand he's headed your way. It's damned important. His life may be in danger."

The man behind the bar smiled, shifting valleys of tired flesh. "Hell, you think I give a shit? I gave up trying to keep track of him two years ago. He settled in with me two nights ago, then disappeared again. I don't know where he's shacked up. He's in and out of leather, not a regular. You want to find him during working hours, that's easy enough. I hear he took a job at Suzette's. Don't bother going there, though; you'll never make it inside."

Stewart frowned. "Yeah? Says who?"

The bar owner shrugged. "The shrewd midget lady who runs the place, Suzette, that's who. Garrett's an exhibitionist. He's found his spot all right, in her all-male exotic revue. It has a ladies-only audience, get it? Kind of the opposite of what we have here. Your girlfriend can get in." He turned to Carlie, squinting. "Hey, wait a minute. I recognize you. Channel Three news lady. Can I buy you a beer?"

An hour after the C-11 press demonstration, Motti Barak emerged from the underground concourse connecting the two buildings of Washington's National Gallery of Art. He paused to check his watch. Pleased that he was five minutes early, he took his time heading for the French Impressionists exhibit. He patted the two tape cassettes in his pocket, pleased that the miniature mikes in the ball-point pens had functioned so well.

The gallery wasn't crowded. Relaxing on a settee in the middle of the hall, Barak's eyes methodically swept over the visitors. Mostly schoolchildren. A few adults on tours. Several long-robed monks, earphones clamped over their heads and guided-tour tape players slung over their shoulders, paused in front of Degas's *Madame René de Gas*.

Barak looked up, carefully studying the monks, making sure none of them carried a copy of *Paris-Match* under his arm. He laughed at the prospect of a Russian agent going that far for a clever disguise. He watched, as the monks, their brown robes rustling, moved off to the next corridor.

Almost immediately two men approached, gazed intently at the Degas oil, and began whispering. One of the men carried a recent copy of *Paris-Match*. The recognition signal. Good, but why two men? Glancing around, making sure the immediate area was quiet, Barak rose and stepped forward. As he approached the pair from behind, he heard them conversing in fluent, hushed English. Their voices bore only the slightest accent.

"Good day," Barak called out. "I see you enjoy the Degas,

yes? Have you also seen his works in the *Louvre?*" Barak had dispensed with the code word; a specific, equally innocuous response would prove their bona fides.

"No, my friend," said the younger man. He had a thick brown beard, wore a twill jacket and khaki slacks, and might easily be cast in the role of a young Fidel Castro. His accent, though slight, was unmistakably Russian. Continuing, he said, "But we have seen his paintings in New York. *La Toilette* at the Metropolitan is particularly interesting."

Barak smiled, taking in the second individual, who was older, had a square jaw, a slight paunch, and the wide hips typical of Russian men. Barak wondered why two operatives had been sent when one would have sufficed and been less conspicuous. Perhaps the ambassador didn't trust him, or possibly the KGB didn't trust Mikhail Grotski. His superiors were making a summit meeting of a routine operation, Barak thought, his sense of injustice and personal affront even stronger than usual.

Once again, Barak wondered if he was doing the right thing, this duty above all else. Should he have first turned his incriminating tapes over to the newspaper reporter and given duplicates to the KGB much later? Kirk Stewart should be here, but it was too late for such considerations. The two intense men expected him to produce, and he no longer had a choice. Back at the Soviet compound, Ambassador Grotski would be waiting. The Russians would get their copy first.

The older man looked impatiently at Barak. "Enough of this decadent art," he rasped quietly. "We are waiting, Comrade."

Barak smiled. "Perhaps the capitalists have Impressionist art in order not to die of the truth."

The two men looked at him grimly. Barak glanced nervously around him, reached in his pocket, and extended a cassette. The one with the beard took the tape, thrust it quickly into his pocket.

They were alone, so Barak spoke swiftly and softly in Russian. "The conspiracy is of greater proportions than we suspected. It has alarming possibilities. The outcome depends on the reactions of the President, any loyal friends he can muster in the Military, and the FBI. The American news media also may be of help, but only if they move quickly enough." Barak exhaled slowly and looked away, toward the paintings on the far wall. He smiled and added, "I suggest you take in the rest of the French Impressionists at another time. Degas, Monet, and Renoir may stir your emotions, but the information on that tape, I fear, will stir the world."

The two Russians nodded.

Barak moved closer to the man with the beard and whispered in his ear in Russian. "The capitalist tiger, I'm afraid, is changing its stripes. It could become a far more dangerous cat."

The contact looked back at him and quietly scoffed. "The aggressive nature of the imperialist does not change, and it does not frighten us, Comrade. The tiger is a beast of prey, but it never attacks the elephant."

Barak nodded, turned, and walked slowly out of the gallery.

Stewart saw his reflection in the phone booth's glass, his boyish face suddenly haggard, with lines under his eyes. He looked every bit as beat as he felt. Tap Nelson's clipped voice on the line from Washington made him even more tired and irritable.

"Who you kidding, Kirk? Only damned reason you haven't broken your story yet is that you're waiting for the big sting."

Stewart ignored Nelson's abrasiveness and glanced at Carlie. She was staring at him from outside the booth. He smiled, tossed her a kiss, and again spoke into the phone. "What happened to the ski trip, Nelson? Were the bunny slopes at Stowe too much for you?"

The voice at the other end of the line sounded irritated. "Up yours. The boss called me back early. We've got hell breaking loose everywhere, your bullshit included. What's with you, for chrissake? Why haven't you returned Oliver Wright's phone calls? You plan on fleeing the country or going underground?"

"Tap, I'm sorry. I know it looks bad." Stewart paused, considering whether to tell Nelson about the phone number that belonged to Condor's board chairman. No. The FBI line might be monitored.

"Stewart, you still there?"

"Yeah. I need your help."

"You've got it, but first things first. Where are you staying? I've been trying to call your office and your apartment for hours."

Stewart stiffened, shrank back in the booth like an animal that has seen the shiny steel beneath the meat. "No offense intended, pal, but I haven't decided where I'll sleep tonight. When I do, I'll probably keep it to myself. What's more, I can't talk now, not on your office phone."

Nelson's voice sharpened. "What the hell you talking about?"

"Either Oliver Wright or some of his men are in this mess with Singer."

There was a long silence. "Jesus Christ, Kirk. Come off it. You believe that? Impossible."

Stewart limited himself to a negative grunt. Quickly, he said, "Okay, listen. Where's the nearest pay phone booth at your end?"

"Downstairs, in the visitors' lobby."

Stewart's jaw clenched. "No, not in the FBI Building, you imbecile!"

There was another pause; then Nelson said, "Kirk, you're crazy. I'll hike down the street if it'll make you happy. But what you have to say had better be good."

"Fine. Pay attention now and think hard. Do you remember the name of that small New York bar where I introduced you to Shira a year or so ago? The time we had double margaritas?"

Stewart glanced sideways, distracted by Carlie as she opened the booth's folding door and squeezed inside.

Nelson responded. "Yeah, of course I remember."

Carlie snuggled close to Stewart, looking up at him with worried eyes.

He said into the phone, "All right, I'm heading there right now. When you find a public phone, get the number of that bar from New York information and call me there. In half an hour. No later. I have too much to do this afternoon to stand around getting pie-eyed."

Carlie's fingers circled Stewart's hand, squeezing it tight.

Stewart hung up the phone without signing off. He looked down at her. He kissed her, this time without qualm.

27

THE TWO CIA men who had accompanied Sam Wadislow to the top of the Potomac Plaza had departed, returning to sit in their car on the street far below. The hotel roof was cold, a stiff wind blowing over the capital from the northwest. Cursing the microwave relay reflector that had slipped from its mount, Wadislow dug in his toolbox for another wing nut. The electronics engineer didn't see the workman in blue coveralls who had slipped quietly from the air conditioning enclosure and come up behind him. He sensed something; he wasn't sure just what. Too late he turned, and saw only the quick blur of pipe wrench before it crashed down on his head with a dull thud.

The man in coveralls deftly dislodged the large microwave dish, managed to ease it over so that it hid Wadislow's body. The workman then probed through the engineer's toolbox, removing several VCR switches, half a dozen patching clips, and a roll of black plastic tape. Once more double-checking the tools in his pocket, he glanced around the roof. The area was quiet. He carefully examined the coaxial cables that led from the remaining parabolic antennas, then followed them to the edge of the roof. A narrow window-washing rig, equipped with heavy hemp lines and geared block and tackle, was suspended just outside the parapet.

The workman gingerly climbed aboard, steadied himself, then began cranking the platform down the building's glass facade.

Inside the Committee's improvised headquarters on the thirtieth floor, the conference was into its second hour. Walter Singer was growing increasingly impatient. He rocked back and forth in his swivel armchair, eyeing the others. "Now that Gifford's Citadel crew has repaired that interference satellite, I'm absolutely confident," he said. He managed a smile and added, "It'll be like taking a toy from a sleeping baby." Singer glanced at his watch. He would spare the group another fifteen minutes before leaving.

Jimmy Hallowell spoke up from the end of the conference table. "I'm impressed, gentlemen, although some of our operational staff's solutions strike me as a bit ruthless."

"They're workable solutions," snapped Singer.

Hallowell persisted. "God help the minorities."

Karl Frober laughed. His hands shook where they were folded across his girth. "Good! Let God help them. The damned government's been helping them long enough."

At the center of the table Norman Gifford sifted through several manila folders and waved one in the air. "I suggest we get back to the state capital portfolio. The computer printouts for tomorrow are missing." Gifford looked at Singer. "Your CIA people indicated that Massachusetts and Oregon presented problems."

Singer leaned over the table, scrawled a notation on the document before him, and slid it to Gifford. "No longer," he snapped. "This morning I did a little housecleaning."

"He means 'forceful persuading,'" added Frober, grinning.

Gifford picked up his chairman's gavel and was about to strike it; he scowled instead.

Frober chuckled. "Relax, Norman. You'll get used to the words after you become secretary of state. You'll be up to your ears in it in Central and South America."

The defense plant chairman didn't appear pacified, thought Singer. Frober and Gifford were like two peas in a pod when it came to politics, but their personalities were poles apart.

Gifford suddenly asked, "What about the governors then?"

Singer looked up. "They haven't a chance in hell." He rose,

went to the blackboard, pointed to a series of numbers he'd written there earlier. "The shock teams assembled at state level are small, but highly trained groups. We've already taken into custody the governors who won't be in their offices tomorrow. Harriet of Connecticut, was at his ski condominium. Mitsui of Hawaii was picked up after he deplaned in San Francisco. Myers of Idaho was about to take off on a fishing trip. It's a matter of moving in rapidly with the others; we'll also hold any subordinates who are authorized to call up National Guard units at the state level."

Jimmy Hallowell looked annoyed.

Singer watched the minister push back his chair, imperiously get up, and walk over to the wall of glass that overlooked the river.

Slowly, Hallowell said, "I still question the Nazi cadres wearing their swastika arm bands. We need their muscle, but not that kind of publicity." Hallowell glanced up, startled by the traveling window-washing scaffold that slowly descended in front of him. The workman on it nodded to Hallowell as he tied off the platform outside the suite.

Singer lit his second panatela of the day, at the same time studying the man outside the window through a haze of blue smoke. The workman, he noted, ignored the activity in the hotel room and went about his business immediately. Apparently an electrician, not a window washer. The man fastened several windblown wires back in place, carefully examined and marked others with colored tape.

Jimmy Hallowell turned from the window to face Gifford. "One of your Condor electronics people, I trust?"

Gifford nodded. "He probably works for Wadislow."

Frober looked toward the window, then back to Gifford. "I thought he was CIA, one of your men, Singer."

Gifford didn't appear concerned. His eyes were on Hallowell. "Now, about those swastikas, Mr. Hallowell. It's not—"

"Just a minute," Singer interjected, his gaze still fixed on the window. Easing away from the conference table, making a deliberate effort to appear casual, he picked up the phone connecting the suite to the small office the CIA had set up at the end of the hall. The others watched him, perplexed. After a short wait, he said into the phone, "Perkins, this is Singer. The man outside this suite, on the scaffold. Is he one of Wad-

islow's assistants or one of your men? Whoever he is, call him
off until we're finished. I'm uncomfortable with electricians
working outside my window when I'm in the middle of a
conference." Singer listened briefly, then frowned. "Hell, no.
I don't recognize every last employee on our payroll. Look
into it." He hung up the phone, shook his head, and rolled his
chair back up to the table.

"Relax, Walter," soothed Gifford. "He's all right." He turned
to Hallowell. "Now, about those arm bands."

Frober interrupted. "Whether any of you appreciate their
banners or not, those Nazis are important to us, because of
their numerical strength and their enthusiasm. They're one of
our strongest fibers."

Hallowell came back to the conference table, looked hard
at the fat man. *"Fiber?* I'm sure Walter here feels his CIA
deserves that credit. But as far as I'm concerned, the gossamer
thread of this so-called American renaissance is the *Bible.*"

Frober groaned, then whispered in an animal snarl, "Renaissance, my broad ass. Political power stems from the barrel
of a gun."

"Quiet, both of you," Singer said bluntly. "Screw the petty
rhetoric and get on with business."

Directly across from the Potomac Plaza, the two CIA agents
inside the parked Ford sedan exchanged puzzled looks. The
man behind the wheel rasped into the radio microphone. "What
are you talking about, Perkins? All our men are here in the
car, except Singer and yourself. We've got no electrician on
the job today, and nobody should be on that roof now but Sam
Wadislow." He paused, listening to the reply. "Singer said *what?*
Just a minute." The agent dropped the mike, reached under the
seat for his binoculars, trained them on the upper floors of the
hotel. Sweat began forming on his forehead.

"Cocksuckers," he said slowly, as he handed the glasses to
his front seat companion. "If that's not a Bureau man, I'll—
oh, shit!" Retrieving the microphone, he snapped, "Perkins,
you're right. Get your ass up to the roof. Don't ask questions,
and don't take the time to call the boss back. Just eliminate
that snoop before he can doctor up those circuits. Yes. we'll
cover you. Use your brains, damn it. Make it look like an
accident. Hell, grab a fire ax."

• • •

Singer tried to ignore the man working outside the window. He looked around the conference table. "Gentlemen, let's stop playing games. We need the Nazis, the Freedom Militia, and the Klan, as well as our other conservative allies. If the Nazis need a symbol to rally behind, the swastika's easier to eyeball than a red star. I say let's not panic over a damned arm band."

"Why frighten people unnecessarily?" Hallowell asked quietly.

Singer scowled. "We've got to frighten certain elements, make our presence known."

Leaning forward in his seat, Frober added, "Most of the country will fall in line like sheep at a slaughter, but I'm still concerned about the blacks in Detroit and Cleveland. And we could have problems in San Francisco."

Singer blew smoke in the air. "Moving on. Norman, what about initial contacts with the West European legations?"

"I'll do that when we arrive back from New York. While I'm in Manhattan I'll touch on several aspects of our proposed foreign policy during our network telecasts."

Frober looked sharply at Gifford. "You've discussed this with Vice-President Chandler? He's anxious about the Soviets."

Gifford smiled thinly. "With good reason. Russian Ambassador Grotski's playing a cunning wait-and-see game."

"Paul Chandler should be at this meeting," complained Hallowell.

Gifford frowned. "Impossible. It was difficult enough to sneak the CIA director into this hotel, let alone the Vice-President. I had my doubts about using this conspicuous location in the first place."

"Looking for skeletons in the closet, Norman?" Hallowell was smiling for the first time. "This isn't the Watergate."

Ignoring the spat, Singer looked at his cigar. It had gone out, and he relit it. "The price is right," he said flatly. "I like the location."

Frober shot Gifford an indignant look. "Your own Condor men checked out the facilities and approved them. Sam Wadislow tells me he installed the best debugging and scramble gear money can buy." Sweat glistened on his scalp beneath his crew cut as Frober turned and pointed to the window. "Look outside. They're still perfecting it. We're in the most secure spot in Washington, and I'm not puffing just because I own this hotel."

"Frober's right," snapped Singer, with finality. "Next subject?"

Jimmy Hallowell welcomed the opportunity for a conversational broad jump. "What if the President doesn't resign? Suppose he decides to fight?"

Singer calmly puffed his cigar, yielding the floor to Gifford.

"It's too risky forcing him off to Haiti with the others. All we need is a damned government in exile. I suggest that we intern him for the balance of his term at Condor's Citadel in California."

There was a moment's silence in the room. "We could help some nut assassinate the bastard." The soft voice was Frober's. The others ignored him. Hallowell, especially, sat stony-faced. Singer bit back a smile.

Norman Gifford eased back in his chair, folded his arms before him. "The apartment inside the Citadel is comfortable. It's closed off and entirely self-contained. I've stayed there myself on several occasions. The area's as tight as a drum and well-guarded. His detention there could be kept top secret." Gifford looked at the others, waiting for a response.

It was only a slight noise, a quick blur that didn't belong, but it caused all the committeemen to suddenly look to the window. Staring in amazement, they saw the scaffold drop at one end. The workman, his face twisted in horror, reached out, clawed at the air, then slid helplessly off the end of the rig and hurtled toward the sidewalk thirty stories below. The rigging rope, frayed at one end, slipped past the window, snaking its way after him.

"Between five and six," the New York City librarian had told Stewart, "the microfilm room will be quiet." She was right; he had the files virtually to himself. Under ordinary circumstances, Stewart would have used the facilities at the *Times*, but he couldn't chance it now, not until the police and FBI had been called off and Murphy gave him the green light to return. Worse, Arnold Metz might be watching the office. Hiding and going about one's work, Stewart found, were irreconcilable tasks; the fear made haste all the more imperative.

He glanced at the stack of photocopies he'd made of articles about the chief executive of Condor Defense Industries. At least a dozen so far, and he was only beginning. Norman Gifford appeared to be a controversial figure. Stewart didn't have time to read them all now; he would take the lot back to Carlie's apartment and work there until she returned from the studio.

Stewart pulled another reel from the file, went back to the microfilm machine, and threaded it. He pushed the button, and the motor whirred. News copy flashed before him along with full-page ads for computers, Rolls-Royce automobiles, reduced transatlantic air fares. Stewart was in a low mood. His eyes were weary, and his shoulder had started to ache again.

The *Wall Street Journal* was proving more fertile than *Speeches in Print* or the *New York Times*. He found material on Condor Industries, a news article reporting an illegal trade of weapons through third parties. Stewart remembered the incident from two years earlier. He also found stories about some kind of swap of foreign properties belonging to Worldwide Hotels Corporation—hotel structures in Libya and Iraq, development property in Haiti, deals that had been hotly debated by the State and Defense departments. Stewart put in a coin and activated the built-in copier.

Across the aisle a young woman took a place at another viewer. She gave him more than a casual gaze. She went through the motions of examining the microfilm, but her eyes repeatedly left the screen. A trifle too often?

Stewart felt a sudden uneasiness. He pondered over the young woman's presence. There were plenty of women agents in both the FBI and CIA. Why was she interested in him and pretending otherwise? His heart beat faster. He knew he had to leave. There wasn't time to weigh the possibilities.

As casually as he could, Stewart gathered up his reference materials, turned off the microfilm machine, and left the room. He took his time strolling out of the library. Once outside, he waited across the street for several minutes. The woman didn't follow.

I'm becoming paranoid, Stewart thought. I've got to get control of myself.

The early evening traffic in Manhattan was light, and Carlie made good time to Suzette's all-male exotic revue on Forty-ninth Street just off Broadway. Carlie's new bodyguard-driver insisted on going with her into the club, but at the entrance quickly discovered that the Ladies Only—Early Show sign meant what it said. Men were being turned away.

"Stay with the car," Carlie said, dismissing him. Kirk had already agreed to remain in her apartment and wait for her call. She paid the cover at the ticket window and climbed a long flight of stairs. At the landing she paused beneath a garish prism chandelier, then bravely stepped inside the club. The music was loud, and there was shouting and applause.

Carlie joined several other women who appeared to be alone at the main bar. The floor show in the brilliantly lit chamber was already in progress, and no one took notice of her. All eyes were on the sparsely clad young men spotlighted in the center of the room. The busy bartenders, too, ignored her; finally a tall, red-haired waiter in a black satin jockstrap, white dickie, and formal bow tie, took her order. She asked for a tequila sunrise. The waiter teasingly brushed against her knee as he departed. Carlie smiled, rubbing her arms to brush away the tiny goose bumps beginning to form.

She had purposely arrived late, aware that Dennis Garrett was scheduled to appear in the final segment of the show. She watched, fascinated, as three men dressed as Parisian gendarmes teased the all-female audience. Tossing aside their capes and nightsticks, they disrobed, and the women became ecstatic. By the time the smiling, muscular men had stripped to their bikini briefs, the audience was clapping in unison. The room was so crowded that some women were kneeling on the edge of the dance floor. Carlie watched two fat girls in the front row rise, ponderously crash forward, and land at the dancers' feet. They screamed, made promiscuous gestures, tucked cash into the men's G-strings, and finally returned to their places.

The waiter brought Carlie a drink, and she tipped him liberally. She laughed, having to admit to herself that Suzette's was definitely an interesting place. Carlie was pleased that no one had recognized her. The anonymity pleased her. The stage show commanded all their attention. She sipped slowly at her drink as an appealing, dark-haired dancer—a John Travolta look-alike—pushed a baby carriage to the center of the floor. He wore only white cotton bikini briefs edged in silver sequins. He bowed unctuously, pulled aside a white veil from the carriage, and called, "I introduce you to Madame Suzette!"

Her hair a tangle of frizzy salt-and-pepper ringlets, a pug-nosed midget woman crawled upright and placed her tiny hands on her hips. She emitted an unladylike belch, pulled a silver compact from her pocket, and proceeded to touch up her garish lipstick. Smiling, smacking her ruby mouth, she accepted the microphone from her assistant.

"I am Madame Suzette," the tiny woman lisped in a gravelly voice over the microphone. "You all like men, yes?" She wiggled her hips and legs.

The audience cheered and applauded; a few women gave her the Bronx cheer.

"And you like them hot, yes?" Suzette laughed, digging in the baby carriage and retrieving several red and green peppers. *"Arriba!"* she shouted, skillfully juggling them. Suddenly, she turned and thrust them inside the briefs of the Travolta lookalike. He pretended to be startled. Grinning, he danced his way offstage.

"Welcome to Suzette's!" the woman shouted, jumping down from the carriage and strutting with her microphone to the corner of the room. The spotlight followed her, while a chorus of male dancers pushed a miniature red barn—a prop hardly larger than a doghouse for a Saint Bernard—to the center of the floor. The band struck a discordant theme, and the audience held its breath.

"Ladies!" Suzette commanded. "I'm pleased to present not only the most debonair young men in Manhattan but variety as well, yes? Meet the newest member of our troop, Hunky Hayseed! What every woman would secretly like to find in the backwoods of Appalachia!"

Abruptly, the red and white doors of the miniature barn flew open. A muscular youth, clad only in a tattered straw hat and cut-off Levis, leaped out, holding a pitchfork. The band somehow managed to come up with a noise that was a cross between a cow's moo and a foghorn.

Carlie laughed and took a quick sip of her tequila sunrise. So this was Dennis Garrett. She watched him begin his provocative dance and toss aside his cut-offs. Carlie considered his face, suddenly coming back to reality, remembering the purpose of her mission. She would head backstage immediately following his act.

The young "farmboy" danced with absolute abandon as the drummer stepped up the tempo. Garrett moved closer to the women at the edge of the floor and, one after another, removed several pairs of briefs. The audience screamed, called out to him. Some laughed. Others squirmed forward on their knees, tucked five and ten dollar bills in Garrett's G-string. Madame

Suzette's ever-present shriek, almost lost in the keening female voices, kept repeating above the music, "Don't forget, ladies! No touching of the merchandise."

Carlie was startled to see Garrett leap from the stage and dance over to the bar, the spotlight following. Suddenly he was before her. Involuntarily, she edged backwards. Had she been recognized? The insolently bulging muscles, the carefully rehearsed smile meant nothing to her. Was it Garrett's practiced sensuality or some instinct warning her that inside this dancing Adonis's body was an evil, dangerous person?

The audience's hysteria did not die out until the sweating Garrett bowed and retired to the wings. But then the bedlam began again as two burly, weightlifter types took the stage and lifted Suzette to their shoulders. She laughed, a wild Gypsy cackle, as she introduced them. The men danced, and Suzette retired to a place at the bar.

Time to get down to business, Carlie thought. She edged along the bar toward Suzette. Luckily, the woman recognized her and willingly listened to her request to meet Dennis Garrett. She led Carlie backstage, pointed to a dressing room, and left her alone. Carlie knocked.

Garrett opened the door and stuck his head out. "Yes?" There was a towel around his neck, and his face was still covered with perspiration.

"Hi. My name is Carlie Chavez. Do you have a minute so we can talk?"

He looked at her speculatively, then edged out into the hallway. "Sure. I recognize you. The NTN news lady. I'm flattered. So what are you doing in a dive like this?"

Carlie looked around her and smiled. "This is a fun place, but I'd like to talk to you privately. No cameras, no tape recorders or notes. Off the record." She pointed toward the dressing room.

Garrett grinned, reached behind the door for a robe. "Sorry. I'm just a member of the chorus, not a star. Couple of dudes dressing in there. Let's go outside on the fire escape. The alley's quiet enough."

Garrett nodded to the backstage watchman by the door and escorted her outside on the landing. "Now then?" he asked. "Go ahead, I'm honored."

"This has nothing to do with your performance," Carlie said, her voice taut.

"I'm listening," he said cautiously.

Carlie blurted out her questions. "Do you know a Karen and Wanda in Washington, D.C.? Do you also know a Tim Harris?"

Garrett's jaw dropped. "I don't understand. Why—"

"They're all dead. Murdered. Also Congressman Schmidt." He looked at her incredulously, then stiffened.

Carlie exhaled slowly. "You've made a mistake, Dennis. A bad one. Look, I'm not going to pontificate. You know the President of the United States is in trouble, right? You've done a con job, and your buddies seem to think it has a chance of working. You really think he's going to resign?"

Garrett looked at her stonily. "Look babe, I'm not into politics. I don't know what you're talking about. This is only my third night in this toilet, but it's getting more bizarre by the day. Jesus Christ, who's the troll that sent you in here to bug me?" He turned to leave.

Carlie grabbed his arm, pulled him back. "Look, muscle boy, do I look like the type to waste time screaming platitudes in a place like this? I couldn't care less about these bulging biceps or your pretty face. Right now, all I want to do is prevent the damned government from falling on its face, protect my own job, and keep you from winding up in a block of cement."

Garrett looked at her, bewildered. "Cement? What are you talking about, lady?"

Quietly, she explained. "Unless you cooperate, you're a dead duck. It's not my friends who are after you; it's yours. Remember Arnold Metz? I don't have time to tell you how many people he's already killed, but you could be next."

Garrett's face looked pale. "How do you know Metz?"

"I don't. But a reporter friend of mine does. And the FBI, furthermore, knows all about your little plot. What none of us know, is who you and Metz work for."

He looked at her, started back into the club, then reconsidered.

"Who do *you* work for?" he asked flatly.

"Only the TV network. My friend who talked to Tim Harris in Washington—he's a reporter for the *New York Times*. If you cooperate, we'll get you the protection you need."

Garrett sneered. "I don't know what the hell you're talking about."

Carlie moved closer. "You made an incriminating videotape

that I'm going to expose tomorrow morning as a big lie. You'll have every reporter in the country down here by late afternoon waiting for you. But I suspect that Arnold Metz will get to you first."

He studied her face. "What do you want?"

"An exclusive videotape interview in which you admit your mistake; it will go to the President only. And the names of the men at the top—the Committee. This in return for your protection. We'll hide you until it's safe."

Garrett's hands were trembling slightly. His eyes looked away. "How do I know I can trust you?" he asked nervously.

"Dennis, I'm not an extremist or a psychopathic killer. Metz is. And he works for this employer of yours." She paused, looked at him. "Who paid you?"

"A former employer. Sorry, I'm not sure I can trust you. Tim Harris is proof of that. He should never have confided in you."

Carlie felt a flash of anger. "He didn't. Kirk Stewart was with him, and saw what happened to Karen and Wanda. Will you talk to Kirk?"

Increasingly apprehensive, Garrett hesitated. His face paled even more as he slowly shook his head. "I should have gone straight to Los Angeles."

"They'll hunt you down wherever you go."

"All right, all right. Can the FBI protect me?"

"Don't count on it. We're not sure who's legit there. But Kirk and I will both help if you just tell us who's on that committee."

Garrett's mouth opened, then slowly closed. Finally, he said, "Bring your friend here. I'll meet you both after my late show. Don't worry. Men are admitted after ten o'clock. If this Kirk Stewart is convincing, I'll tell you who set me up. Maybe even the plan. Are you sure Arnold Metz is headed for New York?"

Carlie nodded. "He doesn't give up easily."

Garrett wiped the sweat off his forehead. "Come back at ten. One thing I don't need is money. They gave me plenty of it. But be prepared to get me out of here to a safe place."

28

STEWART FINISHED SHAVING, rinsed his face with cool water, and looked in the mirror. The shower had refreshed him, but his eyes were still dull and red-lined with fatigue. He had a story, but Mike Murphy and the *Times* hierarchy probably wouldn't like it enough to give it a banner or two-column spread. He needed more facts; speculation on what might happen wasn't good enough. Tap Nelson was right: Stewart needed a sting—a powerful one.

Stewart put on a navy blue pullover sweater and went into Carlie's living room. He had talked to Tap earlier and gotten nowhere. Nelson was stubborn, convinced Oliver Wright was playing it straight; moreover, the press secretary had informed him that Wright had an early morning appointment with the President, at which time the FBI chief planned to put all his cards on the table face up. But saying and doing were different things. Was Wright to be trusted?

And where was Motti Barak? The Israeli embassy had finally acknowledged that he was staying there and would return Kirk's call. But when? First Barak had asked him to catch a plane. Now Tap Nelson, too, wanted him to return to Washington in the morning, to forget his news story for the present. File it after the President's speech, he had suggested. Stewart wandered over to Carlie's liquor cabinet, poured himself a heavy scotch with a splash of Calso water. Finding no ice in the silver thermos, he headed toward the kitchen. The phone rang. Pulse quickening, he nervously glanced at his watch and picked up the receiver. It was Carlie, shouting to make herself heard over a noisy background.

Stewart listened carefully to her instructions, then said, "You told me the place was for women only."

"Just the early show. Get over here, Kirk, but be careful leaving the building. I'll send my driver to pick you up."

"No. Keep him down there with you. How long until the next performance?"

"Half an hour," she shouted. "I'll wait at the bar. Garrett's here, working under a stage name. He's agreed to talk if we can provide protection."

"May not be easy, but we'll have to try. I'm on my way."

"Kirk, please hurry."

He hung up, grabbed his coat, and headed for the door. The phone rang again as he was about to leave, and Stewart hurried back to it. "Still here," he said lightly, half expecting Carlie had forgotten something.

No voice. Only dead air. Finally, there was a click, followed by a dial tone.

Thursday night at ten the uptown traffic was light, and Stewart made it by cab to Madame Suzette's in short order. The hang-up phone call still rattled him. Glancing in both directions he saw no sign of Carlie's chauffeur-bodyguard. Apparently, he had parked farther up the block. The ticket woman's eyebrow quivered slightly when he asked for a single admission.

"You a method actress?" he asked smartly. "Just give me the ticket, okay?" Stewart ignored her smile and headed up the long flight of stairs, taking two at a time. Entering the club, he went directly to the bar and strolled its length. The floor show was well under way.

No sight of Carlie. She was probably in the powder room, he thought. Stewart turned, ordered a scotch on the rocks from a less than friendly waiter, then considered the men on stage. He felt uncomfortable, but looked on curiously, even managing a slight smile.

Two numbers went by and still no Carlie. Stewart began to

worry. Perhaps she had stepped out to make a phone call. Damn
her. He felt awkward standing there alone. Stewart edged down
the bar, once more searched all the tables, studied the eager
women around the dance floor. No Carlie Chavez. He looked
into the foyer, toward the lounges and phone booths. Empty.
Reentering the main room, he went back to the bar, started to
order another scotch, changed his mind. He had to keep his
head clear, and he was tired enough. He ordered a glass of
Perrier with a lime twist and listened to Madame Suzette's
spiel.

Dennis Garrett's number was beginning. The midget woman's voice rose to a grating crescendo as a miniature red barn
was pushed to stage center. A spotlight focused on it as two
actors opened the door, accompanied by a fanfare.

But a smiling, muscular young man did not leap out and
bow, as Stewart and the audience expected. Instead, eyes frozen
in an obscene stare, Garrett tottered forward and dropped like
a rock to the floor. Straw hat fallen to one side, he lay sprawled
face down, and deeply imbedded in his nude back were the
shiny tines of a pitchfork. Rivulets of blood oozed to the floor.
A shiver racked Stewart. It didn't take much to reconstruct the
grisly attack.

Several women in the audience screamed. The band stopped
playing. A silent, ominous pall fell over the room. Stewart
hastily made his way to the exit, taking the stairs to the street
two at a time. Behind him, he could hear chaos erupting.
Spotting the doorman by the ticket window, Stewart grabbed
his lapels. "Look, I need your help. Carlotta Chavez, the network newswoman. She was to meet me tonight, at the bar.
You know what she looks like?"

The doorman pulled away, trying to see what the commotion
was about at the top of the stairway. He glanced back at Stewart.
"Yeah. I saw her leave. So what? I mind my own business."

"When did she leave?" Stewart fumbled in his pocket, planted
a crumpled ten in the doorman's hand.

"Just before the second show began. She was pretty bad
off. I never figured she was the type to go heavy on the sauce.
Her boyfriend had a hell of a time getting her down the stairs."
The doorman backed away from Stewart, attracted by a shout
from the stairway.

Stewart frantically grabbed him again. "Wait! This friend
of hers. What did he look like?"

"Hell, I don't remember. He slipped me a twenty to leave his car in the loading zone when he went upstairs. Then I helped him slide the lady into the front seat. He was my height, dark hair, I think. Oh, yeah, the car had D.C. plates." He pushed Stewart away and hurried inside. Stewart wanted to shout something after the doorman, but all he could do was hold up his tightly clenched fist.

Stewart took off at a run toward Times Square. Pounding along the sidewalk, he felt his breath catch in his throat. Not enough sleep. Don't worry about it now. At the corner he turned to cross the street and saw Carlie's NTN staff car, her bodyguard asleep at the wheel. Running over to it, he rapped on the passenger side window. No response. Stewart went around to the street side, knocked again and called out. No movement. The door was unlocked. As he opened it, his eyes widened. Beside the driver's pinstripe tie, a crimson pool trickled all the way down his shirt.

Stewart swallowed hard, bit back his anger. Checking the street, he groped inside the car, struggling to heft the driver to the other side of the seat, then pushed the body down under the dash. The keys were still in the ignition. Stewart looked at the seat. The bullet had gone right through the man, ripping the upholstery. Ignoring the blood, he slid behind the wheel, started the engine, and headed out into traffic. He shouldn't have been surprised, he thought. He was a fucking amateur driving a road race for professionals, and the pro drivers were forcing him off the road! Stewart was sweating now. He could feel the moisture running down the back of his neck.

Minutes later Stewart parked in the shadows outside Carlie's apartment building on Sixty-first Street. Circling the car, he double-checked to see if the dead man on the passenger side could be spotted from the sidewalk. Satisfied that the body was well hidden, Stewart strode into the building.

"Back so soon, Mr. Stewart?" the doorman asked in a bored voice.

"Yeah." Stewart shrugged. "Is Carlotta home?"

"No, sir."

"Thanks." Stewart stepped inside the elevator, nudged the button. In anger he pounded the side of the car with his palm, knowing now that he had brought a cloud of death over Carlie Chavez.

As he approached the door to her apartment he heard the

telephone ringing inside. Fumbling with the keys she had given him, he turned both deadbolts and crashed into the apartment. The strident ringing ended before he could reach the phone in the living room. Irritated and exhausted, Stewart fell back on the sofa and stared blankly at the ceiling. He felt cold and began to shiver. His throat was as dry as dust.

Shira Bernstein had probably died swiftly, he reasoned. He was dying slowly by the process of grim discovery. They had taken Carlie alive. Why? They could have killed her on the way to Suzette's, in her car, along with the driver.

Stewart mulled over the options. His editor at the *Times* would need to know what had happened, as would the NTN news department. The police would want to get out an all-points bulletin, but he couldn't stick around to help them, not with a price on his own head. He would let Mike Murphy call the cops. Stewart rose, headed over to the phone. About to pick it up, he was startled by its ring.

"Hello."

"Kirk Stewart?" The dull-metal voice sounded like a roll call of the dead. There was a short silence.

"Yeah. Who's this?" he asked irritably.

"My name's unimportant. Let's just say I owe you a thirty-eight-caliber slug between your eyes. But now, you nosy bastard, it appears we have a more clever method of keeping you in line."

Behind the voice Stewart heard heavy traffic—a pay phone near a major highway, he calculated. Holding his breath, he pressed his ear to the receiver and continued to listen.

The threatening voice came to him again. "Your TV celebrity friend is safe as long as you do as you're told. But make one slip, and we roll her up in a rug, secure it with a chain, and heave the lot into Chesapeake Bay."

Stewart's stomach was in his throat. He felt his face begin to redden. Why Chesapeake Bay instead of the East River? Where was Carlie? Angrily he said, "Metz, I know it's you. Come and get me and leave the woman alone, you goddamned coward."

"I'm playing it smart, Stewart. You don't have a story, and you won't have one before noon tomorrow. What little you do have, you're to keep to yourself. No headlines, nothing in the morning edition. You're batting zero, understand? And Carlotta

Chavez is off the air for a couple of days. We'll see to it she calls in sick."

"Where is she?" Stewart shouted. "What have you done with her, you bastard?"

"She'll be safe, providing you cooperate with us. In the morning she'll get to meet the Committee in person."

"Where?"

"The capital, where else? We're headed there now, and I'll release her sometime Saturday *if* you do what I say. Don't follow us. Play it safe, asshole. You might just live to file a real story. With *real* heroes."

"I don't believe you, Metz. You're an assassin, a hired butcher."

There was an uncomfortable pause, then Metz's voice came on again, colder and more deliberate. "I follow orders, Stewart. My instructions are to keep Carlotta Chavez alive as long as you and the Israeli stay out of our hair. And don't even think about calling your city editor. We'll deal with him and the *Times* tomorrow afternoon. If you alert the police or FBI, I'll kill the woman and then blow your brains out."

Stewart swallowed hard. The uncompromising words cut him like a scalpel. "Metz, I don't trust you. Let me talk to Carlie."

"I figured you'd ask. You sure as hell better recognize the voice. One sentence. Ask about her condition only, then hang up."

Again, a long pause, with only the sound of heavy traffic in the background. Suddenly, Carlie's frightened voice shouted. "Kirk! I'm at Howard Johnson's Numer One and—"

Steward heard a muffled shout and then a sudden click followed by a dial tone. Slamming down the phone, he swore softly and checked his watch. He still had time to catch the last air shuttle to Washington. Then he remembered: That Howard Johnson's was only twelve miles out on the New Jersey Turnpike. Metz had to be driving south. He might stop again for food, gas, phone calls. It was a long shot but worth a try.

Grabbing his overnight bag and the camera Carlie had brought him, he hurried downstairs and cautiously ventured out on the street. Until now, Stewart had denied himself the luxury of any deep-seated emotion, reasoning there would be plenty of time for that later. But now his eyes clouded and his apprehension mounted. The tears he shed rose out of helplessness, guilt, and anger.

Wheeling the NTN staff car away from the curb, Stewart drove around the block, found a quiet area a good distance from Carlie's, and opened the door. As rapidly as he could, he pushed the bodyguard's corpse out on the curb. He'd explain it all later to the authorities. Stewart quickly pulled the door closed, accelerated, and checked the fuel gauge. It was nearly full. Pain mixing with fear in every muscle in his body, Stewart leaned forward over the wheel and fixed his eyes on the road. Turning down Lexington Avenue, he headed for the Lincoln Tunnel.

The night was cool and growing colder. Fear sharpened Carlie's wits. The effects of the drug Metz had given her at Suzette's had worn off completely, and once more her brain was functioning. The facts sorted themselves out, slowly, uncomfortably; she was on her back in the rear seat of Metz's car, covered with a blanket, and her wrists and ankles were bound. Had it been daylight she might struggle upright, signal to passing cars, possibly take a chance and cry out. But dare she try it now in the darkness, in the fast, blurred night traffic of the toll road?

Metz had warned her to stay down, get some sleep if she could, threatening that if she didn't cooperate he'd shoot her, dump her body on the shoulder of the turnpike, then go back after Stewart. He reminded her that one or two more deaths meant nothing to him, that she was small change. Carlie didn't panic easily, but she detested confinement; it was her only phobia. Lying helpless and cramped in the back of Metz's car, she tried to fight back her worst fears of what might happen when they left the toll road. Metz had told Stewart on the phone that they were going to the capital. The Texan was using her, but for what reason? A hostage to keep the *Times* and the network silent?

Metz turned on the radio, playing it loudly. A country music station. Good, she thought, dreading any further dialogue with her thus far talkative captor. Metz's silence didn't last long. He suddenly turned down the volume, reached around, and once more tugged the blanket up over her face. "Another toll booth ahead. Freeze." His voice was quiet, utterly calm. "If you so much as wiggle a finger, I'll shoot the attendant."

From under the blanket, Carlie pleaded, "No more killing,

please." She felt the vehicle slow down, heard the window roll open. Metz paid the attendant and immediately accelerated. Seconds later, he flipped the blanket away from her face.

"You're learning," he said icily.

Carlie thought hard, trying to come up with a way to escape from this madman. She wished he wouldn't turn around and look at her, relishing her helplessness. There was a violent excitement in his yellow eyes that made her shudder, and his smile had a switched-on quality.

Several cars passed them in the fast lane. Obviously, Metz wasn't in a hurry. At this pace, they'd never attract the attention of a turnpike patrol car. She tried once more to wriggle out of her bonds but realized in despair it wasn't possible. Despite the hour, sleep was out of the question. Metz terrified her. All she could do was wait, fight back the fear, and pray.

29

STEWART WAS BEAT. He had kept going on adrenaline alone. It suddenly came to him that this was Friday, the day of reckoning. It was four o'clock in the morning. The cold moon and clear sky over Manhattan had been replaced by a heavy overcast; light rain had fallen intermittently from the time he had crossed the Maryland state line. The rain let up as he drove through Washington, D.C.

Twenty-second Street was silent as he coasted up to the Israeli embassy and parked in the loading zone. Stewart got out of the car. Smelling of smoldering leaves, a brisk northeast wind swept the city, pushing away the early morning dampness. Stewart's nerves were numbed by the tedious drive from New York. Shivering with cold, he pushed the embassy's doorbell.

The door opened almost immediately. A uniformed young man guardedly asked, "Yes, what is it?"

"I need to see Major Barak immediately. It's important."

The man ushered him inside the lobby and brusquely pointed to a bench by the wall.

"Sit over there, please," the duty man instructed, going to the reception desk and dialing a number. The guard conversed softly in Hebrew for several seconds. He listened, said a few more words, then hung up. "You must wait," he said to Stewart. Then he ignored Stewart and perused a magazine on the desk before him.

Stewart sat through five minutes of uncomfortable silence before the familiar face of Motti Barak came into view. The Israeli wore a white bathrobe, and his eyes were glazed and puffy from sleep. Barak looked at him and gave up a long sigh. "You have a habit of suddenly appearing at the least propitious of times, my friend." He looked at his watch. "You do realize the hour?"

Stewart wearily climbed to his feet. "All too well. I'm beat myself." Sighing impatiently, he swiftly added, "I'm sorry, Major, to ruin your sleep, but there are serious complications. They've taken Carlotta Chavez."

Barak frowned. "You were going to call me back earlier, at eleven. I was prepared to play the tape recording," he scolded.

"I'd planned to phone immediately after talking to Dennis Garrett. Unfortunately, he's dead. Arnold Metz beat me to him. And now he has Carlie. It's been a matter of first things first. Motti, we've got to find her."

Barak was wide awake now. Collecting himself, he asked evenly, "Where do you propose we begin?"

Stewart liked Barak's style. As usual, the Israeli was steely-nerved—steady, calm, regardless of the hell breaking loose all around him. He looked at Barak and said quickly, "I talked on the phone with Metz. The bastard claims he's taking her to Committee headquarters for safekeeping. Somewhere here in Washington." Stewart paused, slowly shook his head. "I was skeptical at first, but now I'm running scared. Not just for Carlie, you, and myself—we're just small wheels—but for the whole damned country. They're organized out there, Motti. More so than I ever thought possible. Organized, armed, and fanatic." He waited for Barak's reaction. None came. Stewart felt light-headed and confused, as if a few of his cerebral gears were somewhere else. Still back at Carlie's? "Dammit, Major, are you listening?" he queried.

Barak glared back at Stewart defiantly. "I'm listening. You want me to wear a hat?"

Stewart was too tightly wound to be shut off. "I had plenty of time to think on the drive down from New York. These people aren't simply anti-Semitic, Motti. They're after the Catholics and snapping at the heels of the moderate Protestants as well. They're also fired up against blacks and other minorities. And the Klan's working double-time stirring up hate. On top of this we've got Jimmy Hallowell and a dozen others of his ilk. These TV snake-oil salesmen with their mail-order prayers and testimonial bumper stickers have monopolized the media."

"Slow down or sit down, before you fall over," urged Barak. "You're tired, remember?"

Stewart shook his head. "If you listen closely to what they have to say, Motti, you quickly realize it's nothing new they're telling us. They're exploiting high technology, yes. But the message, the style—it's the same. The inspirational Chatauqua meetings of Wilson's era filled a void; the tent revivals of the Depression did the same thing." Stewart paused to catch his breath. "And remember the films of those huge Nazi rallies in Nuremberg? All of those events, Major, had everything in common with the electronic church of the eighties. It's another form of mass hypnosis."

Barak shrugged, put a hand on his shoulder. "Out of the blood and fire Judea will fall, and out of the blood and fire will rise again. The prophecy for Israel will come true. Perhaps there is a similar fate for America, my friend. But each sect sees the prophecy in a different light, yes? Now the real majority must fight for what they believe is good and right."

"I'm not interested in prophecies, Motti. We've got to find Carlie Chavez."

"We will. I have some contacts who can help us. But not at this hour."

Stewart exhaled slowly and rubbed the stiff muscles at the back of his neck. "I'm meeting with a couple of senators in the morning. But I want to hear the tape first."

"Sorry, when you didn't call, I sent it to the White House. An Air Force general came by to pick it up. Bernard Colloran. I suspect when the President hears it, he'll call us both in."

Stewart stiffened. "Has the Israeli government become involved in this?"

"Quite unofficially. Only from the standpoint of sympathetic intelligence." Barak smiled, hastily changing the subject. "Now that you are here, you must tell the President or his aides what happened in New York."

"Sure. In the morning. Right now we've got to find Carlie. Motti, listen to me. If you won't help, I'll go alone."

The atmosphere in the lobby was heavy. The guard at the desk watched them both, his features revealing no clue to his thoughts.

Barak frowned, glanced again at his watch. "A problem of time? You're right. Come, I'll find you a sofa to get a cat nap. We can do absolutely nothing now. And you will be useless to me later if you are not alert." He led Stewart down the hallway.

"But the President should be warned and—"

"Yes. He needs his rest as well. From what I heard on that tape, today will be a long one for all of us," Barak said with finality.

In his room at the Andrews Officers' BQ, Colonel Pete Reddick flung his pillow aside and rolled over again. He looked at his watch. Five o'clock, and he had slept only fitfully. Staring at the ceiling, he once more considered Arnold Metz's proposal. It was madness, of course, but Reddick clearly had the ability to carry out the technical phase and get away with it. But the final stroke had serious ramifications. In the end, could he trust Walter Singer? Would the staff-level Pentagon reward be worth the risk? God knows, the country would be better off if he followed through as suggested. He was not afraid to do it, but what if—. Too many ifs. He was in this up to his neck. If he didn't volunteer, what then? They could eliminate him as easily as the others. Men like Arnold Metz would relish the opportunity.

The phone beside him rang shrilly.

"Reddick here."

"This is Lynx. You're awake and alert?"

"Unfortunately, yes. A helluva time to call, but I'm listening."

"Get up, Colonel. It's going to be a big day. Have you considered my superior's suggestion?"

"For lack of something better to propose, I have," Reddick grunted. Clearing his throat, he added, "But it sounds like something out of World War Two. A goddamn Gestapo final solution."

"An *accident*, remember? The country's future depends on

it. And we're depending on you."

"It's fucking murder."

"A more acceptable word might be 'elimination.'"

The CIA head showed his credentials and slipped into the back of the auditorium to observe the proceedings. It was one of several stops Singer would make this morning for a last-minute review of the various assault teams. At least a hundred Klan leaders were gathered in the hall. On the podium, Exalted Archon Bobby Harrington looked his way, nodded, and puffed on a cheroot.

Singer glanced around the room. He knew each of the Klansmen assembled before Harrington represented a team of two dozen or more men, all of whom had come to the capital champing at the bit for action. Bobby Harrington and his Invisible Society would get their chance. All their preparation and training would now be put to the test. Singer knew that throughout the South and in other sections of the country, thousands of Klan members would take to the streets on Sunday morning to prevent blacks from assembling at church services. Harrington and his followers would make sure no aspiring Martin Luther King or Jesse Jackson used a pulpit to organize resistance to the takeover. Singer suspected the Klan's task wouldn't be an easy one, but he had not discouraged them.

Their assignment in the capital, however, was more important, and Singer was determined to double-check the arrangements himself. He watched Harrington tap the lectern and wave a khaki-clad arm for attention. Like the others present, the Exalted Archon wore battle fatigues; their white ceremonial robes would be far too cumbersome for the work ahead. Harrington put his cheroot aside.

Singer listened intently to his pep talk.

"Gentlemen, you've all had the opportunity to look over the computer printouts on your targets, the rendezvous times, and locations. Hear this. It's imperative your groups be on station, ready to move out, prior to the President's speech. Some of you have the assignment of taking legislators' wives into custody. You'll be firm, but treat them with courtesy." Harrington smiled wryly, looked around the room. "There are a few good-looking ladies in the lot, so don't let any of your men get wild ideas. Any hanky-panky and we'll cut off their balls in a kangaroo court."

Singer heard the men laugh. He didn't think Harrington was funny at all.

The Exalted Archon continued: "Others of you will bring in the remaining family members—young folks from public and private schools. I can't emphasize the importance of each four-man team finding its assigned hostage, going after the brief, signed statement, and detaining the families until those planes are off the ground. It's the only way General Brady's men can load those 747s promptly without spilling blood. Our congressional guests have got to be convinced that the safety of their families is dependent on their cooperation."

Harrington looked toward Singer, saw that he was satisfied. Smiling wanly, the Exalted Archon started pacing in front of the delegates. "Gentlemen, don't be too impressed by the show of military strength. The Klan, too, has an important job. We were chosen for this assignment over the Freedom Militia, the Nazi shock troops, even the mercenaries—the so-called professionals. We've got our special work to do; they've got their assignments. But I don't want anybody to make the Klan look bad."

Singer glanced around the room, pleased with the enthusiasm of the men.

Harrington continued: "Those of us here in Washington will be in the limelight, gentlemen. No slip-ups, hear? We've got to set an example for every klavern in the country. Go with God, brothers! A Bible in one hand, a weapon in the other. If every Klansman does his job right, we'll flush the Catholic, Jewish, Mexican, and black votes down the sewer where they belong."

The gathering whooped and shouted its approval. Singer left the hall, satisfied with what he'd seen and heard. He still had two other groups to check.

Feeling halfway refreshed after his brief rest, Stewart stepped outside the Israeli embassy. The weather was still dismal. Barak joined him. Together they looked at the towaway ticket on the illegally parked sedan Kirk had driven from New York. Stewart hesitated, aware that by now the body of the TV network's driver would have been discovered back in Manhattan; the staff car would be reported missing. He and Barak needed transportation, but the New York car was hot. He decided not to chance it. Retrieving his camera from the trunk of the car, he joined Barak at the curb. They hailed a taxi.

Just down the block, a gray Cadillac limousine with four men in it waited until the cab had turned the corner, then slowly pulled away from the curb and followed it at a distance.

30

KARL FROBER SHARED the elevator to the penthouse level with
a huge bag of pastries, a treat for the troops. What they didn't
consume, he'd finish himself. The doors slid open, and Frober
ambled down the hall. The door of the suite was guarded by
two MPs; a woman Army officer sat nearby at a small desk.
Frober showed his identification, smiling at the woman captain.
While she examined it, he nibbled on a jelly roll, leaning over
to keep powdered sugar off the canopy that was his size fifty
suit. He offered the guards a pastry, but they politely refused.

With her keys the woman admitted Frober to the suite.
Inside, she pointed to the dark-haired, unshaven man asleep
on the sofa. "The night guard claimed he arrived four hours
ago from New York with the woman. She's in the adjoining
bedroom."

Frober went over to the sofa, shook the sleeping figure.
"Wake up, Metz. We have work to do."

Startled, Metz jumped to his feet, gun drawn. Blinking, he
looked at Frober, then over to the Army captain. His face
relaxed, and he put the gun away.

Pushing out his chin, Frober looked the disheveled Texan
up and down. "Get yourself some pressed clothes and a shave,

291

Metz." Frober grimaced. "You look like hell. You'll stand out
like a sore thumb."

The woman officer went back to her duty station outside
the door. Frober hastened to the adjoining suite, gently eased
the door open part way. Looking inside, on the bed he saw a
woman curled under the blankets, sound asleep. He smiled and
closed the door.

"Fortunately, she's out of it," he said to Metz. "But I don't
like the idea of Ms. Chavez having the run of the room. There
are windows; she could possibly signal."

Metz looked in Frober's direction and smiled. "I agree. You
employ considerate interior decorators, Frober. The elegant
brass headboard was a convenient place to handcuff her wrist."

Frober grimaced. "Fine. But what do we do when she wakes
up?"

Metz ambled over to the desk with its battery of colored
telephones. "Patience, Mr. Frober. Which one of these do I
use for a local Washington line?" He started to pick up the blue
telephone.

"None of those, you fool. They're all priority bypass lines.
Use the hotel phone beside the sofa. It's secure."

"Touchy, touchy. Haven't had your coffee yet this morning,
Fatty Arbuckle?"

Frober glared back at him. "See here, Metz. Your impertinence—"

"Fuck off!" Metz withdrew his wallet, found a card with
the phone number he needed, and quickly dialed. Seconds later
he grinned and said, "Frieda? This is Arnold. *Jag älska Dig*—
I love you, baby." He paused, listening. "What? I know it's
early and your flyboy colonel isn't staying there. I don't want
Reddick; I need you." Metz waited again, this time frowning.
"Yes, damn it. I know the massage parlor doesn't open until
ten. That's not what I'm after. Listen, you silly Swedish ding-
bat. I'm in town on important business and need you. Pull
yourself together and go easy on the plunging neckline. Hustle
over to the Potomac Plaza on the double. I need some of that
Scandinavian muscle of yours to watch over a lady prisoner."

The route they took to the old Senate Office Building was
circuitous, Barak surprising Stewart by insisting it was first
necessary for him to stop at the Soviet embassy compound.
Stewart was more curious than annoyed by the delay, but the

more questions he asked, the stronger the rebuff from the Israeli. Barak remained in the building for less than ten minutes, then returned carrying a large manila envelope. Smiling wanly at Stewart, he dismissed the incident too lightly, as if it had never occurred; his only words were, "Trust me. The chameleon assumes many colors out of necessity."

Damn Barak, Kirk thought. The Israeli's sincerity was unquestioned, his emotions seemed right, but what, or who, motivated him? Barak was making him increasingly uncomfortable. Worse, Stewart had the distinct impression they were being followed by a gray limousine five cars back. Piqued, he continued to argue with Barak over his secretive manner all the way to Capitol Hill, even up to Senator Vince Hartman's door. Only the inquiring gaze of the senator's shapely secretary prompted him to put the incident aside.

The petite, hazel-eyed brunette was pleased to see him. "Hello," she beamed. "You're going to be a trifle disappointed."

For a split second, Stewart didn't care. Her smile had a magnetic quality that he liked. Strange, he flashed, how men gravitate to women when they are in trouble or afraid.

Barak nudged his shoulder.

Stewart said swiftly, "I'm Kirk Stewart. This is Major Barak."

"I know; you spoke with me on the phone. Senator Hartman asked me to give you a message. He and the other two senators had a last-minute change of plans. But they've agreed to meet with you late this afternoon, after the President's speech and the Andrews Air Base flight demonstration. Could you come back around five?"

Stewart felt sandbagged. He looked at Barak, then back at the secretary. "Why the cancellation?"

The woman kept her poise. "*Postponement*, please. The senator's a very busy man," She paused, studying Stewart. "Why do you look so shaken?"

Stewart frowned, tapped her desk lightly with his knuckles. "It was important we meet *before* the President's speech. Hartman promised—"

"Your anger is unwarranted. I suspect it's a matter of not enough time before the joint session begins. Or possibly it had something to do with the CIA director stopping by. The senators did leave with Mr. Singer."

Stewart's shock showed in his stance; he looked at Barak,

who only shrugged, as if he'd expected as much.

Kirk collected his thoughts and turned to the secretary. "Mind if I use your phone?"

With the President in the Oval Office were the commander of the Air Force and the director of the FBI.

The man simply isn't afraid, thought Oliver Wright. How could he make the President understand the complexity and size of the situation as well as the imminent danger?

The room was quiet, ominously so.

"Absolutely incredible," the President said somberly, finally looking up from the small tape recorder General Colloran had brought in and played for Wright.

With a slight gesture of his hand and a flick of his eyes, Wright let the President know he wanted to talk in private. Bernard Colloran glanced awkwardly at Wright, then back to the man slumped behind the broad walnut desk.

"Do you wish to meet the Israeli major and the newspaper reporter sir?" Colloran asked.

The President nodded, waving his hand with impatience. "Yes, definitely, but not now. There isn't time before my address. I'll see both of them after the joint session. Do me a favor, General? I believe Mr. Wright has some personal advice for an old friend and would like some privacy."

"Of course, Mr. President."

"And while you're out there, try to get the Secretary of Defense on the line from Walter Reed Hospital. Find out if he's well enough to talk."

Colloran nodded and drifted out of the room.

"What else, Oliver? It's been one hellish morning already. Knowing you, I suspect the FBI has saved the best—or should I say the worst—for last."

Wright leaned forward in his seat, then straightened his big frame. The uncertainty he had observed in the President bothered him. Still, he had to get it all out, every ugly detail. In the silence of the Oval Office Wright could hear the President breathing heavily. He could even hear his own heart pounding in his chest. Wright withdrew a charred metal box from his pocket and nudged it across the President's desk. "From my men in Houston, courtesy of the National Air Safety Board investigators at that DC-10 crash site."

The President put on his gold-rimmed bifocals, picked up

the scorched, badly twisted box. After examining it at length, he shot Wright a puzzled look.

"Mr. President, what you have in your hand is an EMR homing device. The receiving end of a short-range, anti-personnel and anti-tank weapon, used for espionage work and fired from a standard rifle. Perhaps you remember the controversial audit on this Army procurement program a year ago?"

"I remember. Condor Industries seems to be constantly under GAO audit. But I saw only drawings. This hardly—"

Wright stood, approached the President's desk, and pulled another small box from his pocket. This one was shiny, stainless steel. "Perhaps, sir, you'll recognize the undamaged unit." He put it down beside the scorched box. "The Houston plane was shot down by an EMR. Our enemies used it ruthlessly once; there's no doubt in my mind they'll use it again." Wright let the President examine the intact EMR beacon for several seconds, then took it back and tucked it in his pocket. "A dangerous device to leave around," he said grimly.

"God in heaven," the President said, rolling his chair back. He stepped quickly to the window and looked across the South Lawn toward the Ellipse. He watched the morning inbound traffic, still heavy on Constitution Avenue. "To think it has come to this," he said sourly.

"You will, of course, cancel your appearance at the Andrews demonstration?"

"Certainly."

"Mr. President, when you leave Capitol Hill after your speech, I suggest you ride in my personal car. I'll accompany you back to the White House. I realize you prefer Secret Service men, but I'm asking you to trust my judgment this time. I'd like you to tell only Givens, Burroughs, and Robertson that you intend to make a last-minute change of vehicles. Swear them to secrecy."

The President turned from the window, his gray eyebrows arching upward. His face was drawn as he looked at Wright, started to speak, then changed his mind. With a slow nod, he lowered himself into his leather chair. His voice was hard and even as he said, "I gather from the tape that my only allies now are an Air Force general, the head of the FBI, and what's left of my Cabinet."

"And the press, provided you pull no punches in your speech."

The President nodded. "Fine, but moving the media to a

great exposé will take time." He paused, looked at Wright
thoughtfully. "General Colloran will need help. I'll have to call
the National Security Council together—without Singer, of
course."

Wright shook his head vigorously. "No. That could be dangerous at this point, sir. Your defense secretary is incapacitated.
Also, Colloran will have to be cautious when passing the word
to the strategic and tactical command levels. Aside from Singer,
Admiral Palmer, and General Brady, we still don't know the
precise military makeup of the enemy camp."

"Come off it, Oliver. Venture a guess as to who's on that
Committee."

"At this juncture, your guess is as good as mine, Mr. President. Renegade senators or congressmen, business leaders—
I'm still not sure. We're working on it. Whoever they are,
they're pulling the strings while Singer, Brady, and Palmer
dance. I suggest, sir, you call an emergency meeting of your
Cabinet, along with the House and Senate leaders immediately
following your speech. In the meantime, other than confiding
in General Colloran and your White House aides, it may be
safer to keep quiet about that tape."

The President looked back at him, his face forlorn. "Precisely my own thoughts." He picked up the phone, hesitated.
It was the cue for Wright to leave.

"I would like permission to reinforce your Secret Service
staff with a dozen Bureau men, all to serve at your pleasure."

"Suit yourself," said the President.

"Good luck, sir." Wright headed for the door. He paused,
adding, "I'll be waiting at the House chamber's side exit to
escort you to the motorcade." Wright wet his lips, hesitated,
then added with a wry smile, "Your State of the Union address,
under the circumstances, may require some ad-libbing, Mr.
President."

The President held up a pen. "If you'll kindly exit and get
back to work, I'll do likewise," he said with a diluted smile.
"Be careful, Oliver. Don't take any chances until reinforcements arrive."

Wright left the room, hurried down the corridor of the White
House diplomatic wing, bound for the limousine that would be
waiting for him under the canopy of the south driveway.

• • •

"Mike, get off my back. If the senator had been here, I would have had those quotes! You could have gone to press immediately. I need another hour. We're still trying to get into the White House."

Stewart listened for the city editor's grunt of disapproval. It came, and sounded like a belch. "Big deal, Stewart. In another hour the man's State of the Union speech will be public domain. I want a scoop."

"You'll get one, I promise. But in the meantime keep the lid on this Carlie Chavez thing until I get back to you. An hour, tops."

"Stewart?"

"I'm listening."

The editor continued: "About the material you gave us last night. The Condor Defense angle is dead in the water unless you can prove Gifford's involvement. But that Bund in Yorkville and the body in the river—it all ties together. Our man who's working on your leads is wondering if there's a link to the Odessa, what's left of the German SS. Frankly, I'm curious myself."

"I considered that," Stewart replied. "I doubt it; at best, the link would be indirect."

"Don't be so sure," Murphy chided. "They're everywhere, not only in Germany. The damned of the old order waiting, biding their time. From what I hear, they're convinced, like the Farmer's Almanac, that there's a proper time to sow the seeds for a new thousand-year Reich."

Stewart winced. The senator's reception office was uncomfortably quiet. Both the secretary and Motti Barak were staring at him with confused looks.

"Mike, it sounds plausible, I know. Anywhere else in the world, maybe. But in America?"

"Hell, where else can the election process be so easily bought?"

"No," Stewart said firmly. "Not the Odessa. They're old men now. Even the paper in their Nazi scrapbooks is crumbling with age. Shira used to tell me about it, Mike. Their children, though still active in the movement, are comic book characters who do little more than picnic together and sing the *Horst Wessel* song. The Odessa may have agents everywhere, and they could be prompting from the wings, but—"

"Save it," Murphy snapped, cutting him off. "Nevertheless, work on it." The editor wasn't about to be put off. "Get some good background material."

"Whatever you say, Mike, but in my opinion, the movement's indigenous. And it's just as fanatical, our own American Reich."

Oliver Wright paused at the door to the White House portico. To his surprise, both the car and the four FBI aides who had accompanied him were missing.

Wright's heart thudded.

A Secret Service agent, one he had seen before around the President, came quickly up to him. "Mr. Wright?" The man blocked his way. "Mr. Singer called from CIA headquarters in Virginia. He would like to meet with you immediately."

Wright straightened his big frame, looked down at the Secret Service man. "What's going on here?" he asked irritably. "Where's my car? And my assistants?"

"Sorry, sir. The CIA director said it was imperative you come to see him immediately. I've taken the liberty of sending your driver and the others on ahead, just as he instructed."

"You take orders from no one but the President, God damn it. And my men answer only to me. What's more, how the hell does Singer expect me to get to his office?" Wright felt apprehensive, a little afraid; all he could do was mask his fear with a display of anger.

The Secret Service agent pointed toward the South Lawn. "Mr. Singer sent his helicopter to pick you up. It's on the President's helipad, waiting. The CIA director implied you would prefer these arrangements."

I don't need any CIA arrangements, any time, any place, Wright thought, making a quick mental note to remember this Secret Service face. It wasn't one of those he would trust to protect the President when the showdown came.

"Look," said Wright smoothly. "I'd better tell the President where I'm going. He's expecting me to return immediately to FBI headquarters."

"Sorry, sir." His escort smiled, pointed impatiently toward the helicopter. "I suspect Mr. Singer has already alerted the Oval Office. If not, I'll pass the word."

"No, I'll do it myself." Wright said uneasily.

Three more men came up from nowhere, stood behind the

Secret Service man. Wright recognized the faces: Walter Singer's aides. They drew no weapons; CIA agents thought of themselves as Ivy League gentlemen, but the implication of threat was in their eyes. Sullen-faced, Wright walked out on the South Lawn.

Bastards, he thought, feeling a gnawing frustration for the first time. The Huey helicopter's engine was running, and the two-man CIA crew was aboard and waiting. Crouched over, the White House Secret Service agent escorted Wright to the aircraft, made sure that he was buckled in the rear seat, then backed off across the lawn, nodding to the pilot with a thumbs-up gesture. The Huey rose, banked sharply, and headed in the general direction of the CIA compound at Langley.

Out of the jungle, into the lion's den itself, thought Wright, bristling. He had no intention of shouting, making idle conversation with the two somber faces in the front seat. His plans had suddenly been shot to hell, he knew. He had intended to organize a task force, and immediately following the President's speech send them to the Potomac Plaza, take the hotel apart room by room, if necessary. The Bureau man working undercover there had not fallen from the building by accident; of that he was sure.

The helicopter banked again, heading not northwest in the direction of the Virginia suburbs, but instead toward the river and the towering hotel on Virginia Avenue—the Potomac Plaza roof helipad!

Wright felt under his jacket, wishing this once he had a small automatic in a leg holster above his ankle, not the bulging Walther beneath his arm. He suddenly remembered the EMR homing beacon in his pocket. No, he didn't want to be caught with the device in his possession. Not yet. There was a chance Walter Singer had no idea how much Wright and the FBI knew about his operations. The Israeli, Barak, had assured Colloran that the CIA head was unaware of the secret tape recording made at Andrews. Wright had to think quickly. The Huey was settling toward the hotel roof, where he could see four more CIA men waiting. Unobtrusively, he slid the EMR unit under the helicopter seat, hiding it between the flotation cushions.

The roof of the Corcoran Gallery of Art offered an excellent view of the Treasury, the Executive Office Building, and the White House—especially the rose garden, south portico, and helipad. The two Soviet undercover agents who had been hiding behind the parapet since shortly before dawn shivered and drank coffee from a thermos. Occasionally they raised their binoculars. Posing as roof repairmen, twice they had taken up their tools as government helicopters had soared overhead at close range.

The Russians made careful notes on who entered the White House, their time of arrival and departure. Both men were surprised when the FBI director's limousine and two waiting assistants had been summarily driven off by several men in civilian clothing. Now the Bureau chief himself had been escorted to a waiting helicopter. The Russians conversed in agitated tones.

"The morning's events are escalating, Comrade. Again, an unexpected turn."

The second man did not reply, his binoculars continuing to track the CIA helicopter with the captive FBI man inside. He watched it move away from the White House, race across the city, and finally descend on the Potomac Plaza roof. The Russian put aside his binoculars. "We are fortunate. We have only to observe and file reports. This Baroski is in the thick of it."

"Barak, you fool. You must always call him Barak."

"These Americans will kill each other, and for what? Barak is in great danger. They will kill him as well."

31

CARLIE'S CAPTORS HAD turned on the TV in the bedroom, assuming she would want to see the President's State of the Union address. Under more auspicious circumstances, her journalist's instincts would have kept her attention glued to the set, but now her mind wandered, desperately trying to come up with a plan for escape. If only she could talk them into opening the draperies she would have some idea where she was.

The bosomy blonde named Frieda who sat across the room filing her fingernails didn't look bright, but she didn't have to. She was tall, big-boned, and tough. The door was locked from the outside. Several times Carlie had made an effort at conversation, but each time the smear of lipstick that was Frieda's mouth curved downward in a silent sneer. A small poodle at her feet looked equally disagreeable.

Carlie sighed, sat back on the bed, and focused on the television coverage of the joint session. The President's speech had begun.

Stewart looked around the crowded House chamber. They sat on the right side of the gallery; Barak had obtained two passes from a New York senator who owed the Israeli legation a favor.

Stewart leaned forward in his seat, absorbed in the proceedings. He had never attended a session of Congress before. The room was warm from the capacity crowd and banks of TV lights. As usual, the State of the Union speech was being telecast by all the networks simultaneously.

The President—poised, steady-voiced, showing no signs of fear—had been speaking for over twenty minutes, and had yet to be interrupted by applause. Stewart could guess why. This was the same Chief Executive who four times this year had seen his vetoes overridden by Congress. Still, the senators and representatives on the floor were politely attentive. Under the flag, just behind the President's podium, the Speaker of the House looked benign, but beside him, Vice-President Chandler was scowling.

Stewart's eyes wandered over the Supreme Court justices, scanned the crowded semicircle of desks on the floor, and darted up to the gallery on the opposite side of the chamber. Wives, family members, special guests, he suspected. Then he saw a familiar face—Tap Nelson, sitting in the back row of the gallery. He had tried to reach Nelson, both at home and at FBI headquarters earlier, without any luck. Why was he here? Could he possibly signal him in the opposite balcony? The FBI press director didn't look Stewart's way. His eyes were riveted on the President. Stewart wondered if Nelson had been dispatched here by Oliver Wright. And for what reason?

The President appeared to be winding down his address. "Fiscal restraint without complaint has to be first in the mind of every U.S. citizen. Just as you have come together for this joint session, I now ask you to unite, to join forces for the common good in supporting the upcoming budget."

The President suddenly placed aside his prepared speech, scanned the audience intently. His eyes went to the TV camera, remained there.

"If you will permit me, my fellow Americans, I would like to depart from my text and speak extemporaneously to a subject that is of grave concern to me. What I am about to say will be difficult. I have always been skeptical about the accuracy of political polls, particularly those which claim to accurately index an incumbent's popularity. Still, I'm aware that the majority of Americans are impressed, if not influenced, by these polls.

"I'm sure you are well aware of the substantial shift toward isolationism, the drift in American political philosophy and national temperament since I took office three years ago. I readily acknowledge that some of my grass-roots support has eroded, that many Americans appear to be marching to a different drummer.

"My opportunity to appoint two new justices to the Supreme Court of the United States has created far more opposition than I expected. Certainly, I did not envision my veto of the Robinson Immigration Bill would provoke such an avalanche of hate mail. Nor did it occur to me, at the time of my inauguration, that my private life would be the subject of such controversy. You will recall that often, at press conferences, questions regarding my marital status far outnumbered intelligent queries on pending national policy."

Even from where Stewart sat, the President's growing discomfort was apparent. This man, Stewart thought, hardly fit the image of the most important leader in the country. Slightly stooped, hollow-cheeked, his iron gray hair gone white at the sides, he could easily pass for a mild-mannered watch repairman at Macy's or Gimbel's. Still, if nothing else, the Chief Executive's voice was commanding, and his words rang with conviction.

"Now, my fellow citizens, I must tell you of a serious problem that confronts us. A small cabal of wealthy businessmen, aided by certain evangelistic religious leaders have organized themselves to oppose the government and the nation. As a part of their conspiracy, they have attempted to blackmail me into resigning."

A sudden eclipse of the sun could not have caused a more deathlike hush than the one that fell over the chamber. No one coughed, stirred, or even breathed. Stewart, too, was frozen. He watched the faces of the men and women on the chamber floor. Most of the legislators appeared drained of color, completely thunderstruck.

The President continued: "I am reminded of the words of Samuel Johnson, who said, 'Differing from a man in doctrine was no reason why you should pull his house down about his ears.' I will not be intimidated, and I will not resign. I am not afraid."

The chamber burst into applause. The President waited for the bedlam to die down, then said soberly. "You have nothing to fear, my fellow citizens. But the scope of this conspiracy appears to be broad. We will keep you informed as the investigation continues in the hours and days ahead. The FBI will devote all of its resources to this crisis. The National Guard may be placed on alert."

Stewart grimaced. The President was putting things mildly, to say the least. He looked across the chamber at Tap Nelson in the opposite gallery. Nelson looked agitated and suddenly nervous.

"I can tell you now that these enemies of democratic American diversity are on the move. Let me say to them: No group of citizens in our land has the right to assume righteousness over any other. There are charlatans among us who would tell you most Americans have become lazy and will be easily manipulated; that there is a vacuous majority out there who will readily set sail to any new wind, regardless of where it will take them. I don't believe these soothsayers of failure, and neither should you. The basic American spirit, nourished by a great diversity of religious spirit, will not change.

"Yes, there is violence and restlessness in our land today. There is also hunger and injustice. We will address these problems. As for extremists, America absorbed them and their excesses in the eighteenth century and the nineteenth, and will continue to do so in the twentieth. Communism has no appeal for the majority of the American people. And neither has fascism, whatever its seeds. We cherish our individuality. We're never complacent, easily satisfied, or open to manipulation. We'll continue to tolerate others as long as they don't infringe on our rights." The President paused, looking around the chamber. "I regret there will always be fanatics among us who prefer to shout and pound the table rather than exchange ideas. Dark passions must be confronted in the light of day, the light of reason."

Arnold Metz smiled in fiendish satisfaction as he glanced toward Pennsylvania Avenue and once more considered his trajectory. An easy shot, he mused. An Army corporal had parked the canvas-back truck on Seventh Street, a short distance from the route the President's motorcade would take back to the White House. Metz dismissed the young driver, waited until he had departed in another military vehicle, then climbed in the back of the truck and opened the wooden case containing the EMR weapon. The task ahead of him was definitely a one-man job; he didn't need assistance, least of all witnesses. Only three others knew what he had planned: Walter Singer, Lynx, and Colonel Reddick, who would have a surprise of his own in store for the Committee.

Metz unrolled the rear tarpaulin and let it drop to the tailgate. After examining his equipment again, he looked out and checked the target zone. The odds for a clean kill were excellent. His truck was parked some hundred feet down the side street, near the National Archives. At the intersection of Pennsylvania Avenue four Army jeeps waited. Though the men in them were ignorant of his mission, Metz knew they were under orders; in the event of trouble in the presidential convoy, they were to immediately seal off Seventh Street. Clever planning on Walter Singer's part, thought Metz. After the presidential limousine exploded, the motorcade's police patrol would be prevented, at least temporarily, from investigating the side street. There would be time to escape, maneuver the truck into the collection of other Army vehicles on Capitol Hill.

Metz felt a warm satisfaction as he carefully attached the EMR charges to the two telescopic-sight M1-A Springfields. He planned to steady the rifle on the truck's raised tailgate. He wouldn't get a second chance for reloading or adjustments. If the first shot failed, the backup weapon would be beside him, available instantly.

Metz smiled to himself. He was ready now. Fully prepared to make a name for himself in history. All that was left was to wait patiently, cross his fingers that the CIA head had placed one of the small stainless steel boxes in the President's limousine.

Stewart suffered with the President. He knew the man at the podium was battling with his vulnerability, feeling for the first time the fragile nature of his purportedly powerful office. He looked haggard.

Stewart's eyes drifted away from the President. Across the gallery he saw Tap Nelson look at his watch, rise from his back row seat, and hurry to the exit.

The President lowered his voice. "No, my fellow Americans, I will not resign. I have asked the two retiring Supreme Court justices to stay on an additional six months until the election. I will not make replacement appointments, but leave this to your next President. I will not seek an additional term of office. Your feelings regarding the political philosophy of the replacement judges can best be expressed at the nominating conventions and the ballot box. Forgive me for delivering what may appear to be a State of the Presidency rather than a State of the Union address, but these things had to be said today. Thank you, my fellow Americans, for your time this winter morning. May God bless America during this crisis."

Stewart and Barak stood, applauding along with the rest of the gallery. Turmoil broke loose on the chamber floor. Most of the legislators were on their feet, clapping loudly.

Stewart whispered in Barak's ear. "What do you think, Major? Does he have a fighting chance?"

Barak leaned toward him. "With all the controversy surrounding him, this popularity battle is one fight he'll have to win on his own."

"I suspect you're right. He's just one man. Here today, gone tomorrow. The crisis now is over what he represents. The institution of the presidency."

Barak nodded. "More than that. Over two centuries of American constitutional government are at stake."

Stewart thought briefly about the balance of power between the executive, legislative, and judicial branches, the often divergent postures of military and civilian leaders. He wondered about the effectiveness of the Sedition Laws. With the showdown ahead, it was time to dust them off. Stewart watched the activity on the floor below. The President shook hands with the dignitaries at the rostrum, but did not venture into the aisles. Secret Service men flanking him, he hurried to a side exit.

32

FIRST TO COME under the iron fist of the takeover were the shuttle subways connecting the Capitol with the Senate and House office buildings. Electric power had been cut after the President's speech, the darkened entries now guarded by somber Marines wearing blue arm bands. The legislators leaving the joint session in the House chamber had no choice but to spill outside into the East Plaza.

At one end of the plaza parking lot Admiral Sandy Palmer looked at his watch, then slowly rolled down the window of his staff car and called to General Brady, who sat in a jeep a short distance away. "Give the signal, Brady. Let's see how fast you can move those troops."

George Brady smiled thinly and waved.

An instant later a sergeant posted at the top of the Capitol steps blew a shrill whistle. Immediately, several hundred armed soldiers dispersed from the olive-drab trucks surrounding the plaza. The troops wore helmets, fatigues, and bulletproof jackets; each man carried an M-16 and had a gas mask strapped to his waist. Many carried teargas canisters and riot clubs.

His Canon A-1 swinging from his shoulder, Stewart walked out of the Capitol rotunda alone. Motti Barak had excused

himself, ostensibly to make a phone call to one of his mysterious contacts. Stewart no longer cared; he'd made up his mind
to rely on his own devices. Right now he was trying to spot
Tap Nelson in the crowd. Around Stewart, the members of
Congress spilling out on the Capitol steps were unusually subdued, their faces solemn. He suspected that the senators and
representatives were worrying about the President's revelations
and planning their own next moves. Stewart felt a sickness in
his chest.

He stopped, eyes widening. Stewart looked with amazement
to the bottom of the steps where the men in uniform were
scattering quickly to surround the plaza. He raised his camera,
took several pictures, then edged back out of foot traffic. The
maneuver he was witnessing only added to the worst of his
earlier fears. This is America, he told himself. It can't happen
here.

Stewart retreated to one side, partially hiding behind a door.
He looked out on the plaza, and his stomach muscles tensed.
Over a dozen charter buses were parked bumper to bumper at
the bottom of the steps. He heard a voice suddenly echo from
a portable public address system.

"Testing. Testing," came the well-modulated, authoritative
voice of an announcer, rising above the babble of the crowd.
"Your attention, please. Honorable Members of Congress, Dignitaries, and Officials, if we may have your cooperation. This
is an unannounced red-alert evacuation, a drill pursuant to
Defense Directive Fourteen-A, with which you are all familiar.
For your own safety and the effectiveness of this critical personnel movement, you are requested to immediately board the
waiting buses for transport out of the target zone. This is a
drill. You will be sent to an emergency briefing area. Senators
and representatives are asked to board the buses immediately.
Guests, family members, and staff employees will stand by at
the north end of the plaza. Additional vehicles will be here
shortly to transport you after all members of Congress have
been safely evacuated."

Stewart looked on in amazement. He listened as a murmur
of discontent swept over the crowd. Most of the legislators
stood absolutely still, exchanging bewildered looks. A few
yards from Stewart, the Democratic senator from California
shouted at a passing capital page, "Who authorized this drill?"
The page did not answer, instead running off, apparently with

fears of his own. The senator turned, shouted across the plaza, "It's a goddamn takeover!" Swiftly, an angry murmur rose. Stewart lifted his camera as two congresswomen tried to push their way past the Army cordon. They were roughly escorted to a waiting bus.

Stewart's shock gradually subsided. The other correspondents had rushed to the press room to prepare their stories on the President's revelations. Stewart appeared to be the only newsman outside. He had to get the whole story. Hurriedly, he threaded his way through the throng and down the steps to get closer to the loading buses.

General George Brady felt resplendent in his tailored dress uniform with its row after row of ribbons. The brass stars on his dark blue helmet glittered, his shoes and gun belt were polished to perfection, and the scarf around his neck was pleated in all the right places. Standing at the top of the wide marble staircase, watching his troops move in on the agitated dignitaries, he whispered orders into a walkie-talkie.

Brady looked up as two familiar senators elbowed their way up to him: Barton of Illinois and Melchior of Vermont. Brady had met both men when he appeared before a Senate Armed Services Committee—an uncomfortable time just prior to his expedited retirement, when he had been reprimanded for making inflammatory speeches that had caused international repercussions.

"What the hell is all this about, Brady?" asked Barton, his face red with anger. "I've been sitting on the Armed Services Committee for two years. No one ever mentioned any surprise evacuations. And why today?"

Brady kept his silence. Senator Melchior stepped in front of him, obscuring his view of the troops. "We're expecting an explanation, General. Immediately. What military contingent is this? Those Marines downstairs in the subway aren't locals from Quantico. And why the guns?"

Brady smiled calmly. "Everything will be explained en route to Andrews. Would you mind stepping out of my field of view, Senator? Relax, before you wet the pants of that fine Italian mohair."

One of Brady's assistants, a Marine bird colonel, came up beside him and and swiftly ordered, "Board the bus, gentlemen, please. This is only a test. Most of you were on your way to

Andrews for the open house and lunch anyway. The troops will expedite your bus trip and bring you back later."

Brady brusquely dismissed the two senators and followed his aide to the center of the portico. His troops, he noted, weren't working fast enough. The legislators and others who milled around him were growing rebellious, and that was dangerous. Sensing their anger, Brady strode down the steps to join his armed men. At his urging, the troops began prodding with their guns, urging the crowd to move faster.

Brady now took over the public address microphone. Coldly and emphatically, he said, "Board the buses immediately, with no further delay!"

Stewart threaded his way down the steps. Around him, no two people seemed to be reacting the same. Stewart passed an angry Nisei he recognized as a congressman from Hawaii. The legislator raised his fist. "Bullshit, this is no drill!" Stewart took his picture.

A gray-haired, immaculately dressed woman beside him, apparently also a House member, grabbed the congressman's arm. "What can we do?" she asked.

The man from Hawaii spoke softly, but Stewart heard the reply: "One does not argue with M-sixteens." He took her arm and gently led her down the steps to the waiting buses.

Like a drawstring, the expressionless soldiers gradually tightened their circle around the crowd. Stewart heard a commotion behind him and looked up the steps. A group of Marines, led by a white-helmeted major, came out of the rotunda doorway, escorting several somber but dignified Supreme Court justices. The Marines broke a path through the crowd on the steps, pushing their group toward the third bus in the line. Stewart raised his camera, got off three good shots, then quickly held it down and out of sight.

None of the justices appeared to resist. The major climbed aboard the bus with the judges and a minute later came back out. He herded ten more people aboard, then signaled the driver to pull away.

Stewart tucked his camera under his corduroy jacket and slipped along the line of transports. At the door to the sixth bus Senator Morris Dixon, his jaw set in silent fury, balked. Stewart knew the senator's reputation for being short-fused and egotistical, obsessed with himself and his public image. Back in his home state of Wyoming Dixon was an important man, the owner of the largest cattle spread in the Rockies and a former governor. Now, framed in the bus doorway, he refused to move. Stewart suspected that Dixon wasn't the type to be pushed easily, guns or no guns; only a week earlier he had made news by conducting a noisy, table-pounding filibuster that would have sent a less rugged legislator to the hospital, then topped off the event by punching an annoying reporter in the face.

Stewart wanted to take a picture of the man, but he didn't dare; the troops were too close, watching him edge through the crowd. Indignant, Dixon refused to ascend the bus steps, instead spitting at the feet of the burly MP beside the door, demanding to speak to his superior. Stewart was roughly pushed aside as two more guards came up, guns at ready. Fearlessly, the senator nudged the gun barrels out of the way and started to step out into the crowd. One Marine pulled him back by the collar; the other blew a bos'n's whistle. Almost immediately, a paramedic with a red cross arm band appeared, glanced quickly at the struggling senator, then maneuvered around him.

"Bastards! Let go of me," rasped Dixon. "I demand to see your commander."

Stewart looked on in amazement as the guards grabbed Dixon's flailing arms and held his body. Coming up from behind, the paramedic expertly rammed a syringe through the senator's pants. Dixon's mouth shot open in surprise; his body jerked forward only slightly. The two Marines didn't wait for the Amytal Sodium to take effect. To the shock of the others in line, they strong-armed the senator aboard the bus. Through the windows the crowd saw them slam him into a seat. Several passengers scrambled to their feet, shouting angrily and clogging the aisle. Facing leveled guns, they eased back into their places.

Stewart's stomach muscles tensed.

The Marines and the paramedic backed out of the bus, a new urgency in their eyes as they resumed their places around the boarding line. Stewart prudently backed away, retreating up the steps to the rotunda. Breathing hard, he struggled to the top. Fewer troops here, but they were still closing in from all sides. He waited for a distraction, then edged through the milling bodies, finally slipping unobserved through a gap in the cordon. So far, so good. He broke into a run, through the rotunda, past the statues of Washington and Jefferson, to the hallway and staircase leading to the press room. Stewart took the stairs two at a time, his mind shuffling through his priorities like a fast card dealer, his head pounding. He needed Barak after all. He had to get to the President. Find the Committee headquarters. Locate Carlie. God, Carlie! She headed the list. He also had to call in a report to the *Times*.

General Brady was pleased. He watched as one bus after another left the driveway, two armed guards in the front of each. When all the frightened, dazed government officials had finally departed, an awkward, unsettling silence fell over the plaza. Brady wasn't finished. He had to wait for additional buses. His remaining troops would now herd up the Capitol press corps and intern them temporarily at the Washington naval base.

Several breaking patches of blue appeared in the sky, which had been dark and threatening all morning. The weather was cold, almost too cold to rain. Good, Brady thought. Fine weather for those flying down to Haiti.

The general strode to the north end of the plaza's parking lot toward the Pentagon staff car parked a short distance from the President's limousine. Admiral Palmer climbed swiftly out of the vehicle to meet him. Both men saluted.

"I've checked the side entrance. The President didn't leave," the chairman of the Joint Chiefs said irritably. "He's gone into seclusion with the Cabinet in the House Speaker's office, with two dozen FBI men and as many Secret Service personnel guarding the door."

George Brady unfastened his chin strap, tilted back his helmet, and wiped the sweat from his forehead. "How do we handle it? Teargas?"

Palmer looked at him narrowly. "No. Singer doesn't want us stirring up a wasps' nest. The President could be holed up with those vermin for an hour, maybe longer. Sooner or later he'll head back to the White House; we'll be ready for him there. Take my car and get on with the operation out at Andrews. Walter Singer's picking me up by chopper as soon as we get that press facility closed up."

"What are we going to do with the President?" Brady asked quickly.

"Norman Gifford has a stand-by plan; it has to do with the Citadel at his plant in California."

Brady grimaced. "No Haiti resort vacation with the others?

What happened to that beachfront penthouse suite and the balmy Caribbean breezes?"

Palmer smiled thinly. "He won't be that lucky. Singer insists we let him go back to the Oval Office unmolested. When he arrives, he'll find all his communications dead. The White House is out of business, General. The entire city, for that matter, is effectively isolated.

Brady nodded, satisfied. Activating the walkie-talkie, he said into it, "This is Sunburst-One to Alpha Control."

"Go ahead, Sunburst One. We read."

"What do you have from the contingents at National and Dulles?" Brady took off his helmet, tossed it in the back of the staff car. He ran his fingers repeatedly through his thick gray hair and waited for the response.

The radio crackled. "Affirmative, Sunburst One. They report all runways closed on schedule. No departures or arrivals. All obstruction aircraft are in place. Over."

"Message received, Alpha," snapped Brady. He shoved the radio back into his pocket and nodded to Palmer. "A piece of cake, Admiral. Colonel Reddick placed several F-15s at strategic spots on the field. Same at Andrews and Patuxent."

"Good," said Palmer. "I'll take over here. Get your ass out to Andrews, Brady. The sooner those two jets are loaded, the faster we can mop up."

Stewart entered the press room in the Capitol basement and shook his head. The scene was pure bedlam. The President had dropped a multi-megaton bomb, and the reporters were making the most of it. All too quickly the world would hear a full report of the horror confronting the country. But why had the reporters remained here? Didn't they know what was happening outside? Stewart pushed through the crowded room, searching for one of the *Times* Washington bureau reps.

A gentle tap on the shoulder startled Stewart. He turned. Eyes glistening behind gold-rimmed bifocals, the Washington Bureau manager herself faced him. Penny Kubitz had seen plenty of crises; she looked more concerned than frightened. They conferred briefly, then flipped for first use of the *Times* direct circuit. Stewart won the toss and a minute later had Mike Murphy on the line.

"Mike, did you hear the man's words? Any more doubts? Listen, I'm with our Washington Bureau manager. We're both filing stories. Here's what you don't know, what's going on outside on the plaza. General George Brady's been pulled out of retirement and he's—"

"Hold it, for Christ's sake!" Murphy shouted, so loud Stewart had to ease back from the receiver. Stewart had rattled off his thoughts so rapidly he had failed to hear the city editor repeatedly try to interrupt.

"Kirk! Forget it. Both of you, as of now."

Stewart's eyes narrowed. "Forget it? Are you crazy, Mike? I'm ready to break loose with—"

"Kiss off, junior reporter. We've got trouble. Bigger headaches to sweat over here than your goddamn byline. And tell Penny the same applies to her crew. Jesus! Right now our entire staff is staring down the barrels of Uzi automatic carbines. The building's overrun from roof to basement with damned blackshirts."

Stewart swallowed back his bile. *"Blackshirts?"* Stewart repeated. He had been afraid of news like this.

Murphy raised his voice. "You heard me right. Crazy bastards. What's more—"

The line clicked. A second later there was a jarring busy signal, then static. The circuit abruptly went dead. Stewart looked around the room. The other reporters held receivers away from their ears, looking at them quizzically.

"The lines. They're cut!" a young woman shouted as she continued to depress the line buttons on her phone. The press room erupted in an angry clamor.

Eyebrows knitting, Stewart put down the receiver. He had to find Barak.

"Take this," he said to Penny Kubitz, handing her his camera. "Get the film processed. "Where I'm going, a camera could be the kiss of death."

He ran out into the hallway, there to be nearly run down by Motti Barak. Stewart blinked. For the first time the Israeli looked genuinely excited.

"They moved faster than I anticipated," Barak said. He looked around him, frowned, and shouted to the other reporters. "There's no story in here. They're taking House and Senate members forcibly." He looked at Stewart. "Why didn't you tell them what was happening? You were there, on the steps."

"I'm a competitive reporter, Major. The bureau rep and I

were trying to file a first." Stewart couldn't help feeling a measure of guilt.

The press corps stared at Barak and Stewart, then suddenly broke out of the room and down the hall as a group. Stewart watched the reporters go, the *Times* Washington bureau chief among them. Most of them were running, not walking. Last man out of the press room was a pale reporter in his fifties with two Nikons strapped around his neck. He puffed up the stairs after the others. The hallway was quiet.

Barak shrugged and said to Stewart, "I have the information we needed. My observers tell me the FBI director was abducted, taken by helicopter to the roof of the Potomac Plaza. I suspect the Committee is headquartered there."

Stewart started for the stairs, but Barak caught his arm.

"Kirk, you have to wait for the President's summons. Explain everything to him, especially the events you uncovered in New York. Tell him about the Potomac Plaza. I have to get out to the air base."

"Now?" flared Stewart. "What about Carlie? Our work's just beginning!" He was crestfallen.

Barak looked at him stonily. *"Your* work."

Stewart's mind reeled. "I don't understand."

"You will, at a later date. We have dissimilar roles in this. Different cues to leave the stage."

"Motti, damn it. You're not making sense. There's just—" Stewart wasn't able to finish. Barak had raced off behind the reporters, hurtling up the stairway. Still tightly clasped in his hand was the large manila envelope he had acquired at the Soviet embassy.

Obtaining the Sparrow air-to-air missiles had been the greatest challenge facing Colonel Reddick. Arming the rest of his squadron with 25mm tracers before they took up stations at National, Dulles, Patuxent, and Andrews had been accomplished easily enough, but for Reddick's own plane and one other, he needed the new AIM-9 air-to-air missiles—the twelve-foot Sparrows.

Reddick checked his watch. He knew his ground crews needed time to load the under-wing weapons and run pre-flight data checks. With the help of the armory's duty sergeant, Reddick and his men had surveyed the rack of missiles, noting model numbers and weight classifications. Turning to his crew chief, he ordered, "Half a load only on each fuselage. Use the inboard pylons. And hurry. This is a balls-out operation."

The armed sergeant in charge of the armory had taken Reddick's counterfeit sophisticated weapons orders to a telephone, apparently to check with a superior. Reddick was perturbed. Time was running short. The sergeant was returning now and appeared ready to confront him.

"I'm sorry, Colonel. I can't comply with your request. I contacted Base Ops for an oral confirmation of your orders. There's an irregularity in the computer printout, and Colonel Thomas would like you to call him immediately. I've been instructed that your men should leave the facility at once."

Reddick flared, his initial apprehension turning to outright hostility. Ignoring the sergeant, he faced his crew chief and pointed to the hangar doors. "We'll load as planned. Fetch the weapons carrier." He watched the crewmen take off at a run.

Clenching his teeth, the duty sergeant reached hesitantly for his pistol, then took his hand away, instead retreating behind the dispatch counter. He stared at Reddick as a buzzer sounded and the large security door of the building rolled back. The ground crew drove two weapons carriers inside and approached the missile storage bay where Reddick stood waiting. Immediately, they went to work.

Reddick could see that the duty man was both angry and confused. Slowly, the duty sergeant reached for the phone on the wall. "Sorry, Colonel. You can't do this."

Reddick threw the man a menacing look. "Sergeant, I wouldn't use that telephone again."

The duty man ignored him, continuing to dial.

"That's an order, Sergeant. Drop that phone." Fool, Reddick thought, as he cocked an ear and listened to the scream of a jet engine just outside the armory. Slowly, he reached inside his tunic. Christ, he thought. It had come down to this. He could only cross his fingers, hope to hell his crewmen would understand. Had they been indoctrinated thoroughly enough? It was a risk, but he had no choice. Not now. Withdrawing his hidden service pistol, he aimed it carefully at the sergeant's head.

Eyes widening, the duty man went for his own gun.

Reddick fired, the noise lost in the sound of the jet. The sergeant's face blossomed in blood. His body plummeted to the floor. Reddick exhaled slowly, steadied himself. He replaced the telephone on the hook, shoved his smoking automatic into his shoulder holster, and strode across the armory to the door. His ground crewmen, standing beside the weapons carrier, stared at him and held their breath. Reddick offered them no explanation for his actions, instead simply glared at them until they opened the armory-hangar door and drove out to the flight line with the Sparrows.

Walter Singer's helicopter roared over the George Mason Bridge, bound for National Airport. The pilot and a bodyguard were up front; seated in the back with Singer was Norman Gifford. Both men wore intercom headsets so they could talk without shouting. The Condor Defense executive put out one cigarette only to light another.

"Relax, Norman," Singer urged. "In less than four hours, your name and face will be familiar in every home in America."

Gifford looked back at him, wincing. "'Laverne and Shirley,' 'Magnum, P.I.,' and 'Happy Days' with Norman Gifford." He thought for a moment, finally smiled. "I'm not impressed, Walter. What good will a Committee meeting on national TV do if all the members aren't in attendance?"

Singer smiled. "We'll feed ourselves piecemeal to the public. That's the best we can do. Frober has to remain behind to manage the communications. I've got my hands full here as well with the Pentagon. I'll join you and Hallowell tomorrow after the military picture is consolidated."

"Does Vice-President Chandler still plan to sit in with us?"

"Yes. As quickly as you can work him in, but not on the panel shows. The networks will have to cut him in directly from his Washington office."

"Comforting. Less lonely with three on the griddle."

"Damn it, Norman, don't worry about it. Just walk into that TV studio and talk softly. You've got the indoctrination films. No lament over the past, no lofty promises, easy does it. Plenty of others to carry the big stick and play the roughrider role." Singer looked out the helicopter canopy, pleased to see below that armed sentries were guarding the Jefferson Davis Highway approaches to the Pentagon. Good, he thought. Palmer's staff was in firm control of the complex. Turning back to Gifford, he quipped, "Champagne's in order for tonight, Norman! You can toast me from New York. I didn't realize we would achieve our goals so easily."

Gifford shifted in his seat, adjusting his earphones. "Champagne may be your talisman for continued success, but I'm taking a wait-and-see attitude. Washington, D.C., is one thing. Let's hope the show plays as well in Spokane and Syracuse."

"Meaning?"

"We're still not sure how our Novocain will work in New York, let alone the rest of the country. If everything's coming up roses, why the hell are you flying Hallowell and me off to the Big Apple now instead of on Sunday? What was wrong with the original plan?"

"Calm down, Norman. New York, not the capital, is the country's financial heartbeat. You're a businessman, not a politician. Need I test your financial sensibility? Concentrate on the salient points."

Gifford looked annoyed. "I'm fully aware and concerned about Wall Street. I've made all preparations and worked out the details with over a score of other business leaders. But that's for Monday morning."

"Precisely why we need the weekend, plenty of lead time to soften the public up. And that's where the Moral Confederation comes in. Provided our master of ceremonies meets us at the airport as scheduled." Singer looked out the window. The Huey was circling, making an approach at National. Singer continued. "If I've learned one thing from Jimmy Hallowell, it's that the church is good for business, and business is good for the church."

Raising an eyebrow, Gifford forced a smile. "I trust your intelligence expertise pays off, Mr. Singer. This is a time for professional acumen, and yet we rely on that soothsayer."

The helicopter went into a banking turn, approaching the flight apron from the west.

Singer frowned. He wanted more confidence and enthusiasm out of Gifford, but he wasn't going to get it. Not yet. Slowly, he said, "Listen close, Norman. There may be jubilation out there tonight in some quarters, but we'll also be contending with despair. And that's where Hallowell will pay off for us. Damn it, I know he's good. This Moral Confederation is grass roots, and it's real. It's frightening if you're on the other side. Hallowell uses high-tech communications—even satellites— to push the belief in a supernatural Jesus and a supernatural Satan who will rise above the sordid scene of the day. The easily intimidated, the easily oppressed, the frustrated, the superstitious—hell, they'll all sit up and take notice. And God, how they listen to him! If this takeover is going to be a continuing force, we have to let Jimmy Hallowell console the doubting millions."

Gifford grunted, looked down at the nearby field. His private jet was below, waiting. "Despair makes the world go around, Walter. I say let the losers wallow in self-pity."

Singer tapped his knee and glanced at Gifford with annoyance. "When the exchanges open on Monday, I'm expecting renewed confidence and total enthusiasm. Our broadcasting network takeover will make or break the movement. Hallowell will soften the ground, prepare the soil. We've got to mellow out our TV audience, prepare the way for Paul Chandler's swearing-in ceremony on Sunday."

The helicopter slowly descended to the tarmac.

Singer continued: "What's more, Hallowell's got a ground swell of support from the other evangelical networks as well. Half a dozen TV preachers are behind him."

Gifford impatiently flipped away his seat belt. "All right. Fine. So where's your Bible-waving spellbinder now?"

"Hallowell's driving up from Richmond. He'll be here shortly." Singer gestured toward the waiting JetStar. "Have a good flight, Norman, and give my regards to Broadway."

The silver Rolls-Royce Corniche purred north along Interstate 395. It had already passed Alexandria, and the Washington National Airport was just minutes away. Behind the tinted windows evangelist Jimmy Hallowell sat in the suede rear seat, going over his speech for the Committee's New York telecast. The driver, accustomed to Hallowell's last-minute, en route rehearsals, kept silent, his eyes fixed on the highway.

Hallowell's voice continued to rise and fall in grand opera tones: "My friends, we are in safe hands at last. The Committee's goals are basic: Return to the value of the individual, install inspired leadership, back to national strength, back to patriotism, and back to biblical morality. Americans, wherever you are out there tonight, you must know there is no middle ground. You are either with us or against us. The Bible says: 'If my people shall humble themselves, pray, seek me, turn from their wicked ways, then will heaven forgive them and heal their land.'"

"Pardon, sir," interrupted the driver. "We're approaching

the airport terminal. Which airline?"

"None," said Hallowell, leaning forward and pointing to an access gate. Go to the side of the United Freight Terminal. I'm leaving on the Condor corporate jet."

Ignoring the driver, the evangelist adjusted the mirror in front of him, brushed off his lapel, and continued to rehearse his monologue. "Today, you've been witnesses to a great political rebirth in our land. For over three decades, the United States of America has not been committed to victory and world greatness. We lost the spirit of nationalism, the desire to be strong, and as a result, we have not won any of the wars we have fought since 1945. Now the time has come to stand and join ranks, to become soldiers of the Cross. We're going to start winning again, my fellow God-fearing citizens!"

Hallowell smiled, wiping the perspiration from his forehead with a clean white handkerchief. He looked in his practice mirror, pushed back the shock of silver hair over his right eye, and smiled. This was going to be his finest performance, he knew. Absolutely his finest hour.

33

"YOU'RE EXPECTED," the Secret Service man outside the House Speaker's office said. "But you'll have to wait."

Stewart's heart sank.

The agent pointed to a seat across the hallway. The corridor was filled with FBI and Secret Service men, more than Stewart could count. Several bore machine carbines. They all looked tough and resolute, but he suspected that in the long run they would be no match for heavy weapons and a military assault team determined to take the building.

Stewart sat down to endure the gradual tightening of the knots in his stomach. His meeting with the President and his aides seemed inconsequential. He was concerned now with finding Carlie. But he had been ordered to wait, and one didn't disobey an order from the President of the United States. Stewart idly wondered if the man was, in fact, still the Chief Executive.

Stewart tried several times to start a conversation with the untalkative Secret Service men who sat on the bench beside him. Finally he gave up, resigned to sit mutely and cool his heels.

• • •

Carlie Chavez looked away from the mirror in annoyance. Again there was a loud knock at the bathroom door.

"Carlotta! Your lunch is getting cold." The female voice with its Swedish accent sounded irritated. "You've been in there long enough, hear?"

Carlie ignored the summons. She calmly dried her hands, rubbed them with lotion, and once more examined herself in the mirror. Her penthouse prison was obviously one of the hotel's most lavish suites, she reasoned. The bathroom walls were covered with onyx and Carrara marble. Touching up her lipstick under the ornate crystal chandelier, Carlie swung her head to inspect her profile. The usual sweep of dark brown hair fell across her left eye so that she had to push several locks away. Ignoring the pounding at the door, she casually combed the silky strands, her thoughts drifting back over the events of the past twenty-four hours. The fear had eased, replaced by impatience and a growing irritation. They had permitted her to watch the President's speech on television. After what she had already learned from Kirk Stewart, the words echoing from the House chamber had hardly come as a surprise. But why hadn't her captors released her, now that the news had been broken? And Arnold Metz—was he still after Kirk? Should she still be afraid, after all?

Frieda, the Teutonic batwoman who guarded her, was tall and strong, and the bedroom door was locked from the outside. Still, wasn't there something to the phrase "The bigger they are the harder they fall"? The tall blonde, surprisingly attractive for her size, had to be a weight lifter or wrestler. God, possibly she changed truck tires for a living. The high-strung poodle accompanying the wardress seemed to have a fickle disposition. Left alone, it would wag its tail and come up to Carlie, but when near Frieda it would protectively snarl if anyone drew near. So much for sneaking up on her and delivering a quick zap on the head. To make matters worse, Frieda had taken away her clothes. All she had was one of the hotel's terry-cloth robes.

Pulling herself together, Carlie opened the bathroom door and padded barefoot out into the bedroom. A quiz program was on TV, and the draperies were partially pulled. Frieda was slouched in a chair by the window, her dog sharing her lap with a box of Kentucky Colonel chicken. Glancing up, the blonde said sourly, "Your lunch is on the bed."

"I'm not hungry," Carlie retorted. "I want to see Mr. Frober, now."

"Fat chance. He's busy with his damned computers. He expects us to remain in here. And quietly."

Carlie strode up to the television, abruptly turned it off, and glared at Frieda. "Now listen to me." She felt her anger rise, uncontrolled. "Open that door or I'll start shouting at the top of my voice." She leveled a trembling finger at the big blonde. "And believe me, you won't like what I'm prepared to bellow out. They'll think you're after my body."

Frieda shot her an incredulous look and laughed. She dropped a chicken leg back into its box, casually wiped her fingers. "Big deal, sweet." Her voice turned to a hiss. "I've had women before. And I get what I want. You, I can do comfortably without. I suggest you shut your trap or I'll gag that big mouth of yours with your pantyhose. Understand? Now turn that TV back on." She took a big bite of chicken and spoke with her mouth full. "What gives with you? You don't like 'Family Jackpot'? It's one of your own network's shows."

Carlie started to edge closer to Frieda. Again, the dog snarled.

"Quiet, Raphael!" Frieda looked up at Carlie, glowering. "Turn on that tube, you conceited news reporter bitch."

Ignoring the blonde, Carlie ran to the door connecting the bedroom to the main suite. It was locked, as she suspected. Banging her fist loudly, she shouted, "Mr. Frober!"

Frieda was on her feet immediately, lunging toward her. Carlie called out again, continued to pound on the door. Her knuckles hurt. Frieda came up to her. With a smirk of pleasure, she put the weight of her shoulder into her fist and struck Carlie in the solar plexus.

Whap! She hit again, harder. *Whap!*

Turning white, Carlie gasped for air, doubled up in agony.

The lock gave up a click, and the door opened. Karl Frober's corpulence took up the entire doorway, while behind him, several staff workers looked on curiously. Frober's rubbery lips parted as he stared at her. "And what have we here?"

Carlie's hands covered her face. She was still trying to get air.

Frober finally said, "Young woman, you're disturbing our work. What is it?"

On the edge of tears now, Carlie swallowed hard, tried to calm herself. "Look, Mr. Frober, you and your friends have made your point. I want to go." Gasping for breath, she slowly added, "There's no need to keep me here any longer."

Frober shot back a fleshy smile and shrugged. "The CIA director believes otherwise. Until our takeover of the networks is completed and we have absolute cooperation from the production personnel—your NTN crews in particular—we may need your assistance."

"Help?" she asked, grudgingly. "The proper term, I believe, is 'coercion.'"

"You won't be alone. I suspect we'll be holding other members of the press as well."

Warily, Frieda stood to one side, her arms held out like a wrestler's.

Frober smiled. "Mr. Singer's arriving soon. You can address your complaints to him directly. Enjoy your lunch, Carlotta. But no more outbursts or our masseuse here may be forced to sit on you." He pulled a pair of handcuffs from his pocket, tossed them to Frieda. She caught them, turned, and sent Carlie a dry smile.

"I suggest you lock her in the bathroom. But if there's any more noise, handcuff and gag her," ordered Frober.

Arnold Metz looked at his digital watch. Sitting in the back of the truck, he waited patiently like a cobra for his prey to cross his path. Down the street, the intersection at Constitution Avenue was still blocked, the Army troops patiently standing by for the President's motorcade. Slumped against the truck's sideboards, for the first time Metz felt impatience and a degree of boredom. Though his neck muscles had unknotted and his facial lines relaxed, the hatred he felt in his heart was as strong as ever. Why had the President been delayed? Was the real action elsewhere? No, that wasn't possible. Walter Singer had promised to let him know of any change in plans.

Metz opened a small wooden matchbox. Only one red devil left, he noted. Quickly, he tossed it in his mouth and swallowed hard. He heard a helicopter. Glancing out of the truck, Metz looked skyward and immediately recognized the approaching CIA executive Huey. The chopper didn't land nearby, instead hovered a short distance away from his truck. Metz could clearly make out the two occupants. Sitting beside the pilot was Walter Singer himself, and he was signaling. Singer nod-

ded, waved, and pointed toward the distant Capitol. The high
sign.

Metz watched the helicopter bank and sweep upward, move
off in the direction of the Pentagon. Good, he thought. The
President's convoy would soon be under way. Metz took his
place behind the EMR-equipped rifles. A feeling of success,
absolute power, and control once more enveloped him, sending
a satisfying, heady flash through his body.

Motti Barak found it easier to move around the Andrews base
perimeter than he had anticipated. The Army and Marine troops
were interested only in the passengers stepping off the chartered
buses. Unchecked, Barak was able to make his way up close
and crawl beneath one of the last transports to arrive. He watched
as an Air Force colonel with a distinctly familiar face shouted
instructions to several assistants, demanding a speed-up of the
747s' boarding process. The first of the two giant planes was
already loaded and ready to taxi away from the staging area.
Several Marines with automatic carbines sauntered up to the
officer, addressed him as Colonel Reddick. Suddenly it came
to Barak. The picture he had pulled from Arnold Metz's wall—
the pilot beside the U-2 spy plane! The same set jaw, the same
fierce-looking beetle brows.

Barak listened as Reddick assigned additional civilian and
military guards to the passenger jets; others were sent to take
over flight operations and the tower. In the distance, he saw a
car pull up to one of the ramps, a Marine general climb out.
Swiftly, the officer climbed up the 747's boarding ramp and
disappeared inside the plane with several aides, apparently in-
tending to make a final inspection.

Barak eased back out from under the bus, dusted off his
clothes. He knew now that the wad of plastic explosive he had
brought along would be a drop in the bucket for the job at
hand. Diversionary fireworks at best. He needed another plan.

A large group of idle bus drivers stood by, waiting for further
instructions. Barak strolled among them, and no one took notice
of him. Unobtrusively, he moved in as close as he could to the
jeep occupied by Colonel Reddick. Barak watched as a young
Air Force captain came running across the tarmac and saluted.
The two officers were now less than a dozen feet from Barak,
and he easily heard their words.

"Colonel, both fighters are loaded. I checked over the yellow sheets with the crew chiefs myself. We're set to go."

"Fine," grunted Reddick, glancing at his watch, then at the closest jumbo jet. "I'm on my way to the ready room now. You stay on the ramp until that second 747 is buttoned up, then get over and pick up your own gear. Do you have the mission absolutely clear in your mind?"

The captain nodded, his eyes sparkling with excitement. "Yes, sir. Visual flight rules, twenty-two thousand as far as Charleston. Reassigned there to instruments for the Miami leg if that Gulf weather front continues to close in. You'll follow the first passenger jet. I'll escort the second aircraft ten minutes later at twenty thousand. Right?"

Reddick looked back at him, obviously pleased. "Keep your eyes and ears open. If it comes down to choosing between air traffic control instructions and my explicit orders contradicting them, you'll know what to do."

The captain seemed to tense. He lowered his voice. "About the Sparrows, sir. What purpose do—"

Reddick clapped him on the back. "Later, Captain. All in due time," He looked back toward the civilian airliners. "Make sure that second plane's loaded; then gear up on the double. Call me on the military VHF frequency when both you and the passenger plane reach cruise altitude. I don't want those civilian pilots listening to our in-flight dialogue."

Barak watched the colonel's jeep drive away. He knew now that he had to alter his plans drastically. When he first arrived at Andrews, Barak had intended to steal a rifle and blow out the landing gear tires of both airliners. A dozen or better flats would delay their departure by several hours, for there were no overhaul facilities or spares for the giant Boeing planes on this base. New tires or replacement aircraft would have to be brought in from other facilities. If nothing else, that maneuver would have bought some time. But Barak was forced to shelve that plan, because the planes were parked too far apart. Even if he managed to get out near the runway, he could shoot at the gear of one plane, perhaps, but not both. The armed men would quickly be on to him, and he would be caught.

He needed another plan, and quickly. Time was running out. Why were F-15s accompanying the VIP-loaded planes, and why were the fighters armed with the deadly Sparrow air-to-air missiles? Who was Reddick expecting to encounter on the flight? Odd, Barak thought. Very odd.

Less than ten minutes later, Barak watched Colonel Reddick taxi his own F-15 Eagle across the apron and join the first 747 at the end of the runway. Both planes immediately took to the air and headed southeast.

Barak saw a food service truck back away from the second 747. The aircraft was almost finished loading. Reddick's second, the young Air Force captain, headed across the tarmac. Glancing quickly at his watch, he hastened into the nearby ready room. Barak followed.

The waiting outside the House Speaker's office was intolerable for Stewart, made worse by the FBI and Secret Service men who gazed at him as if he were a leper. Making up his mind to find the Bureau man in charge, Stewart walked down the hallway. After a couple of inquiries, he found a supervisor, a Slavic type who introduced himself as Vosberg. Stewart looked speculatively at the agent, wondering if the man knew anything at all about the Potomac Plaza. "What leads you have on Oliver Wright?"

Vosberg looked at him narrowly. "Nothing. We're waiting for orders from the President."

"Where's Tap Nelson, the press secretary?" Stewart asked, deliberately changing the subject. "I need to reach him."

"Don't we all? Take a hike over to the FBI Building," he replied glumly. "I understand that he and the deputy director are barely able to hold down what's left of the fort there. We're completely cut off. The telephone circuits are dead, and our backup radio communication is being jammed. Good luck, buddy."

There was a slight commotion at the end of the corridor as several Secret Service men hustled a trio of civilians with swastika arm bands up the hall in Stewart's direction. They stopped outside the door leading to the impromptu Cabinet meeting, where a Secret Service supervisor and Bureau man Vosberg confronted them. The smug-faced Nazis were all in their late twenties or early thirties and were dressed in identical gray corduroy suits, black shirts, and white ties. Their polished shoes gleamed like glass. Stewart looked at the disturbing red, white, and black swastika arm bands and thought, for the first time in his life, how good it would feel to have a double-barreled shotgun in his hands.

"We're an official delegation. We demand to meet with the Secretary of the Treasury and the Secretary of State." The impertinence came from the apparent leader of the group, a tanned, blue-eyed man with brown curly hair and a bushy handlebar mustache.

"You don't say," agent Vosberg replied. "Who the hell do you motherfuckers represent?"

"The two hundred members of the armed Nazi Alliance of America who are now occupying the State Department Building. Over one hundred and twenty more of us are guarding the Treasury Department. We have more hostages than you would care to count."

Stewart inhaled so swiftly he almost choked.

At Andrews, the pilot's ready room was deserted except for the young Air Force captain. The pilot, who had almost the same build as Barak, didn't notice that he had been followed to the locker area. Barak knew now what he had to do. It occurred to him that he could take over and fly one of Reddick's F-15s himself. He knew the plane well. A Soviet trawler would be waiting to pick him up at sea when his work was finished here. What difference did it make how he got out there?

Barak thought again about the two 747 passenger jets. He was puzzled. Where were the big jets loaded with congressmen going? And why the fighter escorts? And why the Sparrows?

Barak stepped quietly across the ready room.

The captain had the locker open, his hard hat in his hand. Quickly, Barak brought down his gun butt on the young man's head. The white helmet with the mirrored, reflective visor clattered to the floor, the pilot collapsing in a heap beside it.

Quickly, Barak pulled the unconscious captain around behind the lockers. This would be another wearisome masquerade, he flashed. From Russian KGB sleeper to Israeli major to American fighter pilot. What was next for him? Barak swiftly pulled on the Nomex anti-G suit, added the survival vest and harness with its underarm life preservers, and grabbed the oxygen mask. Retrieving the helmet from the floor, Barak checked the flying suit's leg pocket to make sure the en route aeronautical charts were in place. He then opened the manila envelope he had picked up at the Soviet embassy, withdrew another chart, tucked it in with the others, and zipped the pocket.

Stepping over the unconscious captain, he headed for the

operations desk at the end of the building. Barak was about to enter the room when he changed his mind. No! They would notice his accent. Besides, there was not enough time. He had no time to worry about the pilot coming around, either. He had to get the F-15 airborne immediately, breaking every rule in the book if necessary. Barak suspected he had a few things going for him: The aircraft would be ready, the APU working, the ground chief standing by. The mirrored, reflective visor of the helmet would hide his face. But suppose he was forced to speak. Would the ground crew be alerted by his accent? Would his walk and mannerisms give him away?

Leaving the ready room, Barak snagged a jeep from the transient pilots' parking line and drove it across the apron. The McDonnell-Douglas F-15 sat on the line, its broad fuselage, slab tailplanes, and yawning, sharp-edged engine intakes giving it an alien, dangerous look. Parked among several cumbersome transport aircraft, the F-15 Eagle—America's answer to the Russian Mig-25 Foxbat—looked restless, like a thoroughbred in a pasture full of workhorses. Barak knew the aircraft well and had come to appreciate its sophisticated performance, its remarkable ability to make tight, sustained turns without loss of speed.

Haste, he concluded, would be the only way to deal with the ground crew. He parked the jeep close to the jet fighter. Barak ran to the cockpit, gestured to the power generator, and silently hurled himself up the assist steps. Sweat ran from his scalp down into his eyes, and beneath the hard hat he could hear his pulse in his eardrums. The crew chief looked surprised by his haste, but said nothing, assisting the man he assumed to be Colonel Reddick's assistant squadron commander into his seat.

Barak buckled himself in and cinched his mask. He closed the canopy as the starting engines shrieked. Turning on the radio, he listened to the field traffic. Barak glanced down the flight apron and saw that the second 747 appeared ready to taxi. Ground control was trying to raise him, but Barak didn't respond. He turned the radio control to the UHF frequency the civilian pilots would use, and listened intently. Seconds later he heard the 747's pilot: "Andrews GC, this is United charter aircraft zero two. VFR to overfly Miami, clearing for Port-au-Prince, or some damned mud flat nearby. Request taxi instructions."

Barak heard the tower come back: "United zero two cleared to runway five. Wind northwest eight. Altimeter three-zero-point-zero-five. Your ATC clearance is two thousand lower than the sister aircraft you will follow. Separation interval one hundred miles. You reading clear?"

"Five by five. Any information on that second Air Force fighter assigned to escort us?"

"Sorry, United. No flight plan filed here. We see him sitting out there on the taxi strip, but can't raise him. Over."

Barak smiled, but kept his silence.

The pilot came back: "Ground Control, my orders were to clear the field by thirteen-thirty. I've got a planeload of VIPs, and the armed security personnel keep insisting we get under way. Any suggestions?"

"Go ahead, United zero two. You're cleared for taxi and takeoff. No response from that F-15 escort."

Motti Barak watched the huge 747 lumber across the field and head for the end of the runway. He continued his pre-flight check. The F-15As he had flown in Israel, although basically the same, had been conspicuously modified for the peculiar needs of Middle Eastern warfare. The missiles under his wings now were Sparrows instead of Sidewinders. The extra fuel tank of the Israeli version was missing. Barak knew his travel distance and time in the air would be severely limited, compared to that of the planes he had flown out of Etzion Air Base in the Sinai. The cockpit was initially confusing. It took Barak a few minutes to familiarize himself with the U.S. Air Force version. Not good, he thought, but there was hardly time for a familiarization flight now.

The twin turbofans screamed steadily. Signaling away the APU and chocks, Barak released the brakes and bobbed down the taxi lane. The radio squawked as ground control summoned him repeatedly, but he ignored the calls. Barak felt his stomach tighten.

The crowded 747 roared past him down the runway, finally easing into the air at the seven-thousand-foot marker. Barak maneuvered his F-15 out on the runway after it and paused only briefly for the cyclonic turbulence to subside. He pushed the throttle forward, satisfied that there wasn't any rustiness. Barak felt better; he was as smooth as he had been ten months earlier. The F-15 Eagle shot down the runway, soared into the sky as easily as its namesake. Now the real test, thought Barak.

He would pour on the afterburners and make time, passing the second 747 and catching up, unannounced, with this Colonel Reddick.

The meeting between the young Nazis and the combined force of FBI and Secret Service men had reached a standoff. Stewart slowly shook his head.

The Nazi spokesman tugged at his mustache and smiled fatalistically. "I repeat. We come in peace" Both hands shot out at his sides. "What do you want, a flag of truce? Send out those Cabinet members."

Before anyone could respond, the outer door of the Speaker's Office flew open. Framed in the doorway, Air Force Commander Bernard Colloran surveyed the crowd in the hallway.

Stewart looked at the four-star general, whose chest was covered with ribbons. Colloran—with his wavy gray hair, heavy and somnolent eyes, button nose, and jaws like a bulldog— reminded Stewart of his college crew coach a dozen years earlier.

Colloran glanced in both directions down the hallway. "Where's the newspaper reporter, Kirk Stewart? And Israeli Air Force Major Barak?"

The Secret Service and FBI men stepped aside, clearing a path for Stewart.

"I'm the reporter from the *Times*. Our Israeli friend sends his regrets. He left suddenly for Andrews Air Force Base to attend to some unfinished business."

Colloran frowned, gesturing for Stewart to step inside the office, but his eyes lingered on the three men with the Nazi arm bands. "What's this scum doing here?"

FBI Agent Vosberg stepped forward, erect with authority. "These men claim to have taken State and Treasury. They want to talk."

The general's eyes widened, his mouth twisting. "They'll have to wait," he said in a rumbling voice. Colloran beckoned for Stewart to follow him inside the reception office, then slammed the door on the others.

Stewart, the general, and an older Secret Service agent were the only occupants of the room. The Cabinet meeting was apparently still under way beyond the inner door; Stewart heard loud, agitated voices but wasn't able to make out the words. The more Stewart thought about being called before the Pres-

ident, the more he felt naked, as if he were about to be turned
over hot coals.

Colloran broke the uncomfortable silence. His tone was dry
and dead serious as he said, "The President told me about you,
and I've heard your Israeli friend's tape." He hesitated, rubbed
his chin, and added, "We'll lick the bastards, Stewart, once
we determine where they're headquartered. Apparently it's not
the Pentagon. Sorry to hear they've taken your friend Carlotta
Chavez as a hostage, but I suspect that's just the beginning."

Stewart stepped forward. "Sir," he anxiously began.

Colloran didn't yield the floor. "We've got one hell of a
snake on our hands. It's not venomous; it's a damned constric-
tor. The slow, persistent squeeze can be just as dangerous as
poison. A part of this serpent is convoluted around the nation's
communications—both military and civilian." Colloran
shrugged. "I once scoffed at the idea that whoever controls the
computers also controls the country. Now I believe it. Our
cunning enemies have planned for a long time, and I'm forced
to admit they've done a brilliant job. They control Comsat
Three and Four, as well as the big one, Argonaut Twelve."

Stewart glanced nervously toward the Secret Service agent
who sat at the receptionist's desk. Colloran, sensing Stewart's
reluctance to speak in front of a third party, asked the man to
wait outside. The agent departed.

"Sir," began Stewart warily. "Major Barak claims that the
Committee is headquartered in the Potomac Plaza Hotel. The
FBI chief was taken there, not to CIA headquarters."

The general stared with astonishment at Stewart. "Are you
sure of this Barak?"

Stewart nodded. "I see no reason not to trust him."

Colloran stiffened and pursed his lips. "Some immediate
reshuffling of priorities is in order." He thought for a moment,
then stepped toward the inner door. "This can't wait. The President and the others have to know about that hotel now."

General, one second, please," said Stewart, feeling his self-
confidence soar. "Before we go in, I have a suggestion."

"Shoot, but make it fast."

"You mentioned a snake. If you cut off a snake's head, it
wiggles for a while, but it's doomed to die. By now the Potomac
Plaza's probably guarded by a battalion of crackerjack troops.
That hotel's filled with innocent bystanders, not to mention the

two hostages. This Committee's not playing in the minor leagues."

"Now hold on, Stewart. You're out of line."

"General, just hear me out, please." Stewart gestured over his shoulder with his splinted finger. "Out there in the hallway are three would-be pretenders to the throne of Hitler, complete with swastika arm bands. The assholes probably have some I.D. in their wallets. I say bring them in here, along with some Bureau muscle, and strip them down. Then we use their clothes. Give me a couple of men you and the President can trust. Together, dressed in those Nazi costumes, we'll penetrate that hotel."

Colloran came up to him, his face clouded. "You see too many movies, Stewart." He shook his head. "Three of you wouldn't stand a chance in hell. Besides, the President can't spare the men. Not now."

"It may be our only chance."

"Stick around, and I'll show you how to fight a war."

Stewart wasn't about to be put down. "Sure. Send in a paratroop division, and the innocent hostages will be killed, Carlie Chavez and Oliver Wright included. God knows how many more they're holding elsewhere, as you said yourself. With communications severed, you don't even know what's happening at state and local levels. They do. Seems to me the first priority is to get those phone circuits and satellite relays back in order."

"The plan is too risky," grunted Colloran. "The President won't buy it."

"You don't have a choice." Stewart started to press. "Look, I know what Arnold Metz and Oliver Wright look like. I understand how Carlotta Chavez thinks. I've been in that building before." Stewart's mind raced, adding up the pros, dismissing the cons. He knew he had a weak one, but still . . . "General, I've already lost one friend, a woman journalist, by sitting back on my ass when the extremists first came calling. I've read everything she ever wrote about American, German, and South American Nazis. Damn it, General, if I can't play this role, no one can."

Bernard Colloran, from the dour look on his face, clearly didn't share Stewart's optimism. He didn't move, only continuing to stare Stewart squarely in the eye.

"Well, General?"

Colloran snorted. "If I took this to the President, he'd bust me back to a colonel. Stewart, I'll give you exactly one hour; then I'm moving in with troops."

Stewart was genuinely puzzled. "Troops from where?"

"Thirty-one years in the Air Force should have taught me how to short-circuit Pentagon bureaucracy. It would be impossible to bring in heavy-duty transports from Texas and California in a couple of hours, but by God, I'll have loyal reinforcements by nightfall. In the meantime, it's not numbers that count; it's quality."

"What about the White House?" Stewart asked quickly.

"The Air Force has a couple of those new STOL transports at Andrews. Blocked runways won't mean shit to them. I'm sure the pilots would look forward to showing off a little, dropping those birds down on either Virginia or Constitution Avenue. Hell, we could even land on the south lawn in a pinch." Colloran paused and thought for a moment. "There's also General Hart, the commander of the Marine barracks at Quantico. He's a personal friend, and I talked with him earlier. Hart was as surprised as the President over what Singer, Brady, and the chairman of the Joint Chiefs are up to. There's plenty of brass in the Pentagon going along with Palmer, but just as many hedging their bets. If we can get a message to Hart, he'll be with us."

"But there are Marines outside," Stewart interrupted.

Colloran frowned. "They aren't Quantico troops. God knows where Brady and Palmer rounded that force up. Brady has some pals, a few generals who teach blind obedience, but I suspect Hart will show us some real Marines. Men who can fight *and* use their heads."

Stewart exhaled wearily. "They may have to do just that, General Colloran. Let's hope this isn't an eleventh-hour effort, too little too late."

"It's all we have, Stewart. You give your best shot to freeing the hostages, and I'll start rounding up the military."

"General, you're aware that all of the senators, congressmen, and Supreme Court justices were forced aboard buses and taken to Andrews Air Force Base?"

Colloran nodded. "Yes. The FBI so informed the President. Why this happened, we can't figure. But there's not a damned thing we can do until we deal with the trouble at the Pentagon."

Stewart liked the sound of the Air Force general's voice, throaty and strong, with a directness that suggested honesty. "One more thought," Stewart ventured. "You're positive about the loyalty of each Cabinet member inside?"

"Absolutely. We're convinced that Walter Singer's the only turncoat appointee. The President has agreed to remain here in the Capitol temporarily. Vice-President Chandler's volunteered to go back to the White House and test the waters there. He'll take the presidential limousine and police escort. We'll make it look as though the President himself is returning, just a little behind schedule, to the Oval Office. That will confuse the opposition, if only briefly." Colloran frowned and added, "We've got to buy time."

Stewart felt galvanzied for action. He'd talked with Colloran long enough. "General, do I meet with the President now or later?"

"Later. Do a job for us and I'll see to it he gives you a goddamn medal. Now let's get those Nazis in here."

34

WALTER SINGER'S HELICOPTER took off from the Pentagon helipad and banked sharply, heading across the river. The CIA pilot eased back on the throttle, slowing his speed. Singer noted the roadblocks on the Rochambeau and George Mason bridges, military checkpoints he and General Brady had set up a half-hour earlier to monitor the movement of government personnel in and out of the capital. They had established similar barricades at the other bridges across the Potomac, as well as the Anacostia River and the main roads serving the city from the north.

Singer adjusted his headset microphone and turned in his seat. To the pilot beside him, he said, "You're sure you can pull Metz out of there safely? If you have any doubts, he'll have to fry. We can't let the opposition take him alive."

"No problem. I'll get him away."

Singer pointed to the radio. "Good. Patch me in with the chairman of the Joint Chiefs. And bypass Frober and that damned Committee communications center."

The pilot nodded, swiftly reset a dial on the instrument console. He glanced at Singer. "Go ahead. You're linked to the Pentagon war room."

"This is CIA One. Put Palmer on the scramble horn."

Admiral Palmer's voice came on the transmission. "I'm standing by, Singer."

"We're checking out the presidential motorcade, Palmer. In the meantime, I suggest you send some men over to Pennsylvania Avenue. Close down and guard the White House underground command facility." Singer knew the President would never make it back there, but all he needed now was for some genius kid with a first-class ham radio set to join forces with a stray Air Force or Army general. Setting up shop, they could establish three-way dialogue among themselves, STRICOM, and NORAD. Singer planned to control every foot of the White House, especially the basement with its sophisticated electronics.

The reply came back from Palmer: "I read you. Brady has his hands full at Andrews, but I'll put General Garlock to work on it immediately."

Singer thanked Palmer, turned off the scrambler, and switched back to the cabin intercom. He pointed to the string of red blinking lights leaving the Capitol and proceeding down Constitution Avenue. "There he is. How close can you get?"

The pilot looked at him askance. "You positive this chopper's cleared with the Secret Service?"

Singer smiled, slowly stroked his mustache. "It is today. You could land on the roof of the President's limo, and no one would give a shit." Singer looked down on the police escort, the President's bubble-top limousine, and two more vehicles filled with agents and aides. The press cars, he noted, were conspicuously missing.

The pilot eased back almost to a hover, taking a position behind the motorcade and to the left. Singer watched the procession angle off into Pennsylvania Avenue, move past the Federal Trade Commission and the National Archives. He looked for the row of military vehicles he knew would be on the side street. Singer saw them, as well as the one truck parked a half-block away from the others. He tapped the pilot on the shoulder and pointed.

They watched Arnold Metz in the rear of the personnel carrier as he pushed aside the rear tarpaulin and tied it back. Now he was setting up the EMR equipment, carefully lining up the trajectory. Singer smiled. So far, so good. "I suggest a tad more space between us and the limo," he said calmly to the pilot.

Beating the air furiously, the helicopter climbed another two hundred feet. Suddenly, Singer felt a sharp concussion below. He looked down. Beside him, the pilot paled and slowly shook his head. So much for bulletproof Plexiglas tops, Singer mused, staring at the charred carnage on the street below. He signaled the pilot to move in closer. The shattering blast had torn the presidential limousine apart, flinging bodies and smoldering debris the width of Pennsylvania Avenue. A column of searing flames and smoke shot into the air, momentarily blinding the CIA pilot. He quickly banked the Huey. Below them, a motorcycle patrolman had been hit. His bike lay on top of him, wheels spinning. Several other police on motorcycles circled the area like angry ants. The Secret Service men were out of their cars, running, but the driver of one limousine was looking up at the helicopter, frantically signaling and pointing to the radio mike in his hand.

Singer immediately recognized the face. It was one of his own undercover men on the Secret Service staff. Trouble, thought Singer. What kind?

"Shall I cut in the ground radio frequency?" asked the pilot.

"No!" Singer's stomach muscles tensed. "Something's gone wrong. Put me down and I'll talk to him. Then you go in there after Metz, and fast."

The pilot quickly put the Huey down in the street. "You want me to pick you up after?"

"No. Get the hell out of here. I'll have our limo driver take me back to the Pentagon." Singer climbed out of the chopper, slammed the door, and ran toward the waiting Secret Service agent.

The pilot quickly got the Huey back in the air. Immediately he found the truck he had observed a short time before. He watched Arnold Metz abandon his weapons, jump down from the tailgate, and walk swiftly up the street. The helicopter was close now, near enough for a man on the ground to feel the wash of its rotors. Distracted, Metz stumbled and fell; he crawled to his feet and started running.

The pilot pulled a pistol from inside his jacket and placed it on his lap. Just in case. He tried to signal the fleeing Metz, but the assassin looked quickly away, frightened.

Suddenly, two D.C. motorcycle police screeched down Seventh Street from the north, leaped off their bikes, and drew their guns. The CIA pilot could see that they were ordering Metz to stop, trying to shout over the thunder of the helicopter. Their quarry didn't comply, instead turning and darting in the opposite direction toward Pennsylvania Avenue and the scene of the explosion. The patrolmen aimed and got off several shots, but Metz dodged behind parked cars.

The pilot had to get in closer, from the opposite side. He watched as Metz drew a heavy .45 from inside his coat, carefully leveled it with both hands, and fired. The nearest officer's stomach caved in, erupting in blood. Dropping the Huey between Metz and the second officer, who had run for cover, the pilot threw open the cockpit door.

Metz saw him and sprinted.

The pilot watched helplessly as a Secret Service man less than twenty feet away from Metz braced himself with both feet and fired his shotgun. The blast picked the assassin up, spun him in midair, and dropped his riddled body on the curb.

The CIA Huey leaped back into the air immediately, the pilot anxiously scanning the street beneath him. Additional Secret Service and FBI men swarmed over the truck from which Metz had fired on the presidential motorcade. The pilot watched, distracted, as an old man seated on a park bench, apparently shaken by the commotion that had frightened off the squirrels he'd been feeding, wandered fearlessly over to Metz's body. Examining it with disinterest, he looked up at the helicopter and waved. The pilot glanced back to the truck with the Secret Service men surrounding it. Their eyes were on the chopper. He had to move, fast. But as he looked down he saw one of the agents kneel to steady himself and point an odd-shaped weapon in his direction.

The helicopter clawed the air, rising rapidly. Wiping the sweat from his brow, the pilot felt relieved. Staring down the barrel of a rifle was nothing new. He'd seen it all before in 'Nam. He also knew the CIA chopper was a production design proven there; he had plenty of sheet steel under his ass. He looked back, smiling to himself. At this distance, the gunman didn't stand a chance.

Any relief he might have felt disintegrated in a blinding flash and doomsday crack. The Huey exploded with devastating vehemence. Broken rotors flailing meaninglessly, what was left of its burning hulk plunged from the sky. The CIA pilot saw his severed leg whip past him. In his twilight consciousness, he felt what was left of his body falling through searing hot air. The suffocating smoke around him became darker. The earth rushed up to meet him, but even before the impact, there was nothing.

Stewart stared over the shoulder of the FBI driver in the front seat. Good God, no! The explosion five cars ahead had been deafening, and now a column of black smoke from burning gasoline and rubber marked the place of the Vice-President's rendezvous with death. The powerful blast had been meant *not* for Vice-President Paul Chandler, but the President himself!

There were two other men in the car with Stewart. Conversation had thus far been limited, with only their last names exchanged. With him were Vosberg, the agent he had talked to in the House Chamber hallway, and a new face, Givens. Stewart was pleased with the FBI men Colloran had selected to accompany him to the hotel; they looked not only determined but tough as well.

Their car made a U-turn in the center of Pennsylvania Avenue, turning away from the carnage blocking their way. Vosberg, the driver, didn't need to explain why. Stewart understood. Others would investigate the incident; the FBI men had their own priority assignment. Timing was critical. The general had given them only an hour.

Stewart looked out the rear window, considering the turmoil in the street. Despite his fear, he had come to realize that he was getting used to the violence, the cruel realities facing him, the spilled blood at every turn. He only wondered when, or if it would end. As if to answer his question, a second explosion, even more deafening than the first, erupted behind the car.

FBI Agent Vosberg slammed on the brakes.

They all looked back, saw a disintegrated helicopter fall in flames. Stewart's hands trembled, only slightly, but enough to make a mockery of his budding self-confidence only seconds earlier.

Inside the Committee's thirtieth-floor suite at the Potomac Plaza, Karl Frober had lost all track of time. The day's events had unfolded at breakneck speed; too quickly, he thought. Frober stared at the red, green, and yellow images on the computer display screen, but his eyes could no longer focus on the glowing print and dimensional graphics. Closing his eyelids briefly,

he let out a tired breath. He was hungry and tired. Not only
were his brain and body beginning to feel sluggish, but for the
first time Frober felt a tinge of resentment over his assignment.
Important, critical, Singer and Gifford had stressed. Perhaps,
but properly he should have been allowed to fly to New York
with the others to appear on the national television panel. After
all, he'd furnished two hotels to the cause and donated large
sums of money; moreover, he'd worked harder and more diligently than Gifford or Hallowell. And he was just as dedicated
as Chandler and Singer.

Frober pushed out his thick chin and frowned. A corporate
executive didn't belong at a computer keyboard, he reasoned,
no matter how secret the input and readout information. America had become little more than an assembly line, whose attendants were bored with pushing buttons. Now he, too, felt
like a robot. Even as he sat hunched over Condor Industries'
sophisticated TV-9000 console, Frober knew that control of it
wasn't his alone. The national situation reports were being
simultaneously printed out at two other locations: CIA headquarters, and the Pentagon war room.

The longer Frober stared at the monitor, the more irritated
he grew. It hadn't occurred to him that he might be so down-
graded. At least, he thought, the statistics clattering out of the
printers were encouraging. Across the country, the takeover's
problems thus far had been minimal, nothing the field forces
couldn't handle. Again, he reviewed the incoming data.

Most of the newspaper offices around the nation were either
locked or guarded, their staffs in a state of shock. An over-
zealous Nazi cadre in Atlanta had shot one publisher and his
managing editor. Governor Hambre of North Dakota and Governor Swall of Virginia had both disappeared, and were still
missing. Michigan's first black governor had barricaded the
executive mansion and surrounded himself with state troopers
and local police. A dissident faction in Admiral Ellington's
Seventh Fleet—some eleven ships, including a Trident missile
submarine—had put to sea from Pearl Harbor, the commanding
officers demanding a clarification from the White House. Frober
wasn't worried. He suspected these mavericks would recant
soon enough, once a few military heads started to roll.

The Air Force was still an annoying bone in the throat,
thought Frober. Why hadn't the chairman of the Joint Chiefs
given him an updated report on that service? Where were Gen-

erals Colloran, Hockmeyer, and Tufts? And what was happening with the Army's counterinsurgency forces—Delta and Gamma? Was Brady in control? Frober once more faced the control console, exhaled swiftly, and rested his plump hands on the keyboard. He typed the word "STRATCOM," followed by two subcategories, "Military Relays Mount Lee" and "Civilian Long Lines Beddington."

The screen flashed back: "Hold for Revisions." This programmed response meant that information was being changed at this very moment. Frober waited, shifting his bulk in the swivel armchair. At last the summary appeared on the screen:

> Update Five / Strategic, Tactical
> Commands Diverted to Mount Lee,
> Colorado, and Bangor, Maine / All
> White House circuits diverted to
> Joint Chiefs war room / Satellite
> matrix effectiveness ninety percent.

A row of coded numbers moved up the screen, indicating more information was being processed. Frober felt better. General Brady had the situation well in hand. Events were going smoothly and looked highly successful indeed. He scanned the screen, looking for negatives. This time he saw none:

> Civilian long lines no change /
> International phone circuits
> monitored at Beddington / Direct
> dial interstate inoperative / COMSAT,
> TRIAC units ready for additional
> programming / New code authority
> required / Details follow.

Code authority? Whose bullshit was this, he wondered. Frober looked at the video screen irritably, wondering why the clarification was taking so long. Someone at the Pentagon was working an intercept. Admiral Palmer? One of his staff men? There was a burst of transmission relay, then a red line of copy flashed across the tube.

As of 14:30 additional change elements
accepted only from CIA director
Singer / End transmission.

"You pricks!" Frober said under his breath, backing away from the computer. Too many of Singer's hatchetmen were standing by for him to shout the words. Damn Singer, he thought. What the hell was the CIA up to?

The blue telephone on the desk behind Frober buzzed. An assistant picked it up, code-screened the incoming caller, then handed the receiver across the table.

"Yes?" Frober asked, not bothering to identify himself.

A halting voice grated in his ear. "This is Lynx. There's been a temporary setback."

"Yes. Go ahead, I'm listening."

"Metz attempted to assassinate the President, but he exterminated the wrong man. Paul Chandler is dead."

Frober tensed. He stared at the telephone mouthpiece, too shocked to respond. Swallowing with difficulty, he finally choked out, "The Vice-President was killed? Christ almighty, how? What now, and who'll—"

"Stop babbling like a simpleton. Who do you think will take over the helm? Not you, Gifford, or Hallowell by a long shot. Who else has the intelligence, courage, and strength? The individual you should have endorsed in the first place—Walter Singer."

Frober listened, open-mouthed, numb with disbelief. The CIA director was a ruthless, self-centered megalomaniac. Lynx's voice came at him again before he could dwell on the thought.

"Sorry, Frober. That's not all. Arnold Metz and Singer's pilot have been benched as well. They're out of the game. Permanently, and a bit untidily at that."

Stewart's mind raced furiously. Sitting in the unmarked FBI staff car accompanied by three other identically dressed men, he felt half supersleuth, half fool. His companions had provided him with a small automatic and two extra clips, and had demonstrated how to use it. The only place Stewart had fired a gun was at an amusement arcade. He hoped he wouldn't have to use the weapon, but he knew this would depend on the effectiveness of his deception.

Because he was the tallest member of Colloran's hastily

organized team and since their Nazi captives had all been men
of average height, Stewart's pants were over an inch too short.
So much for bad casting, he mused; now for some bad acting.
He was glad Shira Bernstein couldn't see him now with the
repulsive Nazi arm band. Initially he felt as if he were bound
for some beer hall putsch; the bizarre venture had seemed
almost a lark. But with the gut-rending explosions behind them,
Stewart's mood had turned irreversibly serious. His FBI companions, too, were grave.

Following the blasts, their car had pulled out from the end
of the convoy and taken side streets across town to Virginia
Avenue. It was different for the Bureau men, Stewart thought.
Vosberg and Givens were primed for confrontation, even bloodshed. When Stewart thought about it, most of the violence he
had experienced in his lifetime was compressed into this past
week. He reminded himself to look for gray hairs the next time
he found a bathroom mirror.

The Potomac Plaza loomed ahead. From here on in, he
thought, he would need his concentration. He couldn't leave
even the slightest margin for a faulty decision, a stupid mistake.

Motti Barak tipped the F-15's wing slightly and looked down
and back. The North Carolina coastline was behind him, the
Atlantic below in gradations of gray and dirty blue. He turned
on the plane-to-plane TBS radio, settled back, and waited,
knowing that at any moment Pete Reddick would try to contact
him. He hoped no one on the ground or in the 747s would be
listening to their intercom conversation. No, they wouldn't
have the military TBS, he remembered.

Less than a minute later, the colonel's voice came through
loud and clear. "This is Able Frank two three one seven. Forget
the code, Captain. If you're in posit, how do you read me?"

Barak went rigid. If ever he wanted to pass for an American,
and not an Israeli or Russian, the time was now. The fewer
words the better. He eased the transceiver dial ever so slightly,
enough to pick up sideband static. Muddying the background
might help, he figured, pushing the microphone button and
saying just three words: "Loud and clear." He had worked on
the "r" but suspected it still had a slight roll to it.

Reddick's voice shot back: "Can't say the same for you.
Not reading five by five. Fact is, you sound like hell. So just
listen. I'm picking off that first 747 as soon as it's a hundred

miles farther southeast. I'll pull a high-speed sweep of the area first to make sure no shipping is in the immediate vicinity. I suggest you wait until I confirm a hit before moving in on your own target. Sparrows don't come cheap, Captain, so let's try to get the job done with one missile each. Over."

Barak could not respond. His voice was locked in his throat. His suspicions were confirmed; either the Air Force colonel had gone mad or in some way the system had accepted and then promoted the lowest level of humanity. Never in his life had he felt more alone, and never had he felt less like the Israeli Motti Barak and more like Laurenti Baroski, the Russian whose education, professional training, and culture had taught him to look unfavorably on Americans. Had his feelings now turned to unadulterated hate? No. Colonel Reddick was far from the typical American! He planned to fire an air-to-air missile at the 747, blast it out of the sky!

Rejecting the idea in horror, Barak swore softly under his breath, glanced at the altimeter, and put the fighter into a slight climb. Calmly, with more determination than he had ever felt before in his life, he adjusted the scanner radar, searching for the two blips that would be the lead 747 and Reddick's F-15. Already he had left the second passenger jet far behind him. Barak was closing fast on the other fighter. He would have only one chance. If he missed, the slower 747 jet would be a sitting duck for the depraved colonel.

Pete Reddick cursed the radio transmission with his companion F-15, chalking up the bad reception to the Bermuda Triangle. His second in command had been thoroughly indoctrinated on the ground and had already confirmed his instructions for firing his AIM-9 Sparrow. All Reddick could do now was hope the young captain didn't go buck fever on him. Thus far none of the squadron's hand-picked complement had questioned his instructions. Reddick often wondered if it was the electric, galvanizing quality of command in his voice, or whether, just possibly, they considered his judgment godlike. Maybe his men were mindless robots. Whatever, it didn't matter. His subordinates followed his orders to the letter, without question, regardless of their ability to comprehend them.

Reddick completed a long, sweeping turn around the large passenger jet. The 747 was doing over 500 knots, and he had poured it on at almost three times that speed. The ocean below him was free of ship traffic. Excellent, he thought. With the upheaval in the capital vanishing behind him, Reddick felt limitless, unhampered power. Like a soaring hawk, he felt masterful, determined, free, controlled only by his iron will.

Sweating slightly, Reddick knew that the time had come to fulfill his patriotic dream. The promise of the future would soon take form and substance. The enemy had never been so confused, gullible, completely helpless. Two jumbo passenger jets were filled with weak, double-talking legislators and misguided Supreme Court justices. Even the senators and representatives who had professed to be true conservatives had failed the cause. The cancer that was eating away at America would now be eradicated, once and for all.

Reddick felt a strange exhilaration rushing upon him, battering down his final barriers of self-doubt. Filled with a loathing for the evil that must be destroyed, he released the safety switch on the infrared sensor brackets and slowly lined up behind and slightly above the 747. The air was smooth, the fighter rode easily in the clear blue sky. He turned on the missile's radar seeker terminal, checked the target illumination and data links. He was ready. *Now,* he thought.

His finger never closed around the missile's release trigger. In his last instant of life, Pete Reddick himself came to know the awesome destructive force of the Sparrow AIM-9. The explosion that disintegrated his fighter, tearing his body to pieces, was deafening, all-consuming—a giant, remorseless ball of fire.

Motti Barak had seen Sparrow missiles perform before. He knew what they could do. He felt no contrition for his surprise flanking attack on Reddick's F-15. Swiftly, he banked his fighter, flicked the firing controls for the remaining Sparrow on safety, and adjusted the aircraft's trim to compensate for the weight differential from the one empty weapons pylon.

Barak thought long and hard. The passenger jets were free to travel on to their Caribbean destination without interference. For the present, they would be safer there than back in the capital. Barak had at least eliminated the egocentric, misguided Colonel Reddick; he would leave the homicidal Arnold Metz to the FBI. Kirk Stewart would be safe enough with the President and General Colloran, both of whom had been alerted in time. They would have their hands full rescuing the FBI chief and the newswoman, but numerical strength was on their side. The one who really worried Barak was Walter Singer.

Barak felt cheated. All his efforts to preserve the status quo in America had cost him his cover. Back at the Israeli legation it had become apparent that Mossad Intelligence was probing, asking the wrong kinds of questions. Under the circumstances, Barak's value to Soviet Ambassador Grotski was ended. The KGB had assigned Barak a new cover in London, and he had been ordered not to remain in the U.S. for another day. Unfair, he thought. My work is not completed. It now occurred to him that he might be able to launch his last Sparrow on the CIA building itself, directly into Walter Singer's office. Was it possible? And afterwards, could he expect to get away? By returning to Washington, he could help Stewart and the woman, if nothing else. Later, he could make his way out to sea and be picked up by the trawler. The ship had orders to remain on station, waiting, if necessary, until two hours after daybreak tomorrow.

Barak weighed the challenge of returning to Washington against the safety of following orders. If CIA headquarters wasn't a propitious target, he could at least do some heavy damage to Reddick's squadron on the ground at National. Barak thought for a moment, then withdrew from his calf pocket the aeronautical chart the Soviet embassy had supplied him earlier. Unfolding it, he noted the position of the trawler some fifty miles off Cape May. Closer than he had figured. Barak was also surprised to see, beneath the marked coordinates, a scribbled notation in Russian from Ambassador Grotski himself:

Perhaps, with more men like you, Laurenti Baroski, we can prove to the world that the nationalities question is not the Soviet Union's Achilles' heel. Good luck Mikhail Grotski.

Barak smiled to himself. He felt pleased, wondering if a similar commendation might be placed in his KGB sleeper's dossier. He also wondered if exit papers were already being expedited for his parents back in Ivanovo.

Barak checked the F-15's fuel consumption. Better than he had originally estimated. He made up his mind. The powerful Sparrow missile would only be wasted if he ditched now. He slowed the Eagle to 500 knots and, deliberately ignoring the

UHF channels, turned his radio to the civilian ATC band. It was his only chance—double-talking the flight controllers, letting them assume his radar blip was one more private jet in the Northeast Corridor.

The white FBI sedan drove past the lobby entrance of the Potomac Plaza without stopping or slowing. Stewart turned and stared back at the half-dozen men standing vigil outside the hotel. As the car moved on, he saw three personnel carriers loaded with soldiers in combat gear a short distance down the street. So that's the scene, he thought. Low profile out front to avoid attention; inside business as usual. The hotel was a nice cover, and there were heavy reinforcements on standby, ready to move in at any sign of alarm.

"No chance at the lobby entrance," agent Vosberg said from behind the wheel. "One of the men out front is CIA. He knows Givens and me." Vosberg slowed the car and turned the corner. The vehicle crept slowly around behind the hotel.

Stewart set his jaw in determination. Ahead was what looked like the convention center and lower-level entrance to the hotel. Men were unloading crates and exhibit materials from trucks.

"Park the car," he urged the driver. "There has to be a way into that Committee stronghold."

"We don't even know where they're holed up," groaned Givens. "The Potomac Plaza has thirty floors and over eight hundred rooms, for chrissake."

Stewart adjusted his swastika arm band and reached for the door handle. "Before the three of us go inside, I'm checking out the terrain. Alone, okay? At least I don't have a face that'll be recognized."

The FBI men looked at each other, shrugging. Vosberg said quickly, "No more than a fast walk around. If you're gone more than ten minutes, we'll move in."

"Relax," Stewart replied. "I'll reconnoiter the lobby, the basement, and the freight elevators." Not waiting for any more advice, Stewart got out of the car and headed across the parking lot. Striding past several off-loading trucks, he wandered into the hotel's exhibit hall and found it filled with workmen preparing for a convention. They looked at him curiously, noted his arm band, but said nothing. Stewart passed a registration table, noted a banner that read "Arcade Amusement Industry

Convention." He walked out through the foyer, along the service ramps opposite the catering kitchen. Two Marines standing beside a roped-off freight elevator were the only sign of takeover surveillance in the area. Stewart paused near the guards. They were checking the delivery documents of a truck driver with several cartons marked "Electronics."

Stewart climbed the flight of stairs leading to the lobby and reception level. The activity in the main corridor appeared normal—except for one detail. Four of the elevators, he noted, were available to hotel patrons, but the fifth one was guarded by three burly civilians and an army lieutenant holding a clipboard. Stewart watched a Marine general with a bulging briefcase flash his credentials, go through an electronic gun detector, then step briskly into the elevator. The doors closed.

Stewart stood off to the side, pretending to wait for one of the other cars, but at the same time his eyes scanned the floor indicator lights above the guarded elevator. It stopped at the thirtieth floor, the penthouse level. Getting up there wouldn't be easy, Stewart calculated. The stairwell would be guarded, and it was too long a climb anyway. Still, there had to be a way in. An idea began to gel in his mind. *Deliveries*.

Stewart took the next down car, got off at the lower floor, and again took a shortcut through the exhibit hall. As he passed the Midway, Bally, Sanyo, and Atari displays, he saw two workmen trundle a two-foot-by-six-foot game machine called Godzilla and the Geisha out of a reinforced cardboard shipping crate. Stewart hesitated, eyed the video game curiously, then looked at the shipping container. His mind sharpened. The labels on the box read:

> Fragile—Delicate
> Electronics Equipment
> Tanaka Videomedia Mfg Co.

Below, in smaller stenciled letters, were the words, GODZILLA AND THE GEISHA, MODEL II.

Stewart turned back to the machine, watching, fascinated, as one of the workers activated the unit. It gave off a terrible, bestial roar, then alternated between heavy breathing, electronic beeps, and coquettish, feminine giggles. A kaleidoscope of pornographic cartoon characters flashed across the screen.

Stewart put away his smile and went up to the workmen. He didn't need the machine, but he had a definite use for its shipping container.

The Washington, D.C., Air Route Traffic Control Center at Leesburg was on the air, busy diverting inbound flights away from the sealed-off capital area airports. One communication in particular caught and held Motti Barak's attention as he flew his F-15 westward at twenty thousand. The controller's voice from Leesburg, he noted, was terse and emphatic.

"Condor Industries JetStar three zero one one. We have no authority to clear private aircraft for corridor traffic en route New York. All flights from National Airport are to remain grounded until further notice. Do you copy?"

Barak then heard the Condor pilot's voice come back: "Washington ATC, this is three zero one one. You're wrong, Mac. We've already been cleared by National Ground Control at runway three six, and we're holding. What's the delay?"

"Sorry, Condor. All private and passenger aircraft entering the corridor must have official approval. Some damned Committee's orders, funneled through the Pentagon. There's a four-hour exit and entry quarantine on the capital."

An angry voice came on. "Suggest you stick to your radar scopes, Leesburg. Who the hell do you think we have aboard this plane? Half of your Committee, that's who. Do we get a VFR clearance or just turn you off? You reading?"

Barak smiled. So much for eavesdropping. He listened intently to the ATC's prompt clearance, making a note of the assigned corridor. He felt a sudden chill as he realized that here were two, possibly three leaders, the very heart of the cabal— the men he and Kirk Stewart had tried in vain for a week to identify.

Barak descended another three thousand feet and adjusted his course. Already he could see the Anacostia River where it converged into the wider Potomac. Beyond it was National Airport. If he strained hard enough, he would probably see the Lockheed JetStar on its takeoff run. Inside it were the brains, the driving force behind the movement, Barak reasoned. Apparently headed for New York to survey the spoils of their conquest and participate in the news media takeover Kirk Stewart had predicted. There was a strange kind of evil aboard that plane—an incalculable evil that defied the reasoning power of reasoning men. He was faced with an opportunity to alter history.

Barak had to think quickly. If he didn't do the unpleasant job, it was only a matter of time until others did; the process might be slow, the ugliness and pain extended. Millions would suffer. The Sparrow missile beneath his wing, on the other hand, would be sure and swift.

Barak watched the JetStar rise from the ground like a phoenix, its dreadful significance overcoming his sensiblities as it climbed higher in the sky over the capital. He blinked from the rivulets of sweat rolling down his forehead into his eyes. Barak pushed his silver visor up, wiped his face. His F-15 was tracking the executive jet, gradually closing the gap. He felt a gnawing uneasiness in his stomach. In sudden replay his eyes saw the DC-10 explode mercilessly on takeoff from Houston's Hobby Airport, and in the same instant he knew he didn't have the will to turn his back on retribution, that he couldn't run away. Fate had ruled otherwise. But his act would be seen from below; getting away would be difficult, if not impossible. Barak thought about the safety, the comforting security of the Soviet trawler waiting for him. His superiors would never order him to commit such an act, but if he was successful, they would commend him. And then possibly give him a reward. And his KGB obligations—possibly they would be satisfied forever.

Swiftly, he mumbled a prayer in Hebrew: *"Miyom kipper zeh ad yom kippur habo olenu l'tovoh."* The very old traditional Jewish plea to be absolved of his vow to God, the prayer of the people who are not free to make their own decisions.

Completing his firing sequence, Barak pushed the AIM-9's release trigger.

The Sparrow rocketed forward, immediately found its target. An explosion lit up the sky.

Barak felt every muscle in his body tighten. Immediately, he banked the F-15, completed his turn, and lit the afterburners. The plane slammed into his back and limbs as he felt the anti-G suit compensate. He didn't look back or down. The Eagle's mach-meter started to climb upward as he raced away from the scene.

But he was too late! The F-15 shuddered as a fusillade of 25mm tracers struck his left outboard wing. Only then did he see the other Eagle scream off in a tight, climbing turn. One of Reddick's men. How long had he been following and observing Barak? The other F-15 bore no Sidewinders or Sparrows, only cannon armament.

Barak's heart beat erratically. Some of the controls were gone. He had to slow the plane, try to guide it to an unpopulated area. Where? He was headed south. There was only the Potomac, if he could lose more altitude and maintain course.

Seconds, then minutes passed. The second plane, confident of its kill, didn't return. The river was below. Barak throttled the trembling fighter back as close as he could to stall speed and checked the altimeter. He watched in dismay as the vibrating wingtip broke away. Zero control now. Straightening himself against the cockpit seat, he pushed the automatic canopy release and eject button.

35

STEWART LOST A quarter of an hour negotiating for the shipping container, rounding up his Bureau companions, then convincing Vosberg and Givens that his plan would work. It took another five minutes to move the empty crate to a secluded spot, tape over the Godzilla label, and have the FBI men drive several small nails in place, temporarily securing Stewart, as well as all their weapons, inside. They had drawn straws to flirt with claustrophobia, and Stewart had won—or lost.

After the close surveillance Stewart had seen outside the hotel, in the lobby, and at the freight elevator, he knew that if they were to be admitted at all to Committee headquarters, they would face a weapons check—either an electronic scan or a frisking. The Potomac Plaza's outer perimeter of security, at least, was clear to them. Uncomfortably so. Their guns would be secure inside the crate. Stewart had also requisitioned a roll of heavy duct tape from one of the exhibit builders for possible later use on captives.

It was dark inside the container, and Stewart had to crouch slightly. Already his shoulders had started to cramp, and he wondered if he'd made the right decision. Suddenly, it occurred to him that he'd forgotten to make air holes in the cardboard, and so with a ball-point pen he made several small punctures in the top and a small one in the front of the box. He grimaced as his sore shoulder slammed against the side of the container. The FBI men were moving him. Vosberg's borrowed hand truck tilted at a precarious angle.

Seconds later Stewart heard a terse conversation between the two FBI men and the Marines guarding the freight elevator. Stewart stared out through the small hole in the cardboard. As he suspected. Vosberg and Givens, despite their swastika arm bands, were being searched for weapons. Stewart watched nervously as they presented their bogus credentials. After some argument, one of the sentries admitted he didn't want to interfere with the delivery of computer equipment needed upstairs. He said he would accompany them in the elevator and turn them over to the security personnel who guarded the thirtieth floor.

A double perimeter of security, thought Stewart. He clenched his teeth as his shoulder again hit the side of the box. His casketlike container was being wheeled inside the elevator. He heard the doors close, then silence. Trying to avoid thinking about his discomfort, Stewart fixed his mind on Carlie. He was more determined than ever and had to admit to himself not only that he wanted to rescue Carlie Chavez but also that he had an insane desire to find out everything about the ugly cabal. He was amazed by the secrecy and obedience the conspiracy had thus far generated, right down to the guard on the elevator. Idly, Stewart thought of Vietnam, then Central America. His brain began sifting through words like *duty, patriotism, unquestioned obedience*. A vision of National Guardsmen at Kent State came to mind, at the same time a quote from Shelley: "Power, like a desolating pestilence, pollutes whatever it touches."

No one in the elevator spoke. Stewart heard only a steady disconcerting hum.

Inside the Pentagon, Lynx stepped rapidly down the busy D Ring corridor, turned off into a quiet, narrow hallway. He found the inconspicuous door with its coded push-button lock. Lynx pushed the correct sequential numbers, and the door opened, revealing a small lobby with an elevator and armed guard. Showing his identification, he was promptly admitted to the special car that would plummet down to the large concrete cube far beneath the ground, the subterranean conference room where Walter Singer, Admiral Palmer, General Brady, and several other staff-level officers would be waiting for him.

Lynx wasn't concerned over the death of Vice-President Chandler. And as far as Metz was concerned, it was so much good riddance. But the fiery explosion of the executive jet he had just seen was another matter. The Condor Industries plane had gone down in Arlington Cemetery, and there had been no survivors. He debated how to break the news to Singer.

Lynx brooded. New faces were about to shape the destiny of the United States—the world, for that matter. Though the takeover had just suffered a serious setback, Lynx remained confident. He knew that Walter Singer would effectively take command; in the end, this was what they had intended anyway. Lynx also knew that his own efforts over the past year had earned him the right to be at Singer's side for the big finish.

Swinging slowly from his parachute like a marionette on strings, Motti Barak sucked in huge lungfuls of air and tried to untighten his nerves. His head had finally cleared from the noise and force of the ejection catapult and subsequent separation from his seat, and he was still in one piece. The F-15 had cartwheeled end over end, splashing into the Alexandria side of the river just north of the Highway 95 bridge.

Ears singing with a strange quiet, Barak searched the sky but saw no trace of the plane that had attacked him. Mission accomplished, it had probably returned to base. The pilot was toasting the victory, Barak guessed.

Patting the pockets of his flying suit, Barak took inventory of his belongings. A small Beretta pistol. A folding knife. He still had the twelve-ounce mold of explosive plasticine. Everything else, including his wallet, he had foolishly left in his jacket in a locker at Andrews. He looked at the plastic that he had intended to use for ground sabotage at the air base, wondering if he should continue to hold on to it. Suddenly it occurred to him that he hadn't a coin on him, and he'd need money for a crosstown cab fare. Barak felt more annoyed than concerned. If necessary, he'd sell the expensive pilot's hard hat to the driver, and if worse came to worst, back up any fare argument with his Beretta.

The ground came rushing up. Barak had drifted westward with the wind, and thankfully was over land, not the river.

With luck, he'd fall in a large schoolyard or the park just beyond it.

Inside his box within the freight elevator, Stewart felt as if he
were in a suffocating cocoon. Was it worth it? He was close,
so very close to the mysterious Committee and to Carlie. His
fiery obsession to find her was stoked now, burning ever hotter.
Back down. Cool it a little, he thought. He had to think clearly.

Stewart pondered. He thought of what Metz had done to
others who had obstructed his superiors and their sick cause,
the lives he had snuffed out like so many birthday candles.

Stewart felt sticky with sweat. Why were freight elevators
notoriously slow? At least the main body of troops guarding
the hotel were behind them. Even as they had proceeded to the
elevator, two additional Marine personnel trucks had arrived
at the rear of the hotel. If he and his two companions failed to
infiltrate the headquarters in an hour General Colloran would
keep his threat and move in. A bloodbath. Carlie and Oliver
Wright wouldn't stand a chance.

He was close, very close. When he reached the top floor,
one wrong move could be his undoing. Colloran had ordered
Vosberg and Givens to cooperate, give him the support he
needed. They had both shot him dubious looks of appraisal.
What was going on in their minds? For the present, the two
FBI men were unarmed and could make no precipitous moves.
The ploy with the crate had worked perfectly thus far; it had
allowed them to sneak the weapons past the gun detectors. The
Bureau men couldn't function until the box was opened. Stewart, through his peephole, would have ample time to size up
the situation.

Suddenly, Stewart felt his crate receive a sharp nudge. Again,
this time harder. Now a loud thud. The elevator floor shook,
and he heard a scuffle. There was an outcry, quickly muffled,
followed by the sound of a heavy object striking the side of
the car. Stewart's heart raced. He looked through the hole, saw
a limp form slide past him to the floor.

Stewart could only listen to his imagination. Was it the guard
or that of one of the Bureau men? The battle in the elevator
made his claustrophobia worse.

"It's okay," he heard Vosberg say breathlessly. "Unwind,
Stewart. I stopped the elevator between floors to clean house."

•   •   •

The subterranean concrete cube beneath the Pentagon was more than a bomb shelter; it was the strategy center for military planning in case of war, the place where decisions were made by the Joint Chiefs of Staff and the Secretary of Defense. Officially, it was known as the big board room, but the holdover seniors from the Korean and Vietnam conflicts still called it the war room.

Not all of the usual faces were currently seated at the conference table that flanked the room's illuminated wall. The commander of the Air Force, General Colloran, was conspicuously missing. His chief of staff, General Talbert, sat in his place, but was still wavering on a commitment to the group. Harold Lockwood, the secretary of defense, was conveniently in the hospital. The CIA director sat at the head of the table in the defense secretary's customary place. On one of the large wall screens Singer and the other men in the chamber watched a space data analysis. Satellite transmissions were normally fine-tuned to Russian ICBM sites and other strategic points of interest. But now the Samos 21 orbiting three hundred miles above the earth transmitted intricate scans of several U.S. military installations. Singer and the others were particularly interested in what was happening at Colorado Springs, Omaha, and Fort Bragg. What Singer observed in uncanny, intricate detail was being transmitted instantly, without a moment's delay. The Pentagon was in fact spying on its own people.

An army colonel entered the chamber and handed Singer a document. The CIA head read the blue flimsy prepared for him by the communications staff upstairs and frowned, already aware of the news the message contained. Now that the facts had been released, he'd have to tell the others. Singer signaled the technician operating the Samos unit to conclude the presentation. His face stiffening, he looked at the others. "Gentlemen, about the assassin's target. I'm told it wasn't the President he killed but rather Paul Chandler. The Vice-President is dead."

No one spoke or breathed. Singer squared his shoulders and continued: "As you're aware, Chandler and I were not particularly close. He was the Committee's choice to replace the President, not mine. I might even afford you half a smile for the occasion were it not for an accompanying footnote. My personal pilot has also been killed." Singer paused, watched the shocked faces of the officers at the conference table, then once again examined the communication before him. "Arnold

Metz, too, has perished, though that loss does not upset me."
He smiled thinly. "Gentlemen, dwelling on the past is destructive. With your support, I intend to move forward, not back."

Singer looked at the others, then reached for the red telephone in front of him and patted it thoughtfully. Somberly, he
rose to his feet. "My place is no longer here, but in the White
House command room. I have no intention of allowing the
President to return and attempt to reestablish control from there."

The confused faces around the table stared at Singer. Chairman Palmer looked ashen as he swallowed hard and poured a
glass of water from the silver decanter in front of him. General
Brady scribbled feverishly on a notepad. He was the only Army
representative at the table; two of his in-line superiors had
refused to attend the meeting. Across from Brady, a Marine
general and a Navy admiral whispered briefly with their staff
aides. The mood in the chamber was heavy. Too heavy, thought
Singer.

Admiral Palmer broke the uncomfortable silence. "Singer,
you've just given us some shocking news." He hesitated, glanced
around the table, and spoke in collected tones. "I think we
should reevaluate the situation in light of this severe loss."

Singer wanted to laugh, but contained himself. Glaring dag-
gers at Palmer, he kept his silence.

General Brady's forehead knotted, his mouth curving in a
satiric smile. "Loss?" he rasped, suddenly leaning forward.
"You're talking like a loser, Admiral. When a couple of sixteen-
inch guns on a battleship are out of action, you call it quits?
Hell, you've still got ample firepower, plenty of fuel, and most
important, steerage."

Stroking the ends of his mustache and smiling sagely, Singer
headed for the door. "I'll let you deliberate in privacy, gentlemen. Of course, you'll consider the consequences of retreat.
We've come a long way together. Too far, I'm afraid, to pull
back now. If you go your separate ways, the hunter may well
become the hunted. We can learn from the wolves, my friends.
Stay with the pack. We must eradicate our enemies once and
for all. Not only for those of us here to survive, but for the
nation to endure."

The room was silent, the tension as heavy as ever. Admiral
Palmer withdrew a package of Winstons and nervously lit one.
The others stirred and looked anxiously in his direction. Ex-
haling smoke slowly, Palmer finally said, "Anyone care to

venture a suggestion?" He gestured toward the red telephone at the end of the conference table. "How do we go about installing a new Commander-in-Chief?"

Singer fought down the urge to throw Palmer out of the room. Pausing in the open doorway, he gazed icily back at the chairman of the Joint Chiefs. "Nothing has changed, Admiral. Not a goddamn thing. Do I make myself clear?" Singer looked threateningly at the others. "Gentlemen, I suggest you get on with your work. Discuss the alternatives, if you must, but let's have no equivocating. I prefer immediate action. I have adversaries on my back who need attending to. When I've secured the White House underground command center, I'll contact you." Singer forced his lips into an uneven smile. "Be prepared to answer *my* new red telephone, gentlemen."

Feeling a surge of power, Singer walked out of the room and closed the heavy metal door behind him. He strode across the corridor to the elevator. Singer was about to push the call button when the pale green doors slid open.

Lynx stepped out of the car.

Singer stiffened. Wagging his hand, he pushed Lynx back into the elevator. "We're going back up. And you're late. My men have already given me the facts about the Vice-President and my pilot."

Lynx looked at him. Without flinching, he said, "Sorry, there's more to report. Gifford's corporate jet was shot down by an air-to-air missile from an F-15. Curiously, one of Reddick's planes."

"Shit!" was all Singer could manage to spit out before his breath jammed in his throat. Slamming a fist into his palm, face flushing with anger, he quickly asked, "How could this happen? The opposition's been well covered for the past two weeks. Oliver Wright couldn't possibly have set this up, Lynx. You know that." Singer paused, slowly let out his breath, and collected his thoughts. "He's still being held at the hotel?" His deliberate tone made it more of a statement than a question.

"The FBI director is under close guard," replied Lynx. "But there are others, and they may be trying to join forces with Wright."

Singer's frame tightened. His mind raced. How could he possibly be everywhere at once? Incompetence in the ranks. He now had to compose himself, plan very carefully. He should have disposed of Wright and the TV newswoman at the outset.

In addition to the pair at the Potomac Plaza, there was the problem of what to do with the President. A very alive President. It was too late to send him to Haiti. Now, with Norman Gifford dead, Singer couldn't trust the Citadel. No, he'd personally have to eliminate the Chief Executive; it had come down to that. As for Frober's high-rise hotel and the hostages . . . Singer looked at Lynx and spoke softly.

"You're not only reliable, Lynx, but innovative, too. You've done damned fine work, and I'm indebted to you. Our late friend Arnold Metz, despite his unsavory reputation, had a point: Intimidation alone won't work; we have to be ruthless, use force. No remorse. If you want to win, you have to play for keeps, my mother used to say. She was right, Lynx. My mother was always right. It's time to take off the white gloves and get our hands dirty. From now on, we strike swiftly, resolutely, and like Metz, without remorse. For the good of the nation, my friend."

The elevator came to a stomach-rending halt at the ground level. Lynx looked at Singer expectantly. "Your instructions?"

"Go to the Potomac Plaza. Bring the FBI director to me. He'll be eliminated soon enough, but first he may be of value to us in convincing the rank and file at the Bureau to cooperate with us."

Lynx thought for a moment. "What about the network newswoman and her reporter friend, Stewart, who's been dogging us for a week?"

"With our velvet-gloved Committee out of the way, I no longer have to bargain with the media. Both journalists are now expendable. Terminate them."

The mood inside the Potomac Plaza's freight elevator was heavy with anticipation. The doors finally rolled open at the penthouse level. Between floors Vosberg had pushed the emergency stop button, halting the car. Agent Givens had changed into the Marine sentry's uniform and tossed his gray corduroy suit out of the elevator's ceiling escape hatch. The unconscious Marine, his wrists bound with a necktie, stripped down to his underwear, had been hoisted out the same opening and left on the roof of the elevator.

The plan now was for Givens—in his new elevator sentry role—to protect their flank and keep open a route of escape. He would have no difficulty surprising and overcoming the second Marine who waited in the basement.

Vosberg checked the hallway and whispered to Stewart. "Here we go again," he said ominously.

Seconds later, peering through the small hole in the front of the carton, Stewart saw that halfway down the corridor a small table had been set up outside a doorway. A woman Army captain sat behind it, and flanking the door were two attentive MPs. As Vosberg approached with his cumbersome container marked Tanaka Videomedia, one of the sentries leveled an automatic carbine.

Stewart watched the woman straighten. Quickly, she warned, "That's far enough. Do you have clearance for this floor?" Her eyes took in Vosberg's Nazi arm band with uncertainty. The woman, Stewart noted, had a cold, suety face framed with black, close-cropped hair, and she wore no lipstick. Her voice was coarse and mannish.

Vosberg hesitated, eased forward slightly. "My orders were to deliver and hook up this computer equipment immediately. We're completing a data link between here and our National Socialist group policing the State Department."

Stewart watched the female captian look hard at the agent. She pushed her shoulders back authoritatively and said, "Your identification."

"Again?" Vosberg snorted. "Lady, I've already gone through this twice. Once downstairs, again in the elevator. I'm telling you they're waiting for this equipment inside. You're wasting critical time."

The woman gestured to the two MPs with a flick of her wrist. Immediately, they began frisking Vosberg. Finding no weapons, they resumed their places at each side of the entrance. The woman glared at Vosberg. "You wait here." She opened the door marked 3010 and strode inside, closing it behind her.

Karl Frober ran a hand through his crew cut, giving the woman captain an annoyed look. "Don't bother me with details. Just send in the delivery."

"Whatever you say, sir. But my orders were to admit only shipments scheduled a day in advance. I don't understand."

Breathing heavily, Frober glowered at her. "Before Wadislow's death, he did say additional relays had been ordered. And our data links with those Nazis at Foggy Bottom aren't what they should be. Is this man a technician?"

"So he claims, sir."

Frober exhaled. "Let's see what the hell he has."

A moment later, the outer door opened. Frober pursed his thick lips as he watched a man with a swastika arm band hand-truck a tall cardboard carton inside. He gestured for the MP guards to remain in the hall. The Army captain at his side, Frober walked around the container, eyeing it with an increasingly perverse curiosity.

He was inside! Pleased with himself, Stewart had to choke back an urge to laugh. The ruse had worked. Stewart felt like a voyeur at a Pigalle peep show. He watched through the hole as the fat man who seemed to be in charge stood back and shook his fleshy jowls.

"This is a patch-in terminal? A mistake, surely. Jesus! It's as large as an entire circa-sixties data processor!" He leaned forward, eyes flashing, suddenly curious about the piece of tape Stewart had placed over the carton's label and model number. As he ripped it away, his eyes widened, and he stammered, "Godzilla and the Geisha?" He shrugged, his wet lips half-open as he looked alternately at the captain and Vosberg, beside the crate.

Squinting through his peephole, Stewart, and his reporter's knack of instant orientation, wasted no time sizing up the scene. He couldn't see the FBI agent beside the carton; he could only assume that Vosberg was poised and ready.

There wasn't a sign of Carlie Chavez or Oliver Wright. The room was spacious, probably thirty feet long by twenty wide, with a floor-to-ceiling north-facing window running its length. Closed doors at each end of the suite, Stewart speculated, led to adjoining bedrooms and baths. The captives could be there. Two expensive sofas had been pushed into the corners to make room for several tables loaded with computer and communications hardware. In addition to the fat man in the expensive Italian mohair suit and the woman officer, there were three shirtsleeved young men in the room, all preoccupied with telephones and computer keyboards. They looked innocent enough, but Stewart suspected otherwise. The overall scene reminded him of one of those fund raisers for community-supported television. Stewart studied the men at the work tables. Even without Porsche sunglasses and trench coats, they looked like CIA operatives. Vosberg's timing, thought Stewart, would be critical.

"Should we open it, Mr. Frober?" the Army captain said in a suspicious, uneven voice.

Stewart watched her back away from the crate as if it were a questionable delivery from a sorcerer's shop. She'd called him Frober. Of course! The face came back to Stewart. The *Wall Street Journal* news article—the hotel executive who had allegedly colluded with Condor Industries. Karl Frober. The man who had masterminded the Libyan arms trade.

For the first time in a week Stewart felt cautiously confident. He knew where he was going and what he had to do. Not that he didn't know fear. But he now had a clearer picture of the enemy. Much clearer. The puzzle was almost complete.

Outside the container, the corpulent hotel executive looked nervous, as if he were considering calling the sentries back. Stewart waited for the rap of knuckles on the side of the crate, Vosberg's prearranged signal to pounce.

36

STEWART KICKED HARD. The cardboard that broke away from the crate's wooden frame flattened on the floor as he stepped out into the room, gun ready. At the same instant agent Vosberg grabbed Frober, clamping an arm around his neck. Stewart blinked to adjust to the light, but his Beretta didn't waver, steadily intimidating the technicians at the computer tables. With his free hand he passed the FBI man a second pistol.

"Not a movement. Nobody says a word, nobody gets hurt, understand?" ordered Stewart, for the first time feeling a handgun's mantle of authority. He felt no pleasure, only strength, along with a measure of disappointment at the frightened faces before him. The penthouse suite's occupants looked like office workers, not the bevy of corporate executives, political kingpins, and powerful military leaders he had anticipated.

Vosberg eased his choke-hold on Karl Frober, whose sweat-covered face had turned sickly green. He checked the crew-cut executive for weapons. Finding none, the Bureau agent retrieved the roll of duct tape from the empty crate, came up to Stewart, and said softly, "Before penetrating those inner doors, I want to immobilize the lot. I don't turn my back for a split second with these odds." He turned to the computer operators. "All of you, against the wall, hands behind your heads."

Stewart waved his gun at the nervous but alert-eyed Army woman. "Those men. Bind their wrists and feet, Captain." He looked hard at her. "What's your name?"

"Dorothy." Her voice quavered. "Captain Dorothy McNeilly."

Vosberg handed her the roll of tape. He pointed his pistol at Karl Frober's head. "Tell your friends to cooperate, blubber-butt, or the real noise goes off behind your ear."

A pall of silence descended on the room as Stewart went to the door and listened. Backs against the wall and seated on the floor, the three CIA men glared at him. The tension built. Stewart was pleased; despite her trembling hands, Captain McNeilly worked surprisingly fast with the tape. "Don't forget their mouths," he instructed.

Vosberg found guns on two of the men, emptied the car-tridges into his pocket, and tossed the weapons aside.

Stewart turned to Frober, firmly pushed him into the swivel armchair at the computer console. "You're familiar with this equipment, I assume?"

Frober nodded glumly.

Stewart beckoned to Captain McNeilly. "Tape this man's ankles only. He'll need to use his hands."

"And his mouth, to do a little talking," added Vosberg, joining Stewart. The agent gestured toward the outer doorway and in hushed tones said, "I'm not so much concerned over the presence of two sentries outside as by the firepower of their automatic carbines."

Stewart nodded. Vosberg was right; they needed to protect their flank before proceeding. Pushing the frightened Army captain before him to the door, he said to her, "Open it partially. Ask the guards outside to enter." Stewart nodded to Vosberg, who pressed himself behind the door.

McNeilly obeyed, and oblivious to the trap, the two MPs entered. Instantly, Vosberg pushed a pistol snout against the first man's forehead. "Quiet!" he rasped, slipping the MAC-10 automatic from the guard's hands. At the same time, Stewart just as easily relieved the second man of his holstered pistol. Vosberg slammed the door, leaving the hallway unat-tended. So far, so good, Stewart reasoned. The score was improving, and they still hadn't been forced to punt! But with both guards and the woman missing from the hallway, they would have to move faster or call in reinforcements. At least Givens was outside in the freight elevator. Captain McNeilly repeated the tape-binding process on the guards. When she was finished, Vosberg bound her, too. With the machine carbine in his possession, the FBI agent looked more confident as he and Stewart approached the two doors on opposite sides of the suite. When they were both in position, they gently released the handles and threw both doors open at the same time.

Inside the doorway he had opened, Stewart saw the FBI director. Handcuffed to a brass bedpost, Oliver Wright looked up, startled, but instantly relieved. Stewart's eyes flashed to the opposite door. He heard a woman's shriek and a dog barking. Standing before the open door, Vosberg, his carbine at ready, was greeted by a small poodle poking its bow-decorated head around the corner. A second later, a tall amazon of a blonde, still struggling into a lavender slip, swaggered out of the room. Boldly, she nudged the barrel of Vosberg's MAC-10 aside. "What the hell's going on?" she asked abruptly, in a Scandinavian accent. "Ever hear of knocking, you lout?"

Stewart fought back a grin as he watched Vosberg's eyes widen in disbelief.

The FBI man stood his ground. "Who the hell are you?" he asked awkwardly.

"Frieda." Her tone suddenly softened as she glanced around the room and saw the half-dozen bound and gagged captives slumped along the wall. She looked at Frober, who only gazed back at her helplessly. "Oh, my God," she whispered, both hands going to her cheeks. She scooped up the dog and stepped nervously back into the bedroom.

Agent Vosberg wasted no time obtaining the keys to Oliver Wright's handcuffs from the hotel executive. As Stewart approached Frieda's bedroom the agent and the FBI director conferred in hushed tones. Vosberg immediately armed Wright with one of their captives' handguns and a clip of bullets. Wright tucked the weapon into his empty shoulder holster.

All Stewart could think about was Carlie as he edged through the second bedroom's doorway and pushed past the confused blonde. "Nice dog," he said flippantly, stroking the head of the poodle cradled against her ample breast. The animal growled and let out a high-pitched bark. Stewart ignored it and looked around the deserted bedroom. "Where is she?" he snapped. "Carlotta Chavez!"

"Kirk! I'm locked in here!" The shout, a trifle too casual, came from the bathroom.

Stewart tried the door, found it locked. He looked at the big blonde, extending his hand.

Frieda glowered back at him, dropped her dog, went over to the bed, and started to fumble through her purse.

Impatient, Stewart stepped back from the bathroom door. "Stay away from the door, Carlie." He crashed against it with his good shoulder. The door hurled open. Stewart stared into the bathroom, dumbfounded.

Carlie smiled up at him, her face surrounded by a chin-high sea of fragrant bubbles. She raised one of her perfect legs out of the tub, curled her wet toes, and waved them. "Hi, sweet," she said, her voice thrilled with relief and excitement. "Took long enough for you to rescue me. I've been going crazy with boredom. What kind of scout troop you leading, anyway?"

Leaning against the broken door, Stewart rubbed the back of his neck and slowly shook his head. "Beaver Patrol," he replied tartly. Thank God she was safe, but this? He smiled at her. For both of them the worst was over. "Unfortunately," he said slowly, "this scout doesn't get merit badges for thirtieth-floor rescues of foxy ladies in distress." Frowning, he gestured to the door. "Let's go. We're getting out of here. *Now*. Peculiar time for a bubble bath, isn't it?"

Carlie looked back at him with an ambiguous grin. "I always head for the tub when I'm upset. Some women wash their hair when they panic. I bathe. Wipe off that silly grin and toss me a towel."

Stewart pulled one of the royal blue towels with the Potomac Plaza crest off the rack, flipped it toward her. Carlie grabbed it with one hand.

Stewart shook his head. "The country's crumbling under our feet and you take time—"

"Forget the lecture. What should I have done? Sit on the floor and practice yoga?" She winked at him. "Relax, Eagle Scout. Find my clothes and I'll be ready to go to work." Rolling her eyes at Stewart, she climbed to her feet and draped herself in the towel, but it fell away briefly, revealing her full round breasts and perfect nipples. She looked back at him, smugly aware that her body held his eyes. Bad timing or not, Stewart felt aroused.

Frieda's dog wandered into the bathroom, came up to him, wagging its tail and sniffing.

Relax, Kirk, old pal, you're moving too fast. Too much hell breaking loose to worry about your love life. Not now.

Stewart heard a harsh female voice behind him.

"Raphael!" shouted Frieda. "Stop that this instant!"

Stewart turned to the big blonde. "Bring Carlie's things. Now." He glanced down beside his leg, then back into Carlie's eyes. Stewart ignored the aroused animal at his ankle and gave the TV reporter a kiss on the lips. She pulled him closer, and he ran his fingers through her wet hair. Looking down at the dog, she giggled softly. Stewart shook his leg repeatedly, trying to free himself from the poodle's clutches, but neither Raphael nor Carlie was willing to give him up.

Coughing politely, Oliver Wright pushed the blonde woman aside and stood in the doorway. Stewart looked at him and backed away from Carlie.

Eyes shining, she held both men's smiles. "Give me three minutes to rinse off these suds, gentlemen, and I'll follow you anywhere."

Stewart winked and followed Wright back out into the main suite. Raphael trotted along at this heel until Frieda snatched up the dog as Stewart was about to shoo it away.

Stewart turned to Agent Vosberg. "Do me a favor. Bind that blonde and leash the mutt."

"I underestimated your tenacity and cunning," Wright said dryly, extending his big hand.

Stewart shook it. "The pleasure's not entirely mine, Mr. Wright. The Israeli major, remember?"

Wright smiled. "Another puzzle. I'm still curious about where his expense money originates." He hesitated, studying Stewart. "I'll say this much. You're a persistent bastard. As for myself, I've learned more up here in captivity than I did during the Bureau's six months of investigating this conspiracy."

Stewart nodded. He pointed to the room's mass of computer equipment. "High technology, Mr. Wright. Not only have the military communications networks been tapped, but the civilian phone lines are down as well. Vosberg and I have just come from the Capitol Building. The President's with the Cabinet, apparently safe enough for the time being. General Colloran's with him. But he's cut off, isolated in the House Speaker's office."

Vosberg swiftly added, "Vice-President Chandler's been assassinated. We figure that was a mistake. The Texan Arnold Metz is dead, too, and the CIA has lost a helicopter in an explosion."

Wright whistled through his teeth, his eyebrows furrowing. "Walter Singer's personal Huey?"

Stewart nodded. "Why do you ask? Did you know the pilot?"

"No. I left a small package under the seat." Wright smiled softly and changed the subject. "Now, the question is, who's left on the opposition's team and how strong are they?"

Stewart shrugged. "I suspect the fattest rats are holed up in the Pentagon."

"Probably the big board room," added Vosberg.

Wright rubbed his jaw and shifted his huge frame to look down at Frober. "Who else is on your Committee? Where are they now?" He turned to Vosberg. "I think it's time we motivate our hotel chain executive here to do a little vocalizing." To Stewart, Wright instructed, "That table lamp in the corner. Remove the shade and bulb, then bring it over here."

Stewart was confused. He retrieved the fixture and removed the bulb, as instructed. Wright winked at him.

"Stewart, turn off your reporter's eyes and ears. Whatever happens next is off the record, got it?" Wright gave a nod of understanding to Vosberg, who promptly jerked Frober to his feet and nudged the automatic carbine barrel against his ear.

"What do you want from me?" Frober snapped, trying to hide his fear. "This is only a communications center. I'm just a functionary, like the others."

The big lie, Stewart thought.

Wright persisted. "Kiss my ass, Frober. I want names. Which men at the Pentagon are with you? Who's supporting Singer?"

"Ask the nosy reporter. I don't know." The tone of Frober's response wasn't convincing, and his face took on a trace of panic.

Stewart winced as Vosberg slammed the fat man back into the chair at the computer console. He handed the MAC-10 to Wright. Wordlessly, Vosberg unbuckled Frober's trousers, pulled them down, then took the light fixture from Stewart and quickly plugged it in. Frober's face drained of color.

Stewart was about to say something, but Wright sharply waved his hand.

"Start talking, Frober, before we ram this hot socket over your cock," Wright warned, his eyes leaving the hotel executive and scanning the computer console. He ran his hand over one of the three colored telephones. "This instrument," he snapped, pointing to the blue one. "What's it connected to?"

Frober swallowed hard, slowly replied, "CIA headquarters in Virginia. Walter Singer's office."

"Good." Wright picked it up, thrust the receiver in Frober's hand. "Get the prick on the line. Quickly."

"He's not there." The hotel man pointed an unsteady finger at the video monitor.

Stewart followed Frober's alarmed stare. Several lines of updated information filled the screen. Two lines blinked urgently, indicating a need for immediate confirmation of receipt. Stewart remembered something Colloran had told him. "I suspect, Mr. Wright, that by now the CIA director's in the White House basement."

Frober's eyes confirmed Stewart's supposition.

Wright came up beside Stewart. Together, they read the video display:

> Priority to Committee Control /
> Activate communication from
> White House to Pentagon big
> board center / Joint Chiefs,
> Palmer commanding / Acknowledge.

"*Acknowledge what,* Frober?" asked Stewart curiously. He waited, but got no response from the fat man.

Vosberg cursed softly and slapped Frober's face.

"The cut-out relays are all computerized and controlled here." Frober's flat voice was barely audible.

Stewart wandered over to the next table, examining the sophisticated video transmission equipment he recognized from a recent news story in *Time*. Wright joined him. The system had two-way control. "Do you have transmit cameras in both underground facilities—the White House and the Pentagon?" he asked Frober.

The hotel executive nodded.

Wright looked at Stewart. "Untape his ankles and get him over to this console."

Stewart worked on the bindings, whispering in Frober's ear. The Bureau boys don't look too friendly to me, pal. If I were you, I'd cooperate."

Wright pointed to the video unit. "Okay, Frober. Get this gear keyed in to the Pentagon fast. And play it smart. No sound or visual transmit from here or you're a dead man."

Frober obeyed, pushed several buttons. Stewart watched the screen, and an instant later several flag-rank military officers appeared, seated around a large conference table. Their eyes appeared to be riveted to a display monitor on the wall opposite them.

Stewart shook his head. "Singer's not there. Let's try the White House camera."

Frober shrugged nervously, looked up at the FBI chief. "I'm in my underwear," he pleaded. "May I pull up my damned trousers now?"

"Not yet, asshole. Change channels," growled Wright.

Frober keyed another set of buttons, and the video monitor changed images. The CIA director appeared behind a desk. His lips were moving, but there was no sound.

"That's the President's desk. Singer's in the provisional office, the subterranean chamber under the White House," said Wright.

Stewart leaned over Frober's shoulder, found the volume control, and turned it up. They all listened. Singer's words were being directed to the brass back at the Pentagon big board room.

"Gentlemen, you can relax. Sixteen hundred Pennsylvania Avenue is occupied by my own men and a contingent of Marines. The staff's been dismissed. The truth is, this underground facility is a tad lonely. Thanks to your foresight, Admiral Palmer, the duty officer here obediently follows orders. No sign of the President returning, but if he does, I'll be ready for him. I suspect he's still up at the Capitol Building. He has to show up soon."

Stewart looked at the TV screen closely. Walter Singer's ice-cold, manipulative stare raised angry images in Stewart's mind. The CIA director would still be big trouble, every bit as dangerous as a trapped wild animal.

Singer paused, glaring down at the desk before him. "My console light indicates I'm now being received at Committee headquarters as well as at the Pentagon. Frober, you took your pleasant time about reactivating this White House video link. Is the staff asleep over there? I suggest you be more attentive and mind that control board yourself, if necessary. Also, Karl, I'm sorry, but there's bad news for you regarding three of our associates. If you'll pick up the red telephone, I'll confer with you privately. I'm cutting off my transmission with the Pentagon."

The red telephone behind Oliver Wright buzzed. Stewart started for the phone, but Wright held his arm. Frober, too, had started to roll his chair across the floor to answer it, but stopped as Wright shook his head.

"Forget that call," Wright said adamantly. "Right now I want you to punch up whatever goddamn code it takes to reactivate the nation's long-distance circuits. And I especially want every domestic line in Washington, D. C., working again, understand?"

Frober spread his sweating plump hands and nervously shook his head. "It's only a matter of pulling switches, but you have to understand that I can't do it. If I revealed the code, Singer would kill me. The circuits aren't to be restored under any conditions until Sunday morning."

Stewart looked away from Frober, distracted by the faint smell of cologne. Carlie Chavez, fully dressed, had wandered out of the bedroom and stood to one side, listening to their conversation. Hastily, Frober tugged at his pants. Carlie looked scornfully at the row of bound captives along the wall, then turned to the FBI chief.

"Mr. Wright? I'm Carlotta Chavez. Without the bubbles." She paused, smiling. "We've met before, at a New York press conference a year ago."

Wright looked at her impatiently. "Yes, I remember you." He hesitated, stared at Stewart, then back at her. Wright looked embarrassed. Awkwardly, he said, "I'm sure you'll be more comfortable waiting in the other room. This is going to be—"

Stewart gestured toward Karl Frober.

Carlie glanced at the fat man and back to Wright. "Nonsense. I've seen men in and out of their underwear before. Besides, it's time I went to work."

Work, mused Stewart. Was she serious? Hadn't she had enough? They could be back in Carlie's apartment in time for dinner if he bowed out now and dragged her back to New York. The hell with Oliver Wright, the President, the rest of the government. The hell with these sophisticated computers, and the hell with forcing Frober to talk!

"The code, lard ass," Wright said sonorously to Frober.

Jarred back to reality, Stewart went to the frightened executive. The room was quiet. It was Carlie who broke the uncomfortable silence. "How about it, Mr. Frober? Why don't you and the others just turn the lights back on, pack up your electronic toys, and go home? Your splendid little war is over."

The fat man was sweating, but he still stiffened. "If that were true, I'd cooperate. You're wrong. Singer's winning." Sickened and trembling, Frober looked nervously at the others, then back to Carlie as if she were a sanctuary. She ignored his stare, bending over to pick up Frieda's dog, now suddenly friendly. Carlie held the poodle, stroking its head. Frieda, bound and sitting against the wall, looked up, her lips curling in a sneer.

The red telephone buzzed insistently. Stewart looked again at the video screen and saw the CIA director's face take on a scornful look. Singer pursed his well-defined lips and leaned forward impatiently. Stewart studied the features. The self-indulgence and the perversity were there, in the eyes and mouth.

Oliver Wright ignored the video screen. He placed the automatic carbine he was carrying on the table and nodded to Vosberg. Wright held Frober's shoulders with his big arms while Vosberg approached with the lamp.

Carlie turned her back and retreated to the window. Stewart clenched his teeth.

"No! Jesus, not that, you bastards. Please," groaned Frober.

Mikhail Grotski lifted the carved amber bishop, jumped a pawn, and smiled across the table. His somber chess partner blinked twice at the board, then nervously checked his watch.

Grotski gave him a look of annoyance. "Your mind is not on the game, Comrade," he snapped.

"I am sorry, Ambassador," the KGB man replied dully.

A woman secretary entered the office, placed a radio communication before Grotski. The bald Russian removed a pair of bifocals from the breast pocket of his suit, swiftly read the message, and rubbed his chin. "The fishing trawler *Mitya* reports our bird has still not come home to roost. He is late." Grotski smiled tightly, looked down at the board, back to his chess companion. "Your general, it appears, will have to wait to retire the name of Motti Barak from our list of American sleepers. Comrade Baroski, I fear, is still somewhere here in the city."

The other man looked up. "Unless he is dead."

"I seriously doubt that. The man is infinitely clever. I suspect he has discovered other aspects to this ill-conceived American upheaval. Perhaps we underestimated the numbers and strength of these fascist reactionaries."

"Comrade Ambassador, Barak must leave the United States immediately. We cannot chance the Israelis' discovering his true identity. The Americans, likewise, might—"

Grotski cut him off with a wave of his hand. *"Nyet!* Enough. It will be dark soon, but I suspect our friend will show up at the trawler at first light. Tonight our work will be finished."

"You trust this man implicitly?"

The ambassador nodded. "What other choice do we have, short of war? And what choice does Laurenti Baroski have?"

"Yes. His parents. Comrade Ambassador, if he is successful and gets out of this, do you then wish—"

"Yes," Grotski interjected. "But all in due time. His new cover is prepared and ready?"

"It is arranged. A new name and a destination. London first, then on to Lebanon." The chess partner looked at Grotski gravely. "Is it concluding, Comrade? Is the madness here finished?"

The ambassador smiled. "Not yet, my friend, but the next few hours—"

The KGB man grimaced. "I still say we should have been more direct and ruthless." The words came softly through his thick red mustache. "A wasted opportunity."

"It is not the Soviet position to meddle in American domestic affairs. Naturally, we frown on reactionary aggressiveness of a violent nature. But dealing with the Americans is like playing chess, Comrade. One must have infinite patience; there is no need to hurry. Let capitalism run its course." Grotski paused, unwrapped a roll of peppermints, placed one in his mouth. He sucked it briefly, then continued. "Our man Baroski—or Motti Barak—his task was to determine the nature of the force attempting to seize power in America. Were they cowards or provocateurs? Cowards cause wars by stupidity; provocateurs incite them."

His opponent looked up from the chess board and said slowly, "Americans treat us like little children, Comrade Ambassador. It is as if Communism were an illegitimate child. They threaten us with scolding sticks, yes? In my opinion, the only difference between the American right and left is the size of the twig. They do not understand that we hold the entire broom and that if they are not prudent, we can sweep them away."

"I am a diplomat. Conviction need not necessarily lead to conflict."

"Our man Barak doesn't seem to subscribe to that."

"Perhaps he lost relatives at Buchenwald, who knows?" The ambassador swallowed what was left of his peppermint, held up his hand. "Some things it is good that I don't know, yes? That is your department. In whatever way, Barak must help to ensure that the Americans do not exchange their scolding sticks for the primitive club of the caveman." Grotski impatiently looked across the table. "I'm waiting, Comrade. Stop delaying the inevitable. Choose. You are about to lose either two bishops or your queen."

The woman aide hurried back into the room. "Excuse me, sir. There is an important development. The American Vice-President has been killed. An apparent assassination. There were other deaths."

The chess board went flying as the KGB man leaped to his feet.

Grotski, still in his chair, glared angrily up at him. "I trust your memory is good, Comrade. Sit back down and replace the chessmen. The American contest is not yet over. It is too early for us to react." Baring a thin smile, Grotski slowly unwrapped another peppermint. "We have all the time in the world. Time to finish this game, and others."

The mood in the penthouse suite was heavy. From outside the hotel, somewhere off in the distance, came what sounded like grenade detonations and automatic-weapon fire.

"Key up that telephone restoration code now!" shouted Wright, his uncompromising eyes bearing in on Frober with the force of javelins.

The frightened executive whimpered and stubbornly shook his head, but when Agent Vosberg started to move in with the live lamp socket Frober shrieked, "All right, you bastards! Rotten perverts! Leave me alone for chrissake." Eyes rolling and tearful, he struggled forward in his chair. With trembling hands he began typing coded commands to the computer.

The red telephone stopped buzzing. Stewart watched the television screen with Singer's likeness fade out to be replaced by an outline of the United States. Carlie came up and stood behind him. Together, they observed as, one by one, illuminated yellow, red, and blue lines appeared.

"Restored long-distance trunks," explained Frober without enthusiasm.

"My God," groaned Wright. "I'm not sure whether it's power-hungry men like Walter Singer we should be afraid of, or this high technology."

Carlie looked up, suddenly shouting, "Kirk, look out!"

Stewart and Wright were so mesmerized by the flashing lines on the video screen that they hadn't seen Tap Nelson enter the room and surreptitiously slide up behind them at the console. Stewart jerked his head around, but he was too late. Carlie had tried to make a lunge for the carbine on the table, but she didn't come close. Nelson's fist met the side of her face, sending her sprawling on the floor. Neither Stewart, Wright, nor Vosberg was fast enough to breach the four feet that separated them from the MAC-10 the FBI press director had snatched up and now cradled menacingly in his arms.

"You, Oliver, more than anyone, should know the extremely rapid firepower of this weapon," said Nelson, sneering. "None of you would stand a chance. Slide your guns, butt first, slowly across the table to Mr. Frober." Without taking his eyes off the men, he said from the corner of his mouth to Carlie, "You can nurse your bruised face later. Get up off the floor. Quickly, over here with the others."

37

STEWART'S VOICE CAUGHT in his throat. He could only stare blankly at his former classmate. Dangerous seconds seemed to hang suspended around the weapon in Tap Nelson's hands. The ugly silence was finally broken by Oliver Wright's sharp grunt of dismay.

"You sawed-off turncoat prick!" Wright snarled.

Carlie climbed unsteadily to her feet, rubbing her sore jaw. She came up beside Stewart. Agent Vosberg, keenly aware of the damage a scatter gun would inflict before he could get halfway to the weapon strapped near his ankle, could only glare at Nelson. Intimidated by a swift jerk of the carbine, both Stewart and Wright slid their own weapons across the table toward Frober. He quickly scooped them into the drawer before him.

Stewart wasn't sure what to do or say. He obstinately held Nelson's gaze, waiting for an explanation, waiting for anything that might clear the air. Stewart glanced down at Carlie, saw that she, too, was puzzled.

Karl Frober's face brightened. Pulling up his pants, he scuttled across the room like a crab. "Thank God, Lynx. You deserve a medal for this," he said blissfully.

377

Stewart frowned. *Lynx?* One of the names in the Metz address book! Stewart looked at Oliver Wright. The shock in the FBI director's eyes was gone now, replaced by a look of unadulterated contempt. "So you're Lynx. You're also a worthless, goddamn traitor."

Tap Nelson glared back. "A traitor to you, and worthless to the FBI, I must admit. But quite valuable and a patriot to others."

Stewart grimaced and shook his head. "Save the theatrics, Nelson," he shouted. *Wait.* Easy, Stewart, he thought. Time to measure the words with care. Nelson's green eyes glittered like emeralds; they looked not only greedy but frightened, too, as if he were waiting for an excuse to kill them all immediately. "Why, Tap?" Stewart asked as calmly as he could. "It's damned hard to believe this is for real. We went to the same school, played the same sports, sought similar career goals, and yet you passed me by. I'm still a city room reporter; you're a ranking government press officer. You've got it all."

Nelson's carbine didn't waver a fraction of an inch as he looked up at Stewart and gave out a harsh, cruel laugh. "Don't waste my time with that crap. I was a scapegoat in college; I'm still one working for Wright. I didn't have the guts to fight for what I wanted before, but I do now. And it's a proper fight."

Stewart frowned. "Don't flip your lid on me, Tap. Put away that carbine."

Wright looked at Stewart impatiently, turned a sharp scowl on Nelson. *"Lynx.* Incredible! And contemptible. Never, Nelson, would I have believed you'd respect the likes of Walter Singer, let alone follow him and his ilk into hell. You're backing a neurotic, selfish cause—an extremist movement that knows next to nothing about the true nature of the American public."

Nelson grinned wolfishly. "We understand the masses well enough, Oliver. As do a few of your own agents who are with us—like one of your capital department heads and the bureau chiefs in Milwaukee and Detroit."

Wright jerked back as if he were wounded.

Frober came up beside Nelson. "You're the one, Wright, who doesn't understand why we'll win. The American people have become stupid, lazy, mesmerized by the welfare state." Buttoning his jacket, Frober pulled himself erect, pushed out his chin. "They're lusting for an explosion; they need an iron hand. We won't disappoint them."

Wright sneered and shook his head.

Seizing the silence, Carlie stepped forward. "You're tragically naive, Mr. Nelson—or Lynx, if you're fond of the soldier-of-fortune tag. It's my business to know my nationwide audience. I say Americans have a strong moral streak. Different faiths, a diverse morality, yes, but the history of the melting pot speaks for itself." She hesitated, her piercing brown eyes glaring at Nelson. "Pluralist thought's an American tradition. You've never heard of the First Amendment, or is that over your stubborn head?"

"The TV newswoman is pretty, except for her big mouth. I suspect the color of her lipstick complements her politics." Nelson's hands had begun to tremble slightly. His forehead was covered with tiny beads of sweat. "I've listened to these bleeding heart liberals long enough, Frober. Get that computer of yours working. Put Singer on the video intercom."

Stewart was glad that Carlie had shut up; it was dangerous to provoke Nelson. Together, they kept their silence and watched Frober pad to the command console and begin typing.

Abruptly, the computer screen went dark. A table lamp in the far corner of the room also went out. Frober got up, quickly tried two switches by the door, then looked into the corridor.

Stewart could see that the outer hallway was dark. The hotel power had gone dead.

The louvered steel door to the ground floor utilities room had blown thirty feet out into the parking lot. Easing around the corner of the building, Motti Barak looked on, satisfied. It wouldn't be necessary to probe through the acrid smoke, check inside to make sure the mold of plastic had done its work on the 4,600-volt step-down transformer. Barak could see from the inoperative lights in the Potomac Plaza's street-level shops, the darkened lobby and corridors, that the explosion was successful. The main power lines leading into the high-rise hotel were gone. The complex of relay antennas on the roof would be out of commission, at least temporarily. Already, troops had jumped down from their trucks and were heading for the utility room. Good, Barak thought. The diversion was working.

Rubbing his curly hair, Barak looked up the facade of the building, wondering just how long it would take him to hike up thirty floors. Thank God he was in reasonably fair shape. He wasn't about to make it a foot race. No telling what he would encounter at the top, and he'd need all his breath.

Dissension, thought Stewart, watching Nelson and Frober glare at each other.

"What kind of operation you running here?" Nelson spat his words at the hotel executive. "Where's the goddamn backup system?"

Frober cupped his hand tightly around the hotel telephone, looked back at him irritably. "Get off my back, Lynx. The Plaza's only two years old, as modern as any hospital. The switchover to auxiliary power should have been automatic." He paused, pressing his ear to the receiver. "What's that? I asked for the building engineer." Several seconds passed as he listened again. "I understand. Well, snap it up; this is an emergency." Frober put down the phone, waved a calming hand at Nelson. "They have to patch a sabotaged circuit. Another five minutes."

Nelson flared, "Jesus Christ, Frober, you think I've got all day?"

"You're going to have all the time in the world in prison, Nelson," admonished Wright.

Stewart kept his silence, trying to put it all together. What was Nelson planning? Stewart tried to imagine the feelings of his adversary. Even back in college Nelson had been hot-collared, an extremist in his politics, but never would Stewart have guessed he was the type who could be taken in by fascism, whatever its banner.

"What's in this for you?" Stewart asked.

Nelson's grip on the automatic carbine tightened, the veins standing out on his hands. He glanced nervously at the darkened computer, back over to Stewart. His eyes seemed to betray some painfully withheld emotion, but when he spoke his voice was flat and unrevealing. "You've worked hard enough to break us, Stewart. You deserve an answer to that one." He hesitated, spared a thin smile. "Cleaning out the Jews alone would be enough. But there's a personal reward, too. I've been promised an important position. Government communications director."

"In what department?" asked Stewart.

"Working directly for the new President."

"How nice for the country," scoffed Wright, wrinkling his

nose. "Another Dr. Goebbels, no less?"

Karl Frober grunted. "Goebbels was extremely effective, Mr. Wright. The Third Reich's propaganda minister was considered a genius by many."

Nelson nodded his head. "Our friends in the media will learn soon enough, Karl." His eyes shifted to Carlie Chavez. "Television and radio in particular. Up until now, American freedom of the press has been no more than the sponsor's point of view, right? Whatever the advertiser or the Jewish-controlled national media might dictate. I'll be in a position to modify that."

Stewart exchanged concerned looks with Carlie, frowned at Nelson. "As ghoulish and mad as the Fuehrer himself."

"And as belligerent and provocative," added Carlie.

"Curb your tongue and be useful," ordered Frober. "Unbind those captives."

Carlie took her time crossing the room.

Stewart watched the small beads of sweat roll down Nelson's face, the red sparks in the dilated eyes that burned brighter than ever. Nelson looked again at the darkened computer screen and frowned. He glanced back at Stewart. "You're a misguided, vapid fool, my friend. Brainwashed to the core. You were naive even when you edited that dull campus newspaper years ago. And what do you know about Adolf Hitler? Next to nothing." Nelson's voice rose several decibels, almost out of control. "Sit down, Kirk." He waved the barrel of his gun toward a chair.

Stewart looked at the weapon and silently took a seat. He felt sick.

Carlie was struggling with the tape around the woman Army captain's ankles.

Nelson continued. "You need to wise up, friend. Germany didn't start the war with America. Hitler's declaration of hostilities merely recognized the truth· the cunning reality of Roosevelt provoking the Japanese to make the first move; our unprecedented warlike policy of sinking German submarines and using the U.S. Navy to convoy military supplies to Britain; supplying Hitler's enemy with warplanes, destroyers, tanks, and ammunition, all at a handsome profit. The war itself and its outcome—that's why we're in the mess we are today. That's the reason I'm standing here." Nelson's tone changed, sounded almost effeminate as he added, with obvious relish, "All the liberals talk about is the horrors of Nazism, the Holocaust. I say there's no proof it occurred."

Stewart wasn't listening. It was no longer a conversation but a rambling monologue.

"You're raving, Mr. Nelson," interjected Carlie, looking up from her work. "I've met and interviewed some of the victims' relatives."

Karl Frober pushed out his chin, scoffing. "Propaganda. All vile Jewish propaganda."

Oliver Wright's index finger shot toward the fat man. "Kiss off, Frober."

Stewart exhaled, slowly climbed to his feet, confronted every inch of the way by the automatic carbine. He looked pityingly at Nelson. "Save the lecture and put away the gun, Tap. Let's have a word outside, alone. It's not too late to talk this over."

Nelson laughed. "Fuck the solicitude. It'd be easy enough to put you and the woman out of business permanently. Singer would like that. Just keep out of my way, and for old times' sake I may be halfway merciful."

"They aren't entitled to mercy," grumbled Frober. "They've tried to destroy us."

"You're both dead wrong and confused," replied Stewart, changing his tone.

"No! This *nation* is confused." Nelson glowered at Stewart. "Fucking puppets marching toward the collective farm. And the godless Russian Communists are pulling the strings."

"Americans pull their own strings," Carlie said angrily. "Winston Churchill summed us up pretty well when he said 'Democracy is the worst system devised by the wit of man, except for all others.'"

The light in the corner of the room flickered, then came back on. Symbols once more flashed across the computer screen. Nelson smiled at Carlie, at the same time gesturing to Frober to return to the control console. "You don't understand the mood of the nation, Ms. Chavez. You're lost, swallowed up by your own muddling objectivity and the success, perhaps, of your TV ratings. The country isn't in the mood for Eugene McCarthys, John Andersons, Gore Vidals, or Rutgers and Harvard types who drive around in old Saabs and pontificate. There's a violent jungle out there, and the guy riding the white charger is going to take over." Nelson hesitated, looked at the others. "You'll all see soon enough. It's a matter of manipulation. We don't need Jimmy Hallowell to pull it off. The people will get what they deserve: a strong leader."

Wright said quietly, "A dictator, you mean."

Stewart watched as Frober tripped several switches and began typing on the computer keyboard. Reappearing on the video screen was Walter Singer's iron-bound face. His look of disapproval slowly changed to an outright leer as he stared at the TV camera. Beside Stewart, Carlie shuddered. Nelson waved the others away with his carbine, went up behind Frober. "Turn on the transmit."

Frober obeyed.

"Can you see me, Walter? This is Lynx—Nelson."

"You're coming in clear. Turn up the volume on your microphone."

Nudging Frober, Nelson looked into the small lens protruding from the console and said, "You can unwind now. The MAC-10 carbine in my hands has not only restored control here, but apparently saved your ass."

On the video screen, the CIA director's face reddened with anger. "What's wrong over there? Your transmissions went dead."

"A temporary power outage," replied Frober.

Oliver Wright edged closer, looking hatefully at the image on the screen. Stewart knew that the time had come for both men to vent their hate for each other.

The FBI chief was first to spit out his contempt. "You're a traitor, Singer!" he shouted toward the console pickup. "I've heard Frober talking, asshole. I know about those chartered airplanes to the Caribbean. You're fucking with the lives of innocent men and women. You and your crowd are a grotesque nightmare."

Walter Singer grinned with enjoyment. He let out a theatrical groan and said, "Do the birth pangs of a new historical age make you squeamish, gentlemen? Come off it, Oliver. Stop playing the moralist. It doesn't become you as a fellow bureaucrat. Politicians have used us too long. It's their turn to take a share of abuse." Singer's jaw visibly tightened. "Frober, I suspect Lynx already has his hands full with his weaponry. Turn off the visual and pick up the phone. I have some proprietary information for you."

Stewart watched the fat man comply. While Frober listened attentively, Nelson said with menace, "You're not moving fast enough, Carlotta. Get on with it. Release those captives."

Carlie started across the room, but paused by the window, looking out over the city. "The White House has visitors," she said quickly. "Are those friendly or enemy forces dropping in unannounced?"

Stewart eased both hands, palms out, away from his body and turned to Nelson. "Mind if I look out the window?"

"Suit yourself." Nelson, too, was curious. Carefully measuring his steps and the line of fire, he eased across the room.

Stewart watched the new STOL transports drop down out of the clouds. Their huge flaps extended, like prehistoric pterodactyls, the C-11s circled slowly around the White House and landed somewhere near the Ellipse. General Colloran's troops coming in on Constitution Avenue, thought Stewart, feeling relief.

Nelson's concerned gaze lingered on the aircraft a second too long. The distraction was precisely what Vosberg, sitting on the floor at the opposite wall, had been waiting for. Slowly, he reached inside his pantleg. His gun was halfway drawn from the ankle holster when Nelson turned, swinging his carbine and pointing it at Vosberg. Before the agent could dive behind a file cabinet, a carefully aimed burst of three bullets riddled the flesh of his leg, went on to stitch the wall with blood.

Frober dropped the red telephone. Carlie, in the process of removing the blond woman's bindings, flattened herself on the floor and covered her head. Frieda screamed shrilly. The poodle yelped and disappeared into the next room. Vosberg doubled up in pain.

It was quiet again. Nelson moved away from the window, came up to the writhing FBI agent, kicked his gun away. Nelson glared at Wright. "Stupid. He shouldn't have tried that. I could have killed him." Voice trembling slightly, he turned to the blonde. "Frieda, pick up that gun and hand it to me. You, Stewart. Release those captives. And your lady friend had better get a tourniquet around Agent Vosberg's leg before he bleeds to death." Nelson's face was covered with sweat as he raised the MAC-10 slightly, waving it at Wright's head. "I'd shoot you right now, Oliver, but Singer wants you alive. Pick that red telephone up off the floor."

Stewart looked at Nelson. *Mad,* he thought. He watched as the FBI chief reluctantly did as he was instructed.

Wright listened at the receiver for several seconds then looked blankly at Nelson. "The line's dead. Singer's not on the wire."

"Hang up the phone," snapped Nelson, taking a seat across from Wright. He'll contact us when he's ready."

Carlie tore off part of Vosberg's shirt, working quickly to bind his wounds. Stewart took his time freeing the woman Army captain. He would definitely save the release of the two angry Marines until last.

Oliver Wright shook his head. "Singer's cornered, Nelson. Those are Air Force planes loyal to Colloran. Your friend's finished. It's all over."

There was a cunning, amused gleam in Nelson's eyes. "Not as long as I have this," he said, patting the gun. "Singer's just begun to fight as well."

Suddenly, from the corner of his eye, Stewart saw a movement at the outer doorway.

"Lynx! Behind you! Watch out!" shouted Frober hysterically.

Nelson whirled the carbine again, but in the wrong direction, toward Frober, not at the door. The hallway door was open, and Motti Barak had slipped into the suite. He held a gun, and it was aimed at Nelson. The roar of exploding ammunition and ricocheting bullets was deafening. Carlie clasped her hands over her ears, ran to Stewart. He threw his arms around her, pulled her down beneath a desk. The captives along the wall flinched, rolled to the floor.

Too late, Nelson turned to confront Barak. Nelson was hit, but not critically. He lurched backwards, his body crashing over a metal computer table, the barrel of his gun snagging on the open drawer of a file cabinet. He jerked it free, pointed the carbine at the entrance, and again clawed the trigger. Bullets patterned the desks, walls, the Godzilla crate, and ricocheted around the room. Nelson finally stopped firing. Barak had disappeared back outside.

Stewart held his breath. The room recked of spent gunpowder and smoke. He opened his eyes and looked up. Nelson, spreadeagled across the table just above him, was protected from return fire from the doorway by a file cabinet and computer equipment. Only one of Nelson's hands was on the automatic carbine; the other clutched a bleeding arm.

"Motti!" Stewart shouted. "Stay back! He's got the doorway covered."

Wright, too, was in the line of fire and powerless. Looking around, Stewart frantically sought a weapon. Anything! Agent

Vosberg looked at him helplessly. Beside Stewart was the bulb-less lamp fixture. It was plugged in. Above him, on the underside of the metal table, he saw the spring and slide mechanism of a center drawer. Stewart quietly disengaged one end of the spring. Turning on the lamp's switch, he grabbed the ceramic base firmly with both hands. Making sure there was a margin of safety between his body and the frame of the desk, he swiftly thrust the lamp upward, ramming the empty socket over the suspended spring.

Zzzzzzzapp! The sound jarred the room. Nelson let out a muffled gasp as his arms and legs did a danse macabre. Spasmodically, his finger tightened around the carbine's trigger, but only three bullets discharged. His body suddenly went limp as the charge short-circuited and tripped a relay.

Stewart pulled the lamp's plug. Wright edged closer, examining Nelson's still form. He turned to Frieda. "Check this man's pulse. If he needs it, make with the CPR. I want to testify at this bastard's trial." Wright looked through the haze of gunsmoke toward the doorway. "You can come in now, Major Barak."

Stewart sighed in relief and climbed to his feet, pulling Carlie up with him. She, too, looked across the room, expectant. Barak came through the door, put his gun away in the pocket of his flying suit. There was a moment's silence as he surveyed the destruction around him, noting the captives by the wall, the bullet-riddled leg of the FBI agent. Then he looked at Tap Nelson, who was beginning to come around.

Stewart smiled at Barak, then glanced at Carlie. She stared at the Israeli in blank bewilderment; her eyebrows arched indecisively, a prelude to either tears of exhaustion or happy relief.

Carlie, meet Major Barak," was all Stewart could say. Words, under the situation, were superfluous. He turned to Frober. "Get that hotel switchboard cracking. We need a paramedic or doctor up here fast."

Frober reluctantly picked up the phone.

Carlie looked at Barak, smiled, and said, "Thank God."

"I seem to have blundered in at the right time," said Barak. "Forgive my sloppy arrival. I wasn't prepared to find a crazed man with an automatic carbine playing king of the mountain."

Wright smiled. "No apologies necessary, Major Barak."

Carlie quickly added, "Your distraction was a Godsend."

Wright scanned Barak's clothing. "Putting in flying time, Major? Did you arrive by combat helicopter or parachute?"

Barak looked at him. "Close enough. There isn't time to explain the details." He gestured toward the windows. "You can't see Arlington. You don't know about the others on the Committee? The crash?"

Stewart exchanged concerned glances with Carlie. Oliver Wright looked perplexed. In the corner, his face a mask of defeat, Karl Frober slumped into a chair and lowered his head. "Singer told me a minute ago," he said, his words slurred.

Ignoring Frober, Barak continued. "Norman Gifford of Condor Defense and the TV evangelist, Jimmy Hallowell, were aboard that plane. There were no survivors."

Stewart's eyes flitted to Carlie, back to Barak. So it had been Gifford. And Hallowell, of all people. Frober. And Singer. So that was the heinous Committee. Aided and abetted by the Vice-President and some Pentagon wheels! Understanding came to Stewart, faintly at first, then with clear logic. "Then it's finished," he said slowly. "All that's left is Frober here and the CIA director. The Pentagon's divided, and outside a few—"

"*A few?*" Barak interrupted. "Across the country, try fifty or sixty thousand on the streets. Who knows how many more standing by at home."

Carlie spoke quickly. "Can Singer communicate with these armed fanatics?"

Barak looked at her, then back to the others. "Where's the CIA director now?"

"Underground. The White House provisional command center," replied Stewart.

Wright swiftly added, "I'd like to leave him be—just move in and guard the above-ground entrances. Like a trapped coyote he'll just sit down there and howl until he gets hungry enough to come up."

Carlie shook her head. "Or until his friends rescue him?"

Barak nodded in agreement. "I suspect you'll want to smoke Walter Singer out immediately, Mr. Wright. A nasty, dangerous character to have burrowing about in the President's cellar."

Wright headed for the phone. "Agreed. As soon as I can get a brace of my own men to take over up here, gentlemen, we'll leave for the White House."

Stewart felt Carlie pull away from him. "Mr. Wright," she said coolly, "Correction. *Ladies and gentlemen*. Reverse the order if you prefer. I've come this far and I have no intention of missing the remaining action."

Wright looked at her skeptically. "I'm sorry, the danger—"

"Chief?" interposed Stewart. "Save your words. She's made up her mind."

Barak shuffled his feet and folded his arms. "I suggest you advise the President to temporarily ignore the renegade Army, Marine, and Navy units inside the Pentagon. Regaining control there should not be so difficult when firm civilian authority is reestablished. With over a thousand self-proclaimed Nazi storm troopers, twice that number of gun-happy Klansmen, and battalions of Freedom Militiamen swarming over the city—even though they're bickering among themselves, searching for the strongest leader—I strongly suspect that—" Barak hesitated.

"We all understand, Major," Carlie interjected. "First Walter Singer has to be muzzled."

"And quickly," added Stewart.

Barak smiled at him. "Still the humanitarian, I see. Singer doesn't appear to be the kind of man to be taken alive. Not now. He's too desperate."

"Then I'll take the traitorous son of a bitch dead," snapped Wright.

38

To Stewart, the White House lawn looked like a crowded marketplace for helicopters. The President's Sikorsky was there, along with a National Park Service Bell 206 and the FBI executive Huey that Wright had summoned. Also on hand was an Army Minerva equipped for rescue and patrol work. The pilots remained at the controls, guarded by the airborne troops brought in by General Colloran.

Stewart had seen plenty of security barriers in his career as a reporter, but never had they been as tight as this. The White House was an armed battlement prepared for a siege. Everyone was keyed to the breaking point—trigger nervous, thought Stewart, as he stood with Carlie under the East Gate portico. They stepped to the driveway as a limousine from the motor pool crept through the ring of guards and pulled up before them. Stewart held Carlie close, kissed her lips, and said quickly, "You positive you want to leave now? Before the final act?"

The driver opened the door for her but she hesitated. Brushing back her hair with both hands, she lifted her chin and smiled at Stewart. "You don't need me to play nursemaid. I'll be back as soon as I can round up a camera and sound crew. I have work to do, remember? This last act needs network coverage."

"Carlie, be careful."

"You, too." She smiled, blew him a kiss.

Stewart looked at her wearily. "Keep in touch. That hand radio the FBI provided you will keep you informed of what's happening here, and it'll help me find you when this is over."

She held up the sophisticated walkie-talkie, patted it thoughtfully. She shoved the unit into her purse, looked hard at him. "Kirk, don't do anything foolish."

"Meaning?"

"You make a better lover than a hero."

Stewart looked at her, unsmiling.

Her penetrating eyes rebuked him. "When you've buried the past, I'm going to have you, Kirk."

"Stewart!"

Glancing over his shoulder, he saw Oliver Wright beckoning to him. Carlie climbed in the back of the waiting limousine. An FBI agent, assigned by Wright to protect her, slid into the front seat beside the driver, and the vehicle departed. Stewart watched the limo slip out into East Executive Avenue, then he turned and hurried to join the Bureau chief who was standing with Motti Barak and several Secret Service men. Somber-faced, Oliver Wright handed him a message from the Bureau's teleprinter.

"Bad news, Stewart. Our people in New Orleans found those victims in that swamp mire. Exactly as you described the scene." Wright's face tightened, and he lowered his head. "I'm sorry. Shira Bernstein's body, too, surfaced a short distance away."

Stewart's hand trembled as he read the message. Confirmation. Proof positive. No more could he shake his head in disbelief. When he looked up, he was angry and fully prepared to vent malice. Stewart saw that the others around him seemed to understand and were waiting for him to react. Their eyes were on his stunned face. He felt sick. Once more Stewart knew guilt; it was like a chainsaw cutting his heart to shreds. Until now the events of the past week had distracted, short-circuited his emotions. And he had encouraged Carlie to play the surrogate.

"Shira," he said in a barely audible voice. Stewart was still turning it all over in his mind when Motti Barak tapped him lightly on the shoulder and gestured toward the White House entrance. The President was waiting for them. His problems were immediate.

Tensing his jaw, Stewart shook his slumped frame erect and followed the others.

The group hastened down the Diplomatic Wing corridor toward the executive offices. His eyebrows arched like caterpillars, Wright looked at Stewart, then to Barak. "Why the hell you two as well as the lady reporter deserve VIP treatment is beyond my grasp. The President wants you to stay on board with us, do what you can." Hunching his shoulders, the big man turned into the hallway leading to the basement command center elevator. "Do me a favor when we get below? Just speak when spoken to, okay? You're both light-years away from being supercops."

"We're not going to the Oval Office?" asked Barak curiously, as they entered the special elevator.

Stewart felt better. He followed the others into the car. Two silent and alert Secret Service men descended with them.

Wright shrugged. "This isn't the time for social amenities. The Deputy Secretary of Defense, Air Force General Colloran, the Speaker of the House, the head of the Secret Service, and God knows how many other advisers are downstairs conferring with the President. Singer's not around. He just disappeared."

Stewart stared at Wright. "What's that supposed to mean? Disappeared?" He glanced at Motti Barak, who also looked confused. Stewart's mind was at work, thinking tortuous thoughts. Supposing the CIA director got completely away. Supposing—.

The elevator door opened at the one-hundred-foot depth. Stewart saw more sentries, this time a half-dozen Marines and as many civilians he suspected were Oliver Wright's FBI assistants. At the end of the hallway sat three grim-faced men, handcuffed and under guard.

"Remnants of the CIA crew left behind to cover Singer's flank when he made his escape," said Wright quietly.

Stewart wondered, escape to where?

They were immediately ushered into the large concrete cubicle that was the President's provisional command office. The chamber was small to the point of being cramped, stuffy with smoke and nervous sweat. Stewart immediately sensed the tension in the room. The Chief Executive sat at his desk, surrounded by his aides. He had a refined face, taut and well proportioned, with a firm mouth, but his eyes were those of a cornered animal—uncommitted, unpredictable.

The only others Stewart recognized were General Colloran and the Speaker of the House. The President stood and came forward. He shook hands with Stewart and Barak, swiftly congratulating them for their services. He then turned and nodded to Bernard Colloran.

The Air Force commander nervously ran his fingers through his thick hair and came up to Wright. He looked uncomfortable and insignificant gazing up at the giant FBI man. Stretching his neck out of his collar, the general exhaled and said, "Singer took the goddamn tunnel. By now he's either halfway down its length, headed for the escape stairway under the Jefferson Memorial, or he's bound for the opposite end, the Pentagon and the Joint Chiefs big board room."

At the desk, the Deputy Secretary of Defense unrolled a topographic map of the city. General Colloran beckoned Wright over to it. The President returned to his chair, wearily sat, and studied the document with the others. Stewart nodded to Barak, and together they edged in closer. No one seemed to object to their presence alongside Wright. Colloran pointed to a structure at the top of the drawing that was obviously the White House, then looked up and gestured across the concrete bunker to a louvered door at the end wall. "He left by that exit. The tunnel has only a five-foot bore and contains a pair of battery-driven golf carts mounted on rails. One of the vehicles is missing."

Stewart boldly stepped forward. "Sir, may I ask a question?"

The others looked startled. The deputy from Defense stared at him scornfully, but the President said, "You may."

Stewart straightened. "I've heard news stories about our emergency control centers in the event of nuclear attack, sir, but no one's ever mentioned tunnels linking the Pentagon with the White House. As a reporter, I'm compelled to ask if this is still proprietary or secret information."

The President smiled, contemplated the map. "No longer, I'm afraid. Too many subway engineers and construction workers know of the shaft. The new Washington subway passes directly over it near the Pentagon. The tunnel was secretly built during the Kennedy administration after the Bay of Pigs scare. Unfortunately both it and the two command centers at each end are technologically outdated now."

The President's face turned glum as he nodded to Colloran. "Continue, General. Explain so that all of us will understand precisely what we're up against."

Colloran slowly traced his finger over the map. "The tunnel leads directly south, gentlemen, with an escape stairway at the Jefferson Memorial, a mile distant. Then it's a little over another mile to the underground facility at the Pentagon. The tunnel was bored at a hundred feet to pass under both the Tidal Basin and the Potomac."

Oliver Wright coughed and sharply exhaled. "So what are you saying? Singer came up at the Jefferson and got away? Or he's burrowed on to the Pentagon to continue the fight?"

The President looked grim. "Sorry, Oliver. We're going to have a battle on our hands."

"I've had men watching that Jefferson Memorial exit ever since Singer first set foot in this command center," said Colloran. "He didn't surface there. That means he's reached the Pentagon and joined forces with Admiral Palmer and the others."

The general was suddenly interrupted by a Signal Corps captain who entered from the next room and handed over a communication. Colloran's face was a mask of concentration as he read the message quickly, then passed it on to the President. Continuing with a frown, the general said, "It's confirmed. Singer's there, and with a death clutch on military communications at that. At least a part of them. And he's got a spotter outside, somewhere over the capital, moving troops like a master checker player."

"Impossible," grunted the President. "One of my Secret Service aides is on the roof of this building monitoring air traffic. We're expecting helicopter gunship support from Oceana or Fort Bragg within an hour, but right now the sky's clear of all traffic. Friendly aircraft or foe, he would have reported it."

Oliver Wright stepped forward and said swiftly, "Mr. President, gentlemen, I'd like a few words. On the way to the White House from the Potomac Plaza I was watchful. It seems our opponents have no interest in massive frontal assaults. They're far too clever, making a thrust here, a strike there. Three hours ago one contingent overran the Capitol Building, then moved off to Andrews Air Force Base. Another group occupied the Justice Department."

The President looked up at Wright wearily, his eyes tired. General Colloran looked impatient. Stewart had a strong feeling of what was coming next.

The FBI director continued: "The Nazi storm troopers invaded Treasury and the State Department, created all manner of hell, then disappeared. As we turned up Seventeenth Street, I noticed a large cluster of them around the Washington Monument. Why would they waste personnel there if the structure had no strategic or tactical value?"

Stewart found himself nodding in agreement. He, too, had seen the men and trucks and had called them to Motti Barak's attention.

General Colloran was silent and thoughtful. Again he studied the communication before him. "The FBI chief makes sense," he said, looking up. "They know our strength, almost to a man. How else could they have seen me transfer four loaded personnel carriers and a command car from here to the Bureau of Engraving?" He waved the paper in his hand. "Singer's been receiving inputs from General Brady, I'll wager my stars on it. That bastard's probably up at the top of the Washington Monument, watching our every move."

The President, like the others, had listened carefully to Colloran's words. "You said some of your Air Force people, General, as well as a couple of staff-level Army generals, are barricaded in your Pentagon office. If I recall, that's on the E-Ring with a view of the river entrance. It has an outside view, so we're lucky. When's the last time you talked with them?"

"Ten minutes ago, Mr. President."

Stewart watched as the Deputy Secretary of Defense strode to a blackboard at the opposite wall, grabbed a piece of chalk. "Go ahead, General, give us what they told you. How many men outside the Pentagon?"

Colloran hesitated, looked slowly around him. There was a mounting, visible tension in the chamber.

"What are the odds?" The President repeated the question. "How many?"

Colloran cleared his throat. "My aides tell me there's well over four thousand well-armed men outside protecting the building. All civilians. American Nazis, Klansmen, Freedom Militiamen, and a couple of other groups they can't identify."

The President cut in quickly, "And according to what we've heard on the radio transmissions, more are arriving every minute. What about General Brady's renegade Marine and Army contingents?"

Colloran looked at him, swiftly replied, "They've taken over inside the Pentagon, sir. Who knows what sections? With seventeen miles of corridors to cover, they've got their hands full. There's one stroke of luck, Mr. President. It's Friday, and most of the building's workers have gone home."

Stewart shuffled his feet. He was getting weary of all the talk when fast, hard-hitting action seemed to be the order of the day. He glanced at Barak. The Israeli, too, looked impatient.

The President leaned forward in his seat. "Thank you, General, for that information." He thought for a moment. "Colloran, you've dispersed one hundred and twenty jet transports with airborne troops. Can't we spare a few of them for the Capitol itself?"

Colloran tensed, glanced at the others, then slowly responded. "Mr. President, I'm doing everything in my power to avoid mass carnage on the streets. The transport troops were needed at state level to bolster activated National Guard units. So far, we've been successful." He looked at the somber-faced civilian aide to the President's immediate left. "Your national security adviser will concur that ninety percent of the governors have regained firm control. The remaining ten percent will be back in business by nightfall. As for immediately bringing the heavy transports into Washington area airports, they'd still have to contend with that rebel F-15 squadron. Colonel Reddick may be dead, but his men will never believe it. Those aircraft must first be eliminated." Colloran's eyes flicked over to Motti Barak. "The major here, I'm sure, can speak firsthand on that threat to our jugular."

Barak smiled sagely. "I would also remind you those F-15s are extremely costly, sophisticated airplanes. Perhaps there is another way out of this, other than force."

Stewart smiled at the Israeli's insubordination.

"I concur," snapped the deputy secretary of defense. "It's worth a try. Talk is cheap."

"And probably ineffective," grumbled Stewart quietly in Barak's ear.

There was a short silence, and it had a different aura. Oliver Wright shifted his massive bulk forward, approaching the desk of the President. He looked down at the map, carefully scrutinizing the Pentagon area. "I assume you're prepared to push in with tanks and helicopter gunships if persuasion fails?"

The President gave up a soft groan. "We're making all the necessary preparations."

Stewart watched the rootlet of concern on Wright's brow grow until the FBI chief's face was completely flushed with anger. "Damn Singer's shit!" The words had slipped out of Wright's mouth. "Mr. President, this could be a bloodbath. And there's the TV and newspapers to consider. What about this media takeover?"

"Your department, Oliver. Get cracking on it. General Colloran and the others here have their hands full with the Pentagon. As for myself, the sooner I return upstairs and meet with the Secretary of State, the better. We've got not only the Russians but the Chinese to pacify. Every time there's an unsettling situation in the West, the Communists start to probe. If I can manage the Reds, you should be able to take care of a few American civilians."

Wright's eyes were dark, sparkling. "The CIA is civilian, sir."

"Then get out to Virginia and clean house at their headquarters. You have my authorization, and Colloran's already assigned two hundred troops to your deputy. What more do you need?"

"Nothing. Thank you, Mr. President." Wright turned to leave, then hesitated. "With your permission, I would like to take the Israeli pilot and the newspaper reporter along. I'll need additional intelligence information."

Behind the desk, the Chief Executive impatiently waved his hand, dismissing them as a group. Oliver Wright turned to Colloran. "I strongly suggest, General, as a precaution against another escape by Singer or any of the others, that you send a demolition team into that tunnel and seal it off below the Jefferson Memorial."

Colloran nodded, dashed out a note, and handed it to one of his staff assistants. The FBI director gestured to Stewart and Barak, and all three of them exited the room. Wright didn't speak until they were in the elevator rising to the surface. This time they had the car to themselves. "Well, gentlemen?"

"You think the general will follow your suggestion?" asked Stewart curiously.

Wright nodded. "Why not? They're hurting for ideas right now. Hell, we could end it in a minute with concussion or scatter bombs, but we'd probably level half of Washington in the process."

Barak looked up at Wright, smiled thinly. "Their anticipated target, your Pentagon Building, strikes me as a tired old filing cabinet, hardly a fortress."

Stewart and Wright both laughed.

"An accurate assessment," said the FBI man. "Still, don't discount the defense possibilities. Those trim lawns and friendly magnolia trees can be deceiving. Behind that gray limestone facade there's plenty of reinforced concrete. It may not be the Maginot Line, but the Pentagon will serve damned nicely as a giant bunker."

Stewart liked Wright's perverse evaluation. Grinning, he said to Barak, "From what I hear, some of the brass inside may be getting a little soft from paper pushing. Could be they're also thinning out on hard combat experience. Or rusty."

"Not a factor," declared Wright. "The action will probably be outside, on the front steps. Except for flushing out Singer himself."

Stewart saw a gleam appear in Barak's catlike eyes.

The Israeli turned to the FBI head, "So? Enough speculating, yes? I say we go after that spotter at the Washington Monument. Then the Pentagon."

The elevator door opened. Wright didn't move; his eyes were still on Barak. Stewart watched them, curious.

"We?" Wright finally chided.

Barak hitched his shoulders and smiled up at the tall man. "If you and Mr. Stewart do not wish to join me, I'll understand your reluctance. But if you'll make arrangements for me to receive a large helicopter and an ammo bag of grenades, I have a plan. I've been considering it for the past fifteen minutes while your leaders below were still trying to focus on the problem. Kirk, if you're feeling brave, I'd like your help."

Stewart nodded, then wished he hadn't. Oh, God, he thought, here we go again!

Impatience flared on Wright's face. "Major Barak. The two of you were there and heard the man. The Pentagon and the Washington Monument are not my problems. *Or yours.*" He started down the corridor.

Coming to Barak's defense, Stewart pulled Wright back by the sleeve. "But the CIA *is* your problem," Stewart said boldly. "And the head of that shop has a knife to the nation's jugular."

He turned to Barak. "Go ahead, Major. Let's hear it."

Barak slowly said, "Eliminate Walter Singer. Without the head the snake's body will die." He looked at the FBI chief through veiled eyes. "Will you find me a flying machine, Mr. Wright? Or should I again proceed with my own requisition technique—effective enough, but time-consuming?"

Oliver Wright made no response, but for several seconds his eyes glinted with a strange sort of amusement.

"His record speaks for itself so far, Chief," Stewart said eagerly.

Wright shrugged his big shoulders. "I'm not promising you a thing, Barak, but curiosity's my big weakness. Spit it out. Let's hear your brilliant plan."

39

THE ARMY MINERVA lurched off the White House lawn, climbing rapidly into the capital sky. Stewart and Barak looked down and saw Oliver Wright toss a mock salute their way, wishing them luck. Stewart knew the Bureau chief would now have his hands full wielding his authority at CIA headquarters. Wright also intended to concentrate his FBI forces on the city's radio, TV, and newspaper offices, to regain control there.

Besides Stewart and Barak, there was a two-man Army crew aboard the helicopter: the pilot and a young rigger in the cargo compartment. At a thousand feet the pilot made a slight adjustment in pitch, and the noisy machine dipped south, moving over the Vietnam Memorial, past the Reflecting Pond, heading for a position where the Washington Monument might be approached from the river side.

Motti Barak nudged Stewart, pointing across the Tidal Basin. They could see that already General Colloran's ground units had forced the armed men at the base of the 555-foot-high monument to seek cover inside.

The Minerva's pilot pointed to the open windows near the top of the white obelisk and nodded. Stewart knew the pilot could tell from the radio traffic that General Brady was still in the observation room, relaying tactical information back to Singer and his group at the Pentagon. The Minerva swung in a wide sweep over the Potomac and the Jefferson Memorial, then the warrant officer at the controls shoved the rotor above him into high throttle. the helicopter clutched the air, struggling for altitude. The windows at the top of the monument had to be approached from as directly overhead as possible.

Stewart watched Barak's face flare with impatience as the rigger fumbled with the drop harness, finally fitting it to the Israeli's body. Barak carefully clipped four teargas grenades to his waist. Stewart tapped his partner on the shoulder, gestured toward a nearby case of grenades Wright had given them.

Shouting over the roar of the engine, Stewart asked, "Are you positive that the smoke will do the job?" He picked up two of the grenades, offering them instead.

Barak nodded and called back, "It's the only way!" He patted the smoke bombs at his waist. "Why destroy your national shrine?"

Stewart shook his head and put the grenades back in the box. The air became more turbulent. He had never been comfortable in choppers. Trying to adapt, find some kind of body rhythm, was out of the question. All the infernal Minerva did was jerk, roll, and vibrate. Stewart's stomach was rattling, too, and every muscle in his body was taut and sore. He wondered how the pilot would ever be able to maintain a fixed hover directly over the structure's apex—a necessary position to avoid gunfire from the observation windows on each side. Stewart watched as, on the ground below, a gathering of troops retreated inside the monument, seeking cover from Colloran's support group across the mall. The helicopter had to move in quickly, do its work, and retreat before Brady could call in reinforcements.

The pilot pushed the control stick forward. Barak was ready; his focus alternated between Stewart, the pilot, and the open doorway. It would be up to Stewart to provide fire cover as Barak descended.

Stewart glanced into the cockpit and read the altimeter. Six hundred feet. He watched, fascinated, as the sharp tip of the monument rushed up to meet the Minerva.

"Closer!" the rigger shouted. "He needs another twenty feet."

Barak pulled on his gas mask and slipped out the door. The

winch shrieked as the cable slowly descended, dropping him along the structure's smooth white face. The tip of the huge obelisk was perilously close. The pilot nursed the controls as Stewart, cradling an M-16, gaped downward. His stomach pushed upward to his throat. Barak was against the side of the structure now, trying to inch as close to the open observation port as his harness and cable would permit. Stewart saw him prepare the first teargas canister, holding it for what seemed forever. Barak was having trouble maintaining his position.

Stewart watched Barak clip his safety belt to one of the large window washer's grommets on one side of the opening. His hands free, he carefully aimed and lobbed the gas bomb inside. Immediately, he reached for another canister. With the deafening noise of the Minerva, Stewart couldn't hear the concussions, but he saw smoke belch from the observation ports on all four sides of the monument. He continued to watch as Barak, apparently for good measure, pulled a third smoke bomb from his belt. Suddenly, through the rotor-buffeted smoke beneath him, Stewart saw a head and shoulders emerge from the observation window; the man pointed a gun in the Israeli's direction. Smoke billowed out through the opening, and Stewart couldn't see to fire. The range was short for the man below, an easy shot!

Beside Stewart, the rigger went for the winch control, but stopped short, suddenly realizing Barak was still secured to the monument. The pilot couldn't even put the Minerva into climb! The smoke cleared briefly, and Stewart fired a burst at the figure in the window, but too late. Barak had been struck in the chest. He dropped his last gas canister to the ground far below. Barak looked up, his eyes staring through the gas mask goggles helplessly.

Stewart and the rigger both frantically pointed to the grommet on the white marble wall. Barak's head slumped. The gust from the rotors blew the smoke away from the nearby window, and Stewart could see that the individual who had fired the gun had either fallen or retreated back inside.

"Is your man alive?" the Minerva pilot shouted.

The sweat rolled down Stewart's face, stinging his eyes. He looked at the line wound around the winch at the top of the cabin, then to the alarmed rigger. "That's it? The only cable?" Stewart was frantic.

"Yes, other than a couple of heavy hand lines and a cargo harness." The rigger started to dig through his equipment along the cabin wall.

Too slow, Stewart thought. His mind flashed. Wright and Barak had taught him lesson one: How to hold and fire an M-16. But they hadn't gone any further, and he was ready for lesson two: Beware of snap decisions, impulsive moves. Getting Barak out of there immediately would mean tearing his body apart in the process. Was the Israeli still alive? Lesson three came to him in a flash: Don't be led into a trap by other would-be heroes. The rigger had found a heavy coil of blue nylon and was bringing it toward him.

The hell with lessons, no time to think. Stewart put down his carbine and shouted to the rigger, "Forget that line. Just give me your gloves!" Spotting several webbed belts on the floor, Stewart grabbed one, wrapped it around his waist, securing the steel winch cable within the loop. The rigger handed him the canvas gloves, and before either he or the pilot could protest, Stewart pocketed two grenades and was out the side of the Minerva. Legs wrapped around the cable, he descended, hand over hand, toward Barak.

Above Stewart, the rigger snapped up the M-16 and kneeled in the helicopter's doorway, covering him.

Stewart's anger drove him downward like a possessed spider on a web. The noise and wind were horrendous, the height above the ground staggering. His heart pounded with fear, but he had to get to that hook. Reaching Barak's harness, Stewart struggled to avoid kicking the limp Israeli with his feet. Lower. A matter of inches! Stewart cursed and arched his body, extending his hand toward the grommet, stretching. His focus alternated between the safety hook and the smoking observation port. The buffeting rotors fortunately blew the teargas fumes down and away, and his eyes were still clear. But he and Barak were both open targets. Was the Israeli still alive? The body next to Stewart felt lifeless. He pulled Barak's mask away to give him air.

Stewart lurched for the hook and pulled the line free. Immediately he reached for a grenade, pulled the pin with his teeth, and hurled it through the observation window. The winch started to scream, lifting them upward. Stewart hurriedly tossed his second grenade.

He felt both concussions, saw the smoke billow out through

the windows. Something had been hurled against the window ledge. A man's body, his silver-gray hair matted with blood. There were general's stars on his tattered tunic, and his face twitched violently as he struggled to look up toward Stewart and bring his pistol to bear. Stewart felt helpless. Above, the rigger was preoccupied with the winch. Looking down, Stewart watched General George Brady's fingers slowly open. The Walther pistol dropped to the ground as if in slow motion. The general's head rolled back, motionless, blood oozing from his lips.

They swung in a wide arc until the painfully slow winch brought them up to the Minerva's door. Stewart climbed back in the cabin first, then crouched and extended his hand. Barak's face was a gargoyle of death as they pulled his limp form toward the chopper and rolled it inside. Slamming the cargo door, the rigger quickly unfastened the drop harness, tucked a folded blanket under Barak's head. Stewart numbly pointed to the blood seeping from the Israeli's chest. The fatal bullet had apparently struck Barak in the heart, killing him almost immediately.

Stewart felt sickened. There was always the one hound who got too close to the trapped wildcat, he thought, but why did it have to be Barak? The pilot looked back, anxiously pointing in the direction of the White House; he was waiting for Stewart's signal to return to base.

Stewart shook his head. "No!" he yelled, his voice breaking. "We go ahead as planned. Head for the Pentagon!"

He stared at Barak's limp body. Anger rushed over him, fierce, black anger at his companion's death. It had been a short but meaningful friendship.

The pilot called back to him, "It's suicide! Too dangerous. You'll never make it alone!"

Staring down at Barak, Stewart felt a strange inner strength roar inside him, one he had never known before. Go back, he repeatedly told himself. Lesson number two: Don't allow compulsion to replace reason. No, you can't go back, Stewart. You're too close. There had to be a weak link. The CIA director was razor sharp on the surface, but how deep did it go? Could Singer be more impulsive than methodical? Might Singer make just one small mistake? He turned to the pilot and shouted, "Move in! We're going to try. You've got the FBI chief's authorization. There has to be a way in!"

The pilot gave a reluctant shrug, turned the Minerva south. The rigger beside Stewart rubbed his hand back and forth across his chin slowly, shook his head, and moaned, "Medical retirement, here I come!"

The air was still rough as the helicopter vaulted over the Fourteenth Street bridges and edged closer to the Pentagon. Less than a minute later they were hovering over the river entrance. The huge, boisterous mob on the ground looked up, and a few waved, but they didn't appear concerned over the arrival of a cargo helicopter. To Stewart's left he could see the Pentagon helipad with its great white Maltese cross. The Minerva's pilot called to him and pointed to it, but Stewart shook his head. "Wouldn't stand a chance!" he shouted into the cockpit. "I don't need a welcoming committee! How about the roof?"

Stewart stared out through the cockpit canopy and saw a long line of tanks parked on Army-Navy Drive, and beyond them, personnel carriers and at least a dozen Chinook combat helicopters scattered nearby on the parkway. Two more choppers approached from the east. The President and General Colloran appeared to be pulling it together, thought Stewart. The Minerva circled the Pentagon. Suddenly, below them, there was small arms fire—snipers with telescopic rifles taking aim at the troops across the parkway. A bullet shattered the side of the Minerva's cockpit. The pilot grimaced and quickly banked the chopper away.

Stewart could see that the tanks in the distance were turning, facing the Pentagon and its snipers as if preparing for an assault. The Minerva swooped over the building's E-Ring, then slowed and hovered over first the D, then the C section. Stewart wasn't so sure about the roof. If the hatches were locked from within, he'd be trapped, a clay pigeon. He gestured for the pilot to move in over the five-acre center courtyard. It was filled with trees, tables, and benches—no place to land. Stewart saw a large group of Marines in dress blues; band members standing by for a performance somewhere in the building. A concert that under the circumstances must have been canceled, mused Stewart. The rest of the courtyard appeared empty. No guns were pointed their way. A chance!

Stewart turned, reverently stepped over Barak's body, and shouted to the rigger. "Can you drop me in there?"

"On a dime!" he shouted back.

Stewart again contemplated the courtyard below. He was alert, as prepared as he would ever be. He looked at the rigger, who already had in his hands the harness Barak had worn.

Stewart shouted, "Your target's a little bigger than a dime. Just drop me in between that bass drum and the Marine with the sousaphone, okay? And make it easylike. At the monument I didn't have time to think about this kind of acrobatics. Didn't even have time to turn green. But I do now."

Carlie Chavez and the remote crew from NTN's network affiliate in Washington, D.C., were twice turned back by intransigent Army regulars. Equipped with automatic weapons, teargas, and Stinger missiles, more combat-ready troops—all loyal to the President—were arriving by the minute. The scene around her was chaotic. Forced to park their news van some fifty yards behind the heavy tanks and armored vehicles confronting the Pentagon, the camera crew adjusted their microwave unit and hastily added their most powerful telephoto lens to the roof-mounted video camera.

Carlie stood at the back of the remote truck scribbling on a pad and periodically looking inside at the phalanx of monitors before the technical director and sound mixer. One of the local newsmen was already interviewing a helmet-clad Army captain beside a jeep. Carlie's turn on the portable camera was next, and she was still waiting for the President's press aide to return for a promised interview. If he didn't show up soon, she had made up her mind to toss protocol to the wind and move her camera crew in on General Colloran himself.

On top of the van, the powerful telephoto camera began scanning the front steps of the Pentagon. The cameraman, alerted by an assistant's shout, panned up to the roof.

Carlie glanced at the TV monitors inside the truck. One of the screens showed a helicopter descending toward the center of the building. A man in a harness swung beneath it from a long cable. Carlie looked closer, saw that he wore brown slacks, a yellow shirt, and a corduroy jacket. Her eyes narrowed. "My God," she gasped, her hand shooting up to her mouth. "Kirk!"

Standing near the cherry trees on the bank of the Tidal Basin, a lieutenant colonel from the Army Corps of Engineers clamped both hands on his hips and shook his head in anger. He and several aides stared in disgust at a whirlpool of water just a few yards out from shore. A good part of the Potomac was being sucked down into the earth in a powerful vortex as if someone had pulled the plug on gigantic tub. The colonel turned to the four-man demolition team that had just returned from the Jefferson Memorial and the escape tunnel. One at a time, the colonel regarded his men. "We asked for a simple explosion, a shaft cave-in, and you give us this?"

The leader of the group wavered, then replied, "I'm sorry, sir. The bore was closer to the bottom of the river than we figured. With water thundering through the shaft at that velocity, at least it's useless for escape."

The colonel frowned. "Or any other use. Thank God we vacated the White House end as a precaution." He looked out across the river. "I pity the poor bastards down below at the Pentagon end."

Walter Singer withdrew a plastic bottle of pills from his pocket. It rattled in his hand as he uncapped it and took out a double-strength Bufferin. His hands had never trembled before, he thought. Not once. Now he had a headache and a nervous stomach to boot.

He looked up as the floor of the subterranean Big Board Room trembled slightly. Singer was in his shirtsleeves now; the room was warm. The others at the conference table looked at him and squinted. None of them could immediately place the sound—a muffled, distant roar. The lights dimmed, went out briefly, then came back on at half their normal intensity. An Army sergeant rushed into the chamber, shouted to Admiral Palmer at the end of the table. "The power's gone, sir! We switched automatically to the emergency generator, but I suspect—"

"The escape door!" cried Palmer, ashen-faced, pushing his chair back so rapidly it fell over.

The half-dozen men at the conference table, Singer included, jumped to their feet. Singer whirled, his eyes following Palmer's alarmed stare. The CIA head knew that the tunnel he had used earlier was behind a double barricade: an outer steel door of the sturdy type found in ship's bulkheads and an inner door of louvered wood to permit controlled ventilation. Singer saw that the steel door stood open, hooked back against the chamber's concrete wall. As a safety precaution it should have been secured!

The roaring sound from the tunnel intensified. Singer and Palmer both leaped for the open door, but they were too late. The wooden door shattered, exploding inward. A wall of water hurled them to the floor. Admiral Palmer grabbed Singer's arm, pulled him out from under the inundated conference table. Both men tried to struggle to their feet as tons of water cascaded into the room. It was rising too fast and they were suddenly swimming.

Singer gasped. His lungs choked with murky water. He had to get to the elevator shaft in the next room or to the circular stairwell beside it. There was no other hope of escape. The wooden conference table was already afloat. Chair cushions and other debris tumbled around him. A chair struck his head, then floated away. Singer cursed, sucked in as much air as he could from the rapidly decreasing pocket of space along the ceiling. A shower of sparks burst from the top of the display screen on one wall.

Singer lost sight of Palmer and the others. No matter. He had to get out. Fighting the boiling, filthy water, he plunged below the surface. Muscles pumping, Singer desperately fought the current, trying to propel himself toward the exit, but there were other struggling bodies in the way. He pulled, with all his strength on a sleeve, vaguely aware of a cluster of stars on the epaulet. Air. He needed more air! Clawing upward, kicking aside arms, legs, stupid faces with glazed eyes, Singer again broke the surface, only to find a fluorescent light fixture pressing down on the top of his head. The light sputtered and went dark.

The water had turned to an ugly black, stinking sludge that made him dizzy. Singer kept his head in the air pocket and thought. The stakes, for the past week, had become bigger with every passing hour. Up until this instant he had governed his mind and body with such absolute determination that anything was possible for him. If he could mold in his hands the fate of the nation, why should escape from a room filled with water be such a Herculean task? No, he thought. Not Hercules. Poseidon was the god of the terrible waters. I'm in your hands, Poseidon, he thought, frantically. He heard a woman's voice beseeching him. "Don't desert me, Walter. Not now. You must survive!" It was his mother's voice, as resolute as ever. "Forget your gods and focus on the task at hand. Survive, survive," she repeated.

Singer shot up again for air, but this time there was no surface, only the solid ceiling. The water had pushed the pocket of air out into the ventilating pipes. *Survive*. Don't panic now. Feel your way through the watery violence. But his lungs ached as if they were bursting, and the roaring sound was gradually fading. Which direction should he swim? Singer's waterlogged surroundings grew strangely quiet. Listening to his pounding heart, all he could do was wearily stroke and kick. Stroke and kick. Again and again. He swam along the wall until the obsidian water that blinded him also smothered his thoughts, closing around him in an abyss of nothingness.

The Marine Band's director, a short, bespectacled major, had been surprised to see Stewart drop down from the helicopter, but now he was more than anxious to show him into the bowels of the giant defense edifice. The band, the major insisted, wasn't interested in taking sides; to a man and woman, they wanted out of the building, back to their barracks or to their homes and families.

Stewart was relieved to discover that there were plenty of civilians in the Pentagon's corridors. He wouldn't appear conspicuous. His goal now was the river entrance, the group of military commanders on the steps, whom he had seen from the air. Even if he never reached Singer, he would make his point with the others. "You sure we're headed in the right direction?" he asked the band director after several confusing turns. A short time ago in the helicopter Stewart had been confident; now he felt lost—emotionally, physically, and geographically. Where was he?

The Marine major grinned. "We're taking a roundabout route to reach the outer E-Ring. I had to avoid restricted areas or you'd have been stopped cold."

Stewart nodded, suddenly remembering he had no badge identification.

"Forget the word 'pentagon,'" the director said. "Think of the building as a monstrous wheel with concentric rims and spokes joining the rims to a hub."

"Dante's Inferno had concentric rings too," Stewart quipped.

Finally they entered the huge shopping concourse and reception lobby that was said to be twice the size of a football field. Stewart noted that the visitors were gone, the banks, stores, and tour center all closed; the escalators were guarded top and bottom by Military Police. A large number of combat-ready Marines, wearing the same blue shoulder patches Stewart had seen on the Capitol steps, stood around the room's perimeter. Gathered in platoon-sized groups, they looked watchful and in a state of readiness, as if they were waiting for orders. Stewart didn't stop to ask questions. Instead he hurried with his escort to the end of the concourse and the Pentagon's river entrance. They arrived there in time to hear a booming voice on a public address system outside. The sound seemed to be coming from off in the distance. They went out under the portico, followed several pointed hands and fixed stares. Stewart looked across the approach roads, beyond Lady Bird Johnson Park to the Washington Memorial Parkway. Traffic had been stopped as armored tanks clattered into position, their gun turrets trained on the Pentagon.

Stewart's spirits sagged. It's like a fucking Hollywood production out of the fifties or sixties, he thought. *Cleopatra, Spartacus, The Alamo,* with twice as many extras as needed and the U.S. President cast as the star. And here he stood, the inquiring reporter, without so much as an Instamatic.

Stewart exhaled swiftly. Powerful speakers were set up beside the tanks across the way, and now they boomed again. The sporadic gunfire ceased.

"We repeat. You have one minute remaining. Put down your weapons and move away from the building entrance. Walk away from the Pentagon unarmed, toward Arlington Cemetery."

Stewart and the Marine major stepped to one side of the portico, hiding among a group of civilian workers. They closely observed the agitated men who had surrounded the building, ostensibly to defend it. The outcries from the crowd came in cyclical bursts: shrieks and incoherent imprecations punctuated by small arms fire. A large delegation from the crowd in front of the river entrance had come forward and was gathered in disarray at the foot of the steps. Section leaders, Stewart reasoned.

He heard orders being shouted behind him. He turned, staring in awe as a group of steel-helmeted military officers—all the services appeared to be represented—argued among themselves at the top of the stairs. An Army colonel tried to calm the crowd without any luck. He passed his battery-powered bullhorn over to one of the civilian leaders beside him.

Stewart swallowed hard. He recognized the man in the blue baseball cap and camo fatigues immediately. It was Bobby Harrington, the racist orator he had seen in the town square in Jamesboro, the Klansman who had arranged the attempt on his life at the hotel. Harrington, the Invisible Society's Exalted Archon!

"You heard the colonel!" Harrington's voice was coarse as he spoke in clipped words through the bullhorn. "We're going to have order here! Fall in behind those cars and trucks. One line behind the concrete bulkhead. I don't want anybody to panic over those tanks, hear? We've got troops up here and more of them inside to back us up. They'll be bringing out napalm and anti-tank guns if necessary. And the chairman of the Joint Chiefs has promised us a dozen fully armed Cobra helicopters. They're heading this way from Maryland. If the rotten system wants to fight us, we'll oblige! You listen close now, y'all hear? Today the white renaissance has begun in this country. Together, we're going to shift gears, change some racial, moral, and political attitudes. You all came to Washington looking for action, and by God, you've found it. We're going to call their bluff! We're in control, and the enemy is outside knocking at our door. Are you ready to reawaken white pride and patriotism? Are you prepared to skyrocket America to new heights?"

The restlessness and irritability of the crowd was building. Finally the angry comber broke. "Yes!" they shouted as one, firing volley after volley of shots into the air.

Stewart shook his head, rubbed his sweating palms on his pants. He tried to concentrate on the task at hand, but felt suddenly lead-footed, apprehensive, and inadequate. *Think, Stewart. You've got to do better than this!* He watched helplessly as Harrington goaded the mob.

"The country's ours. You want to give it back?"

Stewart flinched as a chorus of angry nos echoed along the front of the building. Several guns again went off.

Harrington smiled and put the bullhorn to his lips. "One more time, I say! I want to hear a loud 'Hell, no!'"

The responsive roar from the assembly was deafening. It grated on Stewart's ears, and apparently also on the ears of the tank commander across the parkway. Smoke suddenly burst from one of the gun turrets. An instant later a devastating explosion ripped a jagged crater in the Pentagon steps. From where he stood behind a wide pillar, Stewart and the major were protected from the fusillade of shrapnel, concrete, and dirt, but the men down below weren't so lucky. Over two dozen of them had been standing in the smoking place where the tank's armor-piercing shell struck. Bobby Harrington, at the top of the stairs, appeared wounded and in a state of shock. Stewart clenched his teeth and stared. Beside him, the band director paled, looking sick. Stewart was stunned by the carnage one heavy tank shell could inflict on a target. His heart in his throat, he numbly started to count the bodies—what was left of them.

These were not aliens, Stewart thought, but fellow Americans; reactionaries perhaps, obsessed with their political emotions, but nonetheless fellow citizens. Stewart felt anger at the terrible waste, but sensed it was too late for pity. Americans from the industrial cities of the Midwest, the bayou country of Louisiana, the red-soil farms of Georgia, the crowded tenements of Brooklyn, and the Bible country of Orange County, California, had fallen as one on the Pentagon steps and left their blood on them.

His face and arm bleeding, Bobby Harrington climbed to his feet and stubbornly resumed his post at the head of the steps. Before his trembling hand could raise the bullhorn, the loudspeakers on the Memorial Parkway came to life again. "That was only a warning! Your leaders are dead. Both the Vice-President and the members of the civilian cabal have been killed. The Chairman of the Joint Chiefs and the CIA director will soon be placed under arrest for treason." There was a long pause; then a second voice, distinctly familiar to Stewart, came over the system.

"This is the Speaker of the House. I want you to know that both the legislative and the executive branches of the government remain in firm control. The President has asked me to tell you that the governors, too, have repelled all attempts at local insurrection. We're not out here to force you to retreat from your political persuasion or your ideals. But we do insist you put down your guns immediately, leave the capital, and return to your homes. If you wish to avoid further bloodshed, depart from Washington in a quiet, orderly manner without delay!"

Stewart could see that the crowd was more defiant than ever. The smell of burning cordite and the sight of their dead companions had whetted their appetite to fight, and die if necessary, for their cause. The Nazis waved their banners and shouted obscenities toward the parkway. An angry murmur swept over the Klansmen, spread like a wave around the Pentagon's circumference. Stewart looked down at the Freedom Militiamen and the armed mercenaries at the foot of the steps. In their eyes was a brave madness that frightened him.

The House Speaker was replaced by another familiar voice. "We repeat. You're without adequate leadership." Stewart recognized General Colloran's stern tone. "Avoid any more casualties. Put down your weapons immediately. This is your final opportunity. You will have fifteen minutes to comply."

Stewart felt a sick emptiness. The words on the distant loudspeakers sounded hollow, unmoving. He wondered vaguely how Carlie would react to all this. She had to be out there with her TV crew, somewhere among the ranks on the opposing side.

The band director gave Stewart a quick nudge on the elbow, beckoning for him to follow. Together, they edged closer to a group of agitated Army and Marine officers and listened to their conversation.

"Where the hell is General Brady?" asked the senior man, a full bird colonel.

"No communications from the Washington Monument for the last thirty minutes," shot back an assistant.

An Army master sergeant came running up to the colonel. Short of breath, he gasped, "I can't reach the war room, sir. And the subbasement seems to be flooding rapidly."

"Water? From where?" asked a bewildered Army captain.

"Don't know, sir. But if it rises any higher it will inundate the Army and Navy Records Center."

The Marine colonel tried to hide the concern on his face by scowling at the messenger. "Water seeks its own level, Sergeant. I suspect it'll rise only as high as the Potomac. The hell with the records anyway. Get back and find out what's happening down in the Joint Chiefs' command center. Major Willis, go with him. Captain Franks, take your men to the mall entrance and reinforce those nervous Klansmen who are complaining over there."

Only two officers remained before the colonel. He looked grimly at both men, spoke first to a nervous young lieutenant. "Get up to Signal Corps communications on the double. Colonel Schopke's with us. Find out what's happened to those attack choppers from Oceana."

The young officer took off at a clip. The colonel turned to the last man, his own adjutant. "And you, Major. Pull our men out of the main concourse, put them on the line outside with the civilians. Wait, there's more. The Marine Band is sitting on its haunches in the courtyard. I want them and their instruments here on the front steps standing at attention. Immediately."

"Yes, sir. Any musical requests?"

"Get your ass out of here, Major. Tell them to play John Philip Sousa—'Stars and Stripes Forever,' hell, anything!"

It took two platoons to prod the band members together and force them under escort to the Pentagon's river entrance. The wounded from the explosion had been carted away to the building's dispensary, but the dead remained, laid in rows off to one side, plainly visible to the musicians. Uncomfortably waiting for their leader, the nervous musicians shuffled back and forth on the bloodstained steps.

Stewart put his hand on the band director's shoulder. "You're on stage, Major."

"So it appears." He shrugged and started to move off, but Stewart held him back.

"Do us both as well as your musicians a favor?"

The major shot him a puzzled look.

Stewart glanced at his watch. "The quarter-hour's almost up, and we've got nothing to lose. Play 'The Star-Spangled Banner,' all right? And then just keep playing—anything patriotic—and at the same time march smartly out to those tanks and troops by the river. Don't waver and don't look back."

The band director thought for a moment, biting his lip. He shook Stewart's hand and hastily paced off to join his musicians, shouting for them to straighten ranks on the steps.

Seconds later there was a shrill whistle followed by a clatter of snare drums. Stewart sighed, wondering if this was to be a drumroll for the living or the dead. The anthem began, and the crowd looked up in stupefaction. Flag bearers steadied their banners, and everyone in the area stood at attention. Stewart looked out across the crowd, once more considering the two forces in opposition. Listening to the music, he felt pride well up in him, a strange kind of pride mixed with fear. No one sang the words to the anthem, but instinctively Stewart knew each person in the mob was turning the words over in his mind: ". . . Gave proof, through the night, that our flag was still there. Oh, say, does that Star-Spangled Banner yet wave . . . o'er the land of the free, and the home of the brave."

The anthem concluded, the drums rolled again. The Marine Band stepped forward as one, trooped defiantly down the steps and over the driveway. The drums beat a steady tattoo for several yards; then the band abruptly burst into "The Marines' Hymn." The crowd in front of the Pentagon was deathly still. No one interfered.

Stewart could smell the blood—a sweet, cloying odor that made him pause, hold his breath, and consider the forces around him. He suddenly felt a surge of adrenaline. Stewart thought briefly, then seized the moment.

Before Harrington could summon the confused mob's attention, Stewart ran up to the Klansman, tore away the bullhorn, and brought it up to his own lips. "Listen to me! If there's anybody here with enough guts to roll up your sleeves and go to work for the country, solve its problems with honest sweat instead of guns, then fall in with those Marines! If you want to die here and shame your families and their grandchildren to come, if you wish to go down in history as traitors, then stand your ground!"

A Marine colonel walked up to him. Politely but firmly, he took Stewart's bullhorn away and spoke into it with a calm voice. "Your attention, please. Pass this word around the building. The head of the CIA, the chairman of the Joint Chiefs, and General Brady are all dead!" The colonel shrugged, handed the portable amplifier back to Stewart, and quietly said to him, "The helicopter force from Oceana is loyal to the President's forces across the field. It's over." Exhaling wearily, he straightened his shoulders and strode down the steps after the departing Marine Band. Some two dozen Army, Navy, and Marine officers under the portico conferred briefly in hushed voices, then followed him.

Stewart was about to hand the bullhorn back to Bobby Harrington, but the Klan's Exalted Archon looked away. Clasping a bloody handkerchief to the side of his face, Harrington stared transfixed at the dead men on the ground.

Stewart dropped the bullhorn, watched it clatter down the steps. Wiping the nervous sweat off his face, he strode down the driveway after the band. Several standard-bearers from the Freedom Militia hesitantly came out of the crowd and straggled after him. Stewart wasn't sure what would happen now. He didn't look back again, but after walking less than a hundred yards he heard an unmistakable clatter that quickly rose to a din as automatic weapons—thousands of them—were hurled to the ground.

40

THE PRESIDENTIAL MOTORCADE drove slowly past the John F. Kennedy Memorial Flame, climbed the knoll, and halted near the ugly scar of burned and twisted wreckage. The only recognizable parts of the executive jet that had crashed in the middle of Arlington Cemetery were the tail empennage and the still smoking engines. The police had strung a plastic ribbon around the wreck site. Escorted by FBI Director Wright, his newly appointed Joint Chiefs' chairman, General Colloran, and several Secret Service men, the President left his car and went inside the off-limits area.

The director of the National Air Safety Board hurried up to him and reported. "The aircraft exploded in midair, Mr. President. Several witnesses claim it was struck by an air-to-air missile."

The President nodded, but his eyes were focused a short distance away on the ground. Strolling over to the object that had caught his attention, he picked it up. The Bible was charred black around the edges but otherwise intact. Embossed in gold at the bottom of the cover was the name James Hallowell. The President glanced up at his companions. "I'm grasping, gentlemen, for a suitable biblical proverb, but all that comes to mind is Thomas Moore's poem: 'And hearts that once beat high for praise now feel that pulse no more.'"

Gazing across the Arlington slope toward the Tomb of the Unknown Soldier, the President saw the *Times* reporter and the TV newswoman observing the crash site. He waved back to them, sighed wearily, and pulled the fur collar of his coat up against the sudden gust of wind. Walking back to his limousine, he said quietly to Oliver Wright, "A military cemetery. America's ultimate melting pot, where no man is rejected because of his faith, color, or political persuasion. And yet two bigoted, powerful men who would have subverted everything the nation stands for, died here in a holocaust of their own." The President paused, looked back at the tangled wreckage. "This of all places—soil consecrated to the purest form of democracy. A paradox, isn't it?"

Stewart switched lenses on the Canon, snapping in a telephoto. He took several pictures of the President inspecting the wreckage, then put the camera away. His story was solid. Mike Murphy had already started the wheels spinning on a special edition. The pictures Stewart had taken on the Capitol steps would be syndicated worldwide.

The wind blew the charred odor of the airplane crash away from Stewart. Carlie came up to him, and he wrapped an arm around her shoulder. Together they watched the President's limousine leave Arlington. Then they turned back to the Tomb of the Unknown Soldier. They watched, silently, as the honor guard moved in precise steps from one side of the memorial to the other. Stewart stared at the tomb.

Carlie said softly, "Strange about chiseled stone. Any kind. Now I understand the persistent stories of Mount Rushmore, and how visitors always walk away with a lump in their throats."

The quiet tableau was marred by the roar of a passenger jet overhead. Stewart looked up. Airline traffic had resumed at National Airport.

The gray clouds above them had turned to buttermilk and parted in the west, the last rays of the sun poking through and filling the cemetery with heavy shadows. Stewart looked back toward the Capitol. Traffic on the Potomac bridges was back to normal; the rows of military vehicles guarding them had disappeared. The Lincoln Memorial and Washington Monument were dark; the floodlights had not yet come on. Carlie grabbed his arm, pulling him closer.

"It's over and they've gone home," she whispered, looking up. "But will it happen again, Kirk?"

"I doubt it, Carlie. Americans may be prone to experiment and try new things, but we also learn quickly. This has been a bitter lesson on the ineffectiveness of violence and force." Stewart pondered a moment. "I can't say the same for the prejudice. It'll probably go beneath the surface for a while like a sleeping volcano."

"And come bubbling up God knows where and when," she added soberly.

Stewart looked at her. "If I've learned one thing from this fiasco, it's that democracy has nothing to do with politics. It's an attitude of mind, a condition of the soul. Prejudice was the ugly part Shira understood. She had a sixth sense about what was happening." Stewart felt a lingering emptiness in his stomach.

Carlie sensed his melancholy. "Perhaps she and Motti Barak had a better grasp than either of us on what liberty really means. Think about it, Kirk. Fifty years ago the Jews in Germany believed that Hitler didn't intend to exterminate them. Nobody, they claimed, could be that stupid. Even today, the heirs and survivors of the Holocaust ask, 'How did we let it happen?'"

Stewart nodded. "Shira saw it brewing again, Carlie." He hesitated. "So did your friend Bishop Elliott and that New York monsignor. Also that rabbi up in Yonkers. But too many people saw the danger and said nothing, sat back complacently. It almost happened here."

She thought for a moment. "About Oliver Wright's job offer. Will you accept?"

"The press director vacancy sounds interesting, but a high GS rating didn't do much for Tap Nelson. I think I'll stay in New York and continue to write for the *Times*. I like my job. And your company. The sooner we get back, the better."

Carlie pursed her lips. "Don't forget our touring government in exile. I want to be here with a camera crew when they return."

"If and when the President arranges a return flight."

She looked puzzled.

Stewart grinned. "The President's still a politician, remember? Capitol Hill's never been so peaceful. I suspect he's convinced those hostages are tired and need an overnight rest.

Frober admitted that Haiti hotel's posh and comfortable. So the President takes his time about arranging return transportation. Why should he share all the initial media glitter with Congress?"

Carlie stared at him in disbelief. "Unfair, Kirk. The limelight rightfully belongs on people like Shira Bernstein and Motti Barak."

Stewart exhaled slowly. "Wrong, Carlie. The undercover and mystery people of the world don't need spotlights; they only need a cause."

The wind suddenly picked up, a brisk mare's tail that eddied around the Tomb of the Unknown Soldier. The Marine guard ignored it, keeping perfect balance and not missing a step.

Carlie shivered. "Hold me tight, please, Kirk."

The chill breeze and her low voice lulled Stewart. He smiled and pulled her to him. He, too, felt a sudden need for closeness.

"A dollar for your thoughts," he whispered.

"What became of the penny?"

"Inflation. Go ahead, I'm waiting."

She studied him. "Just wondering if you're the type who gets better looking as you grow older."

Stewart grinned. "You'll have to stick around a while to find out."

Carlie pushed aside the long waves of her hair that blew across both their faces. She looked up at him and smiled warmly.

Stewart continued to stare out in the distance. The flags on the government buildings unfurled, rippled in the setting sun. Then abruptly the gust of wind died, as quickly as it had picked up. Stewart thought once more about what the country had just been through. It wouldn't be easy, he suspected, to convey everything in a few news or feature stories. He would give it his best effort. It was difficult, very difficult, to write on the wind.

ABOUT THE AUTHOR

Raised in the Pacific Northwest, Douglas Muir obtained his B.A. degree from the University of Washington, then went on to do graduate study at the University of Southern California. His career began in the mailroom of a Hollywood film studio, and has since ranged over several positions that underscore his many talents. He was a news photographer for KIRO-TV in Seattle, a studio director for KHON-TV in Honolulu, and a staff film producer at two aerospace firms, before becoming an independent writer-director.

Muir has won multiple awards for documentary and educational films. For "outstanding achievement in bringing about a better understanding of the American way of life", a short subject film *This Land is Your Land* won the George Washington Medal for Distinguished Public Service. In the past dozen years, he's directed TV commercials, developed network projects for Metromedia, Wolper Productions, and PBS, and was an associate producer-writer for "The Undersea World of Jacques Cousteau."

In his free time, Muir enjoys art, carpentry, skiing, and travel, currently dividing his time between Southern California and New York.

The *New York Times* Bestselling Series

BROTHERHOOD

OF

☆ WAR ☆

by W.E.B. Griffin

They are America's fighting men—brave, patriotic,
controversial. BROTHERHOOD OF WAR is their saga
of love, loyalty, victory and betrayal.
Spine-tingling adventure and authentic military lore.

____ **BROTHERHOOD OF WAR I, THE LIEUTENANTS**
0-515-08424-7/$3.95

____ **BROTHERHOOD OF WAR II, THE CAPTAINS**
0-515-08301-1/$3.95

____ **BROTHERHOOD OF WAR III, THE MAJORS**
0-515-08303-8/$3.95

____ **BROTHERHOOD OF WAR IV, THE COLONELS**
0-515-08453-0/$3.95

____ **BROTHERHOOD OF WAR V, THE BERETS**
0-515-08587-1/$3.95

____ **BROTHERHOOD OF WAR VI, THE GENERALS**
0-515-08455-7/$3.95   (On Sale February '86)

Prices may be slightly higher in Canada.

Available at your local bookstore or return this form to:

 JOVE
Book Mailing Service
P.O. Box 690, Rockville Centre, NY 11571

Please send me the titles checked above. I enclose _____. Include 75¢ for postage
and handling if one book is ordered; 25¢ per book for two or more not to exceed
$1.75. California, Illinois, New York and Tennessee residents please add sales tax.

NAME_____

ADDRESS_____

CITY_____STATE/ZIP_____

(Allow six weeks for delivery.)   **BOW**